. . . even from a great distance they could see the huge white dome of the Sun Temple flung into the air as though it were a toy. The whole plateau became a raging sea of fire and the first ponderous waves of molten lava spilled up and over the precipice and down the sides of the old mountain . . .

. . . soon the Temple was gone and the plateau was a lake of seething lava, but the great Golden Gates still stood, and as if by a quirk of godly humor the sun was lancing through the clouds of ash and lighting up the great gates so that they shone most gloriously in that dreadful holocaust . . .

THE
SEEDBEARERS

Peter Valentine Timlett

BANTAM BOOKS
TORONTO · NEW YORK · LONDON

*To BARBARA, my wife,
who would give her very soul
to any who had need of it*

*This low-priced Bantam Book
has been completely reset in a type face
designed for easy reading, and was printed
from new plates. It contains the complete
text of the original hard-cover edition.*
NOT ONE WORD HAS BEEN OMITTED.

THE SEEDBEARERS
A Bantam Book / April 1976

PRINTING HISTORY
*First published by Quartet Books Limited
in Great Britain 1974*

AUTHOR'S PREFACE

This novel is based on the occult legend of Atlantis, which is quite different from the legend as told by Plato in *Timaeus*.

The occult legend still survives in the archives of certain Mystery Schools of the present-day Western Esoteric Tradition and has probably changed but little in spirit from the version that would have been held in the archives of certain ancient Mystery Schools of Greece.

Socrates, from whom Plato derived the tale, was an initiate and therefore would have known of the "true" legend of Atlantis, and yet he chose to make many quite radical and fundamental alterations to the story when he spoke of it. He postulated, for example, that Atlantis had been situated just outside the Pillars of Heracles, whereas the original legend puts it at least 3,000 miles farther to the west. Also his description of the culture made it seem so similar to that of his own beloved Greece that it bore little resemblance to the actual Atlantean culture at all. Perhaps he was bound by an oath of secrecy and had to disguise the "true" story. Perhaps he felt that his audience, despite their wit and appreciation of beauty and poetry, were too young of soul to readily grasp a description of a culture so unlike their own. I do not know. Whatever the facts of the matter, the result was the rather naïve Plato version in *Timaeus,* with all the blind alleys that have thus been created to date.

However, I am equally guilty, for this book is the basic legend plus a great deal of imagery of my own. Also I have omitted a great many "facts" about Atlantis because they were not germane to the plot. This book is not a treatise on Atlantis, but a novel, and as such its primary function is to entertain. The legend of Atlantis has always spoken to the very depths of my soul, and I wish to share with others the excitement and pleasure that I have derived from it.

1

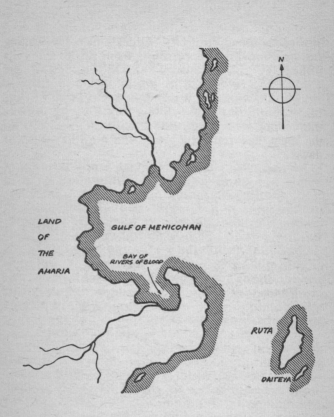

1

Five thousand strong of Vardek's men lay waiting for the sun. Five score ships, their single mainsails furled, lay beached and idle. The beaches of the bay were strewn with campfires. The smoke rose straight and true into a windless sky, and the air was thick with the smell of blood. It lacked but an hour to the coming of the sun, and already the blackness of the night had retreated before the gray half-light of dawn.

No name had hitherto graced this bay in the Gulf of Mehicohan on the eastern shore of the mainland of Amaria—but henceforth it would be known to men as the Bay of the Rivers of Blood. And this army from across the sea, these marauders, these fierce and bloody men from the twin islands of Ruta and Daiteya to the east, sent by King Baralda of Ruta, Lord of the Thousand Isles—these were henceforth spoken of with hate and bitterness as Baralda's Butchers—and the man who commanded the army, the servant of Baralda, was known and feared along the whole coastline of Amaria as Vardek—Vardek the Terrible!

On the center beach lay the main force of the army, three full wings of Toltec warriors, a thousand men a wing. Tall, copper-hued, hawk-eyed men—fierce and cruel, the master race of whence they came. In their midst, surrounded by a company of them, a young Amarian girl of thirteen, naked, lay spread-eagled on her back. Already more than fifty men had raped her where she lay—and they were big men and hard, and she was only small. Her flanks and belly were caked with her own blood, and her breasts were torn and still bleeding from their hands.

"Enough of this," the commander growled. "Cut the whore's throat."

The man on top of her grinned and pulled his knife. He neatly slit the jugular vein and laughed aloud as the blood spurted high and then sank silently into the sand. "What shall I do with the body?"

"Put it on the pile with the rest—no, wait, I have a better idea." The commander nodded toward the northern part of the beach. "Toss her to the Rmoahals —they must be hungry for a woman's flesh."

The man looked doubtful and glanced uneasily over his shoulder. "Vardek has banned the Rmoahals from eating the dead—even the women."

The commander grunted. "The Rmoahals have always eaten the dead, their own as well as those they slay in battle. It will take more than a mere command, even from such as Vardek, to make them change their ways."

The man shrugged and slid off the girl. He picked up her body and slung it over his shoulder. "Are Vardek's commands so empty that even the Rmoahal slave fighters disobey them?"

The commander looked up and fingered his sword. "You can always test the emptiness of Vardek's commands, or mine, Paladek, by disobeying them yourself," he said softly.

The man grunted and turned away to trudge along the beach. The girl's throat hung ragged and open. Already the blood had ceased to flow.

On the northern beach lay the slave wing of the Rmoahal warriors, a full thousand men. Black as night and as fierce as death, no man in their company stood less than seven feet in height, and all Amaria knew them well and feared them more than they feared their gods. No warriors on earth could halt the charge of a battle-crazed Rmoahal line—and no man of Amarian blood would face a Rmoahal black in single combat. But it was not their strength alone that struck fear into the hearts of their enemies, nor their frenzied battle cry, nor yet their custom of eating the flesh of the dead. Dark tales were whispered of their deeds, and grew in the telling to monstrous heights—tales of obscenity and foul acts that took place when the battles were done and the Rmoahals made sport with their prisoners.

But fine warriors though they were, yet were they

slaves to the Toltecs. Each Rmoahal wore a circlet of iron around his throat, and each circlet was stamped with the sign of the Broad Arrow and numbered according to the owner.

Paladek came up to a group of them and threw the girl's body to the ground. "Greetings to the Rmoahals," he growled.

The blacks were clustered around a fire over which an Amarian corpse had been roasted to a blackened hulk. The melted fat from the body had been caught in an iron bowl and the Rmoahals were rubbing the hot fat into their own bodies so that their skins glistened in the early light. Parts of the corpse were missing, and bones and gobbets of burned flesh littered the sand for yards around.

One of the men, huge even by Rmoahal standards, rose from the fire and gave the slave sign. "Greetings, Toltec, from the Rmoahals. We wait your command."

"Not a command I bring, but a gift. May she taste sweeter than the men who knew her."

The man nodded gravely. "It is good, and we give thanks. What can we offer that would be pleasing to a Toltec of Ruta?"

From the center of the wing, a hundred yards away, came the sound of ritual chanting—and Paladek had heard that chant before. He nodded in the direction of the sound. "Give me leave to watch the Dance of Death."

The Rmoahal grinned hugely. "So be it, Toltec—but take care lest you join the dance yourself."

Paladek frowned and put his hand to his knife. "You would also do well to take care, slave! Remember to whom you speak!"

The other Rmoahals had come to their feet swiftly and silently the moment the Toltec's hand had moved —and they towered tall above him. Naked they were, save for the slave collars and belts of leather around their waists that held their weapons and trophies of the war—and their skins glistened and smelled foul and rancid.

The Toltec knew that he would die instantly if he

showed but a trace of fear. "Do the dogs still bark, then?" he sneered. "Have you forgotten, Rmoahal, who is master here and who is slave?" He slowly pulled his knife and placed its point against the black man's stomach. "Speak, slave, lest I thrust and so remind you!"

The eyes of the Rmoahals glinted redly, but for century upon century their people had worn the Toltec collar of slavery, and the habit of fear dies hard, and all knew how many would die if this Toltec were harmed.

Paladek slowly pushed the knife fraction by fraction against the stomach—never taking his gaze from the other's eyes—but not until a full inch of blade had entered the flesh did the man speak.

"I have not forgotten, nor does any Rmoahal forget the collar he wears. I spoke in jest, master, not in threat."

Paladek nodded and viciously twisted the blade as he pulled the knife clear. "Very well, we will not speak of this again, nor will I report your jest—but you would also do well to remember that I am not a jesting man." He thrust the knife back in his belt and then grinned up at the huge Rmoahal. "But we are wasting time— the dance may end before we arrive. Lead on, my friend—many times have I seen the Rmoahal Dance of Death, and always it stirs my blood in a strange and pleasing way."

The Rmoahal nodded and turned to guide the way. The knife cut in his stomach weeped blood, but he did not deign to notice so slight a wound.

In the very center of the wing of Rmoahals a space had been cleared for the Dance of Death. The tall Rmoahal stooped to speak to an old man who sat cross-legged at the edge of the circle. The old man nodded and turned to stare at Paladek. His eyes were black and fierce, his cheeks were scarred with ritual markings, and his lips and chin were wet and red with blood. He offered the iron bowl to Paladek. "Drink, Toltec. None may see the Dance of Death without first drinking the blood of the dancer."

Paladek nodded and took the bowl. He knew the rules, and although he did not relish the taste of hot blood as did the Rmoahals, neither did it make him gag as it did some Toltecs he knew. As he lifted the bowl, the old man rose to his feet and Paladek saw that it was Dracombi, for he had no penis and no testicles—the flesh where those organs should have hung was scarred and puckered like a grotesque caricature of a woman. Long ago in Dracombi's youth he had himself severed the organs from his own body in the initiation ceremony of the Mating with the Dead. The act symbolized that henceforth the new shaman would not concern himself with giving life, but would dedicate himself to achieving total communion with the dead and the gods of the dead. The name that he chose for himself, Dracombi, when translated into Toltec meant "The Eyes Through Which the Dead Look Out."

Paladek drank from the bowl and wiped the blood from his lips with the back of his hand. The old man took the bowl and set it on the sand. He waved his hand toward a pile of headless corpses. "As you can see, Toltec, many have already danced, and they now speak to me from the land of the dead. There are but two only still to dance. Sit among the Rmoahals and watch."

Paladek took a place in the circle, his body a streak of red beech among so much ebony, and the chant began again. A single drummer beat a slow and relentless rhythm, and the deep Rmoahal chant rolled along the sand and echoed bass-voiced across the bay. The Toltec felt his hands tingle in expectation, and his heart began to beat more swiftly. The chant rose a full tone as the last two prisoners were led into the circle, and the single note of the drum began to be accented on the off-beat as the Rmoahals began to slap their thighs in unison.

The first prisoner was a male warrior, a grizzled veteran, and like all Amarians, he was small and light in stature, a mere five feet or so, dwarfed by the giant black who held him. His skin was a light brown, not unlike the Toltec coloring, but without that reddish hue.

Paladek started with surprise as he saw that the

second prisoner was a woman, a girl in fact. From between her legs there hung the loose ends of crude twine that had been used to sew her flesh together, her father's proof to the village that his daughter was still a virgin.

"A girl?" said Paladek. "I have never seen a woman honored by the Rmoahals and given the Dance of Death."

The old man grunted. "Woman she may be, but unaided she stole the life of three Rmoahals, and so by our custom she is deserving of honor as though she were a man."

The Toltec looked at the young girl and shook his head in disbelief. "How could such a one vanquish even a single Rmoahal in battle, let alone three?"

Dracombi turned his dead eyes on the Toltec. "She pretended death, and when a lone Rmoahal passed her by, she sprang upon his back and stabbed twice with her knife in his eyes and so blinded him. She then drew off and rushed in time and again to stab him deeply until he fell and so died. Three times thus she fought until she was captured."

Paladek looked again and marveled at the girl's boldness and courage. "It is a pity that such a one should die—she could breed fine warrior sons."

"Would you rob her of honor?" said Dracombi. "It is her right to be given the Dance of Death, and none may deny her—not even a Toltec," he added.

Paladek looked deep into the shaman's eyes, but what he saw made his courage falter. "A Toltec does not deny honor to one who deserves it," he muttered. "What the Rmoahals do is of no consequence to us—let the girl dance, if that is your sport."

"And yours, too, Toltec," said the old man, "else why are you here? The sport of slaves stirs your blood —many times you have watched the dance, and each time your sleep is troubled for many days with visions of the dead." He looked at the Toltec shrewdly and saw the memory of those dreams flit across the man's eyes. "And how many times have you seen yourself headless dancing among the grinning dead, and felt the fear rise up and bring you trembling from your sleep?"

"Enough of this idle talk of dreams," the Toltec growled. "Let the dance begin, lest the sun rise and bring an untimely end to your sport."

The shaman grinned evilly and laughed. "So be it." He clapped his hands and pointed to the prisoners. "Let the dance begin!"

The chanting rose to a higher key and quickened in pace. Two huge Rmoahals, each wearing the painted insignia of a shaman-warrior, strode into the center of the circle. Each carried an enormous knife with a blade so curved that it formed a three-quarter circle. The drumbeat quickened yet again, and the prisoners struggled in terror in the arms of those who held them. The circle of a thousand Rmoahal slave fighters swayed in rhythm to the quickened beat, and the Toltec swayed with them, his resentment forgotten in the excitement of the moment.

The chant rose to a crescendo, and at its height the two shaman-warriors stepped up to the prisoners, one to each, and grasped them by the hair. With their free hands each whirled his curved knife so fast that the eye could barely follow its motion. In one quick movement each simultaneously sliced the blade around each prisoner's neck in a full circle, cutting through the flesh of the throat and nape, cutting deep but not deep enough to sever the spine—and with a strong upward jerk each tore off the head completely, leaving a few inches of spine and marrow sticking up from the headless neck. At the same time, the guards and shaman-warriors stepped quickly away, leaving the corpses standing headless by themselves. It had happened in a single second—a quick, practiced slice and lift—and the two heads were thrown to the waiting crowd.

The head of the girl came rolling toward Paladek, and the Toltec dived forward and secured it before those on either side could move. The eyes were still open and the lips still writhed in terror. Paladek laughed and kissed the dead and moving lips, and then turned the head so that the girl's eyes faced toward the center of the circle.

The prisoners had been struggling furiously up to the moment their heads were severed, and the movement of their struggles now continued to animate the headless corpses. Each corpse staggered from side to side, the column of white marrow sticking up from the neck whipping backward and forward, and the baying roar of the chant splintered into separate shouts and shrieks as the Rmoahals burst to their feet in appreciation.

The breasts on the girl corpse bounced furiously with the movement of the body, and the Rmoahals laughed and pointed and made obscene gestures. The Dance of Death rarely lasted longer than a few seconds, but just as the corpses were about to fall, a quirk of chance caused the two bodies to collide, and for a full ten seconds the dead Amarians danced together, headless, breast to breast—and Paladek, the Toltec, clutched the head of the girl to his chest and laughed and roared —and then the two corpses staggered wildly and fell to the ground still locked together, and the Rmoahals bellowed with laughter and sweat broke through every pore on Paladek's body and ran in streams along his skin.

The old man, Dracombi, shaman to the Rmoahals, grinned evilly and signaled for the corpses to be dragged away. "So, Toltec, the Dance of Death is ended. May your sleep be free of terror."

Paladek was still breathing heavily, and the sweat glistened on his skin. "It was worth a few troubled nights," he growled. He swung the girl's head by the hair. "Do you think she saw the dance?"

A faint smile touched the old man's eyes. "The dead see more than you think."

Paladek laughed. "This dead one owes you much— there are not many who have watched their own death struggles." He threw the head at Dracombi's feet. "But I do not think she took much pleasure in it," he added dryly. He looked up at the sky and sniffed the air.

"The dawn wind is rising—I must return. We will be sailing soon. Greetings, Dracombi."

"Greetings, Toltec—may the dead leave you in peace."

The Toltec headed back down the beach toward his own lines. The light was growing stronger; soon it would be time for Vardek to make the dawn sacrifice before the assembled army. Paladek quickened his pace—his section commander would accept no excuses for lateness. But when he reached his section there was no sign of him. "He has gone to visit the Akkadians," said one of the men. "His knife is blunt and needs sharpening." Paladek nodded and hurried on toward the southern beach. It was his duty to report to his section commander, wherever he might be, though Paladek suspected that it was more than a blunt knife that drew him to the Akkadian lines.

Banda had long been fascinated by the warrior bond that existed among certain Akkadians—even as he, Paladek, was fascinated by the Rmoahal customs. It was a curious bond, certainly, but Banda had perhaps too much curiosity. The rumors might be right, that Banda had Akkadian as well as Toltec blood in his veins. Paladek, however, was willing to overlook such curiosity, provided Banda did not seek a warrior bond with himself.

The Akkadians were a tall race, though not as tall as the Rmoahals. They were a light-skinned race, even lighter than the Toltecs. Their most distinctive feature, however, was their hair. The Rmoahal hair was jet black and woolly, the Toltec's long and shining black—but the hair of the Akkadians was yellow and fair like the tall grass in summer, and they wore it long to below their shoulders and gathered it at the neck with a pretty band. Their eyes, too, were strange. The eyes of the Rmoahals were the color of mud and the whites of the eyes more red than white, and those of the Toltecs were black and bright like wet black stones, but the eyes of the Akkadians were green and flecked with yellow like the rays of the sun among the high leaves of the forest.

A practical yet strangely dreamy race, the Akkadians. They were not slaves, yet were they ordered and ruled by the Toltecs. They were not as fine a warrior race as the Toltecs and Rmoahals, but fought bravely when the need arose. They were the artisans of Ruta, the master craftsmen, and they knew the stars and the ways of the sea. The weapons of the army were forged by Akkadian craft masters, and the ships were of their design and construction, and the helmsman of each was an Akkadian shipmaster. All Akkadians were skilled in at least one craft, and many knew the secrets of several. Twice a year, at the vernal and autumnal equinox rituals, the Akkadian craft masters took the tools of their craft to the Sun Temple to be blessed by the Toltec priests, and the priests looked with favor on the craft masters, for the Sun Temple of Narada, and indeed the City of the Golden Gates itself, had been designed and built by Akkadian artificers long, long ago.

They were not warriors by nature, but every Akkadian youth was required to serve in the army of Ruta for at least one campaign. Some served as shipmasters, some as craftsmen of weaponry, and others were craft masters of the earth and could advise the army where to seek for the red gold and precious stones required by the King and the Temple. But no matter what their particular craft, all were required to fight like any other warrior, and it was in this capacity that they showed that curious trait of the Akkadian character that so fascinated Banda and many other Toltecs—the Akkadian warrior bond.

Not every Akkadian warrior practiced the custom, but at least half of them did so. The warrior bond, as far as the Toltecs could understand it, was a deep feeling of comradeship that sometimes sprang up between two Akkadian fighting men to such an extent that henceforth they fought together, ate together, slept together, and made love together as did a man to a woman. The Toltecs did not discourage the practice, indeed the Lord Commander of the army spoke of it with approval, for it produced in the pair concerned a battle frenzy that was so necessary to make a good warrior and which no Akkadian could attain any other way. The Rmoahals were in an almost perpetual state of battle frenzy when on a campaign, and the Toltec training had taught them how to acquire it at will, but the Akkadians were either too practical or too dreamy to attain a fighting frenzy at all, except when a bond companion was in danger; only then did their aggressive frenzy emerge.

Banda was standing down by the Akkadian ships talking to a craft master. "I do not doubt that the Akkadian warrior bond is a noble companionship—I just do not understand it, nor does any Toltec."

The Akkadian craft master smiled. "You need to be of Akkadian blood to understand the warrior bond. What *we* don't understand is why the custom causes so much concern to Toltecs—there is no harm in it." He looked shrewdly at the Toltec commander and noted the brightness of his eyes. "The extent of your curiosity is itself curious. Is there another reason why you speak of it to me so often?"

Banda shrugged away the question. "I do not know whether there is harm in it or not—the custom intrigues me, that's all."

The Akkadian's yellow hair stirred in the rising wind. "I might remind you, commander, that the Akkadian warrior bond was considered by the Toltec priests many years ago, and after due consultation they announced that the custom was honorable and that no harm would come of it."

"If I remember the teachings correctly," said Banda, "they said that no harm would come of a companionship between two men provided it was not taken to excess and provided each of the pair fulfilled their duty in normal marriage to a woman."

"True," said the craft master, "and we Akkadians observe the marriage laws of Ruta, and none can say that we do not."

"Yet there is a saying among Akkadians, is there not, that women are a duty and men a joy?"

The Akkadian smiled broadly. "Merely a jest among

the young men only, even as the Toltec youths jest that all wives are a pleasure provided it is not your own."

The Toltec laughed. "You are a craft master of words, Demos, as well as a craft master of weapons!" The smile faded from his eyes as he saw Paladek coming toward them. "Here comes my second-in-command. He is also interested in strange customs. I heard the Rmoahal chant a little while ago—no doubt he has been watching the Dance of Death again."

Demos frowned. "I, too, watched it once, but once was enough. They are truly barbarians, the Rmoahals. Your officer should take care, the dead cling to those who summon them."

Inland from the beach, in a clearing on the very edge of the jungle, were the tents of Lord Vardek, supreme commander of the army of Ruta. Each tent bore the golden six-pointed star, emblem of the Sun Temple, and the very center tent also bore Vardek's own personal insignia of the blood-red five-pointed pentacle on a black shield with a flying reptile in silhouette.

Outside Vardek's tent, a few yards away on a grassy knoll that overlooked the beach, stood the three warrior chiefs. The Rmoahal chief, as befitted his status of slave, stood a little way apart from the other two.

The Toltec chief sniffed the wind and nodded. "The wind holds fair—three days to Ruta if all augurs well. I am not an impatient man, Herakos, but my blood frets to be away from this jungle." His headdress comprised seven feathers of the sun bird, denoting his rank in the Toltec hierarchy. No other Toltec could claim all seven, saving only the Lord Vardek himself. "But first we must wait on Vardek while he plays at being priest as well as warrior. I tell you, Herakos, I do not like this business of the sacrifice—my Lord Vardek presumes too much!"

The Akkadian chief shrugged. "He presumes, certainly, but whether he presumes too much depends on whether there is anyone big enough to tell him so." The Akkadian insignia of rank was not denoted by feathers, as in the case of Toltecs, nor in the number of ritual face scars that adorned the Rmoahal officers, but in the color of the shoulder sash, ranging as it did from the pale yellow of junior command to the rich purple worn by Herakos, chief of chiefs of all the Akkadian fighting force. "Will *you* tell him, Demian, that he presumes too much?"

The Toltec grunted. "Not I, nor any man in my command—only the King himself or the High Priest would risk the anger of Vardek, and even they hesitate, I hear." His hand tightened on his sword hilt and his eyes darkened. "Many times has he defied the priesthood, each time more boldly than the last, and each time they hesitate to invoke the Council of Priests against him—and so he grows more insolent year by year. And now we have this business of the sacrifice. All Ruta knows that only a priest can make the sacrifice, and yet time and again on this campaign has Vardek usurped that role for himself. Surely he has overreached himself at last?"

"Perhaps," said the Akkadian slowly, "but I doubt it. Since our own priest was washed overboard on the second night out he had no alternative but to perform the sacrifices himself—or else have no sun rituals at all, and all Ruta knows that an offering must be made to the sun when the battle is done. That, at any rate, will be his excuse."

Demian was not impressed. "A poor excuse that would fool no one."

"Baralda is an old man," said the Akkadian, "and so, too, is Khamadek—both want their remaining years to be tranquil, and so both will seize on any excuse not to move against one who commands the loyalty of the army as Vardek does. When King and High Priests hesitate, what hope has any Toltec, even one with seven feathers?"

Demian's hand moved toward his headdress, and then let it fall. "King Baralda and Khamadek may look with favor on a seven-feather Toltec who rids them of an embarrassment."

"And what of the Toltec warriors? They follow Var-

dek as though he were a god: Never has he lost a battle,
and always he divides the spoil, even among the lowest
of them."

"Trinkets!" said Demian angrily. "I, too, can buy
their loyalty with trinkets if that's all it takes—and I,
too, can win battles. But what of the Akkadians—how
do you stand in this?"

The Akkadian was on dangerous ground. "We follow whosoever is lawfully appointed," he said smoothly. "If Lord Vardek were to die, we would mourn his
death—and if the Sun Temple were to appoint you in
his place, we would give you our loyalty even as we
give it now to Vardek."

"But you will not assist the Sun Temple in dispos-
ing of him!"

"If that is their wish then we will serve accordingly
—but we require a sign."

"A sign!" The Toltec stamped his foot in anger.
"The strength of our people rests with the Sun Temple
—isn't the fact that Vardek openly scorns the priesthood sign enough that his time has come?"

"Perhaps—but if his time has come, then let the
High Priest so declare it lawfully."

Demian snorted. "By the time Khamadek acts it will
be too late! It does not require a priest to prophesy
that if Vardek is not stopped now then the time will
come when he will straddle all Ruta like a god and we
lesser men will have to pay him homage. Let us
sacrifice him now lest in time we have to make sacrifices
to him!"

They were silent for a few seconds and then Herakos
said softly, "You are a Toltec, Demian, but you are my
friend. Many times on this campaign has your company
of warriors come to our aid when we were sorely
pressed—perhaps I even owe you my life—and so I
will give you advice." He eyed Demian cautiously.
Toltecs did not look kindly on advice offered by inferior races. "You may be right in all you say, but if
you value your life, then do not speak your thoughts
so openly lest you too are washed overboard like
that young priest who sailed from Ruta with us."

Demian turned sharply to face the Akkadian. "So that's how it happened!"

He would have said more, but at that moment the seeress emerged from her tent and came toward them. She was a young girl, very young and very inexperienced. Demian could expect no help from her, except that she was too naïve to play at politics and so would faithfully report to Khamadek all that she had seen. "Greetings, seeress," he said. "Our last day in Amaria dawns—soon we will be in Ruta."

"And in truth I will not be sorry," she said. "Greetings, my lords." Herakos and the Rmoahal chief, Bulambi, bowed low. Demian remained upright, as befitted his race and rank. A Toltec chief bowed only to Toltecs of greater rank than his own, and to a senior priest, certainly not to a seeress. The girl moved closer to the towering Rmoahal and looked up at him. "I trust your people have fed well, Bulambi." Her head scarcely reached his chest, though she was tall for a Toltec woman. "It is not easy to obtain sufficient food while on campaign."

The Rmoahal's voice was deep and gutteral. "Lord Vardek has kept us well supplied with flesh," he growled, "and we give thanks."

"Not human flesh, I trust?"

"No, seeress—prisoners taken in battle."

Demian and Herakos hid their smiles, and the girl flushed. Herakos, ever the diplomat, stepped forward to fill the breech. "Some of the prisoners were women, Naida, some as young as yourself, but none could match you in beauty." She was indeed very beautiful. Her hair was long and shining black. Her robe was of the palest blue, each fold a transparent wisp that floated about her caressingly, but fold upon fold enveloped her beauty so that no eye could penetrate their transparency to her nakedness beneath. "Compared to you, Naida," the Akkadian added, "they were indeed scarcely human."

"Thank you, Herakos—but you should not think of me as a woman but as a seeress."

"It will be difficult," he said dryly, "but I will try."

She tossed her head and drew the robe more closely about her. "And I trust that you will succeed. It is my destiny to mate only with a priest of the Sun Temple, not with a warrior."

Demian laughed. "And if I were a priest, I would fight like a warrior to be the lucky one chosen."

The girl flushed more deeply still and moved away to the highest point of the knoll, where a crude altar had been erected. On the altar, spread-eagled on her back, naked and unconscious, her hands and wrists tied with thongs, lay an Amarian girl no older than Naida herself. "I see Lord Vardek intends another sacrifice," she said, "and again it is not properly arranged. The legs should be together, not wide apart like a whore, and the body should be covered with golden cloth as befits an offering to the sun." She reached forward and placed her hand on the girl's breast. "At least she is still alive, not like the last one." She ran her hand down the girl's body and felt between the legs. She turned to them at last and they could see the fury in her eyes. "This girl is not a virgin!" she hissed. "How dare you insult the Sun Temple by this travesty of a ritual! Know you not that the sacrifice must be clean and untouched by man! This thing is not a virgin, I tell you!"

A voice bellowed suddenly behind them. "Who is not a virgin—and who dares question *my* arrangements?"

The seeress and the three chiefs spun around, and there, standing by his tent, was Lord Vardek, supreme commander of the army of Ruta. A small man by any standards, barely five and a half feet, smaller even than Naida, the seeress. But though short in height, his girth was immense, like an old tree, and his skin was dark and gnarled like bark. Naked, he stood glaring at them, not a stitch of cloth or cloak or belt, and his entire body was covered in thick coarse hair like matted fur. Great knotted muscles stood out on his huge chest and shoulders, and his hands hung low to his knees. A great hooked nose dominated his face, and his brow was low and terminated in craggy eye ridges that jutted out like cliffs from the jungle of his face, and beneath those cliffs his small black eyes glared out cruelly and savagely.

Some said he was born out of season, that he was an ancestor long dead from the times when man was more animal than man, and some said that his mother had lain with the great jungle gorilla, but none ever repeated these things in Vardek's hearing. But savage and repulsive though he was, yet he was a Toltec with all the courage and vitality of that race, and all its arrogance and savagery as well.

"I asked you a question!" he roared. "*Who* is not a virgin? Don't tell me that the seeress has at last managed to get one of you between her legs!" He bellowed with laughter and slapped his thigh. "Great Narada, wait till that old fool Khamadek hears about this! Who was it—tell me—who split the wench? Was it you, Bulambi, you great black hulk? A handful of gold to the man who did it! By Narada, girl, you kept it quiet—not so much as a yelp I heard all night!"

Naida stepped forward, her face white with fury. "You insult me, Lord Vardek, and you yet again insult the Sun Temple! I have lain with no man, and you know it—nor have I any desire to do so, as you seem to think!"

Vardek stopped laughing, and his eyes glinted sardonically. "So!" he said softly. "Our seeress is still tight closed—but not for want of desire, *that* I know." He raised his hands as Naida made to speak. "Don't lie to me, girl. I know women, and I tell you this— you will never make a priestess, Naida, you ache too much to wave your sandals in the air. I have watched you these past six months, and I *know*. Many a time have you stared in your seeress' mirror, not to seek guidance for the army, but to see yourself split asunder by Demian there, by Herakos, by black Bulambi, and even by me—and your thighs ache for it to happen! You may fool Khamadek with your virginity, but don't lie to me!"

The girl was blushing furiously, and all could see

from her face that it was true. She made as if to speak, stammered in her embarrassment, and then ran headlong to her tent.

Vardek roared with laughter again. "There she goes —the most reluctant virgin in all Ruta!"

Demian stepped forward, his face a mask to hide his anger. "She is young, Vardek, but even the young have tongues. "Khamadek will hear of this."

"Not from her he won't! It is *she* who trembles lest *I* speak. Anyway, let us waste no more time, the sun is about to rise. We will sail for Ruta immediately after the sacrifice. Is the army ready to move?"

"Yes, Vardek—they but wait your command. But what of your prisoner?"

Vardek glared up at his second-in-command. "The Lady Pirani is a priestess of her people and a daughter of a king." He jabbed his finger in Demian's chest. "You will treat her with the respect that her rank demands!"

Demian's eyes glittered angrily. "A tribal chieftain is not a king, Vardek, and participation in a few primitive rituals hardly warrants the title of priestess. Our own seeress is more of a priestess than your primitive bed companion!"

Vardek's muscles bunched in readiness; in his youth he would have torn apart any man who spoke to him thus, but the years had taught him discretion. "Take care, Demian!" he said softly. "I am the Lord Commander of the army—so appointed by the Sun Temple. Take care lest you cross me once too often and so come to harm!"

"Like the priest who drowned?" said Demian.

In the background Herakos shook his head sadly— Demian was a fine warrior but a fool.

Vardek stared long and hard at Demian, but all he said was, "Let the trumpeters summon the army to assemble. We will speak of this again, but not here," and he turned and strode back to his tent.

Pirani, captive daughter of an Amarian chieftain, lay on her back on a couch of green linen, naked, her legs apart, admiring herself in a mirror of beaten silver that had been in Vardek's family for centuries. "Doesn't that fool realize, my lord," she murmured, "that he is already a dead man?" Like Naida the seeress, Pirani too was beautiful—not the charm of youth and innocence, but that deadly beauty that ensouls the corrupt. Tall she was, languid and sensuous, utterly depraved. Her hair was long and black, her skin was warm and golden brown, her breasts were heavy, her eyes challenging, and her body gave off that acrid smell of musk perfumes that Vardek found so intoxicating. She knew tricks of the bedchamber that no Toltec woman had even dreamed of.

"I doubt it," Vardek growled. "As you say, he is a fool!" He began to dress himself—a tunic of leather, thonged sandals, and a cloak of red woven cloth. He did not bother with the niceties of dress, of color, of fine weaves, of jewels and gold, as did some of his officers. From outside came the sound of running feet and the fanfare of trumpets. "Get dressed, woman—the fleet sails very soon."

She rose from the couch, stretched, yawned, and ran her hands from her breasts to her flanks. "I could help you, my lord—with Demian, I mean." She picked up a robe of yellow and threw it around her shoulders and gathered it at the waist. "On the journey to Ruta he may eat something that will not be pleasing." Her eyes strayed to the carved ebony casket by the couch.

"He may indeed," said Vardek. "It should not be difficult to arrange." He walked over to her, grasped her by the hair, and placed the point of his knife to her throat. "But let me make matters clear, priestess of herbs. I usually take my pleasure of a woman for a few days and then hand her over to the Rmoahals. What say you to that?"

Her head was drawn back, taut and painful, yet she smiled. "It would be a pity, lord—I could serve you well on Ruta."

The knife moved a little nearer. "You are a woman of many talents, Pirani—see that they are used to serve me and no one else. Remember who spared your life, and remember that a woman of Amaria will not be popular on Ruta. Your only hope of survival lies in my

continued support. Remember that before you even
think of feeding *me* from your hell box of evil plants!
But serve me well, woman, and you will live like a
queen!" He released her and thrust the knife back in
his belt, "Come—it is time."

A few seconds later the army rose as one man to hail

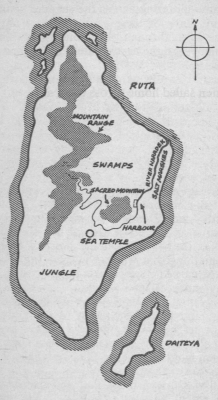

their Lord Commander as he stepped to the altar and
raised high the sacrificial knife. "VARDEK! VARDEK!
VARDEK!"

Behind the Lord Commander stood the three warrior chiefs—Bulambi, black as night, Chief of all the
Rmoahals; Herakos, fair and golden-haired, Chief of

the Akkadians; and Demian, red-brown and angry, Chief of all the Toltec fighting men and second-in-command of the combined army of Ruta. All three raised their swords in salute to the Lord Commander. "HAIL, LORD VARDEK, HAIL!"

As the last echo rang around the bay, the first ray of morning came glittering across the sea and sparkled on the blade in Vardek's hand as he swung it down and rammed the knife through breast and bone to split the heart asunder—and the army roared their salute again.

"VARDEK! VARDEK! VARDEK!"

And thus the sun came, and five thousand strong of Vardek's men sailed home across the sea.

2

The twin islands of Ruta and Daiteya lay east-southeast of the Gulf of Mehicohan from whence sailed Vardek homeward bound across the sea. Islands they were, yet were they merely the summit, the twin tips of a colossal undersea mountain that reared up from the ocean floor many leagues below the waves. Daiteya, the smaller of the two, was a humped-back craggy mound, a mere ridge of broken rock, but Ruta was a magnificent island, a formidable yet savagely beautiful land. Its length was two days' march from north to south and one from east to west. It rose up arrogant and wild from the waters of the sea to tower three thousand feet into the sky. Its southern half was dense jungle growth, impenetrable, hot, humid, and alive with insects of incredible size and color. The northern half was dominated by a mountainous hinterland, the mountain range running parallel to the coast. Between the mountains and the eastern shore an alluvial plain had been formed most of which was only a little above sea level and thus subject to frequent inundations from the sea, making of it a treacherous salt marsh.

The River Naradek rose from a sacred lake in the high mountain range in the background and flowed through great gorges and wound across the plain in a serpentine course. As it drew near to the coast it ran parallel to it for some distance with a narrow strip of land between it and the sea, before finally leaving the marshland to turn eastward into the ocean itself.

At this point, where the land was dry and free of the poisonous gases exuded by the marshland to the south, stood an ancient volcano well clear of the main range of the mountains. Ten million years had passed since it blew off its cone in a dreadful gout of flame and ash, and since then the whole of the upper plateau had weathered flat, undisturbed by further flames, though deep in its belly the old man still grumbled in his sleep.

It was here, on this volcano, on its topmost plateau, on its very slopes, straddling the Naradek at its foot, stood the magnificent, mighty, and ancient City of the Golden Gates, ancestral home of the Toltec empire, last refuge of the subject races who fled thither in ancient times when the great continent was shattered and swallowed by the sea.

Prior to the cataclysm the city had harbored none but the Toltec priesthood, the royal family, the Sacred Clan, and selected warriors for the Temple Guard, but now its population exploded upward with the inrush of refugees. The Toltecs, the royal family, the priesthood, the scribes and warriors withdrew to the topmost plateau to dwell in and around the great Temple of the Sun. The Akkadian merchants and artificers, the builders and craft masters, dwelt on the middle tier of the city, and the Rmoahals, the farmers and agriculturists, dwelt at the foot of the Sacred Mountain.

For a time the people flourished under the ruling principles of the priesthood, but generation followed generation, and the inherent weakness, fed by centuries of inbreeding, caused the breath of evil once more to waft over the land—and the Sacred Clan, the royal family, became weak and ineffective, and the Sun Temple priesthood grew in pride and arrogance.

But there were two temples on Ruta, the Sun Temple and the Withdrawn Temple. Sun worship, as practiced in the Sun Temple, was only the outer aspect of the

Toltec religion, a magical religious cult. The priesthood of the sun cult were magicians and psychics, and the Toltec inhabitants on the topmost plateau of the Sacred Mountain were all initiates of the sun cult in various grades. The dwellers on the lower tiers, the Akkadians and Rmoahals, were not initiated into the Sun Mysteries but did worship at the Sun Temple, for indeed it was a national religion.

But there were deeper esoteric aspects behind the sun cult which were concealed from the general view. This was the sea worship, and only the seers and the highest order of mystical priesthood could attain to its membership. This inner priesthood were the illuminati who dwelt in another temple outside the city, far removed from the political arena. This was the Withdrawn Temple, sometimes called the Sea Temple, and sometimes called the Temple of Naradek, for it was indeed situated on the banks of the Naradek some few miles farther inland from the City of the Golden Gates. Though time and again throughout Toltec history evil had held sway within the people, and within the Sun Temple itself, never at any time had any smear of corruption tainted the honor of the Withdrawn Temple priesthood. The illuminati of the Withdrawn Temple were the real directing influence of the people, but they never dealt in politics, only in the broad spiritual principles of national life.

But this is not to say that the Withdrawn Temple did not watch over the city, or care as to its fate. Watch they did, and with sorrow did they see error piled upon error—greed upon tyranny, cruelty upon pride, lust upon dishonesty—and they could do little save ensoul their prayers with compassion. By the powers vested in them in earth they could have taken over the city, could have dictated to the people as to how they should live and die—but it was not permitted. Man had been given the right to choose between corruption and incorruption, between the infernal and the supernal, and if man chose evil, then he also chose the misery that went with it, and none were permitted to interfere.

At the time of Vardek's rise to power on Ruta, Kumara was High Priest of the Withdrawn Temple and his sorrow was great. For decade after decade he had watched the decline of the city into evil, knowing that there could be but one end.

"Man has a greatness within him that surpasses even He who created him," he murmured softly, "yet does he choose to debase himself, ever seeking to return to the wilds of chaos from whence he rose."

Kumara sat in the high room in the eastern tower looking out over the edges of the salt marsh to the City of the Golden Gates some three miles to the east, and beyond it to the sea. This was Kumara's private meditation chamber high in the eastern turret of the Temple of the Sea—Kumara, High Priest of the Moon, Priest of the Son Behind the Sun, Guardian of the Chalice of the Moon, spiritual head of all Ruta, robed in purest white, the Ring of Power upon his hand, and on his breast the sigil of the Most High.

With him was Marah, High Priestess of the Sea, Priestess of the Grail, Pythoness of the Sun, responsible under Kumara for the spiritual and magical direction and training of all the priestesses and seeresses of both temples—an austere, beautiful woman whose eyes were ever filled with the vision of sorrow, the knowledge and acceptance of all that must occur to man on his chosen path. Tall she was, and perfectly formed, robed in blue as the deepest sea.

"You speak truly, Lord Kumara," she said slowly, "yet I cannot believe that Man will fail. From chaos he arose, and to chaos he will return, and his path is full of tears—yet will he rise on the wings of his sorrow to dance among the stars."

Kumara nodded. "And what say you, Melchadek?" He looked over to the young priest, who stood with arms folded by the seer's mirror. "You who come among us from the days of tomorrow—what say you to this?"

Melchadek, Priest of the Moon, Keeper of the Akhasic Record, robed in simple black, young and yet older than Kumara, who was aged. His eyes were pale, withdrawn, and far away. "To Chaos he will return, and he will surely dance among the stars as you say, Marah —aye, and command them. Out of Chaos was he born, and his mother was the Spirit of the Unmanifest Silence and his father the upwelling force of the Rings of Creation. To Chaos he will return—it is his destiny."

"But not by tracing his footsteps backward through darkness and evil," said Kumara, "but forward in the Light of the Most High."

"And forward he is going, be assured," said Melchadek. "At the close of every age the seedbearers go forward to the new age and those that remain destroy themselves. It was ever thus, and ever will be." He pointed downward to the River Naradek far beneath. "Twice now have the seedbearers set forth from Ruta down the Naradek to the great sea and beyond to the new age, and with them they carried the seeds of greatness that you and those before you caused to be harvested from the flower of this age. Once more the seedbearers must set forth before the waters of destruction are let loose on Ruta."

They were silent for a few seconds, and then Kumara sighed heavily. "What you say is true, Melchadek. You are of the new age and must soon set forth, and I am of the present age and must remain to preside over the destruction of my children. Would that we could all go forward together." He touched the sigil on his breast and closed his eyes. "Seven great ages will rise and fall," he quoted, "and seven times will the Child be born from the flames of destruction ere Man sits on the throne of the Mighty." He opened his eyes and smiled. "Three ages have passed, and the fourth is about to die. To you of the fifth great race of man I bring you greetings, Melchadek."

"Greetings, Lord Kumara," said the young priest gravely. "The greatness of your age will live forever in the memories of those who go forward, even as the waters of the Naradek remember the source from which they sprang."

"Ah, yes, the Naradek, the mighty River Naradek

—soon she will bear my soul to the sea of forgetful-
ness." Kumara closed his eyes and sang softly the beautiful and moving chant from the initiation ritual of
the sixth degree. "Helios, Helios, quanto rhopantanek
—waft thou my soul down the River of Naradek—
bring it to light and to life and to love." He opened his
eyes and sighed. "To light and to life and to love! Aye,
for us, Melchadek, but what of the children of the
city? They will be borne down to darkness, death and
destruction!"

Melchadek would have given much to bring comfort to the old man. "It will pass, Kumara—they will
die and then live again, even as you have done. Where
they stand now, you once stood—the evils that they do
were once committed by yourself. You yourself wal-
lowed in the slime of evil and so suffered. Time and
again you sank into death and destruction and were the
plaything of the Dark Lords. Yet time and again you
rose to be born again—and each time you learned a
little more of your true self, until now you have risen
in the full strength of your spirit, soon to stand before
the Most High to receive as your right the just rewards
of your service. Even as you have risen, so will they
rise. Be assured of that, Lord Kumara!"

The old man stirred, and then smiled. "It is certainly
true that nothing escapes the Akhasic Records—or the
eagle eye of the Keeper of the Records." He cocked an
eye at the younger man. "Was I so very bad?"

"You were the cause of much concern to the Lord
of Flame, whose name you now bear," said Melchadek
gravely.

Kumara turned to the High Priestess. "And what of
you, Marah? Do you remember the days of your foolishness?"

Her eyes clouded with memory. "The vision is ever
before me, Lord Kumara," she said softly. "Often in
foul rites I allowed my body to be used by things that
were born of slime—aye, and often I created monstrous beings of the half-life and ensouled them with
my lust and sent them forth to bring men to their doom.
These and other foul deeds are on my record, and

deeply have I drunk of the sea of bitterness. For many lives have I striven to repay my debts."

"And so you have," said Kumara, "many times over. You have served the lords well, and your just reward will come. Was ever a high priest so faithfully and loyally served by his pythoness! Much honor is yours, Marah, and you will find that the Great Ones will not forget." He turned once more to gaze out toward the City of the Golden Gates, to where on the topmost plateau of the old volcano the Temple of the Sun gleamed golden in the evening sun. "Each of us here in the withdrawn priesthood have known the cup of evil and yet we rose above it and triumphed over our evil heritage and so entered the priesthood and strove upward through the ranks of the Sun Temple until we were found worthy to be withdrawn here to the Temple of the Sea. In all the long history of Ruta, never has a priest or priestess of the Temple of the Sea betrayed the trust that was placed in their hands—never has the breath of evil entered this sanctuary." He pointed to the City of the Golden Gates. "Not so with the Temple of the Sun. It has been many years since a Priest of the Sun was considered worthy to join our ranks. They should be as a great light to the people, but time and again have they led the way into darkness. Man, man, we foolish creatures, why do we choose to suffer?" His face clouded and his voice sank lower. "Melchadek, Priest of the Moon, Keeper of the Akhasic Records— relate again the story of the swarms so that we may understand."

Melchadek bowed and moved to the seer's mirror. His eyes closed and he saw with his inner eyes what was written on the inner plane Akhasic Record.

". . . and having completed his subjective evolution the Logos turned his awareness outward and sought to create a replica of Himself. And He summoned the Divine Sparks from out of Chaos to help him in His work, and they came in their swarms, eager to do his bidding, for by so doing they would advance their own evolutions and so would rise to greatness to be a Logos even as He. And the Most High Logos projected a thought form of Himself, but the earth was void and without form, and darkness was upon the face of the deep."

"Aye," murmured Kumara, "a bargain it was, an apprenticeship, even as a scribe serves a priest and so in turn learns to become a priest himself. But go on with the tale, Melchadek—go on."

And once more Melchadek read the words of fire and brought them through into his consciousness. "And the Logos said, 'Let there be Light,' and He sent forth the first swarm of Sparks to do his bidding. And the Sparks carried the Will of the Logos across the Abyss and made it manifest in the universe—and there was Light. And the Sparks laid down the lines of Light as a framework in accordance with the Will of the Most High Logos. And their work was well done, and they withdrew from the Universe, and the Sparks of this first swarm were henceforth known as the Lords of Flame.

"And the Logos said, 'Let there be a firmament in the midst of the waters,' and He sent forth the second swarm to build the forms of the Universe on the framework already laid down. And again the work was well done and the Sparks withdrew, henceforth to be known as the Lords of Form.

"And the Logos said, 'Let the waters bring forth living creatures,' and He sent forth the third swarm, who laid down the basis of consciousness, and then withdrew, henceforth to be known as the Lords of Mind.

"And of these first three swarms most withdrew utterly from the Universe to continue their evolution elsewhere in the Cosmos. But some remained to give guidance to the subsequent swarms."

Kumara nodded vigorously. "And just as well they did, or else all would have been lost!"

"And then the Logos said, 'Let us make man in our own image'—and he sent out the fourth swarm and gave them a new factor to work out in the Universe, the factor of 'free will,' and when their work is done they are to be known as the Lords of Humanity."

"Enough!" said Kumara. "And there we have it—man's damnation and also his salvation—free will! The freedom to choose between the will of the Logos and the will of man—and so the human Sparks choose to manifest their own will, and so suffer! What we foolish spirits fail to understand until the lesson is driven home by suffering, is that this entire Universe, every stick and stone and every force of nature, was laid down by the first three swarms exactly in accordance with the plan of the Logos. Therefore to align yourself with the Logoidal will is to bring yourself into harmony with all creation and therefore into harmony with all the forces of the Universe. But to go against the will of the Logos is therefore to go against the very nature of the Universe in which we live—and yet time and again must a man be driven to his knees before he will dimly grasp this simple fact. What say you to this, Melchadek?"

"In my opinion," said the young priest gravely, "few men understand the nature of the Logos, or the nature of the Universe in which they live—nor do they understand that they do have free will. They therefore do not deliberately oppose the will of the Logos, but live out their lives haphazardly, and sometimes accidentally run in opposition to the nature of the Universe and so suffer, not knowing why it is they suffer."

Kumara nodded slowly. "You speak truly, but you would think that a man would need to place his hand only once in the fires of evil to know that it hurt—but no, time and again he will plunge it in, and not until the limb is a charred stump will he dimly begin to grasp the fact that the way of evil is the way of suffering."

"But a foolish and ignorant man is not an evil man," said Melchadek, "merely foolish and ignorant. But when he begins to learn of his own nature, and the nature of the Universe, and the nature of the Logos who created it, and yet still persists in his foolish ways and deliberately leads others into suffering, *then* can he be called evil."

"And if such a man is a priest of the temple," said

Kumara, "then he is doubly evil, for he should be as a light to the people, not a guide to darkness and suffering. To such base degrees has the Temple of the Sun fallen. There was a time when the priesthood of the Sun were as Lords of Light to all the land, but now they have fallen on evil ways."

Marah moved forward to stand before the angry High Priest. "And under their example such ruthless and arrogant men as Vardek rise to power. Even now his fleet draws near to Ruta, and my seeress reports that ten thousand Amarians have been put to the sword in Vardek's march along the shores of the mainland. Ten thousand murdered to feed his lust for power!"

"But he was sent to trade, not to murder!"

"But murder he has done, Lord Kumara—not once, but ten thousand times!"

Kumara's face was grim. He turned to Melchadek. "Has the Temple of the Sun invoked the Council of Priests against him?"

"No, Kumara—they hesitate to move against one who commands the loyalty of the army."

"Hesitate! Hesitate!" the High Priest thundered. "How dare they hesitate to oppose such evil deeds!"

Kumara rose from his chair and moved to the embrasure in the eastern wall. He raised his hand and pointed to the City of the Golden Gates. "Then let them die!" he thundered. "For they are not fit to live! Let the new age begin, and let the old perish utterly from the face of the earth!"

In his private meditation chamber high up on the eastern tower of the great Sun Temple on the topmost plateau of the Sacred Mountain, Khamadek, High Priest of the Sun, was jolted from his meditation by a tremendous clap of force that reverberated throughout the lower levels of the inner planes. He staggered to his feet clutching his head in both hands. It had been like a gigantic explosion in his mind, and his senses were reeling under the impact. He lurched across to the couch and flung himself full-length on his back and remained motionless for a full two minutes waiting for the vibrations to die down. At the end of that time there came the sound of running footsteps in the corridor outside, and without knocking and without even the courtesy of the customary obeisance, Baldek, son of Vardek, Priest of the Sun, burst into the room.

"What in the name of the seven Demons of Darkness was that?" he shouted. He ran across the room and stood over the High Priest. "Was that your doing, Khamadek?" He laid his hand roughly on the sleeve of the older man's robe. "The whole temple is in an uproar!"

Khamadek shook his head painfully. "It was not I —some sort of inner plane psychic explosion. I will investigate the cause and inform the Council of Priests in due course. What's this about the temple?"

"The whole place is in an uproar, Khamadek. Every seeress' mirror is obscured by dark clouds, and all contacts with the inner are broken. Only the contacts with the abhuman strata remain open, and even there the seals are destroyed!"

"What was that you said?" Khamadek tried to gather his scattered wits. "The abhuman door is open? Then seal it, and hurry! What are you doing here wasting time! Seal the door! You know nothing of the foul entities that will creep through that opening—not material beings, but practically material—creatures of the half-life! Seal the door, Baldek—and hurry!"

Baldek sneered. "Calm yourself, priest of power!" he said sarcastically. "It is already being attended to— young Helios is conducting the sealing ritual now and will deal with anything that has slipped through. Not that it matters—a priest of the Sun is a match for any abhuman from the slime!"

Khamadek rose and strove to gather together the shreds of his dignity. "You are a fool, Baldek! Ignorant and arrogant like your father! Just because you once invoked a few of the minor creatures and escaped unscathed, you think you know it all! I tell you of my own knowledge that there are entities behind that seal that even a sixth- or seventh-degree adept would have difficulty in controlling, let alone you!"

Baldek's face twisted with rage. "Already I have the secrets of the fifth degree, and . . ."

". . . and that is as far as you will go!" snapped Khamadek. "*I* will see to that! Never as long as I am High Priest will you ever be admitted to the higher degrees!"

Baldek's hands itched to grasp this vain old man by his scrawny neck, but old and weak in body though he was, yet was he still the High Priest and a seventh-degree initiate of the Sun and so commanded too much power for Baldek to deal with as yet. "Mark me well, Khamadek," he snarled, "one of these days I will go through the door that leads to the abhuman kingdom and there command those lumps of slime in their own realm!" He strode to the door and flung it open. "And then we shall see who is a true priest of power!"

Khamadek drew himself up and pointed a bony hand at the furious youth. "Go, then, to the abhumans if you must, but go prepared to die, for die you surely will!"

Baldek strode furiously from the room and slammed the door behind him. Khamadek sank back on to his couch. "Would that he would go now," he muttered, "and so rid us of his vile presence—*and* take his father with him!"

At that moment a soft knock sounded at the door and a young priest entered and gave the sign of salutation. He was copper-skinned and black-haired as all Toltecs, but his eyes were pale, a legacy from an Akkadian grandmother. His expression, as always, was calm and controlled. He carried himself with an assurance unusual for one so young—not the arrogant, overbearing confidence that Baldek displayed, but a quiet, disciplined power. "Greetings, Lord Khamadek," he said.

"Greetings, Helios. What news?"

"The door to the half-world is sealed, as instructed by Baldek."

Khamadek grunted irritably. "He had no right to give you instructions, you are both of the same degree." The old man paused, and then said carefully,

"Indeed, of the two I consider you to be the senior, as you probably know."

Helios smiled. "It is of little importance, Khamadek —the urgency of the moment was to reseal the inner door, not to wrangle over hierarchical seniority."

"Very well. Was the banishing ritual needed?"

"Yes, but only up to the fourth degree—only a few of the lesser entities had begun to emerge."

The High Priest breathed a sigh of relief. "It was well done—thank you. It could not have been easy to conduct such a ritual in that state of psychic confusion. What of Zesta?"

"The High Priestess is in the Chamber of the Seers endeavoring to clear the mirrors. She will report to you as soon as possible."

"Good, then all is well." He strode to the embrasure and gazed out at the early-evening sky. "But what it was, I do not know. The explosion on the inner came as I was deep in meditation and caught me by surprise. All I could detect in the aftermath was that it had emanated from a single human source." He looked quickly at Helios. "Has Baldek been trying some outlandish ritual again?" Helios hesitated, and Khamadek snapped his fingers impatiently. "You may as well tell me, boy—I will learn the details anyway from Zesta."

Helios bowed. "I understand that Baldek has adapted some of the Rmoahal rituals, particularly the one they call 'The Mating with the Dead.' "

"The full ritual? The full physical mating with a newly dead?"

"Even so. The body of an Akkadian girl was purchased yesterday from her parents. The girl had died from a spider bite while out searching for rare herbs in the forests to the south. Baldek himself conducted the ritual and took the part of the consummating celebrant. But the explosion was nothing to do with Baldek; indeed, I understand that the explosion on the inner revitalized the corpse temporarily such that it rose up from the altar and struck him."

Khamadek chuckled. "Good! I would have given

much to have seen that! But by Narada, that boy is a dangerous fool! He knows full well that the inner-plane adepts have expressly forbidden any intercourse with the dead. He will lead us all into harm!"

Helios said nothing. Baldek was a problem that could have been solved easily by a firm High Priest, but Khamadek did nothing save complain. All that was necessary was the Ritual of the Fourth Aspect from the Seventh Degree, which would effectively strip Baldek of all magical powers and so banish him from the temple. But there was a growing feeling throughout the temple that Khamadek had lost his powers and was no longer able to work the rituals of his office. No one was quite sure enough to challenge Khamadek to demonstrate his powers—as was their right—but Baldek in particular grew more insolent every day, as though forcing a challenge without actually making one. Helios felt sorry for the tired old man. The records showed that he had been a good high priest in his earlier days. He could have retired with honor the moment he felt his powers begin to fade—but it was a betrayal of his function to cling to an office that he could no longer perform.

"Well, if it wasn't Baldek," said Khamadek irritably, "then who was it?"

Inwardly Helios shook his head in dismay. All those of the sixth degree had recognized the imprint within the explosion—and so too had some of those of the fifth degree, like Helios. How was it possible that a seventh-degree adept, a high priest of the Sun, could have failed to determine the cause. Helios hesitated, and then said slowly, "I believe it came from Lord Kumara, High Priest of the Withdrawn Temple of Naradek—it was a shaft of his anger against the Temple of the Sun."

"Kumara? Why is he angry? Our rituals are going well, the people are satisfied, we are engaged in profitable trade with the mainland, we treat the seeresses and priestesses with honor—why should he vent his wrath on us?"

Helios sighed. No doubt Kumara knew all that went

on in the Sun Temple and so had good cause for anger. Aloud he said, "Perhaps he has heard of Vardek's exploits—I see the fleet draws near to Ruta."

"Exploits—what exploits? A few lives lost in battle?"

"Not a few, Lord Khamadek—ten thousand slain, if the seeress' mirror shows truly. And hardly a battle with honor—five thousand strong of the pick of Ruta's highly trained warriors against a string of primitive villages."

"Yes, well, you may be right. I shall speak to Vardek when he arrives. Send him to me as soon as his ship is berthed."

"Shall I summon the Council of Priests against him?" said Helios.

"Council of Priests? Certainly not. As you said yourself—five thousand strong of the pick of Ruta's highly trained warriors, and all loyal to Vardek. To move against him now would be to risk plunging the island into civil strife and might cause Vardek to lead the army against the Temple of the Sun."

Helios was appalled to hear the fear in Khamadek's voice. A high priest of the Sun afraid! The idea was almost unthinkable. "But to allow him to continue in his arrogance is to risk undermining the authority of the priesthood, Khamadek. If the people see him defy the temple and go unscathed they may follow his example. Surely the adepts of the Sun Temple can control a mere warrior, even one such as Vardek!"

Khamadek drew himself up. "Enough of this argument, Helios!" he said angrily. "You are a good priest but you know nothing of the politics of government! We of the sixth and seventh degrees are all old and nearing the end of our days, and as you are probably already aware, I have announced that you are to be my successor if your progress continues as it does at present. Until then, do not interfere in matters that do not concern you!"

Helios bowed and left the room; it was his duty to obey, but it was not always a pleasure. Khamadek's powers were waning fast, and as his sun was setting so Vardek's was rising more strongly and so in time would dominate the sky; but what could he, Helios, a mere fifth-degree initiate, do about it—he had neither the powers nor the right to oppose a high priest to whom he had sworn allegiance. And there was also Baldek to reckon with—an arrogant fool, but a dangerous one. If Khamadek allowed Vardek to continue to grow in power in the city, and allowed Baldek to continue to lead the younger priests on the dark paths of obscene rites, then the very Sun Temple itself was in danger.

So immersed was he in his own thoughts that he did not hear the girl come up beside him and walk with him until she plucked the sleeve of his robe. "Helios! Helios! What does all this mean?"

He looked down at the girl and smiled. Netziachos was a year younger than he and a head shorter. A single summer separated them in age, but their chosen path was a wider gulf by far. He was a priest of the Sun, a fifth-degree initiate, soon perhaps to be High Priest after the Order of Narada, the successor to Khamadek—and she was a seeress, a Priestess of the Sea, a child of the Withdrawn Temple, perhaps even to take up the mantle of Marah and serve as High Priestess of the Sea Temple. Every atom of him as a man cried out to this girl, and she to him, but they both knew that such personal things were not for them.

"It means, Netziachos," he said softly, "that the darkness has come again to Ruta." He took her hand and held it in his own. "Are you afraid?"

She shivered a little. "Yes," she whispered, "but I will do what I must do when the time comes." She looked up at him. "But without you I would be more afraid than I am. I am sorry, Helios, I try very, very hard, but sometimes I still think of you as a man, not a priest." She looked away from him quickly. "Especially at night, when the air is still and I can almost hear you breathing beside me, even though you are not there."

"But I *am* there, Netziachos," he said softly, "I am always with you when you think of me."

"But they are dreams, images, Helios—and sometimes dreams are not enough." She kept her eyes lowered and her face turned away from him. "Are you angry with me?"

He smiled and shook his head. "No, for I have the same trouble."

"Do you? Sometimes I wonder." She pulled her hand away. "Every night I pray that we will be chosen to mate, and then at least I will be able to lie with you sometimes."

"But if so," he said gently, "you will have to lie with me as a priest, not as a man. We can never be as others are—you know that."

"I know it, and I accept it," she said sadly, "but I take little joy from it."

"The joy will come," he said softly.

Her eyes were full of tears. "You do not understand, Helios—perhaps you never will." She looked up at him again and smiled. "The path of the ritual priesthood is not the only path to the inner wisdom—there is another path that two can follow hand-in-hand. Would that I could show you my path, but it is not to be, and I accept it. Your way lies through the ritual priesthood, and that way you must go; anything else would be a denial of your destiny."

Helios was very troubled. "But what of you, Netziachos—what of *your* path and *your* destiny?"

She shook her head. "My path is a path for two. One cannot travel it alone, and I will not tread it with any other. I will therefore follow you on yours, because I know that one day the two paths will meet, as all paths meet, and on that day I will bring you a joy that you cannot at present even begin to imagine, for all your priestly powers!"

They were silent for some time. At last he took her hand again and drew her to him and put his arms around her. "What can I say, Netziachos? I would give up everything for you save the priesthood itself. I would give you anything except myself, for I am not mine to give. But I cannot bear to see you so sad."

She trembled in his arms and buried her face in the folds of his robe. "You will bear it because you must Helios. But answer me one question, and answer it truly. When you have fulfilled your path, and when our two paths meet, will you then take me as your companion in spirit, and will we then travel together?"

He raised her head and gazed into her eyes. "Willingly, gladly," he whispered, "I could ask for no more."

She sighed and closed her eyes. "It is enough. I am content."

3

A hundred ships of Vardek's fleet rounded the northern point at first light, and one by one each ship hauled down its single mainsail with its insignia of the six-pointed gold star, broke out the double banks of oars, and one by one in line ahead they swept gracefully into the mouth of the Naradek and began the long trek up-river to the City of the Golden Gates and the safety of the harbor. Across the water there boomed the deep-throated rhythm of the Rmoahal slave-fighters as they heaved on the massive oars and sang the rowing chant of the homecoming warriors, and in descant came the tenor melody of the flaxen-haired Akkadians as they sang of the joy that comes when war is done and a man returns to whence he was born. From the Sacred Mountain ahead, from the City of the Golden Gates, from the great Sun Temple itself, there came the sound of a thousand bells ringing out a welcome for the sons of Ruta home from the sea. Thus sang the Rmoahals and the Akkadians, and thus answered the welcoming city, but the grim-faced Toltec warriors were silent as the night as they stood stern and unbending in their serried ranks on the decks of the long ships of Ruta. Yet silent and disciplined though they were, yet were their hearts full of pride and a fierce possessive love for the city that lay ahead.

As the ships drew near to the berths and landing quays at the foot of the mountain, the rays of the sun fell on the great gates to the third level two thousand feet above them and struck living fire from the inlaid gold and precious gems that encrusted every block of

marble, every buttress, every carven statue of their
structure so that they shone like the golden sun itself
and gave to the city the name that will forever be
known to the races of man to the end of time itself—
the great City of the Golden Gates. The hearts of
the homecoming warriors were lifted by the sight, and
Pirani, the captured Amarian priestess, gasped with
wonder at such splendor. Never had she seen such
magnificence, nor could she have imagined such beauty
though she dream for a thousand years.

The people of the city came down to the harbor to
greet the ships. Thousands upon thousands thronged
the marble quays—the tall black Rmoahal women
naked as trees, their skins glistening, their eyes on fire
for the men they had not seen for many a long night,
their breasts scented with musk, and their eyes laughing with expectation; the golden-haired, slim, white-
skinned Akkadian girls, dressed in flowing robes of
purest white or the blue of the deepest seas, their eyes
dancing with joy, their bodies alive with too much waiting; and the austere, proud Toltec women, naked to
the waist, the tips of their copper-hued breasts painted
with gold, their lips reddened with the juice of the forest
berries, their eyelids silvered, their blue-black shining
hair alive with precious gems like the deep sky at night
—and everywhere the children of the city raced and
chattered like young apes, aggressive and explosive
with too much excitement. Here and there among the
crowd the old men looked and remembered when they
too sailed the seas and came home to quicken the pulses
of lithe young girls now long dead, and the young boys
looked and dreamed of being men in the clash of war,
to sail with the long ships of Ruta and perform great
deeds of arms.

From the topmost plateau there sounded a fanfare
of horns, and through the great Golden Gates came a
long procession of priests and scribes of the Sun Temple, the scribes robed in a simple black, a cord of
white about their waists, and the priests robed in
the deep yellow of the sun. At the head of the procession, borne on two litters inlaid with gold, borne by a

score of young scribes, came the aged Khamadek, High
Priest of the Sun, and the austere and commanding
figure of Zesta, the High Priestess. Immediately behind the two litters came the aged adepts of the seventh
degree, many bearing the weight of their years on the
arm of a favorite scribe. Few there were of the seventh,
for no ordinary initiate could attain to such heights.
Behind these came the phalanx of those of the sixth
degree, and behind them the fifth degree, among whose
number was Helios, named successor to Khamadek,
and Baldek, son of Vardek, strutting disdainfully in
his pride, for was it not his own father they had come
to honor? Behind the priests of the sun came the priestesses and seeresses of the temple robed in the blues
and greens of the sea indicating their loyalty and allegiance to the Sea Temple wherein they were trained,
and behind them came the lay priests and junior scribes
who joined with the priestesses and seeresses and those
of the lesser degrees in singing the Sun Chant from the
third degree.

Along either side of the path that wound around the
mountain, gradually descending from the topmost plateau of the second tier, and from the second tier to the
third at the foot of the mountain, on each side of the
path even unto the harbor itself, were the lines of Toltec warriors, the Temple Guard, who never left the island and whose lives were dedicated to the defense of
the Sun Temple and the Royal Palace. As the litters of
the High Priest and High Priestess passed between
their ranks, each warrior made the deep obeisance,
spear point to the ground, kneeling, head down and
eyes averted.

So perfectly timed was the procession that the litters
bearing Khamadek and Zesta entered the harbor area
even as the flagship was berthing alongside the royal
dock. The people had grown quiet with awe, for this
was Khamadek, High Priest of the Sun, and rarely did
they see him outside the precincts of the temple. Most
were aware that Khamadek and the Sun Temple were
under the jurisdiction of Kumara of the Withdrawn
Temple, but to them Kumara was a remote and almost

legendary figure whom few had even seen, whereas Khamadek was omnipresent among them, the representative on earth of Lord Narada, Lord of the Lords of Light, servant of the Most High.

Thus into a silence born of the awe of ritual power and splendor stepped Vardek, Lord Commander of the Army, to the quayside to face Khamadek, High Priest of the Sun, his enemy. Khamadek rose from the golden litter and drew himself proudly to his full height, and as he entered into the function of his office, his aged face glowed with the majesty and splendor of that which he represented, and his voice vibrated with the power of an office that traced its lineage back through countless millennia, through every initiate and adept who had ever served His altar, even unto the High Temple of the Moon in ancient Lemuria, from whence his office derived, and the words of the ritual greeting rang out across the ancient harbor of Ruta and vibrated in the hearts and minds of all there assembled. "From those who see the Light of the Most High face-to-face," spake Khamadek, High Priest of the Sun, "I bring you greeting!" And as the words rang out, so came the clash of spears as the Temple Guard presented the Salute of the Guardians.

Many times had Vardek heard the ritual greeting given to others, particularly at the vernal and autumnal equinox rituals, when the greeting was given to the entire population of Ruta assembled before the Temple of the Sun, but never had it ever before been addressed to him personally, and in spite of his arrogance and contempt for the priesthood, his heart quivered with the power of it. Khamadek, the man, might be vain and foolish, but Khamadek, the High Priest, was a vessel of power too great for Vardek to deal with as yet, army or no army.

Vardek, Lord Commander of the Army, squat, ugly, and powerful, stepped forward and raised his sword— at which movement, in a single smooth second of flowing action, a score of guards stepped between him and Khamadek, and a phalanx of spears leveled at his throat. The Captain of the Guard strode forward.

"None may approach the High Priest bearing arms!" he thundered. "This you know full well, Vardek!"

The Lord Commander of the Army shrugged. "Do the many fear the one?" he growled.

"The Guard fears nothing—put up your sword, Commander, lest it be taken from you!"

The silence grew deeper, and the hearts of the people trembled at Vardek's daring. The Lord Commander smiled, swept his gaze around the assembled crowd, stared at the sky, looked over his shoulder thoughtfully at the hundred long ships of Ruta still coming upriver bearing five thousand strong of the pick of Ruta's warriors, all loyal to him personally, dragging the moment out to a dramatic tenseness until it seemed that even the Sun itself stood still and held its breath—and then slowly arrogantly, contemptuously, he raised his sword in both hands and broke it in two as a child would break a twig, a feat of physical strength that no man in all Ruta could match. "All know," he growled softly and sarcastically, "the depth of Vardek's respect for the Sun Temple—and there is the token of it!" and he flung the two halves of the sword contemptuously at the captain's feet.

Again there was a stillness, and then the Captain of the Guard barked an order, and the High Guard withdrew so that once more Vardek stood facing Khamadek. The Lord Commander of the Army made the deep obeisance, but he performed the gesture in so exaggerated a fashion that it was an insult. "From the Army of Ruta to you, Khamadek, High Priest of the Sun," he growled, "I bring you greeting." He turned to Zesta and smiled sardonically. "And greetings, too, for the lovely Zesta, High Priestess to every man in my command!"

Zesta raised her arm in salute and smiled secretly to herself—her heart was always stirred by boldness and courage. "Greetings, Vardek," she said, but her eyes said much more, and Vardek was not a man to miss such subtleties. Long had he known that Zesta looked upon him with favor, a favor born of her desires as a woman rather than her powers as a priestess, but such a favor was not to be wasted by a trivial dalliance, it must be used advantageously to aid the realization of his secret ambition. But the time was not yet ripe for such a move, though it drew near.

Khamadek was now flushed with rage, the majesty of his earlier aura now quite gone. "You are as arrogant as ever, Vardek," he said angrily. "Too much power bloats a man with pride, as poison bloats a corpse." He drew his golden robe more closely around his aged body. "You should address the High Priestess with the respect due to her office!"

"Zesta? I have always had the highest regard and respect for the beautiful Zesta!" Vardek deliberately used her personal name rather than her title, for he knew such familiarity would further enrage the High Priest.

The crowd that lined the harbor was tense and silent. Long had they known that Vardek held the priesthood in poor esteem, but never had they thought to see the enmity so publicly paraded. The whispers rippled through the crowd like a wind through tall grass. In the ranks of priests drawn up behind the two golden litters, Baldek, son of Vardek, grew tall with pride as he saw his own father publicly outface Khamadek. Near him stood Helios, his face a mask of dismay and helpless anger.

Khamadek gathered the tattered shreds of his temper and strove to recover the dignity of his office. "Let us waste no more time," he said thinly. "Let the ritual cleansing commence."

The Captain of the Guard and six of the High Guard stepped forward and lined up alongside Khamadek and Zesta—the captain in front and three each of the High Guard on either side. Helios and Baldek, being the two most senior fifth-degree initiates, also stepped forward and took up their position immediately behind the High Priest and High Priestess. From the ranks of the seeresses there came Netziachos to take up her position in front of the Captain of the Guard, thus facing Vardek. This was the first time that she had ever performed this particular function, and the first time that she had ever taken office in a public ritual, and as such she was feeling distinctly nervous. It was considered a high honor for the office to have been entrusted to one so young, and she prayed that she would discharge her task adequately, particularly as Zesta so clearly disapproved of the choice. Normally Zesta, High Priestess of the Sun Temple, was free to make her own choice of the seeresses and priestesses for any ritual, public or private, but the whole temple knew that this time she had received an instruction from the Withdrawn Temple, from Marah herself, to appoint Netziachos.

Zesta watched the girl take up her position and hoped that she would stumble or forget her words, or something that would mar the ritual. Zesta did not like Netziachos. The High Priestess liked her seeresses to be loyal to her personally, but Netziachos dreamed only two dreams, neither of which included Zesta. One was concerned with young Helios and the other with the hope that one day she would be claimed by the Withdrawn Temple to serve Marah, High Priestess of the Sea.

As Netziachos had taken up her position she had tried hard not to look at the black-haired, pale-eyed Helios, whom she loved as a man, but her heart had commanded her eyes, and the vision of him, tall, straight, and commanding, was in her mind's eye as she now faced Vardek. For long seconds she stood frozen in stillness as she wrestled with the image that filled her mind, and all there assembled waited for her to make the opening challenge. Desperately she tried to clear the image and remember the ritual words, but the image of him loomed even larger and blotted out all else—but just as she was about to collapse in failure, the image suddenly changed, and there in her imagination was the figure of Marah, and in her mind the great High Priestess of the Sea smiled at her, and above her head the words of the opening challenge stood out in letters of blue fire.

Netziachos, child of the Sea Temple, stepped forth and challenged Vardek in a voice that rang with power throughout the hearts of all there assembled. "Who is this who lands on Ruta's shores?"

Vardek had been smiling as one who smiles at a

child who is about to recite his lessons, but the power in the girl's voice wiped the smile from his mouth. There was in her voice all the power of the inner plane being who discharged the inner aspects of the office. Clearly he remembered the teaching that stated that behind each physical plane ritual officer there was an inner plane being who used the officer as a channel through which to express all the power of the office itself, an office that came down through the planes even from the throne of the Most High to find expression on the physical plane in the voice and bearing of the ritual officer.

The Lord Commander of the Army drew himself together. "I am Vardek, son of Vardek," he said, and his voice was powerful and full of war.

"By what right do you come among us from across the sea with warriors at your back?"

"By right," said Vardek, "of my appointment as Lord Commander of the Army of Ruta, and these warriors at my back are all the true sons of Ruta loyal to the Sun Temple in the City of the Golden Gates. Long have we traveled in strange lands, and much have we suffered in the name of Lord Narada. And now we come by the grace of the mighty Naradek to our homes again to seek the just rewards of our service."

"Worthily answered, Lord Commander," said Netziachos. "Such are entitled to come among us, but now stand you aside that we may inspect your craft, lest evil has accompanied you from across the sea!"

Vardek bowed and stood to one side, and Netziachos began the ritual pacing to the short gangplank that straddled the gap between ship and shore; and behind her followed the High Guard with Khamadek and Zesta and the two fifth-degree initiates in the midst of them. At the foot of the gangplank she stopped and looked up at the figure of Naida. "Seeress of the Army of Ruta," she challenged, "do you vouch that no evil accompanies this craft from across the sea?"

Naida stepped forward to the ship's side at the head of the gangplank and faced her fellow seeress. Naida, too, was nervous—not because of the ritual itself, but because soon Vardek would be giving his report to Khamadek, and his report might contain accusatory references to herself. But she drew herself together as befitted her office and replied in a strong, confident voice. "I do so vouch. Let none say otherwise!"

"Then stand you also aside," cried Netziachos, "and make way for Khamadek, High Priest of the Sun, and those who accompany him on this his duty!"

Naida, too, bowed and stood aside, and Netziachos mounted the gangplank and went aboard the flagship, followed by the High Guard and those whom they guarded. The ranks of Toltec warriors lined the ship from stern to bow, and on the small poop deck high up by the carven stern stood the three warrior chiefs of the three fighting wings: Bulambi, black as night, Chief of the Rmoahals; Herakos, fair and golden-haired, Chief of the Akkadians; and Banda, copper-hued, tall, and proud, Acting Chief of all the Toltec fighting men and second-in-command to Vardek himself.

The Lord Commander made his way on board and took up position with his three chiefs on the poop deck. "I, Vardek, Lord Commander of the Army, welcome you, Khamadek, High Priest of the Sun, on board this craft. Let none here hinder the execution of your duty!"

"Then let the inspection commence!" said Khamadek.

This completed the first part of the ritual, and Netziachos withdrew with Naida to the seeress' cabin below to commence the examination of the vessel in the seeress' mirror. Meanwhile, Khamadek and Zesta were seated on specially prepared couches on the poop deck to hear the Lord Commander's report. Helios and Baldek, with the three warrior chiefs, stood to one side out of hearing as befitted their station.

"Well, Vardek," said Khamadek, "was your voyage a success?"

Vardek smiled. "Naturally! I am not in the habit of failing. The Sun Temple requested that I obtain certain quantities of the yellow gold and other rare stones and metals of the earth. This request has been fulfilled, and more; indeed, we have brought double the amount asked." Khamadek's eyes gleamed at this news—he had a soft spot for the precious things of the earth. "And in addition," Vardek went on, "I was asked to obtain certain rare herbs. These also we have brought plus many herbs that are unknown here on Ruta. These will be of value to the temple healers."

"You have done well," said Khamadek grudgingly. "The Sun Temple thanks you. And what of the army itself?"

"No commander could ask for better men. They fought bravely and did all that was required of them. The three senior chiefs, Demian, Herakos, and Bulambi, were an inspiration to those in their command. I regret, however, to report the loss of Demian, chief of the Toltecs."

Khamadek eyed him stonily. Long had he known of the enmity between Vardek and his second-in-command. "How was this so?" he said icily. "Did he fall in battle?"

"No, Khamadek, his death occurred on the voyage home to Ruta. Your seeress will have reported seeing him stagger around the ship as one in the grip of the Dark Lords and then fall overboard."

"It was so reported to me," said Zesta, "but the seeress' mirror gave no indication as to what caused his convulsions."

"He was a good warrior, Zesta," said Vardek, "but self-willed and headstrong. He drank heavily of a native drink that was fermented from the roots of certain native herbs. He was warned of the powers of the brew but ignored the warnings, and so died."

"A sad end," said Khamadek, "to one who could have risen to a rank equal to your own." Khamadek would have given much to have known what else had been placed in that brew, and by whom. Demian had been no stranger to mainland native drink. "And what of the Priest of the Sun who accompanied you? I do not see him in your assembly here."

"As you well know, Khamadek, he was lost overboard during a storm that first night out from Ruta. No one saw the incident."

"But the Sun Temple sees all, Vardek," said Khamadek sternly. "Know you that he did not fall because of the violent movement of your ship in that tempest, but because he was pushed, and pushed by one in your command. A dire fate would have waited for that man on his return to Ruta, had he not died in battle and so escaped the wrath of the Sun Temple!"

Vardek's expression was bland. "Had I known, Khamadek, I would have sacrificed him to the Dark Lords as an end befitting so foul a crime!" Vardek well knew the seeress' mirror in the Sun Temple showed only the images of distant scenes but could not discern the thoughts and motives of those who appeared in them.

"But the man was your personal servant," said Khamadek. "Had you no idea of his thoughts of murder?"

Vardek shrugged. "What master knows the inner thoughts of his servant?" The Lord Commander had been particularly pleased that the man had fallen in battle. It had saved him the task of personally dispatching him to the inner planes to seal his mouth from speaking of certain instructions that he had received. "Perhaps he had no love of that particular priest, or of priests in general."

"And in that," retorted Khamadek, "he did but follow the example of those above him!"

"You mistake me, Khamadek. I am not an enemy of the priesthood, as such; is not my own son a fifth-degree initiate of the Sun Temple"—and he pointed to where Baldek stood tall and proud—"but I *am* the enemy of all who cling to high office that they can no longer fulfill. If such are not willing to withdraw voluntarily from that office, then they should be removed, by force if necessary!"

Khamadek flushed with anger at this thinly veiled reference to himself, but before he could speak, Zesta spoke out in an attempt to prevent an open clash. There was much in what Vardek said, but the time was not yet ripe for such a move. She would speak to

Vardek privately later. "And what of Naida, the seeress, Vardek?" she said smoothly. "Did she guide the army well?"

The Lord Commander was tempted to speak openly of the girl's bodily desires, but he chose instead to veil his thoughts. "She is a credit to your training, Zesta. She guided us well in her function as seeress. As to her private thoughts, I believe they do but mirror your own in certain respects."

Zesta raised her eyebrows. "Indeed! And who knows the private thoughts of the High Priestess that he can compare them to those of a mere seeress?"

Vardek bowed. "None but the High Priestess herself, of course, Zesta. And those whom she favors with her confidence," he added.

"But without a Priest of the Sun," broke in Khamadek, "what decision was made concerning the rituals?"

"The seeress Naida will report to the High Priestess," said Vardek, "that I conducted the rituals myself."

"But you are not of the priesthood."

"It was either that, Khamadek, or have no rituals at all. The girl was not competent to perform them herself, not having served with the army before, whereas I have witnessed the warrior rituals of the Sun on many a campaign and know the formulae."

"I do not see what else the Lord Commander could have done," said Zesta. "It would have been disastrous to have abandoned the rituals altogether."

"Very well—it is a decision for the Council of Priests. Let them decide whether the Lord Commander is to be admonished for his actions."

Vardek's own private thoughts at that moment were that it would take more than a council of scrawny priests to administer an admonishment to *him* and make it stick—but he let it ride. "Two further points, Khamadek," he said aloud. "I have on board an Amarian priestess, the Lady Pirani. She is skilled in the use of herbs, particularly the rare herbs that I have brought that are unknown here on Ruta. I claim her as a prize of war, as is my right, and she will be a servant in my household. However, I am willing to place her at the disposal of the Sun Temple. She has much knowledge that she could impart to your healers."

And no doubt, thought Khamadek, to serve as a useful spy for you! Aloud he said, "The Sun Temple thanks you—we are always eager to add to our store of knowledge. Tomorrow is the ceremony of the Mating of the Priests in which girls are chosen from the House of Virgins to be mated with those of the fourth and fifth degrees. Since your own son is one of those to be mated, your presence is required. Bring the Amarian priestess with you, that we may examine her. Meanwhile, she is your responsibility."

"I saw in the mirror," said Zesta, "that she is beautiful, Vardek."

"Some may call her so," said the Lord Commander guardedly.

"*You* seemed to think so."

Vardek smiled at the almost imperceptible note of jealousy in her voice. "I am but an ordinary man, Zesta, and subject to the same hungers as beset other ordinary men. Should a hungry man deny himself a plain meal and wait for the meal of his dreams? He might starve to death before such a dream was realized."

"Agreed. Let him eat when and where he can, provided the plain meal does not dull his appetite for finer fare," said Zesta archly.

"His appetite is not dulled, Zesta, but he sometimes wonders whether his dream will ever be realized, or must he dine on lesser fare forever."

"All dreams can be realized, Vardek," she said smoothly, "if you know the way to aid their realization."

Khamadek looked sharply from one to the other, and he was not displeased with what he saw. It was treason for any man to lie unlawfully with a priestess, let alone the High Priestess herself. The penalty for such a crime was death for both the parties concerned, and that would suit Khamadek very well indeed. Zesta had become much too self-willed of late and was becoming increasingly less amenable to his own jurisdiction—and who would not be glad to see Vardek dead, except perhaps Baldek, his son. "Enough of this frivolity!" he said sharply. "Have you anything further to report, Commander?"

"One small point," said Vardek, wrenching his eyes away from Zesta. "The goods that we carried with us from Ruta were not needed, and we have brought them back with us. I claim half of them for myself and my household, as is the custom. The other half will be delivered to the Sun Temple as soon as they are unloaded."

"Why were they not needed?"

"The natives of Amaria were not willing to trade, so we took by force that which we could not obtain by barter."

"So once again," snapped Khamadek, "you have exceeded your orders! You were sent to trade, not to murder!"

Vardek shrugged. "We encountered resistance—a few lives were lost, no more. Should the army not defend itself when attacked?"

"A few lives? Ten thousand poorly armed villagers were put to the sword, Vardek." Khamadek eyed the Lord Commander bleakly. "Is your lust for war so great that you must decimate a race to appease it? Know you now that the anger of Kumara and the Withdrawn Temple has already fallen upon us because of your exploits!"

Vardek smiled. "It grieves me to hear that you have been reprimanded, Khamadek. Perhaps you would like me to explain to Kumara that you had no control over events and that I acted on my own initiative."

Khamadek rose from the couch quivering with rage. "You go too far, Vardek—your insolence will one day cost you your life!"

"And one day," snapped Vardek, "your incompetence will cost you yours!"

Khamadek, High Priest of the Sun, was so enraged

that he could hardly speak coherently. "You arrogant fool! Do you not realize that I have but to lift my finger to strike you dead!"

"With what—with those?" said Vardek contemptuously, pointing to the seven members of the High Guard. "Bulambi and Herakos alone could handle them!"

"I do not speak of earthly powers!" said Khamadek. "I am the High Priest of the Sun Temple—I have powers that you cannot even begin to understand, let alone resist!"

Vardek shook his head. "I do not believe that the inner plane beings will lend their power for you to give vent to your personal and childish tantrums! Lift your finger if you dare, Khamadek, High Priest of Power, and let us see who dies this day!"

Zesta stepped swiftly between them. "Wait!" she commanded. "If a war is fought between the temple and the army, then all Ruta will be destroyed. Is this what you both want?"

Vardek fought hard to control his anger—his temper had always been his weak point, as he well knew. Open warfare would ruin all his plans. "No one has spoken of war," he said at last. "It is merely the High Priest who threatens the life of the Lord Commander, a commander who was lawfully appointed by that same High Priest himself!"

"And who can easily revoke that appointment!" said Khamadek.

"Then revoke it!" snapped Vardek. "Let us see if the army will follow anyone but Vardek!"

Khamadek, too, was desperately clutching at the shreds of his temper. He, too, knew the folly of this quarrel. He looked to Zesta. "No one speaks of war—this is a personal matter between Vardek and myself!"

"It is one thing to quarrel in private," said Zesta, "but if you do so here in public, the High Guard will leap to defend the High Priest, and the Toltec warriors will leap to defend the Lord Commander—and *that* means war, as well you both know! Look! Even now they finger their weapons in readiness because they see the anger in both your faces. Will you ruin everything by this public brawl?"

Vardek, squat, grim, and ugly, shook his head and tried to clear the blaze of rage. "You are right, Zesta— no good can come of this—but how many more times must I endure unlawful threats to my life from one who would usurp the powers of his office to further his personal vendetta against me?"

"And how long," snapped Khamadek, "must we of the Temple endure your insults and your deliberate attempt to undermine our lawful authority?"

"Long enough, both of you," said Zesta firmly, "to transfer this quarrel to a more private place!" She pointed to Helios and beckoned him over. "Summon the two seeresses immediately!" she commanded.

Helios bowed and hurried below. He burst into the seeress' cabin. "The High Priestess commands your presence, both of you—immediately!" he snapped.

Netziachos and Naida, startled, gathered their robes about them and hurried out. As they were climbing to the upper deck, Helios managed a whispered conversation with Netziachos without Naida hearing. "You were magnificent in the ritual," he whispered. "Zesta herself could not have done it so well. But trouble looms very near. The faces of Khamadek and Vardek are both black with rage—who knows what quarrel they have between them?—but at least Khamadek seems to be standing up to Vardek. But whatever the quarrel, it bodes no good for the welfare of Ruta!"

Naida was hurrying on ahead, and Netziachos dropped back a further pace and clutched at Helios' robe. "I am afraid, Helios . . . I am afraid! I can feel the darkness closing in on all Ruta, even as you said!"

"Don't be afraid," he whispered. "The darkness has not come for you. But come to my chamber at dawn tomorrow—I would talk with you. Now, hurry—Zesta grows impatient!"

Up on deck at last, Netziachos hurried aft to where the grim-faced elders stood, and bowed low.

"Seeress," challenged Zesta, the High Priestess, "do you vouch that this craft is free of evil mists from across the sea?"

Netziachos was startled—this challenge was usually uttered by the High Priest himself—but she answered strongly, "I do so vouch. Let none say otherwise!"

"Then," snapped Zesta, "by the power vested in me in earth, I declare this craft welcome here in Ruta!"

She turned to Vardek. "Stay silent until we are gone," she whispered. "We will talk of this matter in a more private place. Make an official request for a private audience with the High Priestess—we have much to say to each other!" She turned to the High Guard. "Escort the High Priest and myself to the Sun Temple!"

Khamadek made as if to protest at the way in which Zesta had taken command, but then he shrugged and allowed himself to be escorted away.

Vardek stood on the poop deck and watched them go. He had exchanged only a nod and a smile with his son, Baldek, but there would be plenty of time. The boy carried himself well and would be useful. As the last of the procession left the harbor, and as the major part of the crowd began to disperse, he summoned Banda to stand beside him. "Tell me, Banda," he said softly, "would you like your appointment as acting chief to be confirmed to a full chieftainship?"

"I would indeed," said Banda, "and I would serve you most loyally."

"Would you? Tell me, Banda, if I were to visit the Sun Temple and not return, what would you do?"

Banda was no fool—he, too, had seen the rage on Vardek's face. "I would contact your son, Baldek, and if necessary, I would bring the entire army to the temple to demand your return."

"Good," said Vardek. "So be it. Your appointment is hereby confirmed."

High up in the eastern turret of the Withdrawn Temple, three miles away, Melchadek, Keeper of the Akhasic Records, turned from the mirror and came to stand by Kumara and Marah as they gazed out toward the Sacred Mountain to the east. "Events march quickly, Kumara," he said quietly. "Will you now let loose the waters of destruction?"

"Do I need to?" said Kumara. He pointed toward where the Sun Temple gleamed golden on the topmost plateau of the Sacred Mountain. "It seems to me that they themselves have already opened the floodgates. What say you, Marah?"

Marah, the great High Priestess of the Sea, sighed heavily. "I fear you are right, Kumara. The time draws near when we must further our own preparations."

Kumara turned to Melchadek. "Are those preparations completed?"

"All is ready," said the young priest gravely. "It needs only for you to instruct Helios and Netziachos of the Sun Temple as to their function and responsibility during the final phase here on Ruta and during their new life in the lands to the east."

"But you will be going with them, Melchadek, as guide and counselor—you could instruct them yourself."

"True, but I feel that the instruction should come from you as the voice of the old age to the ears of the new."

"Very well. Are we all still agreed that the mantle of the continuing priesthood shall rest on the shoulders of these two, Helios and Netziachos? It is a grave responsibility."

"Even Khamadek recognizes the ability and spiritual development of Helios," said Melchadek, "by naming him as his successor—and the inner planes still approve the choice."

Kumara smiled. "Successor to Khamadek indeed, but not in the manner that Khamadek intends, I think! And Netziachos?"

"She has all the qualities," said Marah, "and her potential is greater than those who at present are more senior than she."

"She did well at the ritual today," said Melchadek.

"Indeed she did," said Marah. "She received my image with good clarity and was able to rise above the problems that beset her womanly personality and fulfill the function of her office in a highly commendable manner."

"And her problems—her personal feelings for Helios?"

Marah smiled. "I called them 'problems,' Kumara, for want of a better word. Her feelings are not those of lust, but are an intuition of a spiritual companionship expressed through the human personality in earth. Her powers as a seeress and priestess are not expressed through the Aspect of Severity of the Most High, which has been the necessary mode of expression throughout this age since Lemurian times, but through the Aspect of Mercy, which will be the necessary mode of expression in the new age to come, and as such she is the most suitable choice—indeed, because of this quality of mercy, this personal love, which is rare even here in the Withdrawn Temple, I think that she is the *only* choice."

"I agree," said Melchadek, "and again the inner planes still approve the choice."

Kumara rose and went to the narrow window. "Very well—so be it—but it is a grave burden we give them."

"Shall I summon them to the Withdrawn Temple?" said Melchadek.

Kumara shook his head. "Not yet. There is still a chance that Khamadek, Zesta, and Vardek will destroy only themselves without involving the army, the people, or the priesthood, and thus avert the destruction of Ruta itself. Even then much harm will have been done, but it would leave the way clear for Helios to restore the spiritual quality of the Sun Temple and lead the people out of their present darkness and so prevent the death of this great age of man."

"A slim chance indeed!" said Melchadek.

"But one that should be given every opportunity," said Kumara firmly. "No, Melchadek, we will wait and watch developments lest our hasty action precipitate the very thing we fear."

The great Sun Temple on the topmost plateau of the Sacred Mountain gleamed white in the darkness with its portico front and domed roof. Three great steps sunk into the ground led up to its entrance, and there rose five pillars bearing its pediment. It was of primitive structure, for like the faith of the Toltecs themselves, it was of extreme antiquity. The main body of the temple was laid out in the pattern of a wheel, with the stone corridors running out as spokes from the hub at its cen-

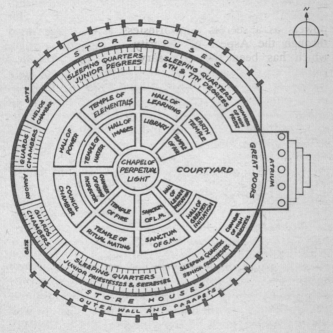

ter, and with the ritual chambers and halls lying between the radii, each chamber with two doors that gave access to the two radial corridors that flanked it. The temple rose to an immense height, and on top of the great dome there gleamed the huge symbol of the Sun placed there by Akkadian craft masters in ancient times.

It was barely first light when Netziachos slipped from

her chamber in the southern quarter and glided through the stone corridors. At varying intervals along each corridor were set burning torches, each one in a niche high up on the stone wall. These flambeaux were tended throughout the night by the temple guards, but now, in the advent of dawn, they had been allowed to die down, and some had already suspired to extinction, plunging that part of the corridor into a gray darkness. The smell and smoke of burned wax hung heavily in the air.

At that predawn hour there were several temple servers gliding through the corridors busy with their duty preparing for the dawn ritual, and so Netziachos was not unduly noticed. On reaching the center she made a brief obeisance to the Eternal Light, as was customary, and then hurried on to the northern quarter to the priests' chambers. When she arrived at the door of Helios' private chamber she did not draw attention to herself by knocking but quietly opened the door, slipped into his room, and closed it gently behind her. The walls of the chamber were built of huge blocks of granite roughhewn even as when taken from the King's quarry in the northern mountain lands of Ruta, and were eight feet thick, as were all the walls of the Sun Temple. There was little furniture or decoration to soften the harshness of the bare stone. It was an austere room, as befitted a man whose thoughts were concerned more with the inner realities than the outer effects. In the very center of the chamber stood an altar, a double cube, and on it the cloth of white linen to represent purity and a miniature replica of the Eternal Light, the Spirit of Flame, to aid him in his contacts. The air was heavy with the smell of stale incense; the burned remains of aromatic gums taken from certain trees in the jungle lands to the south, and Netziachos knew from the density of the aroma and the psychic atmosphere of the chamber that Helios had conducted his own private ritual the previous evening before retiring for the night.

By the eastern wall stood his sleeping couch, and on it lay Helios. The couch stood at right angles to the wall so that Helios lay in an east-west line, as befitted one who had knowledge of the lines of force of the earth. Netziachos smiled softly to herself. His ritual must have taken many hours, and he must have gone late to sleep for him not to have awoken at her entrance. He lay on his back, his arms by his sides, his legs straight and true, and his breathing was deep and steady. He was the youngest ever to have reached the fifth degree, and in sleep he looked even younger than he really was, almost a youth. With his eyes closed he looked almost a pure-blood Toltec, with his copper-hued skin and black hair—it was only his pale eyes that ever revealed the admixture of blood that he owed to his Akkadian grandmother. He wore a robe of white with the waist cord loosened for sleep. His sandals lay on the floor beside the couch.

Netziachos crossed the chamber softly. She stood for a moment gazing down at him, and then she loosened her robe, let it slip to the floor, and naked she lay on the couch and gently nestled close to him. She had hoped that he would not awaken—to lie close to him for an hour, even though he was asleep, would have been reward enough for facing his anger later—but as their bodies touched, his eyes opened and he sat up swiftly. She hid her face in her hands and waited for the blast.

But when he spoke, his voice was soft. "Netziachos!" he said gently. "You are playing with fire! It is bad enough that you are here at all!"

She peeked at him through her fingers. "You asked for me to come to your chamber," she said meekly.

He laughed softly. "I did not mean you to come naked! I did not have a chance to speak to you yesterday, and trouble is brewing fast between Khamadek and Vardek. I wanted to tell you to be ready at a moment's notice to leave the Sun Temple and withdraw to the Temple of the Sea—with me if possible, or without me if necessary. I will arrange for a message to be left in your chamber if things reach boiling point, and when you get that message, you must act immediately. I may also leave a further message for you to deliver to Kumara or Marah. Will you do that, Netziachos, to act immediately you get the message, without hesitation or query? A lot may depend on you."

She nodded. "Yes, of course I will, though I will not be happy to go without you—but I will do it. I expected you to say something like this."

"Good, then it is agreed." He took her hands in his. "But I did not mean you to come naked to receive so grave a message. What would Zesta say if she saw you thus?"

Netziachos wrinkled her nose in distaste. "What could she say! The High Priestess is no stranger to the arms of men!"

Helios frowned. "That is not a pleasant thing to say!"

"It's the truth!"

"Maybe it is, but that's no excuse for you to do likewise. The law states that—"

"I know what the law says, Helios! I am a seeress—I have the law pounded in my ear just as much as you! It doesn't say anything about just being naked; it speaks about having carnal knowledge. I am not breaking the law with you, Helios, but I bet Zesta is not able to claim such innocence!" She glanced at him and then lowered her eyes. "The law goes on to say that a priest must lie only with a virgin specially trained and specially chosen by the High Priest. I have a feeling that Khamadek has already chosen Naida for you, but I tell you of my own knowledge that she does not have the purity required. Her eyes dwell too long on many men, particularly Baldek, son of Vardek—and not with the eyes of love, either, but desire. She is no fit mate for you, Helios. I don't understand how Khamadek could possibly have chosen her for you."

Helios nodded. "I was informed of his choice this morning, but how did you come to know?"

"I am a seeress, remember."

Seeress she might be, but Helios knew that no ordinary seeress could have seen into the mind of Khamadek. "I am not altogether happy with the choice," he admitted, "and I agree that there could have been no finer mate for me than you yourself, for you are as pure in these things as any on Ruta."

"And in addition, I love you—that must count for something."

He nodded. "A great deal, but Khamadek has chosen Naida, and I must obey."

Netziachos rose and pulled on her robe. "If Khamadek is a true priest, then obey him. If not, then seek guidance from the inner." She stood in front of him and rested his head on her breast. "But I, Netziachos, tell you this—if you mate with Naida, you will be tainted and so will fail in the tasks allotted to you. Your heart tells you that I am your true mate, not Naida, but Khamadek says otherwise. Who will you obey, Khamadek or your own inner wisdom?"

4

"You disappoint me, Helios—I expected a more priestly behavior from you!" Khamadek sat in the eastern chair in the Hall of Learning and scowled at his young named successor. "What example is this to the Junior priesthood when you, a senior fifth-degree initiate, cannot or will not perform a ritual properly!" He pointed a long bony finger at Helios. "You will be the object of ridicule if you persist with this nonsense, and I cannot allow that to happen. I forbid you to entertain such thoughts. The mating ritual will be conducted as it always has, and you will perform your part in the usual natural manner. You will *not* use the Instrument of Mating."

Never before had Helios even argued with the High Priest, to whom he had sworn allegiance, let alone disobeyed him, but Netziachos had spoken with such authority and conviction that Helios knew that he must not mate with Naida. Yet at the same time he could not refuse to partake in the ritual at all—such open defiance of Khamadek would not benefit the priesthood or himself. It was only when Netziachos had left his chamber that morning that Helios had remembered the old parchment that described a ritual mating in which the priest had used a wooden phallus instead of his own natural instrument, but Khamadek had flatly refused even to consider the idea.

Helios, however, was equally adamant. "The celebrant was not subjected to ridicule in ancient times when he used the instrument in ritual," he said quietly, "so why should he be so now? Perhaps the junior priesthood will need to be reminded that ritual is both symbolic and sacramental—and since it is symbolic, there is no necessity for an actual mating of the flesh, and since it is a sacrament, it should not be ridiculed."

Khamadek was exasperated. "You are young and healthy, Helios, and quite capable of mounting a woman at any time; you do not have to coax the response, as we older men do—and it's not exactly an odious task we ask of you! Why are you so stubborn, and for no reason?"

Helios was silent for a moment and then said, "Very well, Khamadek, I will tell you. I had hoped you would not insist, or that you would have discerned the reason without the need for such discussion. The reason is very simple. Naida is not my true mate. As High Priest you should have known this—you should not have chosen her for me—but it is too late now, since all the temple knows your choice. There is no inner plane companionship between Naida and me, and to mate with her without that spiritual link would mean that a karmic tie would be forged between us that would not only be detrimental to my work as a Priest of Narada now, but also would take many lives to resolve. Frankly I am not even happy to use the Instrument of Mating with her, but at least it will confine the act to the physical plane alone—the desire nature will not be invoked and as such no psychic vortex will occur and thus no tie can be forged. It is either this or I must disobey you before the whole temple. I will *not* mate with Naida. *I* do not wish it, nor, I believe, do the inner planes wish it."

"And who are you," sneered Khamadek, "to say

who you will mate with, and who you will not! Your
entire function is to serve the inner plane masters—
your own wishes have no significance. You offered
them the unreserved dedication, and that dedication
was accepted; you cannot go back on it now just because you cannot get the woman *you* want! You will
mate with Naida in the natural manner or be summoned before the Council of Priests!"

Helios was calm—his decision had already been
made. "As to who I am, Khamadek," he said, "I am
Helios, Priest of Narada, fifth-degree initiate of the
Temple of the Sun and no mere neophyte that my
words are to be dismissed so contemptuously! I am here
to serve the masters, and it is their wish that I mate
with Netziachos, *not* with Naida. I have offered you a
compromise, not to save your face but to preserve the
dignity and good name of the priesthood so that it will
not be seen that we are at variance on this issue. Frankly, Khamadek, I am appalled that you are unable to discern the inner plane requirements in this matter, and
indeed in other matters of late. It is true that the priesthood is a hierarchical system and that I should give
you my loyal support and confidence even as you give
it to those who are set over you, the inner plane adepts
—but when you command me to an action I *know*
is contrary to their wishes, then I am forced to reexamine the whole question of hierarchical loyalty, and I
find that in the final analysis I owe my allegiance to
the Most High and to the inner plane masters, not to
you! I will *not* mate with Naida—I cannot! I beg of
you to reconsider your decision. You know me well
enough to realize that I would not oppose you unless I
knew the inner plane wishes in this matter!"

Khamadek was silent for a long time, drumming
his fingers on the arm of the chair and scowling at his
recalcitrant junior. He had been counting on Helios
more than any other to support him in the crisis that
was looming near, and now he, too, had turned against
him. Finally he said, "You are asking me to reexamine
the whole question of my ability to fulfill my function as
High Priest. You would have me believe that I have so

little contact with the masters that I have even failed to interpret correctly their wishes in so small a matter as the selection of the correct mate for a fifth-degree initiate. The inference is that if I am so poor a priest even in small matters, then what hope have I of functioning correctly in larger issues? Are you suggesting, like Vardek, that I resign my office?"

Helios shook his head. "I would not be so impertinent. The question of your withdrawal from office is strictly between you and the inner planes. On the earth plane, only Kumara has the right to raise the matter. All I am saying, Khamadek, is that I am fully responsible for every thought in my head and every action I make. If I make a wrong action *knowing* it to be wrong, then I cannot escape the responsibility for the consequences on the grounds that Khamadek commanded me to do so."

"Oh, so now," said Khamadek sarcastically, "you are saying that the heirarchical system itself is imperfect!"

"Not at all, but I do say that the system is only as good as the beings who operate it. The system of a chain of authority and command through the grades from high rank to low is excellent, provided that the officers at each level give the correct commands in accordance with the principles handed down to them. But if a weak link exists in that chain, a link who cannot interpret the wishes of those above him, then the commands that he issues will obviously be subject to error and can lead to chaos in the ranks below him."

Khamadek snorted. "So now I am a weak link! By the Lord Narada, Helios, you go too far! You come in here in your self-opinionated arrogance and tell me that I am incompetent, a weak link in the priestly hierarchy, and that I should resign!"

"I have said nothing of the sort," said Helios patiently. "I came to tell you that I will not mate with Naida because such an action is not in accordance with inner plane wishes. It is *you* who led the discussion to an examination of the principles involved, and *you* who raised the matter of your resignation."

Again Khamadek was silent. He could not afford to

have an open rift between himself and Helios. He had enough trouble already with Vardek, Baldek, and Zesta —and who knows but the boy might be right about Naida? He was certainly confident enough to have taken this adamant position. "Very well, Helios," he said at last, "I cannot change the selection from Naida to Netziachos, particularly as the ritual commences in a few minutes and all preparatory work has been completed—and for other reasons—but I will grant you permission to use the Instrument of Mating." He rose and gathered his robe more closely about him. "I think you are wrong, Helios, but I admire your courage."

The great Hall of the Creation of Life in the southern quarter of the Sun Temple was crowded to capacity. On the canopied dais in the east sat Khamadek and Zesta on carven thrones of red gold. Their ritual robes were red, and gold-threaded with the symbols of solar life. In his right hand Khamadek carried the staff representing the active principle, and in her left hand Zesta held the orb representing the passive principle. To the right of the dais sat those of the sixth and seventh degrees, all aged men, even as Khamadek himself. To the left sat the ranks of senior priestesses and seeresses, among whom sat Netziachos in a flowing robe of sea blue. In the very center of the hall was the altar of the double cube with the light upon it. Circled around the hall were the tiered rows of the junior priests and priestesses, situated such that each directly faced the altar in the center. Not a chair was empty, yet such was the discipline that not a sound could be heard from the hundred there present. Each individually, and yet collectively, was deep in meditation.

In the upper gallery, among the other specially invited guests, sat Vardek and Pirani, the Amarian priestess. Only rarely were noninitiates invited to the temple to watch one of the set rituals. Vardek was there as the father of Baldek, one of the fifth-degree initiates to be mated. Pirani had received a special dispensation to attend, on the grounds that being a priestess she was indeed an initiate of the mysteries in the broad sense of the term, though not of the Order of Narada—and anyway, Zesta had wanted to see this alien priestess from the mainland who had obtained the favor of the grim and ugly Lord Commander.

Although she had been on Ruta a scant twenty-four hours, Pirani had already adopted the fashion of the Toltec women. She wore a loose halter-neck flowing robe of the deep blue of the evening sky. Her breasts were completely free and naked, with their nipples painted gold. Her eyelids were silvered and her cheeks were reddened. Her black hair had been combed long and full, such that it cascaded to her waist in a shining black waterfall that rippled and flowed with every move she made. She pointed down and across the hall to where a group of three middle-aged women and one man sat in a small canopied alcove quite separated from the rest of the lodge. "Who are they?" she whispered. "They don't look like priestesses."

Vardek grunted derisively. "Nor are they," he said gruffly. "*They* are what passes as the royal family, the so-called Sacred Clan. Three bitches who can't whelp, and a dog that can't bark—and the old King lies dying, I hear."

"King Baralda—dying?"

"So I hear, and it's probably true—he's an old, old man."

Pirani pursed her lips in disdain. "I hope he rots with the Evil One forever!" she said viciously. "Baralda the Butcher we call him in Amaria!"

Vardek looked at her and smiled sardonically. "Baralda hasn't sailed the seas or held a sword since your father sucked at your grandmother's breast. What do you know of Baralda?"

Pirani looked at Vardek and bit her lip for having said too much. "Nothing," she said quickly. "A passing comment—no more."

Vardek laughed. "It struck you too late, Pirani, that Baralda knows nothing of what the army does when it raids the mainland, and that the name should be Vardek the Butcher." He reached over and grasped one of her breasts in his huge hand and squeezed until the muscles stood out like thick ropes on his forearm. "That's what suddenly struck you, didn't it? And it is Vardek whom you wish to rot with the Dark Lords, isn't it? Bitch!"

The tears sprang to her eyes as the pain lanced through her chest, but she dared not move or cry out. "No! No, Vardek—I swear it! It was just a name the ignorant used."

The Lord Commander let her go, and the imprint of his hand remained deep and red on her breast. "Not that I mind," he said generously. "In fact, I rather like it—Vardek the Butcher—it has a ring of fear to it, and fear is what wins or loses wars. I am glad your people fear me—they have every cause." He looked over at the last of the Sacred Clan. "When Baralda dies, that will be the end of the kings of Ruta, for even Khamadek will not tolerate that fool there to be crowned after him. Khamadek is a wily dog in many ways; he will think of an official excuse not to proclaim him king."

The pain was beginning to recede, but it would be a long time before she would forget the humiliation of it. "Who, then, will succeed—you?"

Vardek roared with laughter. "Me! You must be mad! The King commands nothing, not even respect, whereas I already command the combined armies of Ruta!"

Khamadek glared up at the gallery as Vardek's laugh rang out. The Lord Commander bowed insolently to the High Priest and placed a finger to his lips. "Khamadek is not pleased with us," he said to Pirani. "We make too much noise for this solemn nonsense of his."

"Nonsense? You believe that all this"—and she swept her arm around to indicate the entire hall—"is all nonsense? It is hard to believe that anything so grand could be as futile as you suggest."

Vardek snorted. "All this grandness, as you call it, is so that a half-dozen randy young priests can shaft a half-dozen equally randy young seeresses! By Narada, I've been shafting women all my life without the need to make a religious ritual of it!"

She didn't answer, but she began to see why Vardek

and Khamadek were such deadly enemies. "Don't you believe in the existence of the inner planes, as you Toltecs call it?"

"Yes, I'm Toltec enough for that, but I cannot believe that they are impressed by all this. Men are born to fight, and women are born to provide more warriors—it's as simple as that."

"Is it?" she said thoughtfully. "Is the warrior life, then, the only life?"

Vardek turned to her. "How long do you think these scrawny priests would last if we were not here to make things safe for them? They would have to put down their so-called rods of power and pick up their swords and become warriors if they wanted to survive —yet do you think that the warriors would be helpless if every priest died tonight? Of course not! Priests need us warriors, but we certainly do not need these priests!"

Again Pirani did not answer. What Vardek had said was right as far as it went, but it did not go far enough. If the priesthood brought no benefit to the community, why, then, did all communities instinctively produce a priestly caste, and why did those priests always rise to an importance greater than that of the hunters and warriors? Every mainland tribe that Pirani knew had its shaman, the primitive equivalent of Ruta's priests, and in each case that shaman held more power in the tribe than did even the chief. She shook her head and abandoned the speculation. Contrary to what Vardek had said, men always seemed to need priests, though what need they supplied was difficult to say.

She leaned forward on the balcony with new interest as she saw Khamadek begin a series of circumnambulations around the altar, pausing at each of the four sides to trace a symbol in the air with his hand and mutter some ritual words that she did not understand. "What is he doing now?" she whispered.

"Invoking the so-called great inner plane beings of the four cardinal points," said Vardek.

"What language is he using?" Pirani had no difficulty with the Toltec language—all languages on the mainland were similar to each other, and similar to Toltec; they had a common origin—but the words that Khamadek was using were completely alien to her.

"Lemurian," said Vardek curtly.

"Lemurian? What race is that? I have not heard of them."

"They no longer exist—they were a very ancient race from whom we Toltecs descended. In the priestly mumbo jumbo it is taught that there have been so far four great root races in man's evolution. The Polarians were the first, the Hypoboreans the second, Lemurians were the third, and we Atlanteans are the fourth. This present fourth root race is said to have lasted eight hundred thousand years—a ridiculous figure that gives further proof of priestly nonsense. Who can trace back eight hundred thousand years to say whether or not another root race was then in existence, let alone give the name by which they were known! Complete nonsense!"

"You spoke of yourselves as Atlanteans—why is this?"

Vardek shrugged. "It is the name given to describe collectively all the subraces, including us Toltecs, who have formed part of the fourth root race of man."

The breadth of the Toltec philosophy was staggering to a mainlander. If the fourth root race had existed for eight hundred thousand years already, and there had been three others before it, then they were thinking in terms of millions and millions of years since man first appeared on the planet. It was a staggering concept. "And how much longer will the fourth root race last before it is finished?"

"Some say that we are near its end already and prophesy death and destruction to all Ruta, but I take no notice of such nonsense! And neither am I going to take any further notice of your incessant questions! Be quiet, woman—your tongue is beginning to annoy me!"

Pirani held her peace and concentrated on the ritual below. Khamadek had completed the circumnambulations and the subsequent ritual responses, still in that same alien Lemurian tongue, and now seemed to be nearing the highlight of the ritual. Four of the young seeresses had stepped forward to stand before the eastern dais, where four couches lay in readiness. At a command from Zesta, the four let loose their robes and lay naked in readiness.

"They are beautiful," said Pirani, "all of them." She looked at Vardek archly. "It would seem that there are some advantages in being a priest!"

Vardek grunted but did not answer. His eyes were too busy elsewhere to meet her look. His hand strayed momentarily to a fold in his tunic, and Pirani smiled knowingly.

Four of the young fifth-degree initiates, including Helios and Baldek, had now come forward to face the waiting seeresses. The junior priests and priestesses had begun the low ritual mating chant, and somewhere a muffled drum had begun to beat with a pounding, regular, incessant beat. The officer of the Southern Cardinal Point, a senior priestess, had left her position and had come forward also, accompanied by a young girl acolyte bearing a vial of holy oil. At a further sign from Zesta, the acolyte began to anoint the genitals of the four waiting seeresses, while the Officer of the South spoke the ritual responses in a clear ringing voice, but, infuriatingly, still in that Lemurian tongue that Pirani could not understand. The acolyte then turned her attention to the four fifth-degree initiates and performed a similar anointing to each of them. The four young priests had not removed their robes but merely parted the folds so that their genitals were also exposed. Helios stood last in line and when the acolyte reached him, she hesitated and looked up enquiringly at the Officer of the South, who gestured impatiently for her to get on with it.

Vardek leaned suddenly over the balcony. "By the Lord Narada, what is *that!*" he said loudly, and pointed to Helios. "He's wearing a phallus!" He roared with laughter. "Now I have seen everything! Poor Naida— even *I* begin to feel sorry for her! All the while on campaign she ached for me to shaft her, or any of my officers, for that matter, and now she is to be plumbed by a piece of wood!" He slapped his thigh and roared again. "By Narada, the healers had better stand by in case of splinters! What is the priesthood coming to when even their men are no longer men!"

Pirani looked closely at young Helios. She was used to the ways of men, and there was nothing inadequate in his body or bearing that would suggest impotency. She then saw the sudden fleeting glance that sprang between Helios and Netziachos who was still seated in the ranks of senior priestesses and seeresses to the right of the dais, and in an instant, instinctively and intuitively, Pirani divined the reason for the masquerade, and her admiration for the young priest rose within her heart. Naida, she noted, had closed her eyes, and her face was red with embarrassment—perhaps she, too, had divined the reason. The other three priests, Baldek in particular, were aggressively normal.

"I see your son takes after his father," she said. "He looks ready to take all four, and Zesta as well if she gives him half a chance."

Vardek chuckled. "Naturally. No son of mine needs any help from a piece of wood!"

The drumbeat had begun to quicken in pace, and the chant slowly began to rise in pitch. At a sign from Khamadck the four fifth-degree initiates stepped forward to the waiting seeresses, and the mating began. The chant rose to its crescendo and the four seeresses jerked convulsively under the force of the climax. For a full two minutes the crescendo was maintained, and then suddenly there was utter silence, and the four priests withdrew from their ritual mates and stood back. Three of the priests, particularly Baldek, were breathing heavily, the sweat beading their foreheads, but Helios remained as cool and calm as he had begun.

Vardek rose suddenly and grasped her arm. "Come," he said roughly, "it is over. They will be leaving soon, and I want to catch Zesta's eye before she reaches her chamber." He hauled her roughly to her feet and marched her from the gallery and down the short stairway. A few seconds later they reached the center, the hub of the Sun Temple, where stood the Chapel of the

Eternal Light, and there they waited. Guards were everywhere, as was the custom when noninitiates were in the temple, but Vardek was careful to give them no cause to attend him.

"You are anxious to see the beautiful Zesta, my lord." Pirani murmured. "Could it be that the ritual has inspired you?"

Vardek grunted. "Just for once, keep your mouth shut! There are more things behind this than you have the wit to see. Keep your ears and eyes open. I did not bring you to Ruta just as a bed companion—I will have work for you to do, and you had better do it well!"

Pirani eyed him thoughtfully. Vardek was a savage and ambitious man, and she was committed to his cause, whatever it was, whether she liked it or not. "My life is literally in your hands," she said. "It is to my benefit to see you succeed. But I could help you much more if only you would tell me what you are planning."

He looked down at her and grinned derisively. "It would frighten you if I told you. I am planning the impossible, and I don't want you as a mass of quivering jelly. If Khamadek saw the fear in your eyes he would probe your mind and discover everything that I had ever told you."

"I don't frighten easily," she retorted, "and the only time I quiver is in bed! Tell me!"

"Perhaps later," he said impatiently. "Not now. Ah, here they come!"

The procession, headed by Khamadek and his personal guard, emerged from the corridor of the southern quarter and turned toward the east. Behind Khamadek came Zesta, and behind her the adepts of the sixth and seventh degrees. Vardek bowed as Khamadek passed, and then made a sign to Zesta. She nodded briefly and motioned him to wait. The procession passed on, and Vardek exchanged nods and smiles with his son, Baldek, who was looking flushed and pleased with himself. Vardek would need to talk to him later. Helios, Pirani noted, was still looking calm and serene as he passed by—Netziachos was fortunate to inspire a boy such as he.

A few minutes later a young seeress, accompanied by a guard came up to Vardek. "The High Priestess commands your presence," she said disdainfully; she did not like warriors and did not approve of her mistress consorting with such ruffians. "And the Lady Pirani. The guard will show you the way." She turned and glided away, her every movement signifying strong disapproval.

Pirani smiled. "My Lord Vardek is not universally popular, I see."

Vardek grunted. "If I did not have more pressing business, I would teach that young bitch a lesson she would not forget in a hurry! All right, guard, lead on."

Zesta was reclined on a couch in her audience chamber when her visitors were announced. "Come in, Vardek," she said softly, "and bring the girl." Zesta had changed from her ritual robes into a soft clinging robe of powder blue. Like Pirani's, her breasts were free and naked and similarly gilded. "Do be seated, Lord Commander." She rose and circled around the Amarian priestess, eyeing her critically. "She is beautiful, Vardek —I could almost forgive you. Yes, beautiful, though a trifle primitive for a cultured taste, I would have thought." Pirani's beauty was indeed that of the primitive, the savage, and the utterly depraved, compared with Zesta's more cloistered beauty. "Does she have talents other than those of the bedchamber?"

Pirani did not like Zesta's manner. "The Lord Commander," she said blandly, "has been so entertained by the talent you have been kind enough to mention, Zesta, that he has not yet sampled the other delights I have to offer."

The High Priestess raised her eyebrows. Here was no uncultured tribal girl. "She has wit of speech as well, I see, and delivered with a barbed tongue."

"No more barbed than your own!" retorted Pirani.

Vardek sat on the cushioned couch and reached for a bowl of fruit. "I did not bring you two together," he said, crunching a wild apple, "for you to fight. There are more important things here than a woman's spite. We could be useful to each other—all of us."

Zesta nodded slowly. "You are right, Vardek." She came to stand in front of the angry Amarian priestess, so close that their breasts almost touched, and stared deep into her eyes. "We understand each other, the Lady Pirani and I—do we not?"

Pirani nodded. "We do," she said briefly.

Zesta smiled. "You have courage—I like that. You are a stranger here—I could order your death this instant if I chose, and you know it; yet you are not cowed by me. I like that. We could indeed be useful to each other. A truce, then, Pirani, till we hear what is in Vardek's mind. My word on it."

"Very well," the Amarian said stiffly. "A truce it is. My word on it as well."

Zesta laughed. "I like you already; the truce may develop into friendship; you bear yourself well." She turned to Vardek. "Well, Vardek, speak your mind—I suspect this is no social call."

Vardek lay back on the couch. "Pirani is wrong in one thing," he said. "There is one other talent of hers that I have sampled. She is a priestess of herbs."

"I know all that!" snapped Zesta impatiently. "You said as much at the quay yesterday. Khamadek has already said that she can work with the temple healers."

"A priestess of *all* herbs," he added calmly.

Zesta looked at him quickly. "Demian? Not drunkenness but an additional ingredient in the brew that led to his death?"

Vardek nodded. He was playing into Zesta's hands a little, but he knew that he was merely confirming what she and Khamadek had already suspected.

The High Priestess looked at Pirani thoughtfully. "But Demian fell overboard, his body unrecoverable from the sea. Had it happened here on Ruta, the healers would have detected the poison in the body."

Vardek shook his head. "It is an herb unknown here on Ruta, and completely undetectable, I understand."

Zesta's eyebrows rose again. "You are right," she said slowly. "We could indeed be useful to each other!"

In that instant Vardek knew that the realization of

his secret ambition was within his grasp—his one doubt had been whether Zesta was bold enough, ambitious enough, and greedy enough to aid him in his plans. The impossible was suddenly attainable. He swung his legs off the couch and stood up. He took Pirani by the arm and led her to the door. "Go back to my house. I will see you there later. Zesta and I have much to discuss."

"But what about our . . . ?"

"Don't argue, woman, just do as you're told—and never repeat what you have just heard, or else you will die a death so foul that even *your* mind could not imagine it!" And he opened the door, thrust her into the corridor, and closed the door behind her.

Pirani leaned against the stone wall of the corridor, a little breathless from the suddenness of her rejection. What were Vardek and Zesta planning that was so impossible? And what had her knowledge of herbs to do with it? She closed her eyes and visualized the comparative simplicity of her life in Amaria before she was snatched up as a prize of war and thrust headlong into the danger and intrigue of the politics of an alien race in an alien city? She had often complained of the boredom and frustration of her life as a tribal priestess, knowing within herself that she was destined for other things, yet never had she imagined anything like this.

"May I be of assistance?" said a calm voice.

She opened her eyes, and there was Helios. He was tall and handsome and very calm and composed. "Thank you. Perhaps you could direct me to the exit— I am to go to Vardek's house and wait for him there. I am Pirani, the Amarian."

"I know," he said gently. "All this must seem a little strange to you. Please follow this corridor until you come to the center. Take the third corridor on your left and you will find it leads to the Great Doors. I would accompany you, but I have urgent business elsewhere. Is the Lord Commander unable to escort you?"

She shook her head. "He is in there—with Zesta."

His eyebrows flickered momentarily. "Is he indeed? Thank you for the information. I regret that I must leave you. Are you sure you can find your way?"

"Thank you, yes—you are most helpful. Are all Toltec priests like you?"

"All human beings differ," he said gravely, "and priests are human, despite some evidence to the contrary."

She smiled. "You're Helios, aren't you? Vardek laughed when he saw the phallus, but I know men, and I know you are not incapable. It's Netziachos, isn't it? You have a pact with her."

He nodded briefly. "You are very discerning. Indeed it is Netziachos who waits for me now."

"Then I must not detain you. You have been most helpful. Thank you."

He bowed and moved away. Pirani watched him go and thought how different he was from men like Vardek and Khamadek—but how insipid. Men like Vardek were dangerous, but life with him was no dull affair! She sighed and began to walk in the direction that Helios had indicated.

Inside Zesta's audience chamber Vardek moved away from the door and crossed to where Zesta lay on the couch. "She spoke to Helios," he said briefly. "He knows I'm in here."

"Does that matter?"

"Maybe not, but of all the priests in the Sun Temple, he is the one who could most upset our plans."

Zesta rolled over on to her side. "And what are these plans, Vardek? I do not remember making any plans with you."

He smiled. "Later, perhaps, we will talk of plans. But first I would dine on the finer fare that you half-promised me." He brushed his hand across her breasts and saw the nipples suddenly stiffen. "Remember?"

"It is death for a layman to lie with a priestess," she said softly, "let alone the High Priestess herself. Have you the stomach for such a meal?"

"Try me!"

She smiled and arched her back; the mating ritual

always made her feel restless, and Vardek was a man whom she found primitively and vulgarly attractive— he was so direct and powerful. She pulled at her robe, and it fell away, leaving her body completely naked. "Come then," she said fiercely. "Let us see what appetite you have!"

Netziachos was waiting for him in his chamber. Directly he entered, she ran across the room and literally flung herself in his arms. "You didn't tell me about the phallus! Helios, you didn't tell me! I knew nothing until I saw you revealed in the ritual! Why didn't you tell me?"

"Gently, gently!" he said softly. "I couldn't tell you because I only thought of the compromise after you had gone. Khamadek was not pleased, but he finally agreed, as you saw. You were right, Netziachos—you were right in all you said. I couldn't mate with Naida in the literal sense, I was not even happy to do so in the symbolic sense—but at least there are still no ties between Naida and me, and it leaves the way clear for you and me to mate properly later at a more appropriate time."

She snuggled in as close as she could to him. "And when will that be?"

He kissed her hair gently, and her forehead. "I do not know. Soon, I think—events march quickly. But we must be patient. We will know when the time is right, but it is not yet."

She pressed herself even closer to him. "You must help me to be strong," she whispered. "I do not want to wait—I want you now!"

Gently he disentangled himself from her. "If you go on like this, it *will* be now—I am a man as well as a priest, but now would not be right. Don't ask me why —I do not know. All I know is that for some reason ours is to be a special mating, and it will require a special time. The inner planes will tell us when it is right."

She sighed and moved away from him. "I never thought that I would ache so much for any man to lie with me, but I want you, Helios, I want to feel you inside me, and want your child, our child. Is it wrong to feel so much?"

He shook his head. When he spoke, his voice was thick and less composed than it had been. "No, it is not wrong—it is only the time that is wrong. You must be patient, and help me to be patient too." He walked to the embrasure and tried to control his breathing. He changed the subject, to move away from dangerous ground. "I saw Pirani, the Amarian princess, just now in the corridor. She has a great deal of evil in her despite the apparent politeness and courtesy of her conversation. Vardek must be planning to use her for some foul deed or other, or else why bother with her at all? Why bring her all the way from Amaria? It was not just as a bed companion; there is no shortage of those here on Ruta for such as Vardek. No, she is here for another purpose—I will stake my reputation on it! And Vardek is even now with Zesta, and what plans those two are hatching, I shudder to think!"

Netziachos frowned. "With Zesta? Does Khamadek know?"

"I doubt it," he said dryly. "Zesta would not advertise the fact that she has Vardek in her chamber."

"They may lie with each other," she said thoughtfully. "It would not surprise me."

"Nor I, though a month ago," he said bitterly, "such a thought would never have crossed my mind!"

Netziachos grew suddenly excited. "But the penalty for that is death!" she said rapidly. "Could we not summon the guard and break into her chamber and surprise them in the act?"

"Break into the chamber of the High Priestess! The guard would not obey such an order. And anyway, we are only guessing—their meeting *may* be perfectly innocent. And even if it was not, even if they *were* in each other's arms, they would have time enough to compose themselves to a semblance of innocence while the guard was battering down the door—it takes only a few seconds to don a robe."

"All right, but why couldn't we then perform our

own ritual, rise on the planes, and overlook them psychically from the inner? At least then we would know one way or the other, and not have to guess."

He shook his head. "The psychic seals on the chambers of the High Priest and High Priestess were put on by Khamadek himself, using a seventh-degree ritual. I am only a fifth-degree—I could not break through the seals, and she would know that the attempt had been made, and by whom—and *that* would cause an almighty uproar, and I would have no explanation for my conduct save an unverified suspicion. No, I'm sorry, Netziachos, we have no alternative but to wait developments. It is hard, but we have no choice!"

In his private chamber Khamadek grumblingly settled himself on his couch for his midday meditation. It had been a trying morning—it would be a long time before he would forget Vardek's impious laughter at the sight of the wooden phallus that Helios had used. The boy was a fool, and he, Khamadek, the High Priest, was an even greater fool for having agreed to it in the first place. Never again! He sighed heavily and cleared these tiresome thoughts from his mind. In his imagination he put his private and personal psychic seals on the four Cardinal Points, and with an ease to be expected from so experienced a priest he rose in his mind to the inner plane lodge—but on his arrival he was astonished to find that the lodge was not empty: a stony-faced Kumara was seated in the Hierophant's chair in the east, obviously waiting for him. Khamadek was suddenly tired of all this interference by Narada; wasn't he the High Priest of the Temple of the Sun, couldn't he be left alone to perform his work in peace?

"Greetings, Kumara," he said icily. "And by what right does the head of the Withdrawn Temple break through my private seals and invade my meditation? Could you not have had the courtesy to summon me to an ordinary physical plane meeting if you are so anxious to see me? Must I tolerate this unwarranted interference?"

"Greetings, Khamadek," said Kumara coldly. "I intrude upon you by my right as spiritual director of all Ruta. A physical plane meeting would take time to arrange, and time cannot be wasted if we are to avoid the catastrophe that even now threatens to engulf my people—a catastrophe, I might add, that has been created only by your own foolishness. Hence my urgent interference, as you call it!"

"Catastrophe! What catastrophe? You are making much out of little as usual. Kumara! I have problems, true—who does not?—but I will deal with them in my own way without interference from you or anyone!"

"The catastrophe of which I speak," said Kumara patiently but angrily, "is the ambition of Vardek—an ambition that will destroy you and the Sun Temple, and all Ruta, if he continues to be allowed to pursue it. You cannot solve the problem of Vardek by pretending that it does not exist, or hoping that by some miracle it will simply go away! In your heart, Khamadek, you are afraid of Vardek, and *this* is why you prevaricate!"

Khamadek was furious. "Afraid! Afraid of Vardek! What absolute nonsense! You must be bereft of your senses, Kumara, to believe such a thing! If Vardek is given enough rope sooner or later he will overreach himself, and *then* I will destroy him!"

"You vain and foolish old man! Do you not realize even now that the rope you give him will soon be around your own throat! How can you be so blind to what is under your nose for all to see! Even the most junior priest in the Sun Temple knows that Vardek is gradually tightening the noose around you—and yet you do nothing! Nothing!"

They both fell silent for some time, and the very lodge atmosphere crackled with the forces they had invoked between them. At last Kumara said quietly, "I could force you to obey me, Khamadek, I have the power to do so, but I am not allowed to use it. I am not allowed to interfere with the free will of the people or that of the High Priest. But I can advise you—indeed, it is my duty to do so."

"And what advice does the great Kumara offer?" sneered Khamadek.

Kumara rose in the east and pointed sternly at the recalcitrant High Priest of the Sun. "Go back and harness what little courage you have left before it is too late! Summon Vardek to appear before the Council of Priests and bring him to account for his evil deeds in Amaria; remove him from his position as Lord Commander; place Herakos, the Akkadian, in temporary command of the army; send the treacherous Pirani back from whence she came; warn Zesta from me to mend her ways or be summoned to the Withdrawn Temple to account for *her* behavior; and finally, expel Baldek from the temple altogether—he is not fit to be a priest of Narada! Do all these things, Khamadek, and the disaster may yet be averted!"

"And if I do not?"

Kumara sighed heavily. "If you do not, then all Ruta is lost—be assured of that!"

Khamadek shook his head. "Much out of little as I have said, Kumara. If anyone is afraid, it is you, not I."

"Yes, I am afraid—I am afraid for Ruta and for my people, afraid that your vanity and foolishness will bring utter destruction down upon them!" He shook his head wearily. "I have warned you, Khamadek; I can do no more. Go now and think on what I have said."

Khamadek, High Priest of the Sun, bowed to Kumara and left the inner lodge, to awake in his own private chamber in the Sun Temple, still trembling with fury at the high-handed attitude of his nominal superior. "By Narada," he muttered, "no one tells me what to do, not even Kumara! I am Khamadek—*I* am master here!"

5

In the center of the open courtyard of Vardek's house there rose a giant statue of a Toltec chieftain grappled in combat with a winged reptile. The carving was crude, primitive, but there was power in it and a type of hideous beauty. Sometimes, especially at night, it seemed so real that the figures moved and writhed and strained in their death struggle—and sometimes, too, when the wind blew westerly from the mountains farther inland, it almost seemed as though the hot and stinking breath of the reptilian monster wafted across the courtyard.

Vardek liked it. He had always liked it, but today he liked it even more; it reminded him of Zesta. Never before had he been matched in ferocity, never before had it been he who first called a halt to the lovemaking, and certainly never before had a woman left his arms still hungry for more. And after the lovemaking they had talked and planned, and again he had found himself matched in ambition, in boldness, and in determination. She was the ideal mate for a man such as he. Pirani was good, and would be useful, but she did not have that same aura of power that emanated from Zesta.

He sat on the plinth of the statue and circled his arm around the stone leg of the carven Toltec chieftain. "Some say he was modeled after my great-grandfather," he said, "but to me he represents all Toltec warriors." The great knotted muscles of his arm rippled as he gripped the statue. "We warriors bow to no one—man, beast, or woman!"

Pirani sat at his feet. "Though we women are sometimes useful to you," she murmured.

He gave a great bellowing laugh. "True, very true! You do sometimes help to while away an idle hour!"

"An hour, my lord? You were three hours with Zesta, and those hours were not idle, I'll warrant!"

He reached forward suddenly and grabbed a handful of her hair and twisted her head viciously backward. "Never let me hear you say that again! What I do with Zesta is no concern of yours!" He released her and pushed her away. "Zesta and I had much to discuss that was not for your ears!"

Pirani picked herself up and brushed the dust from her robe. She knew perfectly well that Vardek had made love to Zesta that afternoon—she could smell it on him when he returned to the house—but she felt no jealousy. Let him lie with whom he liked, so long as he continued to allow her to be part of his household; her very life depended on his patronage. She did not care about the lovemaking, but she would have given much to know what they had discussed. "Three hours of discussion!" she said tartly. "A great deal of talk, my lord. I trust the result was worth the effort."

He nodded. "It was, but I have no intention of telling you about it yet, so don't keep prodding!" He rose and pulled her roughly to her feet. "All you need to know is that my plans are proceeding even faster than I had dared hope. I will tell you your part in them when I choose."

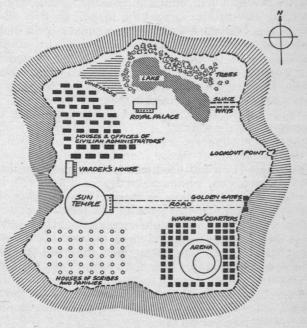

The topmost plateau of the Sacred Mountain was approximately two miles in diameter and housed the entire Toltec race, priests, scribes, and warriors. The afternoon sun beat down strongly and shimmered white on the pillars and dome of the Sun Temple, which stood near the northern edge of the plateau facing east. To the north of the temple were the large houses of those of senior rank in the army, senior civic administrators, and of course the palace of the royal family, the Sacred Clan.

The Royal Palace was a truly magnificent building of white and green marble. Like the Sun Temple itself, great steps sunk into the sand led up to its entrance, where rose five pillars bearing its pediment, but whereas the Sun Temple was domed, the roof of the King's house behind the pediment was flat.

Pirani pointed to it as she and Vardek left the courtyard. "It is very similar to your own house here, my Lord," she said appreciatively. Indeed, the only difference was that Vardek's house was built of black and green marble, not white and green.

"A special dispensation," he said gruffly, "granted to my family for services to the state. All the marble for its construction was granted free from the King's own quarries in the mountains to the north."

"You must be a very important man to have a house second only to the King's."

"And don't you forget it!" he grunted.

Behind the Royal Palace, and beyond the farthest house, there lay a tree-lined lake in what had been the volcanic crater ten million years before. Pirani shook her head. "How can there be trees on top of a mountain?" On the southern shores of the lake she could see a group of Toltec children playing in the water while their mothers washed clothing on great flat stones set in the lake's edge; and behind them she could see the neat rows of the royal vineyards. "And how do the sweet vines come to be up here?"

Vardek grunted impatiently. "The wild trees have always been here—grown from seeds, no doubt, blown here by winds in ancient times."

"And the vines?"

He pointed irritably beyond the mountain to the south. "There are wild vines on the edge of the jungle. Akkadian craft masters of the earth brought them here at the King's command at the time the temple was built."

Near the temple, on the southern side of the plateau, stood a motley collection of houses, diminutive by comparison with the Royal Palace or with Vardek's house, but clean and neatly kept. "Whose houses are they?" she asked, pointing.

"The junior scribes and their families," he said gruffly. "The priests and senior scribes live in the temple itself as indeed do all the priestesses and seeresses."

"And they go to work each day in the Temple?"

Vardek nodded but did not reply. Her incessant questions irritated him, but it was useful for her to know her way around—he might have need of her as a messenger.

"And those?" she asked.

To the east of the temple, stretching as far as the plateau's edge, was a large collection of houses, some hundreds of them. In the midst of them was a huge open arena with tiered stone seating. "They belong to the warriors," he said curtly, "and the arena is for the games and for training."

"Seems a great many houses."

He grunted. "Not counting the aged, the children, and the women, I have over four thousand fighting Toltec warriors; I took over three thousand with me to Armaria as well as one thousand Akkadians and one thousand Rmoahals! We are not a weak people."

They walked toward the arena, and as they approached, Pirani could see many of the warriors engaged in training exercises, each group with a training captain in charge. One group was practicing swordplay, another with spears, and a third was engaged in close-quarter training in wrestling and the use of the short heavy knife that all warriors had strapped to their left arms, their shield arms. Deprived of both shield and sword in a fight, a Toltec warrior was still a formidable enemy if armed with only a single knife. The weapons used in training were not fitted with guards, or blunted, or made of wood; each man used his own personal weapons, and no quarter was given. It was said of the Toltec fighting wing that they suffered more dead and wounded during training than they ever did on campaign; indeed, the lower tier of the arena was already being used to tend the wounded from that morning's session. Here and there among the warriors laid out on the bottom tier Pirani could see at least a half-dozen temple healers moving along the men, applying ointment to cuts and gashes.

Vardek paused in the entrance to the arena and waited for Banda to hurry over to him. Pirani looked up at the tall second-in-command and smiled. Banda was wearing the headdress of seven feathers, denoting his new rank of full chieftainship. "My congratulations on your appointment, my lord," she murmured. She had already learned that the title "lord" was used only in addressing chieftains and very senior civic administrators.

Headdresses were not usually worn at training sessions, but Banda had not been able to resist the temptation to flaunt his new rank. He bowed. "Thank you, my lady." He glanced at Vardek. "I hope to be worthy of the honor."

"You had better!" growled Vardek. "Or else, my lord," he added sarcastically, "you will not remain 'my Lord'!" He swept his gaze around the arena. "Does not seem to be many here. Where are the rest? I will not have any slacking in discipline—I hold you personally responsible!"

Banda swallowed nervously. "The remaining Toltecs are on an exercise in the mountain lands beyond the Withdrawn Temple; they will be away three days." Vardek eyed him bleakly, and Banda went on hurriedly but guardedly, "But I still have more than enough here to deal with anything that may occur—even the Temple Guard, if necessary."

They were silent for a moment, and then Vardek said, "Very well," and Banda breathed an inward sigh of relief. "But what of the Akkadians and Rmoahals?" said Vardek suddenly.

Banda was on safer ground here. "The Akkadians,

for the most part," he said, "are disbanded and are returned to their craft lodges. A few, under Herakos, are supervising the transfer of goods from the ships to the temple and to your house, as arranged. The Rmoahals are cleaning and repairing the ships under Akkadian supervision. It will take about three days, and then they too will be disbanded and returned to their owners."

Vardek gazed around him again and then said, "Very well, Banda, you seem to have everything under control. Report to me at my house tomorrow morning—I have much to discuss with you. Greetings."

Banda saluted. "Greetings, Lord Commander," he said, and turned away with obvious relief.

Vardek watched him go. "Command sits uneasily on the shoulders of those not used to it," he said softly, "but I think he will do."

"He is obviously loyal to you personally," said Pirani, "and terrified of you, I think."

"Good—that is how it should be; the one follows the other. The more a man fears you, the more loyal he is!"

Pirani looked at him thoughtfully. "What was that about having enough men to deal with even the Temple Guard if necessary?"

"Mind your own business!" said Vardek calmly. "And I warned you not to keep on prodding. If you prod just once more, I will prod back again—with my sword!" He snapped his fingers and beckoned over two Rmoahal slave boys. They were arena body slaves, not warriors. Their tasks included the cleaning of weapons, oiling the bodies of their warrior masters, keeping the arena freshly sanded, and anything else that any of the Toltec officers ordered. "Get two others," snapped Vardek, "and a litter. The Lady Pirani and I wish to visit the lower levels and the harbor!" The two boys hurried away and returned in a matter of minutes with two others and a red canopied litter—Rmoahal slaves did not dawdle when a Toltec commanded, particularly one of Vardek's exalted rank.

From the steps of the Sun Temple a broad flagstoned

highway ran due east to the great Golden Gates on the rim of the plateau. Once through the giant gates the road turned sharply left and dipped down to circle the mountain, descending gradually to the lower levels and thence to the harbor. The Sacred Mountain plunged precipitously on its western face, and on that side the road clung precariously to the cliff face, in some parts hewn from the solid rock itself, but the eastern face descended in a series of steps, and although each step plunged equally steeply to the one below it, the flat steps were wide enough to accommodate not only the road itself but also the dwellings and craft lodges of the Akkadian people—indeed, at one point just below the shoulder of the mountain on its eastern face the step was fully a half-mile across. It was here, at this widest part of the descending route, that Herakos, chief of the Akkadians, had his small, austere, but beautiful house; and here, too, was located the Akkadian master lodge, the lodge that controlled all the Akkadian craft lodges and coordinated their efforts. Every week the senior craft masters of the various lodges met in the master lodge to discuss their plans. The meeting was presided over by the venerable High Master, a sage second only to Herakos in importance among the Akkadian people.

Vardek commanded the litter to halt outside the master lodge, and he and Pirani descended. As they did so, a young golden-haired apprentice emerge from the lodge and ran across to them. He bowed low and said gravely, "From Herakos, chief of the Akkadians, and Malekh, High Master of the crafts, I bring you greetings, Lord Commander—and greetings, too, for the Lady Pirani."

Vardek nodded sourly. "Greetings. Where is Herakos?"

"Herakos and the High Master and all the senior craft masters are met in the master lodge. I am commanded to invite you, my lord, to join them in their deliberations."

"Very well, I will come." He turned to Pirani. "Wait here," he said curtly, and he strode toward the lodge.

Vardek had a problem. His officers and men had no more respect for Khamadek than he did himself, and it amused them to see their lord commander publicly defy the High Priest—*but* a feud with Khamadek was one thing, war against the Sun Temple itself quite another. Sun worship had been the national religion for Toltecs and Akkadians for uncounted centuries, and during all that time the Sun Temple had wielded supreme and unchallenged authority over the national life, subject only to broad influence from the Withdrawn Temple. Even *opposition* to the temple was unthinkable to all save the very few like himself, let alone outright war. With four thousand warriors he could put to the sword every priest, scribe, priestess, and seeress, *and* raze the very temple itself to the ground; but the army would not follow him in such a war; indeed, even to attempt to give such commands would mean his finish. No—the matter would have to remain a personal feud between himself and Khamadek.

The problem was, how to get rid of Khamadek without seeming to oppose the temple itself, and how to ensure that Khamadek's successor would be more amenable to temporal influence. If that successor was indeed to be Helios, as Zesta had warned, then the situation would be even worse, for Helios would not tolerate defiance from Vardek as Khamadek did. It was highly probable that Helios would revoke his appointment as Lord Commander of the Army. The problem, therefore, was not only how to get rid of Khamadek, but how to ensure a weak successor. Vardek shook his head thoughtfully—it was time for him and Zesta to bring both Pirani and Baldek into the planning.

The master lodge was a circular building—indeed, the circle was *the* predominating feature of Akkadian architecture. The outer perimeter comprised the private rooms, offices, and library of Malekh, the High Master —the major portion of the building being the enormous central circular hall, and dominating that hall, again repeating the circle motif, was a huge rough-carven round table.

The Akkadians rose as Vardek entered the hall.

"Greetings, Vardek," said Herakos. "You are welcome among us." The craft masters nodded and murmured their greetings. They had little liking for Toltecs in general, and even less for Vardek in particular, but it would hardly have been diplomatic of them, or wise, to allow their opinions to show. "We would be honored if you would join us."

"Greetings," said Vardek, and took the seat offered opposite Malekh and Herakos. "Well, Malekh, High Master of the Crafts, once again the craft masters who accompanied the army served us well, as did the Akkadian warrior wing. I could find no fault with their service."

The craft masters took their seats, one of them helping the aged Malekh. "I am pleased to hear it, my lord," said the old man. "Our training is thorough and only the best are chosen to serve with the army." The High Master might be old, the oldest man on Ruta, older even than Khamadek, but his eyes were bright and his mind sharp and shrewd. "And not a single man lost during the entire campaign."

"No Akkadians, at any rate," said Vardek. "A few Rmoahals, that's all."

"And one or two Toltecs, I hear."

Vardek looked at Herakos. "We were unfortunate to lose a priest on the outward voyage, as Herakos has obviously told you, and Demian, my second-in-command, on the homeward voyage—but none in battle. The sea was not kind to us Toltecs."

"The fault lay not in the sea, I think," the old man observed dryly.

Vardek laughed. "You're a shrewd old man, Malekh, but I will not quarrel with you today! The Akkadians served us well, and that is all that need concern us here. I am well pleased."

The craft masters glanced at each other and then looked to their High Master. "But," he said carefully, "I hear that Khamadek did not share your pleasure— the whole city is buzzing with the account of your meeting on the harborfront when the fleet first arrived. This is news that touches us all."

Vardek's face grew darker. "Some men, like yourself, Malekh," he said gruffly, "grow old with grace; others do not. It may be that a new high priest will serve the Altar of the Sun—what say the Akkadians to that?"

There were startled looks around the table, and Herakos frowned. To threaten the life of the High Priest, even here in the closed chamber of the Akkadian master lodge, was madness. Herakos could hardly believe that even Vardek would be so bold. "I find that very difficult to believe, Vardek!" he said sharply.

Vardek's lips tightened, but Malekh raised his hand to prevent Herakos from speaking further. "Herakos does not doubt your word, my lord," said the old man smoothly, "nor indeed do any of us, but you must understand that this news is startling. Might I inquire the source of your information?"

Vardek pursed his lips and smiled. "It is not exactly 'information,' Malekh—more an assessment. But assuming that assessment to be correct, what is the Akkadian attitude?"

The High Master leaned back in his chair and put the tips of his fingers together and eyed the Lord Commander thoughtfully. "Our attitude is clear, Vardek," he said at last. "If the High Priest withdraws lawfully from office, or is lawfully withdrawn, and a successor lawfully appointed, then we will give our loyalty to that successor, whoever he may be, even as we have given it to Khamadek. Our loyalty is to the Sun Temple and to the lawful priesthood."

Vardek smiled. "You place great stress on the law, Malekh."

"What man of good heart does not? I did not mean to imply that there might be a suggestion of unlawfulness; I was merely outlining the Akkadian attitude, as you requested."

Vardek rose. "We understand each other, old man. Greetings to the most loyal and lawful Akkadians!" He laughed and strode from the hall.

"Greetings," murmured Malekh. He turned to Herakos. "I doubt," he said dryly, "that Khamadek has been informed of his impending departure!"

The chief of the Akkadians looked worried. "You think we should warn him?"

The old man was silent, lost in thought. At last he looked up and said emphatically, "No—definitely not!"

It was not the answer that Herakos had expected. "And your reasons, Malekh?"

The High Master drummed his fingers on the table and gazed around at the assembled craft masters. "As we all know," he said, "the greatest danger to Ruta is the ambition of Vardek himself, and Khamadek has failed to control that ambition."

"But," said one of the younger craft masters, "his successor may also fail."

"In which case," said one of the others, "we are no worse off than we are now."

Malekh nodded approvingly. "And there is always the chance that the Council of Priests will appoint someone who will succeed where Khamadek has failed."

Herakos leaned forward. "Are you saying, High Master, that we should help Vardek to depose Khamadek?"

Malekh shook his head. "No—I recommend that we Akkadians choose not to interfere in Toltec politics."

There were nods of agreement all around the table. Herakos, being basically a warrior, always preferred the positive rather than the negative answers to a problem, but he acquiesced with the majority. "Very well," he said, "so be it."

Outside, in the hot midday sunshine, Vardek and Pirani settled themselves once more in the litter, and the Rmoahal body slaves grasped the poles, lifted, and began to move at a trot along the road. The muscles stood out on their shoulders, and their skins glistened with sweat.

"Well, my lord?" said Pirani. "Was your meeting successful?"

"I learned what I wanted to know, if that's what you mean."

"And that was?"

Vardek settled himself more comfortably in the litter. He seemed more at ease since leaving the Akkadian master lodge, less irritable. "That the Akkadians will not interfere."

"Interfere with what?"

"My plans."

Pirani's eyes gleamed with excitement. At last things seemed to be moving. "Baldek, your son—have you sounded him out?"

Vardek shook his head. "I don't have to. He has no more regard for Khamadek than any of the rest of us. And besides," he added, suddenly grinning, "he will not object to the part he has to play—it is, after all, a part that he has always dreamed of playing."

Pirani did not like enigmatic comments, but she resisted the temptation to probe further. "So the Akkadians will not interfere. But what about the Rmoahals?"

Vardek shrugged. "Firstly, they are slaves and will do as they're told as they have always done; and secondly, they have no great love of the sun religion, they prefer their own gods of the dead—it will not matter to them who is High Priest at the Sun Temple."

As they descended to the lower slopes of the mountain, the air had grown thicker, and breathing had become more difficult. Perspiration began to bead on Pirani's forehead and shoulders and trickle between her breasts. She loosened her robe and shifted uncomfortably on her seat. It was not only that the air was thick, but there was a pungent, choking smell to it. It was not so bad on the seaward, eastern side of the mountain, for there was a constant stream of air that moved downriver—which was why she had hardly noticed the atmosphere in the harbor when she had first arrived in Ruta—but the northern slopes that overhung the swamplands were vile. The entire lower slopes of that side of the mountain were wreathed in the evil-smelling swamp mists.

"And the Rmoahals *live* down there?" she gasped.

"They are used to it," he grunted. Indeed, Vardek himself hardly noticed the change as they descended.

He had long been inured to the Rmoahal swamp mists. As a boy he had often stolen from his father's house to creep down the mountain to sit among the Rmoahals in their rituals of the dead.

Pirani drew her robe across her mouth. "Why *are* we going down to the lower levels?" she said sulkily, her voice muffled. "I can hardly breathe!"

"We are going," said Vardek calmly, "to see Bulambi and Dracombi. When trouble looms, a man must know who will fight with him, who against him, and who will remain neutral." He looked down at her contemptuously. "And he must know who the weaklings are in his own ranks."

"I am no weakling!" She glared at him furiously. "You above all others should know that!"

He shrugged. "You are strong enough in some ways —for a woman—but since you make such a fuss about such a small discomfort, it makes me wonder how you would react in a real emergency."

She snatched the robe from her mouth and pretended to ignore the pungent atmosphere. "Well enough!" she retorted.

"Perhaps, but I doubt it!"

The road plunged precipitously on the last curve and then straightened for the sweep along the eastern foot to the ancient harbor. Here the air was cleaner, the mists kept at bay by the currents of wind that swept around the base of the mountain and downriver to the sea. The harbor was alive with activity. Long lines of Rmoahal slaves were transferring the ships' cargoes to the waiting transport litters, and each vessel itself swarmed with Akkadian craft masters and their apprentices repairing the ravages of a six-month campaign. Already some of the vessels had been beached and lay on their sides, their keels exposed, while apprentices scraped and cleaned and caulked the transverse planking.

Vardek beckoned an Akkadian captain. "What is the position?" he demanded curtly.

The man was nervous; he was not used to addressing so eminent a person as the Lord Commander. "A little over half the cargo has been off-loaded," he said; "the remainder will be completed by noon tomorrow."

"And the repairs?"

"As you can see, some are already nearing completion and will be refloated and berthed today—the rest tomorrow."

"Very well!" snapped Vardek. "Now, where is Bulambi?"

The man pointed. "With Dracombi, my lord—in his hut, down there."

Vardek barked a command, and the litter moved on.

As they skirted the harbor area around to the northern face of the mountain the flagstones of the road gave way to hard-packed dirt, and its width narrowed to that of a mere track that twisted and turned through the maze of tumbled boulders at the mountain's foot to where the Rmoahal compound lay. It was a giant compound, far larger than Pirani had expected, even though she had known that the total Rmoahal population was a little over four thousand. The entire compound was enclosed by a twelve-foot palisade of sharpened stakes—not bound together but set at two-inch intervals that allowed a defender to spear-stab through the palisade to the attacker outside. Its main purpose was to keep out marauding reptiles from the swamps, but it would work equally well against human attackers as Vardek was well aware. If the Rmoahals ever revolted, it would be no easy task to subdue them.

As if reading his thoughts, Pirani said, "The Rmoahals are slaves, but I don't understand how you keep them in slavery. Don't they ever turn on you?"

"They did once, in ancient times," said Vardek, "but they were slaughtered in their thousands, and they have never forgotten it. We see to it that their numbers never rise to a point where they could overcome both the Akkadians *and* the Toltecs."

"But if the Rmoahals and Akkadians joined forces, they could give you Toltecs a hard time. They would not be able to storm the topmost plateau, but they might be able to starve you out."

"True, but the Akkadians would never join with the Rmoahals—for one very good reason."

"What is that?"

Vardek grunted impatiently. "Because although they have no love for us Toltecs, they know that if the Rmoahals rose to power they would slaughter every Toltec *and* every Akkadian on the island, to the last man, woman, and child. From the Akkadian point of view it is an ironic fact that their very continued existence depends on us Toltecs maintaining mastery over both them *and* the Rmoahals—and to maintain that mastery, it is not necessary for us Toltecs to be stronger than both of them together, but only stronger than either. Khamadek calls it the 'balance of power.' That is the reason why we take a Rmoahal *and* an Akkadian fighting wing with us on campaign—it maintains the same proportion of races in the army and leaves the same proportion at home on Ruta. It is a policy that simply cannot fail, provided we control their numbers."

"And how do you do that?"

"Simple. Twice a year, at the vernal and autumnal equinoxes, sacrifices are required for the Sun ritual—sometimes animals are used, and sometimes certain women are chosen to be honored."

"Honored! Yes, we call it that in Amaria, and the fools believe it—do yours?"

Vardek smiled crookedly. "Let us say that the faith of some is stronger than others. In some cases a drug has to be administered so that they can accept the honor without struggling."

The guards had rushed to open the great wooden gate at the first sight of Vardek's litter and now made the deep obeisance as their visitors entered the compound. A runner had gone on ahead to warn the shaman, Dracombi, and Bulambi, chief of all the Rmoahals.

The shaman's hut lay in the exact center of the compound. Vardek pointed to it and said, "The Rmoahals are a barbaric people with little intelligence, a mere grade or two higher than cattle, but not so Dracombi.

The old man is shrewd and cunning and more of a priest than many in the Sun Temple, *and* with more power. The Rmoahals are terrified of him, and so too are many Toltecs and Akkadians, if the truth were known—*and* with good reason!" He looked down at Pirani. "Dracombi—do you know what the name means?"

She nodded. "Dracombi—'The Eyes Through Which the Dead Look Out.' "

"And it is no idle description," he warned.

As the litter crossed the compound, the Rmoahals gathered swiftly and silently, until several hundred were crowded around them, leaving only a narrow lane between them and Dracombi's hut. Pirani was rigid with fear, but she did not allow even a trace of expression to betray her feelings. She had seen the battle-crazed Rmoahal line in action against her own people in Amaria: there was no shame in fearing such ferocious barbarity. She glanced at Vardek. His expression, too, was without fear, but in his case it was probably quite genuine—the man seemed to fear nothing.

The litter halted outside the shaman's hut, and as she and Vardek stepped down, so the giant figure of Bulambi appeared in the doorway. "Greetings, Lord Commander," the Rmoahal said gutturally. "Dracombi saw you coming even as you left the topmost plateau, and bids you welcome."

Vardek smiled to himself. Dracombi had some peculiar powers, but not *that* peculiar. Not to be outdone, he said loudly, "Tell the great shaman of all the Rmoahals that I sent my spirit to warn him of my coming —*that* is how he saw me. The power is the power of Vardek, not the power of Dracombi!"

An evil low chuckle came from within the hut, and Dracombi's voice said, "Dracombi does not question the power of Vardek, and Vardek knows full well the power of Dracombi. Neither of us needs boast as children do, or untried warriors; our powers are too well known to all. Bid the Lord Commander enter. The woman remains outside, and may the dead protect her from the living."

Pirani swallowed nervously and tried to gather her robe even more closely around her. She felt naked under the stares of the savage Rmoahals.

"The dead need not concern themselves," said Vardek arrogantly. "The woman is under *my* protection; any man who touches her will die!" And he strode into the hut without so much as a glance in her direction.

Bulambi followed him in and let the curtain of strung beads fall back into place. Vardek blinked in the darkness, and then, as his eyes grew more accustomed, he saw Dracombi seated cross-legged on a rush mat on the far side. "Be seated, Lord Commander," the old man said, "and tell me what brings you to the foot of the Sacred Mountain to visit the Rmoahals. It is not often you visit us now, though when you were a child you came almost daily and vowed eternal friendship. Does the man deny the vows of the child?"

Vardek grunted and sat opposite the evil-looking shaman. "I seem to remember a certain ugly old man who made similar vows to a child. I could ask the same question of you, Dracombi, but I won't. Let us say that both of us will keep our vows as far as our different responsibilities will allow." He shifted his weight and leaned back casually against the center pole. "You spoke of powers just now—your own seem to be fading if you have to ask the reason for my visit."

The old man chuckled. "Like wine, Vardek, I become more potent with age, not less; my powers are not diminished. For example, the dead tell me that soon they will be joined by two high-ranking Toltecs—so I know that you have not come merely to renew a childhood friendship."

Vardek was startled. He had spoken openly of his enmity with Khamadek, but no one knew of his other plans. It was impossible that Dracombi should know of them. "Either your powers are greater than I thought possible," he said slowly, "or you are guessing."

Dracombi leaned forward. "The dead *see* everything and *know* everything, Vardek. Not for nothing am I called 'Dracombi.' All know that one of the newly dead will be Khamadek if your plans are fulfilled. Let me just say that the other is of even higher rank than Khamadek—and *that* will leave you as master of all Ruta. You have visited the Akkadians to see if they would ever oppose you, and now you visit us. You are worried that the Toltec loyalty will be divided in this matter and you *might* have need of either Akkadian or Rmoahal support. I do not guess, Vardek—I *know!*"

Vardek glanced up at Bulambi standing, as a carved black statue, silent, by the door, and then looked back to the shaman. "Very well, Dracombi, friend of my childhood," he said softly, "assuming that the dead have not misinformed you, where will the Rmoahals stand in this issue?"

6

Naida was nervous. She did not know why she had been summoned to Baldek's private chamber at this late hour nor why it was thought necessary to have a guard standing over her as she waited in the anteroom. Was she under arrest? If so, then why hadn't they taken her to the western quarter to the chamber of the Grand Inspectorate? Didn't Baldek know that she would have come willingly to his chamber at any hour of the night or day without the need for this escort?

At last the communicating door opened and Baldek entered. He pointed to the door. "In there," he said curtly. "You can go," he said to the guard, "and don't mention this to anyone, or you will regret it!" He followed Naida into his private chamber and closed the door behind him. He sat himself carefully in the carved high chair by the eastern embrasure, leaving Naida to stand nervously in the middle of the room. He eyed her bleakly, not a glimmer of welcome or friendliness, not even a flicker of interest in her as a woman.

Naida began to feel even more alarmed. "Why have I been called like this, Baldek?" she said, as calmly as she could. "Have I offended you in some way?"

Baldek eased himself back in the chair. "Indeed you have—not offended me personally so much, but certainly you have offended the Sun Temple."

"How can that be? I have always done my duty to the Sun Temple. My Lord Valdek, your own father was kind enough to praise my services to the army to Khamadek himself, and I have done naught since our return to warrant your displeasure!"

Baldek smiled and put the tips of his fingers together. "My father is a kindly man," he said. "He could have chosen to tell Khamadek the truth, but he chose to gloss over your behavior in his report." He eyed the girl stonily. "But he felt that someone in the Sun Temple should know of your failure as a seeress, and so he chose to tell me in the hope that I could remedy the situation without the need for an official complaint."

"Official complaint? But what have I done? The entire campaign was a success, and in some small measure I contributed to that success—I guided the army well!" There were tears in her eyes now, and Baldek smiled secretly to himself. "I don't understand this at all—I cannot believe that Vardek has any just cause for complaint!"

"Are you saying, then, that my father is a liar?" said Baldek softly.

"No, of course not, but—"

"Or me?"

"No, but—"

"Then what *are* you saying, girl!"

Naida tried to pull herself together. She could feel the tears on her cheeks, and she brushed them away. "It's just that I don't understand." She took a pace toward him. "What is it that I have done—how have I given offense?"

Baldek pursed his lips thoughtfully. "It seems that you spent more time gazing into the seeress' mirror on your own behalf than on behalf of the army."

So that was it! She felt a little relieved; there was nothing they could actually prove. "I submit, with utmost respect," she said carefully, "that since your father is not a priest, he does not have the training to know what I am thinking when I am about my work." She held herself a little more erect. "I am a woman, Baldek, a healthy woman with healthy desires. Perhaps your father recognized my healthiness and merely assumed that I was misusing my powers."

He nodded, seemingly thoughtful. "Perhaps you are right. If so, then you will, of course, have no objection to my reporting the matter to Khamadek. He can then examine your inner self, see the evidence of the purity of your thoughts, and thus settle this unofficial complaint once and for all."

The girl paled. She could not risk an inner probe by the High Priest himself; such a probe would certainly result in her being recalled to the Sea Temple to face Marah and could easily lead to her being banished from the temple altogether; and the thought of spending the rest of her life as a childbearing drudge for some Toltec junior administrator was an appalling one. She would do anything rather than risk that. "No, I wouldn't want that, Baldek," she said. "My thoughts are not evil, but I admit that they are human enough for Khamadek to call them impure—they are the thoughts of any normal healthy young woman." She looked at him quickly. "Or any normal healthy young man, for that matter. If Khamadek were to banish every one with such thoughts, then he would have to banish practically every seeress and priestess in the temple— yes, and every priest, too!"

Baldek folded his arms and eyed her quizzically. "And we can't have that, can we," he said softly, "or else who would remain to serve the temple? But we are not speaking of putting every seeress to the inner test—only you."

He was smiling at her now, arrogantly and sneeringly. "What can I say," she said, "to persuade you that no useful end would be served by having me recalled to the Sea Temple?" She searched his face for some clue. It couldn't be that he simply wanted to lie with her; he must have known for a long time that she would be willing without all this. There had to be some other reason. "Is there no way that I can serve you as a penance for my impure thoughts?"

He eyed her thoughtfully. "Now that you mention it," he said blandly, "there is an operation that I am about to undertake for which I will need the services of a discreet seeress."

She sighed with relief. "Anything, Baldek—I will do anything within reason."

"You are in no position to bargain with me, woman!" he snapped viciously. "You will do anything I tell you, whether it is reasonable or not! Is that clear?"

The change from a mild verbal fencing to this sudden lash caught her by surprise, stunned her, shocked her into a sudden helpless fear. She could only bow her head and wait to learn what was in his mind. There was a crooked twisted power in Baldek; all the temple knew it save the elders, who were too withdrawn in contemplation to see anything outside themselves. Baldek was feared by many of the junior grades, and with good reason.

"That's better!" he said. "It is as well you understand your position. And now to business. As a seeress, I take it that you have had the necessary training in trance control?"

Now she was even more startled; she had not expected this. "Yes," she said slowly, "and it was considered that my ability was above average."

"Good. Then that settles that." He rose and walked to the door. "Go and prepare yourself—a guard will call for you in two hours from now."

She did not move. "But what is it that you want me to oversee? I must know—I must have the points of reference in order to get back to my body."

"That will not be necessary. I will put you in deep trance and send you out in a specific direction. I will then listen to what your lips speak, then erase your memory and bring your astral back so that when you emerge you will have no recollection of what you have seen or what you have spoken."

Naida was now really frightened. It was a method of

trance control that was never used; indeed, it was banned. The normal method was for a seeress to know where she was going before she went out. If anything happened to the operator, or if the seeress' astral encountered any trouble that she could not handle, then she could always return to her body instantly at her own command. But this way the seeress was utterly dependent on the operator to recall her. If anything happened to prevent him, or if he deliberately chose not to recall her, then she would remain in that trance until she died; and if she did meet any trouble and was not recalled immediately, then there was a good chance that she would emerge from the trance later hopelessly insane.

"I know what you are thinking," he said sneeringly, "but you need have no fear. I will not leave your astral out there to betray me by contacting any of my fellow priests as they rise to the inner lodge in their meditations." He smiled crookedly. "Besides, after you have served me on the astral, I will need you back here again to serve me physically—you will be entitled to some physical pleasure as your just reward! Go now—be ready in two hours from now!"

Could she trust him? And anyway, did she have any alternative? She shook her head and walked blindly from the room and made her way back to her own chamber. If she refused him now, it would not be a simple matter of a report to Khamadek; she knew too much—she doubted if she would see another dawn. At least this way she had a chance of surviving.

Back in Baldek's chamber a curtain stirred and Vardek himself stepped into the room. "You handled that very well," he said approvingly. "My faith in you was not misplaced."

Baldek shrugged. "It was easy enough." He was never at ease in his father's presence; a childhood under such a dominant man was not an easy heritage to overcome. "Only the very strong cannot be blackmailed, and she is weak."

Vardek sat himself in the carved chair with an air of royal arrogance, but his squat, ugly, hairy body made him a travesty of a kingly figure. "I have no faith in priestly powers," he said gruffly. "Are you sure she can get you the information you require?"

"Of course—it's simple enough when you know how. I could send her out to any part of Ruta, and she would report faithfully what she could see and hear, and those being watched would have no idea that she was among them."

Vardek grunted. "Sounds like more of Khamadek's mumbo jumbo to me."

"That's because you do not understand the priesthood, nor want to understand." Baldek eyed his father thoughtfully. "Your biggest weakness, Father, if I may say so, is that you always underestimate anything that you do not understand. Don't make the mistake of dismissing priestly powers so contemptuously—they are very real."

"Priestly powers!" snorted Vardek. "Rubbish! Where would your priestly powers be if I ran this sword of mine through your guts!"

Baldek kept silent. Let the old fool wallow in his ignorance. When he, Baldek, was High Priest of the Sun, he would take great pleasure in teaching his father about priestly powers—the hard way! Aloud he said, "Be that as it may, Father, I can do what I say I can do. I will have the information just after dawn."

Vardek rose and stepped to the embrasure. "See that you do; the rest of the plan depends on it." And he squeezed through the embrasure and disappeared into the darkness.

Baldek lay on his couch and composed himself to sleep for two hours only. His father's plan was a bold one; the old man had not been idle since his return. Zesta being part of the plot had surprised him. Baldek had known for a long time that the High Priestess was restless under Khamadek's bumbling administration, but he had obviously badly miscalculated the depth of her dissatisfaction. Trust his father not to have missed it! The old man certainly had a way with women. Pity about Pirani; she would have been a welcome addition to Ruta's social life. He hoped that her knowledge of herbs was not just a woman's boast; it would be embarrassing, to say the least, if she failed in her part. But first he had his own part to play—that part, at least, would go without a hitch.

Two hours later to the very minute he awoke and swung his legs off the couch. It was an hour before dawn, and already the sky was gray with that predawn half-light. A soft knock sounded at the door, and the guard came in with Naida. "Wait outside," he said to the man. "Guard the door—no one must enter, no matter who it is." To Naida he said curtly, "Lie on the couch—I will be with you in a minute."

He busied himself at his work cabinet in the far corner and then came over to her with a beaker. "Drink that," he ordered.

"What is it?"

"A tranquilizing drug—it loosens the bonds between the physical and nonphysical and makes you more susceptible to suggestion."

She looked at it warily but then drank it down. "You will recall me, Baldek, won't you? Don't leave me out there."

"Don't worry," he said impatiently. "I cannot afford to leave you out there—I *have* to bring you back, for *my* sake." He went back to the work cabinet. "And anyway," he added dryly, "I will have more work for you here, the sort of work you most enjoy."

She smiled. "I look forward to it."

"It will be better than being plumbed by a wooden phallus, I promise you." He came back to the center of the room carrying a smoking silver thurible and began pacing out a circle, swinging the thurible by its chains. "You could be very useful to me, Naida, and I always look after those who look after me." The smell of incense began to pervade the room, and already she felt drowsy. "Lie back now and relax. You will find yourself drifting into sleep. Don't fight it, just let yourself go."

She lay back on the couch as she was told. "I have never lain with a man," she murmured drowsily, "at least not properly—only that time with Helios in the Mating Ritual, and that wooden thing hurt me. But I know I will be good at it." She closed her eyes, and immediately she felt herself beginning to drift. "I will be good at it, Baldek, you'll see—you will never have had a woman as good as me."

Her voice trailed off, and her breathing deepened rapidly. Baldek placed the thurible in the exact center of the circle he had paced and then moved the carved chair over next to the couch. He sat down and placed his hand under her breast to feel her heart. He rolled back her eyelids and saw that the eyes had already begun to swivel upward so that soon only the whites would be seen. He nodded to himself in satisfaction; she was indeed very amenable to the trance drug; this would be an easy operation. "Naida!" he said softly. "Naida! Can you hear me?"

Her lips barely moved. "I hear you," she whispered.

"I am going to send you to a place which I shall describe. When you get there, I want you to tell me everything you see and everything you hear. There is no need to be afraid—you are under my protection. Do you understand?"

The girl's voice was very low, a flat, expressionless monotone. "I understand."

He began to speak to her slowly and distinctly, describing the place he wanted her to visit, and as he described it to her, he built the same scene in his own imagination in every detail and held the mental scene steady and vivid with all the power and concentration of his trained mind; and as he did so, he commanded her to go, powerfully and dominatingly, repeating the command over and over again.

Naida hovered over the couch and looked down at herself and Baldek. She felt cold, but then, it was always cold out here. As she looked at the scene, it shimmered and wavered as though it was not quite real, vague at the edges like a dream image, and things moved in the vagueness, half-formed things that were in the scene but not part of it. Blurred, indistinct faces and forms drifted close to her as though curious, but she paid them no heed; she was used to them. They could be a nuisance at times but they were not dangerous. Out there, however, beyond the vagueness, were things of a different nature, powerful, terrifying entities born of the half-life, not physical but nearly physical. They were dangerous, highly dangerous. If she encountered one of them, she would have little chance, and if she lost the struggle, the entity would be able to backtrack her trail to her body, and Baldek would have a demented madwoman on his hands.

She shivered and drew closer to her body, but she could feel the tug of his commands forcing her away. She tried to resist, to cling to her body as the one point of safety, but the commands grew stronger and she felt herself impelled upward and away. The scene of Baldek's chamber vanished, and she felt herself rushed as though in the midst of a shrieking hurricane, a storm of air so violent that the senses are numbed, leaving only the frightening feeling of breakneck speed. It seemed to last forever, and she struggled, panic-stricken, against the claustrophobic dread of being imprisoned; but then the sensation faded, and she felt herself falling, gently, drifting downward until she came to rest.

She did not recognize the chamber, and yet it was somehow familiar. The walls were made of solid stone, and burning torches were set at intervals in niches high up near the roof. The furniture was sparse, a plain carved high-backed chair in the east, a central altar, and a row of plain wooden stools circled around the altar. On the altar itself was a silver chalice half-full of oil, and on the oil a lighted wick floated. The room was empty, but soon the door opened and twelve cowled figures filed silently in and took their places. The one who sat himself in the east began to speak, and Naida recognized Khamadek's voice. She shrank back into the corner of the room, terrified. She knew she was invisible to them, but it seemed to make no difference—she felt vulnerable, alone; if Khamadek even suspected her presence, she would be condemned; none but seventh-degree initiates could attend the inner sanctum of the Greater Mysteries, and the penalty was death by fire.

Khamadek had risen and was addressing the lodge.

"Brethren of the seventh degree, from those on the inner planes who see the light of the Most High face-to-face, I bring you greetings!"

"Greetings!" came the response, and Naida turned to flee. A seventh-degree ritual—she must get away, but try as she might, the force of Baldek held her there powerless to move.

Back in Baldek's chamber the girl's body writhed on the couch as though in agony, the expression on her face one of abject terror, and Baldek guessed the cause. It must have come as a severe shock to the girl to find herself at the highest ritual in the Sun Temple. "Speak!" he urged fiercely. "I command you to speak!" The body moaned and tossed on the couch, but still the lips were tight shut. "Speak, I said!" Baldek was now beside himself with rage; a seventh-degree ritual was in progress, and the wretched girl remained dumb. Soon the password to the seventh would be uttered, and Baldek had to have that password. Initiates were supposed to discern the password by their own efforts, through their own meditations, and without it no initiate could be admitted to the high degrees. The password was always a brief definition of the spiritual principle that governed the work of the higher degrees, and anyone who could discern the principle was held to be ready to do the work. Baldek had failed of his own efforts; he *had* to have that password—without it he could not be declared as the new high priest; and still this wretched girl would not speak. "Speak!" he thundered, and began beating the body with an iron rod. "Speak, damn you, speak!" Thin red weals sprang up on the girl's body, and as he continued to beat her, these ran with blood. "Speak! Speak! Speak!" At each word he lashed the jerking body again; by Narada he would beat her literally to death! "Speak, wretched woman, or by all the powers I will leave you out there to wander in terror forever. Speak!"

In the senior lodge Naida crouched in the corner. She could not feel the blows on her physical body but she could tell from the waves of hate reaching her that Baldek must be demented with rage. More than once Khamadek had peered suspiciously around the lodge as though sensing an alien presence, but so far she remained undetected. This gave her a slight encouragement, and slowly, haltingly, she began to repeat the words of the ritual.

Baldek was bent over the girl's body, his ear close to her lips to catch the whispered response. "Go on, go on!" he urged; and then, at last, barely audible, came the response he had been waiting for—the password to the seventh. Quick, now—get her out of there before she was discovered. Any high priest but a fool like Khamadek would have sensed an alien in the lodge immediately. Baldek had gambled on Khamadek's impaired sensitivity, but it could not last; even that old fool must realize soon that he was being watched. Quick, get her out—get her out!

Naida felt the tug of the recall, and released at last, she fled upward in blind panic, taking no care, no precautions—a blind, headlong flight—and swept straight into the path of one of the horrors of the half-life. Had she been less blinded by terror, had she made her withdrawal more carefully, she could have avoided it, but now it was too late. The loathsome thing enveloped her completely almost before she was aware of its presence. She shrieked and fought like a demented fiend herself, but she could not break free. The stench was appalling, suffocating, and its grip tightened harder and harder and she felt the link to her body begin to tear away. The force of the recall doubled, trebled, as Baldek realized the situation—and priest and half-thing struggled furiously for possession of the girl, a monstrous tug-of-war that was quite literally tearing her to pieces; and then Baldek threw in everything he had, the entire weight and power of all his years as a priest of the mighty Sun Temple, and with a tearing, rending agony that sent shriek after shriek echoing through the half-world, he pulled her clear and Naida crashed back into full consciousness and flung herself from the couch, covered in sweat and blood, still screaming with abject hysterical terror, and Baldek slumped to the floor half-conscious, drained of every scrap of energy.

"It has to be now—tonight!" snapped Vardek.

Baldek shook his head. "I say we wait. Khamadek cannot prove anything, but he is suspicious. He knows *something* is wrong somewhere—he will be on his guard."

"So what—what do I care about that fool's suspicions?"

Baldek turned to Zesta. "What do you say?"

The High Priestess stretched a languid arm toward the bowl of grapes. "I agree with Vardek. "She took a single grape and bit into it daintily. "We should move now before his suspicions become a certainty."

"Some sense at last!" said Vardek irritably; he was not used to having his commands brought into question. "Stick to priestly things, boy, and leave matters of war to those who understand them. The time to attack is when the enemy is uncertain of himself, undecided. Khamadek does not even know from which direction the attack will come; we strike now—both of them— tonight. Let's not have any more argument!"

The four conspirators were met in Vardek's house. It was late afternoon. Vardek, Zesta, and Pirani had spent an uncomfortable morning waiting for Baldek, not knowing whether he had succeeded or not. When he did finally arrive, he glossed over the difficulties he had encountered, but he had to tell them of Khamadek's wariness. Zesta had guessed that there was a great deal left unsaid in Baldek's brief account, but the main thing was that he had succeeded.

Pirani had been present throughout the discussion but had said little. Her opinion had not been asked on any point, but then she had not expected to be consulted. Toltecs did not seek advice from inferior races. "Shall I prepare the herb, my lord?" she murmured. "The same one as with Demian?"

Vardek and Zesta exchanged glances. "Yes, prepare the potion," said Vardek, "but not the one we used on Demian. Use the one you told us about this morning."

Pirani looked puzzled. "But it is not undetectable. It is well known to your own healers—they will know that they have been poisoned."

"I know," said Vardek calmly. "Zesta and I have been thinking. Two dead bodies will be too much of a coincidence—they will suspect poison even if they cannot trace any—and suspicion will automatically fall on you as being a priestess of strange herbs and the only person on Ruta with knowledge of herbs unknown on Ruta; and if you come under suspicion, then automatically so will I. Whereas if we use a poison that is known to everyone on Ruta, then the suspicion will embrace more than one. It is very simple."

It sounded simple, all right, but there was something wrong somewhere; why bring her all the way from Amaria to prepare a poison that could have been prepared by any slave on Ruta. Pirani felt uneasy without really knowing why. She shrugged. "Very well, my lord—if you insist."

Zesta turned to the girl. "But surely you can see the sense of it, Pirani."

The Amarian opened her mouth to say more, but then shut it quickly. Why draw their attention to the fact that they now no longer needed her? Why invite her own death? She smiled. "Yes, of course—call it vanity. I was looking forward to seeing your healers baffled by the deaths." She rose and went to the door. "This way is much better, I agree. The potions will be ready within the hour."

When the door closed behind her, Vardek looked at Zesta and Baldek and smiled sardonically. "The woman is a fool," he said cryptically.

"I must see the King!" Vardek stood, feet astride, arms akimbo, in the great hall of King Baralda's house. "How many more times must I repeat myself, you fool! I must see the King!"

The captain of the King's Guard with twelve men at his back stood his ground barring the way, but he was clearly very unsure of himself. "But, my lord, all Ruta knows the King lies dying. No one is permitted to see him save his personal healer—not even you, my lord."

"Great Narada, will you or will you not stand aside! I

am here on a matter of extreme emergency—an affair
of state that is for the King's ears only!"

The captain looked past him at Pirani. "And the
woman?"

Vardek stamped his foot irritably. "She is concerned
with this matter; the King must hear what she has to
say. By all the seven demons of darkness, Captain,
Ruta itself is in peril, and you stand there waffling
like an Akkadian whore!"

The man drew himself up stiffly. "I have my orders,
and you, of all people, my lord, know that I should not
disobey them—no one, not even you, is permitted to
see the King."

Vardek fumed at this delay. He bitterly regretted not
having brought his own personal guard—he would have
made quick work of this opposition. "Very well, Captain. Step over here; I will talk to you privately." He
led the reluctant officer to one side, taking care that
Pirani could overhear them. He grasped the man's arm.
"Listen to me, you dolt!" he snapped. "You are part of
the Temple Guard and so take your orders from
Khamadek—right?"

"Er . . . yes . . . as you know."

"Well, Khamadek is dead! Who gives you your orders now?"

The man stammered, "Er . . . I don't know . . . the
new High Priest, I suppose."

"There is no new high priest—the whole temple is in
an uproar. The Lady Pirani has information about the
poison used. The King must hear what she has to say
—and, dying or not, the King must make a decision."

The captain could not take it all in. "But there must
be a new high priest—there is always a high priest!"

"Great Narada, I am telling you that there is not!
Can't you get that simple fact through your thick skull!
There is no one fit to take over. The whole temple is
buzzing like an overturned hive of bees. They are all
running around accusing each other! And with no high
priest, you take your orders from me, the Lord Commander of the Army, and I tell you this, if you delay
me by another single second, I shall run my sword

through your guts, guard or no guard. Do I make my-self clear?" Vardek's grip tightened on his arm, the fingers digging into the muscle. "I said, do I make my-self clear?"

"Yes . . . of course, my lord. . . . I didn't understand." He turned to his men. "Make way, there, my Lord Vardek to see King Baralda."

"That's better!" snapped Vardek. "And one more thing, Captain—the King will undoubtedly issue a proc-lamation. If you utter one single word of this to anyone —to *anyone*—before that proclamation is announced, you will die! Is *that* clear?"

"Yes, yes, my lord."

"Right—then stay on guard here. No one, repeat, no one, is to be allowed through on any pretext what-soever without clearance from me personally! Is that also clear?"

"Yes, my lord—perfectly clear. I am sorry I delayed you, but I had my orders."

"And now you have new orders. Carry them out!"

"Yes, my lord . . . of course."

Vardek strode across the hall toward the corridor that led to the King's private bedchamber, snapping his fin-gers for Pirani to follow him. A household servant hurried ahead to lead the way.

"You took a chance," Pirani whispered. "Supposing he finds out that Khamadek is not dead yet?"

"Then we will have some explaining to do," said Vardek calmly.

As they came to the King's bedchamber, a priest in the blue robe of a temple healer came out and closed the door behind him. "What is this?" he snapped.

"They have clearance," said the servant.

"Not through me they haven't! No one sees the King without a signed order from Khamadek himself!"

"You heard the man!" Vardek grabbed the healer by the shoulder and hurled him to one side. "If you don't like it, go and see the Captain of the Guard, but don't bother me!" The man fell heavily, banging his head on the marble floor.

Vardek paused at the door and looked at Pirani. "You got the potion?"

"Yes," she whispered.

"Then let's go!" And he flung open the doors and strode into the King's bedchamber.

"Why this visit at this late hour, Zesta?" said Khamadek. "I was about to do my evening meditation and retire." He fumbled irritably and fussily with the cord of his robe and eased himself into the high-backed chair. "The meeting of the Council of Priests went on until late evening, and I am tired of talk."

Without the regalia of a high priest, Khamadek looked what he was, a tired and irritable old man, too old for the burden of his office. For a moment Zesta felt sorry for him, but then inwardly she shrugged; he could have retired from office anytime he wanted, retired to a position of honor and tranquillity, but he had stubbornly clung on, too proud and too vain to withdraw. "It was about the meeting I wished to see you," she said. "Did the Council discuss my report on the Amarian priestess?"

"They did, but no action is required. She will be watched, of course, but without concrete evidence, an arrest would be both unjust and undiplomatic. Vardek would not like it at all."

Zesta tried hard not to smile; it was exactly the reaction that Vardek had predicted. "You may be right," she murmured.

Khamadek eyed her thoughtfully. "The Council thanks you for your concern—and indeed so do I; your interest in my welfare is touching—and a little surprising."

"Surprising?"

Khamadek grunted and said petulantly, "In the past, you have not shown yourself to be overly concerned; this late gesture is therefore somewhat surprising. Anyway, as to this present business, I feel you may be exaggerating. If she really does have thoughts of taking my life, I would have detected them by now."

"She has them, all right," said Zesta, "which is why I reported the matter to the Council." She leaned forward and spoke firmly, emphatically. "She blames three people for the slaughter of ten thousand of her people —you, Baralda, and Vardek—and she has thoughts of murder for all three. Choose not to believe me if you wish, Khamadek. You have been warned; I can do no more."

"Baralda is dying anyway, and as for Vardek, she would be doing me a service if she got rid of him. She has plenty of opportunity, being a member of his household, but as to myself, she cannot even gain access to the temple without being escorted, let alone get near enough to me to threaten my life. As I say, the Council has discussed the matter, and thanks you, but sees no need for any immediate action."

Zesta smiled to herself; the old fool really thought himself to be safe. "Very well, but would you humor a woman's fears," she murmured, "and allow me to watch over you these next few days in my own personal mirror?"

"Not at all. It would be churlish of me to refuse your solicitude, even though I think it unnecessary."

"When it concerns the welfare of the most important man on Ruta," she said, "nothing must be left to chance." His expression changed, and for a moment Zesta thought she had overdone it, but then she realized that the man was actually simpering. In a few moments, he might even blush.

"You are very kind, Zesta," he said. "Perhaps I have misjudged you."

At that moment a knock sounded at the door and a young seeress entered bearing an earthen jug of wine. "Ah, good—the wine," said Zesta. "Set it down there, girl, and after that, you may retire." She turned to Khamadek. "I hoped our meeting would bear fruit, and in anticipation I arranged for the wine so that we could toast the beginning of a new understanding between us. Will you drink a toast with me, Khamadek?"

"Willingly," he said. "Most willingly, Zesta."

King Baralda, Lord of the Thousand Isles, lay dying. He was still called "Lord of the Thousand Isles," even though but two islands only remained of the kingdom, Ruta and Daiteya. Once the realm really did comprise a thousand islands, aye, and a mighty continent too, but those days were gone. In ancient times the Toltecs had ruled over an empire so vast that no man could ever see the whole of it though he travel all his life, and the Lord Commander led an army of fifty thousand warriors whose vast numbers blackened the earth as far as the eye could see, an army that would fill the hearts of any enemy foolish enough to stand against them with a dreadful fear. And now Baralda, Lord of the Thousand Isles, lay dying, and no one mourned his passing.

He lay on a vast canopied bed, a frail and sickly thing between the covers. He was not old. Khamadek had been a grown man already in the fifth degree when Baralda had screamed his way into the world, but he seemed old, he looked old, and he even smelled old. His face was sunken and lined, his eyes dull, and his hands lay like two withered leaves on the thin twigs of his arms. Vardek remembered Baralda as a huge bellowing hulk of a man, bombasting his way through life, a bull of a man, a fierce and passionate man who had been a true warrior-king, a king who led from the front, not one who issued orders from the rear—a bloody, battle-loving man, always the first in a charge, the first to cleave his way into the enemy ranks, the first to spill blood, his own and theirs, the first to bulldoze his way into drunkenness after the battle was done, the first to drive his wedge between the thighs of captured women, the first in everything, in battle, in women, in drinking, and anything, and now he lay dying of a wasting disease picked up in foreign lands, a disease for which the healers could find no cure.

"Come in, Vardek," he whispered, his voice a dry wisp of sound. "I am never too ill to see old friends."

Vardek advanced to the bed. He felt sad and angry that such a man as Baralda, his boyhood hero, should die like this, in bed and not in battle—but at the same time, he felt a revulsion for the disease-ridden body. "This is no way for a warrior to die!" he said gruffly.

"It is not my choice, Vardek—the healer keeps me alive—but for what?"

"You would sooner die?"

Baralda closed his eyes. "Give me one more fight," he whispered, "one more woman, and one more skin of wine, and I would be happy to go."

"You could not even pick up your sword," said Vardek harshly, "let alone drive it into flesh—and the same goes for a woman—but I might be able to do something about the wine." He turned to Pirani. "Get the wine for King Baralda. Send that servant."

Pirani, too, had been saddened at the sight of the frail and dying king, even though he was the enemy of her people. Baralda the Butcher they called him—all her life her people had spoken his name with fear and hatred; if only they could see the weak and sickly thing he had become. She hurried to the door but returned in a few moments shaking her head. "The healer will not permit it," she said.

Vardek spun on his heel, strode to the door, and flung it open. He grabbed the healer by the throat and smashed him against the wall. "Who are you," he roared, "to say what the King shall and shall not have? Have you set yourself up as master of all Ruta? Get that wine, and get it quickly, or I'll tear you apart!" And he flung the man to the floor.

"Khamadek will hear of this!" the priest said viciously.

Vardek kicked him cruelly and fiercely in the groin, and the man screamed with pain. "By Narada, you priests sicken me! Baralda is twice the man of any priest who ever lived! Get that wine and then tell whom you like! The King rules in Ruta, not Khamadek!" The man scurried away, and Vardek strode back into the bedchamber. "The wine will be here shortly."

Baralda smiled. "You should come more often, Vardek," he said with a wry chuckle. "I feel better already just listening to you. You're a man after my own fashion! But why *have* you come? You are not a man to pay social calls. And who is the woman?"

Vardek sat in a chair by the bed. "An Amarian priestess called Pirani—we captured her in the last campaign."

"I remember those Amarian women as being devils in bed, Vardek. Is she a devil?"

Vardek smiled. Pirani had never seen him smile in quite that way before—it was almost gentle. "I've had worse," he said dryly.

The dying man looked at her, his eyes not quite so dull now. "That I can believe. Would you lend her to me for ten minutes? I believe she would cure my illness."

"Yes, she would—permanently!"

"Ah, but what a way to go, Vardek! Better than lying here day after day feeling the life drain out of you drip by drip. I'd sooner die on top of a woman or on top of a sword than on top of a bed! Anyway, enough of these dreams. Why have you come, Vardek?"

The Lord Commander pulled his chair closer to the bed. "Khamadek is dead."

The King turned his head toward his commander. "What has a dead priest to do with me? Let the Council elect another."

Vardek shook his head. "It's not as easy as that. Khamadek was poisoned. Pirani here is a priestess of herbs and has examined the body. There is no mistake."

"That is true, King Baralda," she said. "No mistake at all."

"We tried to keep it dark," said Vardek, "but the whole temple knows of it now, and each is accusing the other. Only a seventh-degree initiate can be elected as high priest, and all those of that grade are senile old men unfit to take office in these troubled times. Zesta is fearful of a power struggle among the young men of the fifth degree, and she is probably right. Already the Temple Guard is hopelessly split, as each faction is bribed to support one of the fifth degree, none of whom are qualified for the office—all this, and Khamadek has been dead only a few hours! Zesta tells me that by tomorrow there will be open warfare in the temple itself, and no matter who wins, we end up with a high priest unfit for office, and *that* would be disastrous for all Ruta. The Akkadians will not give their support to an unlawful high priest, nor will many of my own commanders. With the priesthood split into warring factions, the Akkadians and Rmoahals no longer feeling the need for loyalty to the temple, and my own army also divided, the result will be chaos, civil strife—it will tear Ruta apart, Baralda!"

Pirani shook her head. Vardek told the lies so convincingly that even she nearly believed him. No one, least of all the King, would believe that anyone could have the audacity to tell such a gigantic lie—so gigantic that Vardek had every chance of getting away with it.

"Where is Zesta now?" Baralda whispered.

"At the temple trying to keep some semblance of order. The Council is twittering like women and is totally unable to control the situation or make any decisions. They themselves are divided, one from the other, arguing as to the best thing to do."

"But what can I do? I am a dying man, Vardek. I cannot rise from my bed and take command."

"You are still the King, and the King rules in Ruta. You have but to issue your commands, and I will carry them out. You know me, Baralda. I am strong enough to command this situation, but I cannot do it without your proclamation—and also there is the question of your successor."

"Successor? But my son will succeed—all Ruta knows that."

"Only if the High Priest agrees to the succession and administers the royal oath. And without a high priest, that cannot happen. And even if we did have a lawfully elected new high priest, I doubt that he would agree to that particular succession."

Baralda frowned, "Why not?"

Vardek hesitated; all would be won or lost on the next few words. "Do *you* think he would make a

worthy king for Ruta, Baralda?" Vardek knew that
Baralda had little love for his son, a spineless effeminate
youth, impotent and useless, more interested in youths
than women.

Baralda lay silent for several long minutes, and then
whispered, "No, though it shames me to say it."

"And his Akkadian pursuits of young men would
make it doubtful that he would ever marry in the full
sense, and so there would be little likelihood of royal
issue. No high priest worth the name could ratify such
a succession. I am sorry, Baralda, but that is the truth
of it."

The King turned his head and looked at Vardek
sharply. "All right, I agree. But who shall be king after
me? You, Vardek? Is that what you want?"

Vardek shook his head. "No, I would not accept the
crown, even if it were offered."

Baralda lay back on the pillows, seemingly satisfied.
Vardek smiled to himself; that refusal had been his
trump card. Baralda would believe that anyone who
would refuse the opportunity to seize the crown would
be a man to trust. Such is the vanity of kings that they
believe their crown to be a prize above all else.

"What, then, do you want?" he whispered.

"Time and a man," said Vardek crisply. "We need a
strong man to take command of Ruta, a man who will
not seize power for himself but who would rule temporarily only, in a state of martial law—a man strong
enough to quell any civil strife both inside and outside
the temple, a man who could give Ruta time to lawfully choose a high priest fit for office and a new
king fit to rule after you. This is what we need,
Baralda—time and a man!"

"You are speaking of appointing a marshal of Ruta,"
Baralda whispered. *"Now* I know why you have come
to me. Only the King can make such an appointment,
and even then, only if there is no high priest. Is that
what you want, Vardek—to be appointed marshal of
Ruta?"

"It was done once before, in ancient times," said
Vardek, "and the safeguard is that the appointment has

to be renewed at each equinox, and can be renewed only by the King or High Priest. And without either, the appointment can therefore last for only six months. And if we fail to produce a lawful high priest or king in six months, then all Ruta will have been destroyed anyway by civil strife. If I succeed, then we will have a new high priest who will obviously feel no need to renew the appointment. Either way, I can be marshal only until the next equinox. But believe me, Baralda, without a marshal, all is lost, and I am the only man in Ruta who has a chance of making the appointment a success."

"Yes, I believe that, but you speak as though I was going to die tonight."

Vardek hesitated. The original plan was to slip the poison to Baralda secretly in the wine, but there might be no need for the secrecy. "Would you not be happy to go?"

Baralda closed his eyes. "By Narada," he whispered, "I would give a great deal to escape this useless body of mine. But what does Zesta say of this?"

Vardek drew a rolled parchment from his tunic. "Here is a plea from her to you personally, Baralda, begging you to appoint me as marshal."

At that moment the servant entered with the wine and placed it on the table and then left. Pirani walked over to the wine and poured three glasses. She drew a vial from her robe and emptied the contents into one of the glasses and then took all three on a tray to the bed.

"I imagine," said Baralda, "that you have the proclamation with you all ready for me to sign."

Vardek nodded and drew it from his tunic. "Of course. If Ruta is to stand a chance of being saved, then the proclamation must be signed tonight."

Baralda smiled faintly. "With no high priest, and with such a plea from the High Priestess *and* the Lord Commander of the Army, and with myself unable to rule as a king should, I have little choice, Vardek. If I give Ruta into your hands, will you swear to serve her well?"

"I do," said Vardek. "And anyway, Baralda, who else is there?"

Baralda sighed. "Who would have thought my rule would have ended like this! Well, Vardek, what must be, must be, I suppose!" He took the proclamation and the brush pen and signed the parchment. "There, Vardek, marshal of Ruta—do what you can to save the kingdom and the people."

Vardek took the parchment, rolled it, and put it back beneath his tunic. "I will, Baralda, I swear it!"

The King looked toward the three glasses. "Which one is mine?" Pirani handed him a glass. He nestled it in his hands. "Will it be painful?" he asked.

Vardek and Pirani exchanged glances, and Pirani said, "No, King Baralda, Lord of the Thousand Isles, it will not be painful compared to what you have been suffering these past months."

"Say that again, girl."

"Say what?"

"What you called me."

Pirani smiled. "King Baralda, Lord of the Thousand Isles."

The dying man smiled. "It was no bad thing to have been," and he drank down the wine in a single draught.

It wanted still two hours to dawn when Zesta and Baldek slipped away from the Temple of the Sun and headed toward Vardek's house, where Vardek himself and Pirani waited for them.

"Well?" barked Vardek as soon as they entered. The waiting had made him irritable. He was literally gambling his own life, as indeed were they all.

"Perfect!" said Zesta. "The old fool did not suspect a thing. He drank the wine, fell asleep, and died. And you?"

Vardek tossed the parchment on the table. "I am now marshal of Ruta, and Baralda is dead!"

Pirani said softly, "He wanted to die. How lonely he must have been these past months, how frustrated, and who knows what he suffered from that disease?" She shook her head. "I have hated him all my life—

Baralda the Butcher we call him in Amaria. I thought I would be pleased to see him die, but I wasn't. But he wanted to die. He knew what was in the wine and welcomed it. He died like a king, with courage. We have murdered Khamadek, but we did not murder Baralda."

"A noble sentiment!" said Baldek. "But now let us reconfirm our next step. We haven't any time to waste."

"Agreed," said Vardek. "Does anyone else know of Khamadek's death?"

"No, but they will at dawn," said Baldek, "when he fails to attend the dawn ritual and they send someone to fetch him."

"Very well, here is what we do. Just before dawn, Zesta will inform the Council of Priests that she awoke and saw in her seeress' mirror that Khamadek was dead, and saw also that even at that moment the murderer was at the palace to slay the King. She will say that she sent a messenger to me immediately to enlist my help."

"Don't forget," said Pirani, "that directly the news breaks, the captain of the Palace Guard will know that you lied to him about the time of Khamadek's death."

"I have forgotten nothing!" said Vardek irritably. "That captain comes off duty at dawn. He will not reach his chamber alive! As I was saying, I will arrive at the Sun Temple just after dawn with the body of the murderer, and the body of the captain, whom I shall say was bribed by the murderer to gain access to the King. I will be very sorry that I had to kill both of them, and also very sorry that I was too late to save the King. Both bodies will then be handed over to the Council to do with as they think fit. I will then tell them that last night, when you and I, Pirani, visited the palace, Baralda had a premonition of his death and so appointed me as marshal of Ruta—priests like premonitions; it will ring true to them. I will then produce the signed proclamation and take charge. Agreed?"

"What about the healer at the palace?" said Pirani.

"Simple," said Vardek. "I will say that it must have been during our visit that you managed to bribe the captain to allow you to come back later to poison the

King, using the wine still left from our earlier visit."

Pirani's face went white with shock. "Me?" she whispered.

Vardek smiled cruelly. "Of course. Who else would want to kill the King? He was no threat to anyone. Only an Amarian would have a motive—all Ruta knows how Amarians hate Baralda."

"One point," said Zesta smoothly. "You said you were going to hand over the bodies of the captain and the murderer. But the murderer isn't dead yet."

"That's right!" said Vardek, smiling. "She isn't, is she?"

7

The Council of Priests were met in the Hall of Learning. It was an hour past dawn, an hour since they had been told the news, and still their faces were dazed. It was an open council meeting, and as such, anyone from the fourth degree upward could attend, and so too could senior seeresses and above—and all were there, all equally stunned.

Deledian, leader of the Council, the most aged and withdrawn of all the sages of the seventh degree, was completely at a loss as to what to do. At first his mind could not grasp what had happened, nor could it formulate any plan of action. For too many years he had lived the life of a recluse, a life of contemplation, leaving the politics and day-to-day administration of the Sun Temple to Khamadek and the eager young priests of the fifth degree. The others of the seventh were similarly placed—all were aged and near to the end of their days, and all had been withdrawn for many years on to the inner in preparation for their departure from physical life.

All eyes were on Deledian at the head of the High Table. The hall was crowded but silent. Helios stood at the rear near Netziachos. In front of him, facing the High Table, was Vardek with Baldek at his side. Zesta, as befitted her station as High Priestess, sat on a carved chair to the right of the High Table, facing the crowded hall.

Vardek was obviously impatient. "Well, Deledian?" he barked. "What is the decision of the Council?"

The old man glanced around the High Table, but the others were clearly leaving it to him. "The Council thanks you, Lord Vardek, for having brought the murderers to justice. It is a pity, however, that you were not able to take them alive. The murder of the Sun King and the High Priest was a crime so foul that only the long death by a slow fire would have been a fit reward for the murderers. A clean death by the sword was much too lenient."

"I have already explained," said Vardek tartly, "that I came into the King's bedchamber only a few seconds after the poison had been given. The King was already in his death agonies. I slew the girl there and then so that the King could see with his own eyes that he had been revenged. As for the captain of the King's Guard, he was armed and had twelve men at his back. I was too pressed to worry about an arrest. The men-at-arms thought it was I who had killed the King, and it was not until I had slain their captain that I had a chance to show them the truth."

"We are not criticizing your actions, my lord— merely stating that it is a pity they died so clean a death." Deledian cleared his throat and picked up the two parchments in front of him. "This," he said, tapping one of them, "is a plea from Zesta, High Priestess of the Sun, to Baralda, the Sun King, asking that Lord Vardek be appointed marshal of Ruta." He turned to Zesta. "In the light of subsequent events, it appears that your fears for Khamadek's life were justified."

Zesta did not like being questioned in public. "I reported the Lady Pirani's thoughts of murder to the Council officially and to Khamadek himself personally —but both you and he chose to ignore my warning. Since a marshal can only be appointed by a king or a high priest, it was obvious that the appointment had to be made while at least one of them was still alive. In the event of the death of both king and high priest, it was obvious that we would need a marshal to maintain law and order and to prevent Ruta from being plunged into civil strife. It was intended as a precaution only and one that has proved to be justified." She glanced round at the assembled priests. "There are plenty here who would have striven to take Khamadek's place, lawfully or not, and without a strong man in command, our island would have been hopelessly split into warring factions."

"You are probably right," said Deledian dryly. "Certainly as marshal of Ruta my Lord Vardek commands both the army and the temple, not just the army, and so can unite the two." He turned to Vardek. "And indeed as marshal you are not even subject to the jurisdiction of the Council. Baralda must have had a great deal of faith in you, my lord. However, as a man of considerable experience you will know that one man cannot rule over others save either by their consent or by some pressure that he can bring to bear on them. What say you to this?"

Vardek was not pleased. Baldek had told him that Deledian was a doddering old man, but the leader of the Council seemed alert enough to grasp the fundamentals. "Firstly," he growled, "let me say that Baralda offered me the crown itself to rule after him as king."

The crowd of priests and priestesses gasped, and a hubbub of murmuring rose throughout the hall. All eyes turned to Chalian, the King's son, the natural-blood heir to the throne of Ruta. Chalian was an effeminate youth, too fond of Akkadian ways to be a leader of Toltecs. His life was spent in idle pleasures with a company of young men equally as effeminate as himself. It was an open secret that both the priesthood and affairs of state bored him to tears of sulkiness, and it was equally an open secret that his father was deeply ashamed for having sired a son such as he. The King's two daughters were also lacking in that regal air of dignity and authority so necessary to rule a people such as the Toltecs. Nathos was cruel and petty and given to childish tantrums. Her one ruling passion was to terrify the Rmoahal slaves by giving them impossible tasks to perform and having them beaten when they failed. Her sister, Daladia, was said to be overfond of husky men-at-arms. It was rumored that half the Temple Guard had lain in Daladia's bed and that it was only the skill of the healers that had prevented the bitch from whelping a dozen times or more. King Baralda had been a brawling, lusty warrior king, a Toltec among Toltecs, and it was a constant source of wonder to all Ruta that such a man could have sired such a litter.

Deledian cleared his throat. "Chalian is the heir to Ruta's throne, as you very well know, Lord Vardek," he said sternly.

"And that heir cannot succeed to the throne without the consent of the high priest, as *you* very well know, Deledian," said Vardek tartly. "And since we have no high priest, then Chalian cannot be crowned."

There was dead silence in the hall for a full minute, and then Deledian said: "What say you to this, Chalian?"

The King's son was lounging against a buttress and could not even be bothered to straighten himself to answer. He waved a hand airily. "It is nothing to me, Deledian—who wants to be king anyway? My father made such a fuss about being king, but to me it is less than nothing. A crown of flowers is no less a crown than one of gold. I have no wish to be king of Ruta; let Vardek be king if it pleases him."

There was an embarrassed silence. Deledian cleared his throat again and shuffled the parchments in his hand. "I never thought to hear such words from a member of the royal house of Ruta, but if that is your wish, Chalian, then so be it. Do you then renounce all claims to the throne of Ruta?"

"Of course I do!" the youth said irritably. "I told my father often that I hoped he would live forever, to spare me the boredom of being king after him. You know perfectly well that all this solemn nonsense is nothing to me. I have far better things to do." He straightened up and strolled toward the great doors. "In fact, I think

I have wasted enough time this morning on this non-sense. If you will excuse me, Deledian, my friends are waiting for me."

Deledian half-rose and bowed as the King's son passed through the doors.

He then seated himself again and paused before speaking so that he could gain control of his voice. "Chalian's attitude is not a crime against Ruta as such," he said gruffly, "and it is not up to us to judge him. To each his own. The boy is answerable to the inner plane adepts—let them guide him in their wisdom." He turned to Vardek. "A more tactful man than you, Vardek, would have announced that news in a more private place; but perhaps you were right—it is as well to have these things in the open. It is true that I have known for some time that Baralda had serious doubts about Chalian's ability and indeed his willing-ness to rule after him, but even so, I am surprised that he offered the throne to you."

"So was I," Vardek growled, "and so was Baralda when I refused. I am a warrior, Deledian—I have no more wish to wear a crown than Chalian does, or sit in idleness in a royal palace, nor indeed do I even wish to be marshal. I am the Lord Commander of the Army, and that is all I ever wanted to be. I refused the crown, but for the sake of my long friendship with Baralda I did promise him to serve as marshal for six months, only should the need arise. I had no idea, obviously, that the need would arise so soon."

Deledian fingered the second parchment. "It was indeed a remarkable piece of timing," he said dryly, "particularly as no one could possibly have foreseen the death of the King."

"Not so, Deledian!" said Zesta angrily. "*I* knew it was a possibility; it was the Council who refused to see what was before their eyes! You seem to be doing your best, Deledian, to cast doubt on the validity of my Lord Vardek's appointment, yet the truth is that if you and the Council had acted on my warning, then King Baralda and Khamadek would not have died!"

Deledian raised his hand. "Peace, Zesta. I am not

questioning the validity of the appointment; and as for your report we of the Council were guided by Khamadek himself, who saw no reason for any action to be taken. Let us not wrangle among ourselves trying to fix the blame for this tragedy. It is always far easier to look back at events than forward to them. There is no doubt whatsoever as to the validity of Vardek's appointment, and the Council is happy to ratify it officially."

Vardek stepped forward. "The appointment does not require your ratification, official or unofficial; the appointment would stand whether you agreed with it or not." Vardek turned to face the crowd, feet apart, arms akimbo. "Whether you like it or not," he growled, "I am marshal of all Ruta, and by Narada I will fulfill that office as I promised Baralda, even if I have all of Ruta against me!" He turned back to Deledian. "You spoke just now of pressures by which a man might rule others without their consent to his rule. I have five thousand Toltec warriors under my command, and a further five thousand Akkadians and Rmoahals. They are pressure enough if I need it. We can do this the easy way or the hard way, whichever you prefer, Deledian. The appointment is a lawful one, as you have said, and as such the marshal should be able to count on the support of the Council of Priests. If he does not get that support, he has the power to disband the Council, by force if necessary. Now, Deledian, do I have your support or not?"

There was dead silence in the hall. Vardek's crude and arrogant display of power caused a wave of resentment, but some of the older priests were willing to admit that Vardek was the only man in Ruta to command the situation, and in truth they were a little awed by his ruthless and contemptuous display of authority. Being priests of power themselves, they could admire power in action even though disliking the man who wielded it. Yet at the same time they were furious that it was a layman, not a priest, who had been given control.

Vardek was well aware of the mixed feelings around him—he had a gift for assessing the temper of a crowd.

He knew that he was the most hated man in the hall, and he enjoyed the feeling of exercising supreme authority in such conditions. "Well, Deledian?" he growled.

The old man shrugged. "Of course you have our support. It is written that the marshal also assumes the role of leader of the Council, and I will gladly yield up my place to you." He rose and offered Vardek his chair. "The Council invites you, Vardek, marshal of Ruta, to take your rightful place at the head of the High Table—and I, Deledian, offer my services as counselor and pledge the support of the entire Council of Priests."

There was a murmur of approval from the assembly, and Vardek nodded. "Well spoken, Deledian." He made his way toward the head of the High Table and took his place in the carved chair. In the whole history of Ruta, never had a layman risen to such heights, supreme master of all Ruta. Vardek was suffused with the feeling of tremendous power and authority, sole arbiter of the destiny of the finest race on earth. He paused for a moment, and then growled, "My first task as marshal is to see to it that a new high priest is lawfully appointed —*lawfully* appointed." He turned to Deledian. "Agreed?"

The erstwhile leader of the Council was both surprised and pleased; he had expected Vardek to delay such a move. "Indeed, yes, my Lord Marshal. The temple without a high priest is like a body without a brain, but there are no suitable candidates. The high priest must be an initiate of the seventh degree, and we of the sixth and seventh are all old men nearing the end of our days; the office requires a younger man. Traditionally, and indeed, ideally, the office is filled by a young man newly initiated into the Seventh. It is held that if a man reaches the seventh degree while still young, he must obviously have qualities far above average—and his very youthfulness is a much needed quality in order to bear the rigors of the office. The weakness in the system is that a young priest, no matter how gifted, to have reached the seventh degree so early, is nevertheless lacking in experience—hence the reason for the Council of Priests, whose duty it is to advice the high priest on spiritual and ritual matters. Khamadek, I remember, was barely twenty-five years of age when he first succeeded to office."

Vardek appeared to ponder the problem for a moment and then pointed to Helios, standing at the rear of the hall. "Helios!" he called. "I have heard that Khamadek named you as his successor. Is that true?"

Helios stepped forward. "So he was good enough to inform me, Vardek, but I am not of the seventh, I do not have the password."

"How long will it take you to get it?"

Helios smiled. "You cannot put a time limit on these things, Vardek. The password embodies the spiritual concepts that are worked in the rituals of the degree in question. It can be discerned only through meditation. It is held that if a priest can discern the password of his own efforts, then he has obviously come to understand the principles concerned. In other words he has already initiated himself on the inner levels—the physical plane ritual intiation is merely the ratification. As to myself, I am of the fifth degree only. I may discover the password to the seventh tomorrow or next week—or it may take me years. Indeed, I may never discover it at all."

Deledian coughed gently. "If I might interrupt, my Lord Marshal—Helios is being modest. He will undoubtedly reach the seventh, and very soon; but whether that is days or months cannot be known. He is quite right—these things cannot be measured in physical plane time; they can only be measured in terms of inner plane time, where time is a measurement of states of consciousness, not the related movement of physical objects."

Vardek gave a short derisive laugh. "I don't know what that means, Deledian, and I doubt that you do either—but let it pass." He leaned back in his chair. "So in spite of Helios being named by Khamadek as his successor, and in spite of the Council's obvious approval of his qualities, Helios cannot be considered as a candidate for high priest simply because he does not know the official password—correct?"

Deledian nodded. "Quite correct."

Helios was puzzled. He could understand an open council to discuss the murder and the appointment of Vardek as marshal, but the selection of a high priest was a matter for the Council of Priests alone; the names and qualifications of prospective candidates for high priest should not be discussed in open council for all to hear. He wondered what deep game Vardek was playing. Several others of the fifth degree were also frowning—all except Baldek, that is. Helios looked to Netziachos and shrugged his shoulders, and she lifted her eyebrows and shook her head in reply.

Vardek turned to Zesta. "And what does the High Priestess say of this?"

Zesta seemed impatient with all this talk. "It is a simple matter, my lord. Since there is no one of the fifth who is ready to be advanced to the seventh, then we must manage as best we can without a high priest. Obviously the first fifth-degree initiate to reach the seventh becomes the automatic choice, subject to the approval of the Council."

Vardek turned to Deledian, and the old man nodded. "I am not happy with it, Vardek, for it tends to turn the matter into a race, but since that is the situation, we must accept it."

"Then so be it!" said Vardek. "Now perhaps we can turn to other matters—"

"One moment!" said Baldek loudly, and all eyes turned in his direction. He strode forward to face the High Table. "I have remained silent so far, waiting to see if Helios would be accepted, since he was Khamadek's choice, but now I must speak." He paused for dramatic effect, and then went on, "It is not true that no one of the fifth knows the password to the seventh. I, Baldek, have had the password revealed to me by an inner plane master during my meditation. I claim my right to be initiated into the seventh!"

There was a stunned silence, and then a babble of disbelief swept the assembly of priests. Apart from Baldek's own circle of supporters, no one believed for one moment that Vardek's son was a true candidate for the seventh. The tumult rose higher and higher as the angry young priests stamped their sandaled feet and shouted their disapproval. It was a scene unprecedented in the temple's long history. There had been arguments before, times when groups of initiates were at variance with one another over vital issues, but always these differences had been resolved through calm discussion and meditation, solutions and agreements reached through objective consideration of the spiritual principles involved; never had a disagreement been voiced so immediately, so passionately, so angrily, and with such overwhelming majority. Vardek was taken aback by the sheer vehemence of this opposition to his son. For several minutes he sat silently in the face of this uproar, and then suddenly he sprang to his feet. "Silence!" he roared. "Silence! Are these the serene priests of the Sun, the mediators of the inner wisdom, the learned men of Ruta? Silence, you pack of yelping dogs! Silence, lest I summon the army to curb your noisy tongues!"

Deledian also was on his feet, and so too was Zesta, both calling for peace, but the contempt in Vardek's voice and the threat of armed warriors incensed the assembly still further. Deledian was horrified; never had he seen the temple priests so angry. For many years his world had been that of contemplation, of meditation, the silence and peace of the inner communion; this outburst was quite beyond his experience and certainly beyond his ability to control it. Zesta, too, was astonished at the depth of the anger. She had known that Baldek was unpopular but had never dreamed that he inspired such opposition as this. The depth of feeling against Baldek threatened the success of their entire plan. She was now wishing furiously that they had chosen someone else to front their plan—Baldek's anger at having been left out would have been easier to deal with than this collective outburst from the majority of the temple—and Vardek's threatening manner was not helping to quell the opposition.

The tumult rose even higher and threatened to erupt into physical violence at any moment. Of the whole assembly, only two figures remained calm—Baldek himself and Helios. Baldek, flushed and angry, nevertheless remained outwardly calm, arms folded, standing firm among the outraged crowd. Firm as he was, he could not have remained so for long, for even then groups of the more volatile young priests of the fourth and fifth were moving toward him. Just as it seemed that the entire scene would explode into violence, and when Helios could see that events were beyond the ability of the seniors on the High Table to control, he moved swiftly and silently through the crowd and sprang onto the rostrum and faced the angry priests. He did not speak at all, not a single syllable; he merely stood with arms upraised, shaking his head calmly and even sadly. The effect was not instantaneous—far from it—but the air of serenity that he radiated, plus the considerable respect that he had always commanded, gradually dispelled the anger, and as the noise died down, he said quietly and gently, "A claim has been made to the seventh. If that claim is unjustified, it will not be upheld. If it *is* justified, then by the law in which we all live, it *must* be upheld and given our support." The shouting rose again, but Helios shook his head. "This is a matter of faith—faith in the law and faith in the hierarchical system."

"But all the temple knows, Helios," one of them shouted, "that Baldek is not yet ready for the seventh, nor is ever likely to be!"

"That statement is incorrect, and you know it!" said Helios reprovingly. "*I* do not know if he is ready, and neither do you—nor indeed do any of us. Only the inner planes can know. *If* Baldek has the password—*if* he has it—then he will be appointed high priest, and you and I will give him our full support." The hubbub rose again, but again Helios calmed them down. "There is one thing you all seem to have forgotten—a newly appointed high priest must, by law, conduct the full ritual of the invocation of the Kings of the Elementals. If Baldek is not worthy of the office of high priest, he will fail to control the forces invoked and so may possibly die. If he succeeds in that ritual, then he will be deserving of our support." There was a dead silence as the assembly digested this information. They still did not believe for one moment that Baldek was a worthy high priest, but allowing him to be appointed might be the quickest way of getting rid of him—the arrogant fool would be overcome by the Elementals, and may the Dark Lords feed on his corpse forever! Helios nodded. "I see you understand the possibilities," he said dryly. "But first the claim must be tested." He turned to Vardek. "It is for you, my Lord Marshal, to put this claim to the test," and he left the rostrum and made his way to the back of the hall again to stand with Netziachos.

Vardek was in two minds. He was pleased that the situation had been brought under control, but annoyed that it had been Helios who had done it—that boy was dangerous! Vardek well knew the temper of the crowd. He turned to Deledian. "Since Baldek is my son," he growled, "I leave it to the Council to test his claim so that all will see that justice is done. Let the Council test the claim according to the law."

The crowd growled its approval—Vardek could have done nothing else. Deledian rose. "So be it!" he said. "Those of the seventh will withdraw to the antechamber. Baldek, son of Vardek, will be summoned in accordance with the usual ritual. Let all others remain until we return."

Deledian, dignified and unruffled, led the aged members of the seventh off the rostrum and through the side door into the antechamber. Zesta, in accordance with the ages-old ritual, approached Vardek's son. "Baldek, Priest of the Sun, initiate of the fifth degree," she cried in a ringing voice, "do you vouch for the worthiness of your claim to be admitted to the secrets of the seventh degree?"

Baldek drew himself up stiffly. "I do so vouch. It is my will!"

"Then let it be done!" she cried, and led Baldek into the antechamber, and the door slammed behind them.

Those remaining in the great Hall of Learning were silent; they had made their protest; now let the law and the inner planes decide. For a full twenty minutes they waited, tense, on edge—and then suddenly the door opened and Zesta, the High Priestess, led the Council back into the hall and onto the rostrum. Baldek came to stand as before in front of the High Table.

Deledian rose. His face was troubled. "Brethren," he declared in a subdued voice, "the claim is just, and as such, Baldek, son of Vardek, is a full member of the seventh degree and the new High Priest of the Sun Temple. Let none here oppose the will of the Council!"

There was a stunned silence, and Helios knew that the cloud that had for so long threatened the Sun Temple had now descended and lay on the very High Altar itself. The dark days had come!

"There was nothing else I could do!" Deledian clasped and unclasped his hands repeatedly, a sure sign of his disturbed inner state. "He had the correct password. I had no alternative but to administer the oath of the seventh!" Immediately after the assembly, Helios and Netziachos had sought an audience with the erstwhile leader of the Council. "If you had not supported him in the assembly, Helios, he would not have been allowed to press his claim; the will of the majority would have prevailed. I am not saying that you were wrong," he added quickly, "merely stating a fact."

Helios shook his head. "I did not uphold Baldek—I upheld the law. I am aware, perhaps more than most, that Baldek was no true candidate for the seventh, but the law states quite categorically that whosoever obtains the password to the seventh is automatically admitted to the seventh. But as I said before, the law also states that the newly appointed High Priest must conduct the full ritual invocation of the Elemental Kings, Baldek has slipped through one safeguard, but he will not find it so easy to slip through the second!"

Deledian looked at him shrewdly. "You are going to sabotage the ritual?"

Helios laughed. "Certainly not! In fact, I will give him every support I can, because the law demands that I do. But don't you see, Deledian, if he is truly unfit for office, then he will fail, no matter how much help he receives, for you know as well as I that in the final analysis the success of the ritual depends upon the states of consciousness of the Hierophant, and Baldek has not created those states within himself."

"Supposing he does?"

"Then he will succeed and indeed be a worthy high priest, for to achieve such states would mean a quite fundamental change in his attitudes, and I for one hope that he achieves that growth in understanding even as I hope that all initiates grow toward their true selves."

"Not very likely in Baldek's case."

"Perhaps not, but he is still deserving of our help."

Deledian drummed his fingers on the arm of his chair. "You are quite right, of course," he said finally. "I am beginning to see why Khamadek named you as his successor. In what way can I be of assistance to you?"

"Netziachos and I require your permission to conduct our own private ritual in the Hall of Images tonight."

"For what purpose?"

"To contact the Kings of the Elementals to solicit their aid on Baldek's behalf."

"Very well, permission granted." He turned to Netziachos. "And what is your position in all this, seeress?"

Netziachos shook her head. "I do not know," she said frankly. "I suspect that my part is yet to come. In the meantime, I am with Helios, for there is a bond between us whose purpose is not yet revealed. All I know is that all this has something to do with it."

"You are under the direction and protection of the Sea Temple. Do they know of your part in this?"

"There is not much the Sea Temple does not know,"

she said. "Marah is close to me always, and often, too, is Kumara. They know everything that is in my mind, and seem to approve."

Deledian pondered as to why the mighty High Priest of the Withdrawn Temple should interest himself personally in a mere junior seeress; there was obviously much more to this than could be seen on the surface. "Very well. Go with my blessing. Please keep me informed of any developments."

"All right," growled Vardek, "what about this ritual that Helios mentioned?" The three conspirators had retired to Zesta's private audience chamber. Vardek was not pleased that Baldek had invoked such opposition. "What's all this about a new High Priest being tested?"

Baldek waved a hand airily. "Don't worry about it —I can handle it."

"That's not what I asked!" snapped Vardek. "What *is* this ritual?"

"The invocation of the elemental forces," said Zesta smoothly. "It is a standard ritual wherein the Hierophant, by means that would take too long to explain, invokes the Elementals and commands them to some simple task to demonstrate his power over them. In the case of a new high priest it is the final proof as to whether or not he truly has the powers of the seventh degree, for if he succeeds, the Elementals will obey him; if not, they will turn and attack him, and if that happens, there is nothing anyone can do to save him, for it happens too quickly. One moment all seems well, and the next the Hierophant is either stone dead or a demented raving mess."

Vardek frowned. "And do you think Baldek will fail?"

"He has enough confidence," she said dryly, "and that is important. The Elementals do not treat kindly one who is unsure of himself. But as to whether he has the other necessary qualities, who can say?"

"*I* can say!" snapped Baldek. "I know what I am doing! As you said earlier, Father—stick to the things you know. You stick to the army and leave priestly matters to those who understand them."

Zesta raised her eyebrows; she had never heard Baldek speak like that to his father before. Vardek eyed his son coldly. "Don't let your newfound position give you exalted ideas, boy—you are High Priest because we made you so, and don't you forget it!" He fingered the dagger strapped to his left arm. "We made you, and we can break you!"

"You wouldn't dare!"

"No?" said Vardek calmly. "We've disposed of one high priest, we can easily dispose of another. Don't think being my son gives you any special protection."

"And by the same token," snapped Baldek, "don't *you* think that being my father gives you the right to speak to me the way you do. I do not tolerate it from others, and I will not tolerate it from you!"

Vardek's temper suddenly flared again. "I will speak to you in any way I please, and you will tolerate it until you are big enough to do something about it. And I tell you this, boy, you will *never* be big enough to take me!"

Zesta's temper, too, was frayed at the edges. "Will you two stop it! I am sick and tired of hearing you growl at each other. We all have our part to play, and none of us must fail. We have done well so far; let's not spoil it by fighting among ourselves. Vardek controls the army, and through it he also controls the Akkadians and the Rmoahals. I control the seeresses and priestesses of the Sun Temple. When Baldek succeeds in invoking the Elementals, he will then control all the priests and scribes. Between the three of us we will control all Ruta. This is what we all want, and this is precisely what we will get, if only you two will stop this eternal bickering. If this goes on any longer, you will find to your cost that the High Priestess has powers of her own that are not to be dismissed lightly!"

The two men glared at her, but she met their eyes with a ferocity equal to their own. Zesta would never back down from anyone, no matter what the cost. Suddenly Vardek laughed. "You are right, Zesta—by Narada, you are right! We are well matched, we three." He slapped Baldek on the back. "All right, all right— I take back what I said. You would be no son of mine, I suppose, if you did not stand up for yourself. But it really is important that you succeed at this so-called ritual, though it sounds a lot of mumbo jumbo to me. You must not fail, Baldek. It is imperative."

"I will not fail," said Baldek stiffly. "I am no novice at this game."

"Good, good. And then," said Vardek, rubbing his hands, "we will control all Ruta!"

Baldek rose and walked to the embrasure. "No, that is not true—we will *not* control all Ruta at all." He pointed to the north. "There is still the Sea Temple."

Vardek's face grew suddenly thoughtful. "Yes, you are right," he said slowly.

"And also," said Zesta, "there are Helios and Netzia-chos."

Vardek nodded. "Also true. Very well, let's take each step as it comes. First, Baldek's ritual. Then we deal with Helios and the girl, and then the Sea Temple—and *then,* my friends, we will truly be masters of all Ruta, aye, and masters of the mainland, for no one, no race, can stand against the combined armies of Ruta."

"And then, Vardek?" said Zesta calmly.

Vardek's eyes glittered strangely. "And then, Zesta, we march eastward and test the might of the Mongol Empire, and after that, who else is left? We will be masters of all that is. Think of that, my friends," he said softly, "masters of all existence!"

"Masters of all existence!" said Kumara sadly. "Poor blind man, not to know that what he surveys is but a fraction of all that is!"

"And a small fraction at that," said Melchadek, keeper of the Akhasic Record.

"Indeed, yes, and the tragedy is that his blindness causes not only suffering for himself but all around him. The whole of Ruta must suffer because of what Vardek cannot see." He turned to the younger man.

"Quote me the command from the Hierophant to the Neophyte from the initiation ritual—the part about eyes and ears."

Melchadek closed his eyes. "Learn to see with the inner eye," he quoted, "and hear with the inner ear, for there are things to be seen and heard within you which are not of this plane of existence."

"Ah yes, the inner eye and the inner ear, but for Vardek, poor man, they are closed—and what say you, Marah?"

The great High Priestess of the Sea remained silent for a moment, and then said slowly, "Vardek has much to answer for, true, but he is blind, as you say. What of those whose inner eyes are open yet who persist in this folly? They have by far the greater responsibility, surely?"

"Baldek and Zesta?" said Kumara. "Yes, you are right—they are of the priesthood and should know better. They will be brought to account for their actions, be assured of that."

"And in the meantime, the people of Ruta must suffer!" she said, and there was a trace of bitterness in her voice.

"The people are not blameless," said Kumara. "Vardek could have been stopped by almost anyone at any time over the past twenty years or more. He was not stopped because those who came into contact with him either became afraid of him or simply did not care enough to change things. If fear and apathy allow a corrupt man to rise to a position of power in a society, then that society collectively is in part responsible for the subsequent suffering."

"That may be true," said Melchadek, "but it is a hard truth."

Kumara shook his head. "Truth is neither hard nor soft, nor is it painful or soothing. Truth is truth, and nothing more. A man may find it hard to face the truth, or easy—he may find it hurts, or he may be comforted thereby, but these qualities are his reactions and are not inherent in the truth itself."

The younger man smiled. "You are right, of course."

"Good. Now, how are your preparations going?"

"We are ready whenever you give the word. The seven long ships are finished and berthed in an isolated bay at the northern end of Ruta. They can be brought around to the mouth of the Naradek in a matter of hours."

"And neither the army nor the Sun Temple know of their existence?"

"Not an inkling. They were built under supervision of two Akkadian craft masters with eighteen Toltec civilians while the army was on the mainland. These twenty men know of our plans, but not their wives or families, and they all know that they are included in the number that will leave Ruta. They are all good men and can be trusted implicitly."

"And the total tally?"

"Of the one hundred and fifty members of the Sea Temple, fifty have elected to remain, leaving one hundred who will sail with the emigration. Among the civilians, just on five hundred have been chosen as being suitable, three hundred Toltecs and two hundred Akkadians, but they will not be told until a few hours beforehand."

Kumara sighed. "It will be hard for them to uproot their families and sail for strange lands at such short notice, but it is unavoidable, I suppose. And what of the Sun Temple?"

"The twenty seeresses and priestesses of the Sea Temple who are currently under assignment to the Sun Temple have not yet been advised of our plans, but all will probably elect to go."

"And the Sun Temple priesthood?"

"Only Helios."

Kumara shook his head. "It is incredible that of all that number, only one is considered worthy. It is an overwhelming condemnation of the once mighty Sun Temple priesthood. So, Melchadek, we have twenty who built the ships, one hundred from the Sea Temple, five hundred civilians, and twenty from the Sun Temple—approximately six hundred and forty spread over seven ships. It will be a tight squeeze."

"The army sail one hundred per ship on campaign."

"True, but our six hundred and forty include women and children, but it cannot be helped. You have done well, Melchadek. Thank you. And to lead this band, we have Helios and Netziachos, with yourself as counselor."

"Yes, shall I summon them to the Sea Temple to receive your advice?"

"No, not yet. Let us wait the outcome of Baldek's attempt to control our brethren of other evolutions, the Elementals."

Marah stirred and gathered her robe. "They know that something is brewing, and they know that they have a special part to play, but neither of them has the faintest idea what it could be."

"And that is as it should be. There is no point in adding to their burden by revealing their new and not inconsiderable responsibility until it is absolutely necessary. They have enough to contend with at the moment. The time will come, be assured, as it does for all things."

The northern quarter of the Sun Temple contained a special chamber devoted to elemental workings called the Hall of Images, or sometimes the Hall of Mirrors. It was used for those rituals wherein the Elementals were temporarily raised to the human sphere of influence to assist in a working concerning human events and human conditions.

Netziachos adjusted her ritual cloak. "I take it that we are not using one of the standard rituals?"

Helios shook his head. "No, we will play this one as it comes. I will put the seals on the four Cardinal Points and open the ritual in the usual way, but when we get to the actual working itself you will have to follow my lead and be alert for any responses I may call for. Basically, once the elemental forces have been brought through into lodge, I will then visualize and describe Baldek as he will be in his own ritual. You will have to hold a very clear image in your mind of what Baldek and Zesta look like. The others do not matter so much, but the image of those two must be very clear indeed."

"In our imagination, then, we are going to play their parts and act out their ritual showing the Elementals as helping all they can—sort of showing them what we want on the day itself."

"Precisely."

The Hall of Images was a smaller chamber than most in the Sun Temple, a circular room some forty feet in diameter. In the center of the chamber stood an altar on which lay a chalice containing the holy oil on which floated a lighted wick, symbol of the Eternal Light. Around the perimeter of the circle were arranged a series of highly polished metal mirrors, each on a pivot allowing the mirror to be adjusted to give the angle of reflection required. Earlier, Helios had already adjusted each mirror to give the reflection he needed. At each of the four Cardinal Points stood a carved chair and above each chair on the stone wall hung a symbol of the element applicable to the quarter; the symbol of Air in the east, Fire in the south, Water in the west, and Earth in the north.

As they entered the empty chamber, both saluted the East and gave the sign of their degree, as was customary, and then Helios motioned Netziachos to take the chair in the west while he took the Hierophant's usual position in the east. For some fifteen minutes both remained silent, deep in meditation, each establishing their inner plane contacts and building up within themselves the state of consciousness, the state of mind, necessary for their working.

At the end of that time Helios said softly but vibrantly, "From those who see the Light of the Most High face-to-face, I bring you greetings!"

"Greetings!" responded Netziachos from the west.

He then acknowledged the standard greeting and contact from the mighty inner plane adepts and invoked their aid. "To this end," he continued to intone, "I must first, by the power channeled through me in earth, sanctify and seal this lodge."

He rose and began the traditional deosil circumnambulation of the lodge, drawing on the inner the line of delineation and sealing each Cardinal Point in the name of the Most High. Then, once more seated in the east, he declared the seven basic principles that governed all ritual workings, and after that he began the actual ritual itself.

It should have been a very simple piece of sympathetic ritual, well within the ability of a senior fifth-degree initiate, and for the first ten minutes or so everything went according to plan. They visualized in their imagination the Temple of the Elementals, its colors, furniture, symbols, and principles, and as they did so the elemental forces began to pour into lodge. An Elemental is a being of one elemental force only, whereas a human being not only comprises all four but is a very much more evolved entity. In a human being the four basic elemental forces are quite balanced, but this balance can be upset by the inrush of the force of one element only, hence the danger of working a single element ritual.

More dangerous than this, however, is the inrush of all four elemental forces which activate the four corresponding levels in the human being. To loosen one of those foundations causes imbalance—to shake up all four can cause the entire edifice to "take off," even as a man can be knocked clean off his feet with one good punch. But even as the warriors were taught to "ride" a blow without suffering permanent injury, so too did the priests of the Sun Temple learn to handle the subjective forces that they invoked.

Helios and Netziachos were well into the ritual when suddenly, with only the slightest of warnings, they were both, in the psychical sense, knocked clean off their feet. But slight though the warning had been, it had enabled them to "ride" the punch, and after a few minutes of wild mental confusion they were able to pick themselves up. Helios immediately brought the ritual to a close, put on the closing seals, made the reverse circumnambulations, and left the Hall of Mirrors and took Netziachos back to his private chamber.

Netziachos kicked off her sandals, flung herself on

her back on his bed, and let out an explosive gasp. "What on earth happened, Helios? I feel as though I've been kicked!" She untied her waist cord and threw it on the floor. "It was all going so well. What on earth happened?"

Helios stood by the embrasure, gazing out at the night sky. "I am not sure," he admitted. "Instead of us showing the Elementals, it was they who showed us!" Experienced as he was in priestly matters, the incident had shaken him far more than he was prepared to show, even to Netziachos. "We were well into our visualization when suddenly the scene we had created was dissolved, and in its place I found myself in my imagination standing on the deck of one of the long ships just offshore at the mouth of the Naradek."

"Yes," said the girl, "so did I."

"That's right, you were standing at my left. The Elementals were really stirred up—the wind was howling a full tempest, the sea was raised in huge waves, tossing the ship as though it were a single leaf. The Sacred Mountain was belching flame and molten lava, and the very earth of Ruta, the land itself, heaved and bubbled, and giant crevices appeared along the shore!"

"But what did it mean, and what were those other ships and all those people?"

"I don't know," he said thoughtfully. "All I remember was a strange priest standing next to me on my right —a man I've never seen before, a young man, little older than myself, dressed in the robes of the Sea Temple, and . . ." Helios broke off suddenly, and his eyes grew wide with astonishment. He turned to the girl. ". . . and he was telling me the password to the seventh, and its Word of Power!"

Netziachos sat up suddenly; her voice was awed. "The seventh, Helios! You mean you know the password to the seventh?"

He nodded, his expression one of complete bewilderment. "Yes—it is as clear in my mind as my own name! Didn't you hear it?"

"No, not a word—it was obviously intended for

your ears only." She squealed in excitement. "But Helios, don't you know what this means? You can now be the High Priest of the Sun Temple!"

8

"From those who see the light of the Most High face-to-face," growled Baldek, "I bring you greetings!"

"Greetings!" came the response.

The all-important ritual, the inauguration of a new high priest, was under way. Baldek, as Hierophant, was in the east, representing the Aspect of Wisdom. Deledian sat to his left and Choldek to his right, both of the seventh degree. These three formed the triumvirate of the east, whose duty it was to bring through into the lodge the far-off contacts of the inner planes.

Immediately opposite Baldek sat Helios, in the west, representing the Aspect of Severity. In the south was Naida, the seeress, representing the Aspect of Mercy. Zesta, the High Priestess, as Pythoness to the order, sat two places to Baldek's right. These, then, were the senior officers.

Helios was uneasy—the atmosphere was all wrong. Baldek, who as Hierophant was supposed to represent Wisdom, merely radiated the aggressive arrogance of his outer personality. Naida, who was supposed to represent Mercy, was quite clearly radiating a personality frustration, the greater portion of which was sexual. Helios had tried to get Netziachos in at south—she knew more about the principle of Mercy and Love than anyone in the temple—but Baldek had refused. But at least she had been given the responsibility of one of the four junior offices, the other three being taken by Baldek's cronies.

It was going to be a shambles, and Helios knew it, and this knowledge did not help him fulfill his own function. Helios, in the west, represented the principle of Severity, the driving Will. But instead of Wisdom and Mercy from the east and south, they had arrogance and lust, and it was little wonder that Helios was uneasy at providing the driving power for this manifestation of human deviation.

Deledian and Choldek, the two seventh-degree initiates on either side of Baldek in the east, were also aware of the deviated imprint on the lodge, but their duty was to the inner plane ritual; the outer ritual was entirely Baldek's responsibility.

Baldek performed the opening section of the ritual well enough—the deosil circumnambulation, establishing the seals, and the exchange of responses with each of the other six officers—and then came the main part of the working, the invocation of the four Elemental Kings.

Again all seemed to go well at first, the elemental forces began to flood into lodge and the atmosphere became charged with that crackling vibrant power which is the hallmark of a good ritual. Helios was not surprised that the opening section of the ritual had been successfully performed. Baldek might not be suitable material for the actual office of high priest, but he was a highly trained ritual officer who had risen to the fifth degree entirely on merit. The moment of truth, however, was fast approaching for him, and it came at a point when Baldek was least able to defend himself. Had the team of officers been better chosen, they might have carried him through, but Naida had already shown her vulnerability; the sweat was pouring down her face as she struggled with subjective forces that she simply could not handle, and three of the four junior officers were in a similar position. The two seventh-degree adepts were far too withdrawn on to the inner to take any action on the outer. Netziachos, although handling her office well, was in too junior a position to have any effect on the outcome. This left only Helios of the outer team who was capable of giving the support that Baldek needed, but the very weakness of the team, its very imbalance, was giving Helios enough trouble of his own without having to bolster up an incompetent magus.

An invocation of elemental forces invariably stirs

up the denizens of all the subplanes, creatures other than the Elementals themselves. They were ferocious, mindless, abhuman creatures, not physical, but practically physical. Although they came in a variety of forms, each form was revolting and terrifying to the human mind. The magus always purified and sealed a lodge before commencing any ritual, and if put on properly, these seals were always effective in keeping the abhumans out. Baldek, however, had slipped up. In tracing the lines of force around the lodge, his mind had wandered for just a fraction of a second, causing a minute gap, and minute though it was, it was enough to let the abhumans through.

The moment came when Baldek was at the altar in the very center of the circle performing that portion of the ritual known as the Elevation of the Eternal Light. It was always an impressive and moving moment in any ritual. The chalice of holy oil on which floated a lighted wick was raised high in the air by the magus for all the lodge to see. The red light in the east, the yellow lights of the candles in the south and west, the deep blue and silver of the chalice itself made to glitter by the light of the floating wick within it, and the shimmering golden robes of the magus himself, all combined into a kaleidoscope of color that never failed to move the hearts of all present. The Eternal Light was *the* most important symbol in the lodge. It represented the inner light of the Most High, the inner Wisdom itself, and no ceremony in either temple was allowed to be performed without that light standing upon the altar.

Baldek stood at the altar, the cup held high above his head, his face upraised, and in a ringing, powerful voice he uttered the ritual command to the officers and all those present. "Brethren of the Order of Narada, illuminate this symbol within your own being!"

For a moment the tableau held, poised, and then without any warning whatsoever Baldek screamed and slowly began to crumple. In that first split-second he tried desperately to remain upright and to keep hold of the chalice, but his willpower was no match for the thing that was attacking him. His hands twisted, slipped, and the chalice fell from his grasp and crashed to the stone floor. The light was extinguished even as the chalice had begun to fall, and the holy oil was flung in a wide arc and stained the robes of the horrified brethren seated in the southwest quadrant. Baldek himself slipped suddenly to his knees, clutching his throat and screaming in pure terror and agony, then fell sideways and began to writhe in a desperate and horrible way.

It all happened so fast. Even though Helios had come to his feet the instant Baldek had screamed, even though he had been half-expecting some sort of crisis, nevertheless he was far too late to save the chalice or to catch Baldek before he fell. The thing that was attacking Baldek was not physical yet, not visible, though it soon would be. Zesta, too, was on her feet, and Deledian, of the seventh, but there was little they could do. Helios, in the west, was the only one, ritually, who was in a position to take any action at all, and there was little he could do either.

Although the creature was not visible physically, Helios could see on the inner that it was in the vague shape of a monstrous swamp toad, fastened to Baldek's throat, sucking out the life force. Mentally Helios visualized himself plunging a sword into the creature's back. It let out a psychic shriek that reverberated throughout the inner lodge, but it would not relinquish its hold on Baldek's throat. Again and again Helios plunged the sword into its revolting body, and the green foul-smelling slime that oozed from the wounds smothered the face and body of the helpless human adept. Helios could see that Baldek would not survive much longer; too much life force was being sucked from him on the inner to maintain life on the physical plane. To the others in the physical lodge there was no sign of the inner struggle. To physical eyes Helios was merely standing stock-still, stiff and strained, his eyes tight-closed, the sweat pouring down his face, but those who could see on the inner knew what was happening, but still there was little they could do.

Again and again Helios plunged his sword into the

monster's body, until at last the foul thing slithered from Baldek's body and turned on its attacker. The creature gathered itself together and flung itself straight at its tormentor, and it was then that Helios summoned his entire strength and rammed the sword straight down the monster's throat as it sprang, and as he did so, he uttered the Word of Power known only to seventh-degree initiates, and as the ringing sound of it reverberated around the inner scene, the creature shrieked in appalling agony, tore blindly at its own throat, wrenched the sword away, fell to the ground with a sickening squelch, and slithered away in helpless rage.

Helios returned to full consciousness with a jolt. His body ached in every muscle, and he was quite literally gasping for breath. The Hierophant was still sprawled full-length in front of the altar, and Helios was relieved to see that the body was still writhing slightly. "He is still alive!" he said quietly but firmly. "Deledian, close the lodge immediately—use the seals from the seventh rather than the fifth. We cannot take any more chances. Hurry!"

Deledian was far more a senior than Helios, but he obeyed without question—he had heard that seventh-degree Word of Power on the inner. A few minutes later the lodge was closed, sealed, and cleared, and the senior healer and his assistants were carrying Baldek in a litter to his chamber.

Helios spoke to an officer of the guard. "Summon the Lord Marshal to the High Priest's private chamber; tell him his son lies stricken, possibly dying. Say nothing to anyone else." He turned to Zesta and Netziachos. "Come with us."

In Baldek's chamber the senior officers remained silent while the healers were examining the stricken High Priest. Baldek's body still twitched and writhed as though in the grip of a foul dream, and occasionally a groan would escape his gaping mouth. At last the senior healer straightened up and shook his head. "There is nothing we can do. I doubt that he will last the night."

At that moment Vardek, lord marshal of Ruta, strode

into the chamber. "What happened?" he growled. "By the seven demons of darkness you so-called priests had better have a good explanation!"

Helios' manner was cold—he had been through enough for one day without having to tolerate Vardek's arrogance as well. "Don't threaten me, Vardek, or any of us! And if you must swear, then swear by our Lord Narada, not by the creatures of darkness. I will not tolerate any blasphemy within this temple! Is that perfectly clear?"

Vardek was taken aback. There was a new air of power from Helios, an air of authority. "*You* will not tolerate it! And who are *you* to give me orders?"

"As to who I am, Vardek," said Helios coldly and calmly, "that will be made clear very soon indeed. As to the explanation you so arrogantly demand, it is very simple—your son made a complete hash of the ritual and has paid the penalty. The healers doubt that he will last the night. It is now quite obvious that his claim to the office of high priest was false. My own opinion is that he obtained the password by the use of a medium, a method of seership that has quite rightly been banned in the temple since Lemurian times."

"*Your* opinion!" sneered Vardek. "A wild accusation without a single shred of evidence to support it!"

"I imagine," said Helios coolly, "that an inner probe of Naida would reveal some very interesting facts indeed and may well provide the evidence that you demand. I will carry out that probe as soon as possible."

Vardek and Zesta exchanged a glance, and Zesta managed to shake her head without Helios seeing the gesture—an inner probe of Naida could prove embarrassing. Vardek turned and strode to the couch on which Baldek lay. "So—a failure! I have no time for failures!"

"Not even your own son?" said Netziachos. She had remained silent so far, the others were so much more senior than she, but the contempt in Vardek's voice had startled her into speaking.

"My dear girl, good intentions are not enough; the only thing that counts is results. A failure is a failure, no matter whose son he is. There should be no room for failures in any scheme of things."

"There is always room for compassion, Vardek," said Helios sharply.

"Compassion! Rubbish! Compassion is the feeling of one failure for another!"

"And yet we all fail at one time or another."

"You speak for yourself! I have never yet failed in any task that I have undertaken—nor likely to!"

Helios shook his head. "Anyway, failure or not, Baldek is still your son. What are your wishes concerning his welfare?"

Vardek shrugged. "If he dies, bury him; if he lives, exile him. Alive or dead, I wash my hands of him."

"So be it. If he dies, his body will be consumed by the Eternal Fire as is our custom in the Sun Temple. We do not bury our dead."

"Make what arrangements you like—it is of no importance to me. What is important is who is to be the next high priest? Who will succeed Baldek?"

Deledian turned to Helios. "You will be the next high priest of the Sun Temple, Helios, even as Khamadek had planned. Do you accept the office?"

"Wait a minute, wait a minute!" said Vardek. "He doesn't have the password—we went into all that before."

"At that time he did not have the password, true, but now he does—or are my senses failing me, Helios?"

Helios sighed. To be high priest in these troubled times was no easy task, but he really had no alternative. "Yes, I have the password now. I will present my claim officially to the Council in due course and will accept the appointment if it is offered to me."

Vardek was furious—the very last man he wanted as high priest was Helios, but not even he could deny the due process of law, particularly as Helios had proved himself to be so popular with the majority of the Sun Temple priesthood. "And no doubt your first task as high priest will be to revoke my appointment as marshal of Ruta!"

Helios' thoughts at that moment were not only to

revoke Vardek's appointment as marshal but also to remove him from his post as Lord Commander of the
Army, but aloud he said, "I will be guided by the
wishes of the inner plane adepts—if they advise me to
revoke your appointment, then revoke it I will! But
Vardek, why do you always so oppose the priesthood?
Ruta needs men of your energy and talent. Much honor
could be yours if only you would willingly support and
cooperate with the Sun Temple. You are without doubt
the greatest Lord Commander of the Army that Ruta
has ever seen, but you are also without doubt the most
bitter enemy that has ever risen against the priesthood.
Why, Vardek, why?"

Vardek spun on his heel, his face a mask of absolute
fury. "I will tell you why!" he said venomously. Although he was obviously beside himself with rage, his
voice was low-pitched, almost quiet, which was very
unusual for Vardek. "Like myself, my father was also
an outspoken man. Like myself he had no time for
failures and no patience with incompetence. He was
one of the first to realize that Khamadek was unfit for
office, and like myself he made no bones about voicing
his doubts, and as such Khamadek feared and hated
him. As you know, my father was also Lord Commander of the Army, but what you don't know is that I, his
only son, was trained for the priesthood. Until I was
seventeen I lived and worked here in the Sun Temple
as a scribe, which is why I know so much about priestly
matters; and if you don't believe me ask Deledian
there, he was in the fifth when I was a boy."

The older man nodded. "It is quite true, Helios—
and whatever may have happened since, during his
novitiateship he was a good scribe and showed great
promise."

Helios frowned. "Then what happened at the showing?"

"Let Vardek tell of it," said Deledian. "His memory
has obviously been kept more vivid than mine."

"Yes," said Vardek bitterly, "and with good cause.
When I was seventeen, I and all the other youths of that
age were brought to the Sun Temple for the showing.

All Ruta was there for the ritual, and at the climax all the youths of seventeen were paraded on the steps of the Sun Temple for the High Priest to decide their futures, whether they were to be priests, or warriors, or whatever. In front of the entire population of Ruta, just to publicly snub my father, and in spite of my years of training as a scribe, that poisonous old fool Khamadek named me as a warrior, and in spite of all my father's protests I had to leave the temple that very day and be initiated into the army!"

So that was it! Helios had known for years that there must be some particular reason behind Vardek's hatred of the priesthood; such hatred is not born unsired, but of all the reasons that he had dreamed up, he had never even come close to guessing the real cause. "And what about Baldek?" he said.

Vardek gave a short, bitter laugh. "When Baldek was presented to the temple, Khamadek did not dare refuse him. I would have killed him there and then on the steps of the temple for all Ruta to see, and Khamadek knew it!"

"If what you say is true, then you have my sympathy, Vardek—I feel I understand you a little better now. I, too, have known Khamadek to make an error of judgment." He looked quickly at Netziachos, but she kept her eyes lowered. "But obviously I cannot venture an opinion as to whether Khamadek was right or wrong in your case, since no man can now know how you would have progressed had you been chosen for the priesthood. We can only see the man who is, not the man who might have been."

"What I have said is the truth!"

Helios frowned. "You are obviously sincere, and yet it is possible that Khamadek may have been quite right in his assessment of your character—he might have seen in the youth of seventeen the type of man who could and would commit murder regardless of what profession he followed; the type of man, for example, who would put ten thousand defenseless Amarians to the sword for no apparent reason other than the satisfaction of his own lust for power. You are not judged,

Vardek, on what you might have been, but on what you are!"

"And who are you to judge me at all?"

"It is not I who judges you. In the ultimate sense, you judge yourself. However, this is all purely academic; let us deal with what is. You are the lord marshal of Ruta, and I will be the High Priest of the Sun Temple. Do we work together, or do we fight?"

There was a long, long silence. Deledian held his breath. The matter had been put squarely—it was up to Vardek now to make his stand. The lord marshal was eyeing Helios thoughtfully, his anger now quite gone in the face of this sudden confrontation. Vardek would rather control a weak high priest than fight a strong one. Civil war did not suit his purpose. Vardek wanted a peaceful Ruta under his own control from which he could venture forth against the world. Vardek did not doubt that he would emerge from any civil war the victor—priests were no match for trained warriors—but to utterly destroy the national religion would cause an upheaval so great that it would be years before Vardek would be able to turn his attention to foreign lands. He would destroy the priesthood if he had to, but it would be far better to have them under his control—but again it seemed that one man stood between him and his ambition. Khamadek had once stood in that position and paid the penalty; maybe it was time for Helios to go the same way. But he needed time.

Vardek's voice was hard and threatening. "I will cooperate for as long as you are fit to hold your office," he growled, "but let me warn you now, Helios—if you are not a better man than Khamadek, then you will find the army at the gates of the temple, and no ritual on earth could then delay your death by a single day!"

"So be it!" snapped Helios. "Though I never thought the day would come when the army would threaten violence to the temple!"

"Not to the temple, Helios—to you personally!"

The younger man smiled thinly. "A fine point, Vardek, since you would have to fight the entire temple in order to get at me. However, I am pleased to see that in your own peculiar way you are as concerned as I am myself about the efficiency of the priesthood. Very well, Vardek—so be it!"

The lord marshal of Ruta turned on his heel and strode from the chamber without another word. Helios turned to Deledian. "So, Deledian, it seems that I tread a tightrope, and if I fall, all Ruta falls with me! Not the most comforting of prospects!"

Deledian smiled. "You will not fail, Helios; be assured of that. Your strength lies in your innate character—there are not many who could or would oppose Vardek—but in addition to this strength, you will also need good ritual work, and for that you need a pythoness worthy of the tasks ahead. I take it that in accordance with the usual tradition you will use the High Priestess as the Pythoness?"

Helios frowned slightly. He did not want Zesta as his pythoness at all; indeed, it was his intention to remove her from office altogether, and since such an action would be no small matter, he would have preferred to tackle the issue after he had been officially appointed and after he had ratified his appointment with a successful Ritual of the Elementals. Like Baldek, he would have to put his claim to the ritual test. But Deledian had unwittingly precipitated the matter and was asking for a high priest's decision before he had even been confirmed in that office. It was pleasant to know that he had Deledian's loyalty and confidence, but it could have been expressed with a little more discretion.

Deledian realized his error, but it was too late to withdraw the question. "There are any number of precedents, however," he went on smoothly, "for appointing a pythoness as a separate office from that of high priestess. One that springs to mind was the occasion when the High Priest and High Priestess were brother and sister, and it was not considered wise for a brother to mate with his sister. As you know, the High Priest mates with the Pythoness, not with the High Priestess.

Both offices are usually performed by one priestess, but there is no reason why they should not be considered as separate offices."

Zesta frowned and said, "Why the hesitation, Helios? I have been both Pythoness and High Priestess for ten years and no one has questioned my competence before."

"Nor am I questioning it now, but I am commanded by the inner planes to mate with Netziachos, and I cannot disobey that command."

"You make it sound such a dreadful task!" said Netziachos.

Helios laughed. "I'm sorry—I didn't mean it to sound like that." He turned to the High Priestess. "I am sorry, Zesta, but we are all under the jurisdiction of the inner planes. It is our function, our choice, our destiny, and for me at any rate it is my privilege and my pleasure. If and when I am appointed high priest, Netziachos will be the Pythoness and you will remain as High Priestess, and that situation will continue until such time as we are commanded otherwise."

Zesta looked from one to the other, and then to Deledian. "Very well," she said, "I have no choice but to accept, but we may speak of this again, Helios," and she swept haughtily from the chamber and slammed the door behind her.

"I fear I have hurt her feelings," said Helios.

Deledian snorted. "I would not lose any sleep over that, Helios! It was high time she was reminded that it is the inner planes who command in this temple! Well, it's been a long day for an old man. If you will excuse me, I think I will retire to my evening meditation. You will make a good high priest, Helios, but it will be no easy task for you."

"Thank you—I think you are right, certainly, about the difficulties, but with help we may succeed. Good night, Deledian."

"Good night."

Helios walked over to the couch and spoke to the healer. "Call me if there is any change in his condition at all, no matter what the hour." Baldek was quieter now, but his body still writhed a little and an occasional groan still bubbled through his lips. His skin was a grayish color and his fingernails were quite white. Helios shook his head. It would be a miracle indeed if Baldek survived. He turned to Netziachos. "Come. As Deledian said, it's been a long day."

The girl gathered her robe and followed Helios out into the passageway. "You are going to have trouble with Zesta," she said. "She does not like the idea of her authority being reduced—and to separate the two offices of pythoness and high priestess is not very practical, either from a ritual point of view or any other. It may have been right in the case of brother and sister, but under any other circumstances it just could not work at all. I am surprised that you are in favor of the arrangement."

"I am not in favor of it. Unless I receive some indication to the contrary from the inner planes, I intend to remove her from office altogether and appoint you as both pythoness and high priestess in her place. I will send her back to the Sea Temple. As Deledian said, it is high time she be reminded as to who commands in the temple."

"And Vardek?"

"Once the business of Zesta has been settled, we can then deal with Vardek. Without Baldek and Zesta, he will have no influence in the Sun Temple. I will then revoke both his appointment as marshal of Ruta and his appointment as Lord Commander of the Army. Herakos can take over the army—he is as good a warrior as Vardek and a more honorable man by far."

"An Akkadian as Lord Commander of a Toltec army?"

"Why not? He is worthy of the position, no matter who his parents were."

"Yes, I suppose so, but it will be an unheard-of precedent."

"Maybe, but they will hear of it soon enough." They came to the door of Netziachos' private chamber. "And when all this has been achieved, the honor of the temple will have been restored."

A few minutes before dawn, Helios slipped into the antechamber to the Hall of Mirrors. Zesta was already there. "I received your message," he said, "but no explanation. Why all the secrecy, Zesta?"

The High Priestess was wearing the long flowing gold and red robes of the Pythoness. "The temple has too many ears," she murmured. Her hair was worn loose such that it fell in a glistening black cascade to her bare shoulders. "I have things to show you and tell you that are for your eyes and ears alone." In accordance with tradition, the robe was cut in such a fashion that it left her breasts completely bare, the nipples painted gold in true Toltec fashion, and then fell sheer to her ankles but was slit to give freedom of movement. Normally the Pythoness would wear an undergarment, but not only was Zesta completely naked under the robe, she had fashioned it to fit so tightly that every movement, every ripple of her body, was clearly revealed. Also the slit was normally only taken to the knee, but Zesta's robe was slit almost to the waist so that she could by a simple movement reveal the mound of her sex if she so desired.

Zesta smiled, rose from her chair, and came toward him. As she did so, the robe fell back from her thighs and Helios had difficulty in keeping his eyes on her face. Her perfume was pure musk, that heavy, acrid, sensuous scent worn only by Toltec women of high rank. She put her hand caressingly on his shoulder. "I see you admire my robe, Helios," she murmured.

Admittedly this particular robe was by tradition designed to be sexually provocative, since it was the mating robe of the Pythoness, but Zesta wore it with an air of sensuality undreamed of by the priestesses who had formulated its design in ancient times.

Although he had been in the room for only a few seconds, Helios could already feel the excitement stirring within him. A detached part of him viewed these signs with some amusement, but it was an amusement tinged with apprehension. A priest, particularly a young priest, is very vulnerable to a sexual attack. Unlike the average layman, he has had no firsthand experience of the art of sexual seduction, and the sudden, often explosive awakening of his own desire can, if he is not careful, quite overwhelm any inner plane consideration. Humanity is but little evolved; he is much closer to his primeval origins than he is to his eventual goal. His grasp on the higher states of consciousness is tenuous at best, and as such he is more easily influenced by the infernal than the supernal.

Helios removed her hand. "That is the mating robe," he said sternly. "No man save the High Priest himself is allowed to see you wearing it."

"But you *are* the High Priest," she murmured, "or soon will be."

"But I have already told you that Netziachos will be the Pythoness—it is she who will wear that robe."

"Will she wear it as well as I?"

"She will wear it well enough!" he snapped. "Now, what is all this about, Zesta? You are behaving like an Akkadian whore!"

She smiled and drew away from him, well pleased with her initial success. The calm, serene, unflappable Helios was suddenly irritable and snappy. So far, so good. "I have been thinking about what you said concerning Netziachos," she said smoothly. "I believe that I have underestimated the girl."

"Well, it's certainly high time someone realized that!"

"So much so," she went on. "that it is now my considered opinion that she should be appointed as high priestess."

Helios blinked in surprise. Whatever else he had been expecting from Zesta, it was not this. His mind circled the statement, looking for the trap, but so far he could not see one. "And what of yourself?" he said cautiously.

She sat herself once more in the small carved chair near the embrasure, crossed her legs, and modestly pulled the skirts of her robe across to hide her thighs. "I have been both High Priestess and Pythoness for ten years, Helios, and I have enjoyed every moment, and I am human enough to have enjoyed the power and authority that the office has given me. But you are not the only one with inner plane contacts. It has been made clear to me that my time has come, and unlike Khamadek I would prefer to withdraw gracefully from office rather than wait to be kicked out. Netziachos will make a fine high priestess—please appoint her to that office with my blessing."

Helios was still suspicious. "What about Vardek?"

"What has Vardek got to do with this? Certainly he is a powerful and dangerous man, and under a weak high priest we had no alternative but to placate him—but under you we will no longer have to tolerate his arrogance and contempt."

Helios remained thoughtfully silent. At last he said, "There is much in what you say, Zesta, and it is certainly handsome of you to offer to withdraw from office. Much honor will be yours for such unselfishness."

She smiled at him archly. "Come, Helios, admit that you have always misjudged me—admit that the very last thing you expected from me was this particular offer."

Helios struggled with himself, his suspicions holding him back. "It is certainly possible," he finally admitted.

Zesta laughed outright. "Oh Helios, what a grudging admission! Is that really the best you can do?"

He smiled and then began to chuckle. "Oh, very well, Zesta—yes, it seems I have misjudged you. Please accept my apologies. However, this still doesn't explain this charade with the mating robe. If I were a suspicious man I would believe that you are trying to seduce me!"

She stopped laughing suddenly. "But I am!" she said quietly.

Again there was a sudden silence between them, and then Helios shook his head. "All right, Zesta—explain."

She rose and went to the embrasure. The half-light of predawn was already growing stronger. "As I said before, Helios, I, too, have my inner plane contacts, some even stronger than yours. You are quite right about you and Netziachos—indeed, you both have a destiny to fulfill together that is greater than either of you has begun to realize. It is also quite right that you are to mate, but what you have not realized is that this mating is to be on a very high level of consciousness, far higher than I or anyone else in the Sun Temple could reach, and that any physical plane mating would adulterate that higher fusion and render it inoperable. If you insist on a physical mating with Netziachos, then you will be denying your destiny merely for the sake of a sexual gratification."

Helios frowned. "Go on—what is your part in all this?"

The High Priestess swallowed nervously; this was the crux of the whole matter. "It is your destiny and your duty to mate with Netziachos on the higher levels, but for her to fulfill her part properly, it must be as the High Priestess to your High Priest, which is why I am willing to withdraw from office in her favor. But all ritual workings must be brought through into earth, as you know; you will still need a pythoness. Mate with Netziachos on the higher levels as high priestess, but you *must* mate with me on the physical plane as pythoness."

Zesta could not look at him directly—so much depended on his initial reaction. If she could only persuade him to mate with her physically, then she could not only abort almost every ritual that he and Netziachos would perform, but she could also have him completely under her control—or so she believed. When she had explained the plan to Vardek earlier that morning, he had disdainfully rejected the idea completely. They had argued the matter for some considerable time, but then Vardek had finally agreed. It was certainly true that Helios had little or no sexual experience, and as such it was just possible that Zesta might be able to exercise some measure of control, but Vardek still doubted that the control would be sufficient or could be maintained. "All right, go ahead," he had finally agreed, "but if you fail, then we kill him immediately!"

Zesta turned to face the young priest. "You are silent, Helios. Does the thought of mating with me shock you?"

"In a way, yes," he admitted. "Netziachos would never agree to it."

Zesta was inwardly delighted that he had even considered the idea—she had expected an abrupt and angry refusal. "Like all of us," she said, "Netziachos is subject to the jurisdiction of the inner planes. If it is their wish that she mate with you on the higher planes only, then who is she to refuse!"

Helios shook his head. "She would not deny the inner planes, but . . . but, I could not . . . that is, perhaps I . . . but, how do I . . . oh, I don't know, Zesta. It is too sudden for me to take in properly!"

She rose and came toward him again. She took his hands and put them on her waist. "Would I not be pleasing to you as the Pythoness, Helios?" she murmured.

"It's not that, Zesta, it's . . ."

"You find me attractive, I know you do," she whispered, "and I am not too displeased at the prospect either."

"Yes, but . . ."

"And since we are drawn to each other physically, isn't that a good indication that the inner planes approve? Why else would our bodies respond to each other?"

"Well, that may be but . . ."

She put her arms around his neck and pressed herself close to him. He could feel the softness of her breasts against his chest, the nipples hard, and he could feel her leg glide between his own. She nuzzled in close to his ear and ran her fingers through his hair. "Don't deny me, Helios," she murmured. "Don't deny the inner planes—this is what they wish, what they command."

"Yes, but . . ."

"Shhhhhh!" she whispered, and moved her mouth onto his and kissed him softly, sensuously, her hands sliding across his back, her thighs moving gently and softly against his loins. His own hands, almost of their own command, began to move across her back, his fingers trailing against her skin. She shivered and moaned softly, and dug her fingernails into his back as though in ecstasy at his slightest touch. She moved her mouth to his neck, to his shoulders, to his chest, running her hands down his arms and trailing her fingers between his legs and up across his chest again. She pulled his head down to her breasts and guided his hands beneath her robe. "How can you doubt that this is right!" she whispered fiercely. "Would you feel as you do now if this was wrong?"

"Oh, Zesta, Zesta," he said thickly, "if only I could be sure!" He raised his head and brushed his lips across hers. "If only there was some way of knowing!"

"But there is," she said. "I can prove it to you."

"How, Zesta, how?"

She drew away from him and left him breathing heavily, hot and flushed, his hands trembling from the touch of her. "If you do not believe me," she said, "and if you do not believe your own body, how it responds to mine, then will you believe the mirrors?"

"The mirrors?"

She pointed to the side door that led into the Hall of Mirrors itself. "The mirrors do not lie, Helios. I have set them up for a mating ritual—just you and I. If you see yourself in the mirrors mating with me, will you then believe it?"

The mirrors—all the temple knew that the mirrors did not lie, that if used properly they would reflect future events. Time and again Helios had used them himself, and always they had reflected truly. "Yes," he said slowly, "I will believe the mirrors."

Her heart leaped with a fierce pang of triumph; it had been so easy; by Narada, these men were so easy to lead along! "Come, then," she said, "come see for yourself. When the mirrors show you deep inside me, then you will know that Zesta has spoken the truth—and then, as the climax to the ritual, we will bring about what the mirrors portend." She took his hand and led him to the door. "Yes, Helios, this very dawn shall see our mating!"

At that very moment, even as the first rays of the morning sun crept in through the embrasure, there came a knock at the door to the antechamber. Zesta, startled, froze into stillness. "I left no word where I was to be found! If it is that wretched seeress I sent to summon you, I will have her flogged! I told her that I was not to be disturbed for any reason whatsoever!"

Helios drew back from her, freeing his hand. "I left word—perhaps it is news about Baldek. I told the healers to summon me if his condition changed, no matter what the hour."

"Ignore it! Whether Baldek is alive or dead is of little importance now. What we have to do, Helios, must not be delayed. Come, the mirrors wait for us!"

The knock sounded again. "I can't just ignore it," he said. "It will take only a few seconds to answer."

Zesta was almost beside herself with fury—to be so close, so near to triumph—a mood destroyed by a single knock! "Leave it, Helios, leave it!"

He shook his head and turned to the door and opened it. Outside, in the stone corridor, was the captain of the Guard. "What is it, Captain—is there news of Baldek?"

The captain saluted. "Baldek died thirty minutes ago, my lord, but that is not my message."

"Died! But I left strict instructions that I be summoned!"

"I know nothing of that, my lord. Since there was nothing you could do, perhaps the healers thought it a pity to disturb your rest."

"All right, all right, what is your message, then?"

"I am commanded to give you this, my lord." And he handed Helios a small parchment.

Helios unwound it and read: COME AT ONCE TO YOUR PRIVATE CHAMBER—AT ONCE—YOUR DESTINY IS FORFEIT IF YOU DELAY. There was a seal and signature that he did not recognize; it was not the scrawling hand of Deledian, or the neat script of Netziachos, nor anyone else he knew. "Who gave you this?"

"One of the seeresses, my lord."

"Very well, you may go." The captain saluted and strode away. Helios turned to Zesta. "I'm afraid I must leave you for a few minutes."

"Why—what is it? What is that parchment?"

Helios rolled the message and put it beneath his robe. "I don't know, but I will soon find out."

Zesta tried to close the door. "Leave it, Helios, ignore it. Deal with it afterward—it cannot be that important!"

He shook his head. "No, I must go." He pushed her gently away from the door. "Wait for me here. I will either return or send a message to you within a few minutes—this will not take long."

Zesta was furious, but she tried to control her anger. "Very well, if you must, but hurry back to me—we have work to do!"

"If what you say is true, then a few minutes will not make any difference." And he turned and left the room.

When the door had closed behind him, Zesta stamped her foot in an absolute blaze of rage and flung herself furiously in the chair. Another minute, one more wretched single minute, and she would have had him! So close, so near—a single wretched minute!

Helios hurried along the corridor toward his private chamber. "At once," the note had said—but who had written it? The corridors were crowded with scribes and seeresses bustling about their duties; the dawn ritual had begun, and Deledian would be wondering at his absence. Many of the juniors nodded and gave him greetings, but he did not pause. "At once," the note had said.

At last he arrived at his door. He stood for a moment to compose himself as best he could, and then opened it quietly and stepped into the room. He froze, startled, his mind hardly able to believe what his eyes could see. There, near the eastern embrasure, stood the tall, benign, regal, and austere figure of Kumara—Kumara, who had never been known to leave the Withdrawn Temple; Kumara, who was believed by most on Ruta to be a legend, not a real man; Kumara, High Priest of the Moon, Priest of the Son Behind the Sun, Guardian of the Chalice of the Moon, spiritual head of all Ruta, the Ring of Power upon his hand, the Sigil of the Most High upon his breast; Kumara, High Priest of the Sea Temple itself!

9

"Come in, my son," said the old man gently. "Close the door. As Zesta said, the temple has too many ears."

Helios did as he was bid and came across to kneel for Kumara's blessing. "You overheard!" he stammered.

"Of course. We watch over you more than you know. Think of me as a father who has just guided his son away from a deadly peril."

"Peril? But what of the mirrors?"

Kumara sighed. "Yes, the mirrors do not lie—they would indeed have shown you mating with Zesta, and it would indeed have come to pass—but the mirrors reflect everything that they see of the probable future, both the good and the evil, the wise and the foolish. What you would have seen would have been the result of your poor judgment, your foolishness."

"But my motive was not evil, Kumara—I truly believed that it was an inner plane command."

"Yes, no doubt you did, but during those few minutes your mind, dominated by your body, dutifully produced the excuse that enabled the body to indulge its desires."

"And what of Zesta—what of her motives?"

"She thought to achieve control over you through your desire for her."

Helios snorted. "That's ridiculous!"

"Is it?"

"I am not a child, Kumara—she could never have done that!"

The old man sighed. "We are all children in one way or another. You had been with her for only a few

minutes and already she had enflamed you into believing
her lies. If I had not intervened, you would be lying
with her at this very moment. The hallmark of a high-
grade initiate is serenity and an unclouded judgment.
Are these hot and sweating hands the sign of serenity?
Were your reaction to Zesta and your subsequent refusal to see the truth really the symptoms of unclouded
judgment? And are those other bodily responses, which
are even now still rampant within you, really the mark
of a high-grade initiate?"

Helios blushed and turned away. "What shall I tell
Netziachos?"

"That is for you to decide."

The boy was silent for some time. "I've been a fool!"
he said at last. "I will withdraw my claim to the seventh
—I cannot accept the office of high priest now."

"You will do no such thing!" said Kumara sharply.
"I did not pull you out of danger just so that you can
indulge yourself in self-pity! It is your destiny to be
High Priest of the Sun Temple, if only for a short
while, and then there is a greater service that you are
required to give. Avoid this useless self-recrimina-
tion, it wastes both your time and mine."

Helios drew a deep breath. "You are right, of course
—as always." He was beginning to feel much better
now. His hands were no longer sweating, and the flush
had gone from his face. "What is this greater service?"

Kumara hesitated. "Yes, the time has come, I think.
But this matter concerns both you and Netziachos. I
would prefer to speak to you together. Go and tell her
of this morning's events and then bring her back here."

The corridor was still crowded. Helios stopped a
young scribe. "The High Priestess is in the antechamber
to the Hall of Mirrors. Tell her that I have been de-
tained on urgent matters. Then find Deledian and give
him my apologies and tell him I will come to him later
this morning."

"Yes, Helios, immediately," he said, then hesitated.
"They say that you are to be the new High Priest. Is
it true?"

Helios smiled. "Rumor travels fast in this nest of gossips," he said. "Who are 'they'?"

"Oh, lots of people."

"Well, you tell 'lots of people' that they shouldn't listen to gossip."

"Some rumors prove to be true and some false," the boy said stoutly. "If this one is true, then I and many of us will be very glad."

Helios laughed. "Do as I bid, take the messages, and don't listen to idle talk. You will all know the truth of it soon enough." He put his hand on the boy's shoulder. "And thank you."

Netziachos was not pleased with the explanation. "You would have lain with her, yet you refused me!" She shook her head. "You men may be strong in body, but you are certainly sometimes weak in the head! And she is so *old* too!" She reached up and touched his face gently. "Still, at least it shows that you are human."

He smiled and took her hands. "It's over now—let's forget it. Anyway, I have much better news—Kumara wants to see us, together. He is in my chamber right now."

The girl's eyes widened. "Oh, at last!" she breathed. "At last!"

When they reached Helios' private chamber Netziachos ran straight to the old man and knelt to kiss the Ring of Power on his hand. Kumara put his other hand on top of her head. "Peace, my daughter, peace. You are trembling."

"With happiness," she whispered, "with excitement, with apprehension, and because it has been so long since I have seen you!"

"Seen me? But you have seen me often in your mind."

"That's what Helios says, but those are dreams, imaginings."

"But nonetheless real on their own plane."

She looked up at him. "But every dream has to be brought right through into earth before it is fully realized."

He smiled. "They have taught you well, Netziachos, but don't dismiss the reality of the inner so easily."

"I don't dismiss it, but there are two realities, the reality of the inner and the reality of the outer, and both are important to me. If I am starved of the one, I *feel* that starvation even though I may be full fed on the other."

He looked at her silently for a long time. "Out of the mouths of children shall the truth be known," he murmured. "Yes, you are quite right, Netziachos." He turned to Helios. "Here is a worthy companion indeed for you."

Helios smiled. "I have never doubted it. She often knows the truth without knowing how or why she knows. All her life she has known of things that it has taken me years of study to realize."

"The knowing that is in the spirit," said Kumara, "is far more accurate than the knowing that is in the mind."

"But you need the mind to create the forms to hold the forces. Force needs a form through which to work. Force without form is diffused and wasted."

Kumara looked from the one to the other. "Force and form—yes, you are well matched, you two." He looked down at Netziachos. "Dreams without forms, Netziachos, are barren." He looked up at the younger priest. "And forms without dreams, Helios, are impotent. Dream the right dreams, then form the right forms—*that* is the true priesthood."

Netziachos rose and went to stand with Helios. "And is that our destiny, Kumara?"

He smiled and waved them to the couch. "Sit down both of you and I will tell you of a dream that needs both of you to give it form." He moved to the eastern embrasure and gazed out at the morning sun. "To understand the conditions from which we sprang, we must use our memory as a mirror—we must look at the image, and the image that lies behind the image, and the further images beyond—back in time to the far past to our most ancient of ancestors. Look deeply then and know and remember that in the fourth subcycle of the fourth root race of man the Manu Narada founded the Temple of the Sun in the City of the Golden Gates, and the people flourished under the guidance of the true priesthood." He paused for a moment. "As you know, that is the opening statement of the lecture called 'The Origins of the Sun Temple.' As a fifth-degree initiate, Helios, you have given that lecture yourself many times in the Hall of Learning to scribes and junior priests. You probably know it almost by heart. The lecture goes on to speak of how twice in our history our people fell on evil ways, and of how twice a great cataclysm rose up and destroyed much of our land and all those of evil heart. It then speaks of how, in ancient times, before each cataclysm the Sea Temple sent forth an emigration to the new lands to the east, each emigration comprising the flower of our race, those who at the time were of good heart, priests and people who would carry the seed of our teaching to foreign lands, each emigration headed by a high priest and high priestess who had the necessary qualities for such a mission. It was no easy task to choose who was to lead the emigrations, nor was it an easy task for those chosen. The particular quality needed was a functional contact with the very highest states of consciousness coupled with a physical plane efficiency, practicality, and common sense. It needed both the inner and the outer wisdom in order to deal with the many problems that would arise in founding a new temple in a strange land. It was no easy task."

Kumara turned from the embrasure. "You both know of the impending doom that hangs over Ruta and of how that doom has come to use Vardek as its instrument—and you both know of how the voice of evil has come to be heard even in the Sun Temple itself through the mouths of Baldek and Zesta and those foolish enough to follow the ways of their darkness. Baldek has already paid the price of his foolishness, and Zesta and Vardek are soon to pay theirs. I, Kumara, now tell you that the third and final great cataclysm is about to fall on Ruta, and that the third and final emigration is about to set forth."

The sun now beat strongly through the embrasure and outlined the figure of Kumara in a frame of light. Helios stirred. "We have known of the impending doom," he said quietly, "but we have not known the hour of its arrival."

"That hour has now come," said Kumara. "The final phase is upon us, and soon the fourth root race of man will perish utterly. The end is very near."

In a very small voice Netziachos said, "Will Helios and I be permitted to go with the emigration?"

Kumara smiled. "Yes, you will be permitted to go, indeed you have been appointed to serve as High Priest and High Priestess of the emigration. It will be your task to lead my people to a new land, to found a new Sun Temple, and to see to it that the Light of the Most High continues to be known to man. As I have said, it is no easy task, and to help you I am sending Melchadek with you to act as counselor—Melchadek, Priest of the Moon, keeper of the Akhasic Record. You have already met him, Helios—on the inner he stood at your shoulder recently and gave you the keys to the seventh. Like you, he is of the future." He looked at them gravely and kindly. "What say you to all this, my children? Do you accept the grave charge that I lay upon you?"

The blood drained from Helios' face, leaving his skin a pasty gray. "By Narada!" he whispered.

Netziachos was too suddenly frightened to speak. She clutched at the sleeve of Helios' robe and stared at Kumara.

The old man's voice was gentle. "It is hard, I know, but I'm afraid that in the last analysis you have no choice—there is no one else!"

"Hey there—Paladek!" Vardek roared. "Isn't this better than the Rmoahal rituals of the dead!" He laughed and slapped his thigh and pointed down the crowded table to where the suddenly embarrassed Paladek let go the girl he had been fumbling. Vardek punched Banda playfully on the shoulder. "Your Captain is as keen on live women, I see, as he is on dead men! Go on, Paladek—a man should always practice the art of the spear whenever he can!"

"And he could do with the practice," said Banda sourly. "Twice he was tumbled at yesterday's exercise. If he does not pay more attention to his work, he will not live through another campaign."

"Small loss then," said Vardek. "And yet you made him a captain."

Banda shrugged. "He is a sour and twisted man and bears no love for either you or me. As a captain he is where I can keep an eye on him. I would not want him lost among the lower ranks. As you have said yourself, Vardek, always know where the enemy is, always keep him in view."

Vardek grabbed a passing girl and pulled her down beside him onto the cushions. "You look a likely wench." He pulled aside her robe and bared her breasts. "And well armed, I see. What's your name, girl?"

She squealed with delight. "Danios, my lord, if it pleases you."

"It does, it does indeed, but these please me even more."

The girl giggled and flung her arms around him. She had been passing backward and forward for an hour or more hoping that the Lord Commander would notice her. "And I have other delights, my lord," she whispered.

Vardek roared with laughter again. "And saucy with it, too! This one is a willing enough prisoner, Banda—what say we keep this one to ourselves?"

His second-in-command grinned. "I doubt that I would get my share of these spoils, Vardek. Can two swords go into the same scabbard at the same time?"

The girl slipped her hand beneath Vardek's tunic. "And can one slave really serve two masters?"

Vardek shouted with delight, grabbed a wineskin with one hand, the girl with the other, drank a full draft, poured a libation onto her breasts, and buried his face and beard between them, and greedily sucked up the drops that ran across her skin. "By Narada!" he roared. "Do you know what would be a marvelous pleasure,

Banda—to stride barefoot over a sea of upturned breasts! Think of it, Banda, a sea of upturned breasts, each one as perfect as these!"

Banda smiled and shook his head. "A perilous sea indeed for any man to sail, Vardek."

The Lord Commander grabbed the girl's robe and ripped it from her. "Did you hear that, girl? Commander Banda thinks you're dangerous. What say you?"

The naked girl squealed and wriggled in his arms. "Oh, I am, my lord, I am—a dangerous woman indeed!"

The men at the long table roared with laughter and banged their goblets on the stone floor in approval. "Take care, my lord," one of them called out. "Banda might be right!"

The laughter suddenly vanished from Vardek's face. "Yes," he said slowly, "he might be right at that. She would not be the first to dream of my death!" Without the slightest warning he whipped his knife to the girl's throat and pressed the point hard against her skin. "So —you are dangerous, are you! Is that why you have flung yourself at me? Are you hoping that perhaps later, when I am asleep, you can steer a knife between my ribs?" The great hall of Vardek's house gradually fell silent. All eyes were on Vardek. The men were grinning, some hoping that he would press home the knife and let the whore's blood spurt. The serving women held their breath, their eyes wide with fear. At one time or another they had all had their lives poised on a knife's point from some warrior or other. It was an exciting life for a girl to be with the warriors of Ruta, but it was a life full of such sudden fear; warriors held all life cheap, but none cheaper than the lives of their women. Vardek tightened his grip. "I asked you a question, girl—answer it!"

Her throat was tight with fear. "I was only joking, my lord—just joking!"

He spoke quietly and carefully as though explaining something to a child. "You must learn that life is not a joke—nor is this knife. If I were to press it home you would not find it at all funny. Or perhaps you think that

I am joking and that I would not dream of sliding it into your throat. Is that it, girl—do you think that Vardek is joking?"

"No . . . no, my lord," she gasped.

"And do you still want to lie with me even though it may not be a joke?" Danios' eyes swiveled, hunting an escape, but there was no way out. The men were still grinning, waiting. They would not interfere. "Yes . . . yes, my lord," she whispered. "Even though it may cost me my life, it will be worth it!"

Vardek smiled sardonically. "You lie, girl," he said softly, "but I must admit that you lie well." He raised the knife high in the air. "I think I will kill you now and sleep alone."

Her eyes sprang open, glazed with terror. "No!" she screamed, but it was too late. The knife came whistling down, the blade glinting, and Vardek rammed it with a sickening thud into the wooden table a hair's width from the girl's throat.

Vardek bellowed with laughter. "You see, Vardek too can tell a joke when it pleases him!" The men shouted with delight, and even Banda grinned sourly. Vardek lifted the girl's head to laugh in her face, but she had fainted clean away. He pushed her aside, and she rolled naked at the feet of the clustered serving women. "Take the wench away," he roared, "and when she snivels back to life, tell her that it is dangerous to joke with me and that perhaps next time I may not be so considerate!"

The frightened women picked the girl up bodily and hastened away, glad to be out of his reach, for there was no way of knowing who would suffer his attentions next, or when.

"And when you return," he roared after them, "bring us some more wine, for wench-baiting is thirsty work!"

"And evil work, Vardek!" thundered a voice from the doorway, and into the great hall stepped a kingly figure robed in purest white, a great ring upon his hand. "Is this the way you misuse the power that is entrusted to you!"

A startled silence fell on the assembly, and those nearest the stranger shrank away, though they could not tell why they did so, for he was an old man with cloud-white hair and obviously no threat to any Toltec warrior of Ruta—yet shrink they did, and sudden fear stilled their noisy tongues.

Banda half-drew his knife, but Vardek stayed his hand. "We need no weapons for one old man," he said softly. Slowly and very deliberately Vardek drank from the wineskin and then reached for the dish of meats. "Who are you, old one?" he said calmly. "If you are hungry, sit with us and eat. If you are thirsty, then drink—there is plenty for all."

"Unlike you, Vardek, I hunger and thirst for the light," said the stranger, "and there is plenty of that, too, though few will accept what is offered."

"Ah—a priest! I can always tell a priest, they have such contempt for earthly things. Gentlemen," he said, waving his hand airily around the assembly of Toltec officers, "I give you a venerable priest of no name, and one who hungers for the light." The men were beginning to recover themselves now, and some laughed. "Old man," Vardek went on calmly, "if it is light you need to still your hunger I'm sure we can spare a candle for you to chew on."

"Contemptuous as ever I see, Vardek," said the old man. "Only a fool mocks what he does not understand!"

Vardek's brow darkened. "I would know who calls Vardek a fool!" he thundered. "If you have a name, then speak it so that my knife will know whose throat it enters!"

"Always ready with a knife, Vardek. Are you then fearful of one old man that you needs must feel it necessary to offer me violence?"

"Not fear, old man, but irritation will guide my hand and silence your impudence! But before my blade reaches out for your throat, I would still hear your name, if you have one."

The old man stepped forward. "I am Kumara, High Priest of the Withdrawn Temple, and I have come, Vardek, to give you your last warning."

Kumara! The name ran around the assembly in awed whispers. The legendary Kumara, the designated spiritual head of all Ruta! The man to whom even old Khamadek had bowed his head. Kumara—a figure so legendary that few outside the temple really believed he existed at all.

Vardek was stunned, but he did not allow his expression to change one iota. He remained stock-still, frozen, the knife still balanced in his hand. "Well, well," he said at last, softly, slowly, "the great Kumara! Do you know," he went on conversationally, "that some of the ignorant even pray to you as a god?" But Kumara did not answer. "And some believe that you are immortal and have lived in the Sea Temple since Lemurian times." Vardek leaned back and scanned his assembled officers. "Gentlemen, just now I said that I give you a venerable priest, but it seems I was mistaken. It seems that I give you something much greater. Behold Kumara, the immortal god!" And again Vardek reached calmly for the dish of meats.

Kumara shook his head angrily. "You never learn, do you, Vardek! All your life you have held the priesthood in contempt. That of itself would be bad enough, but in your ignorance and arrogance you have sought to destroy the temple and everything it stands for!"

"And what *does* it stand for?" barked Vardek. "Incompetence and corruption! It stands for a gigantic lie—the pretense that fantasy is reality—and through that lie you seek to dominate men's minds and live as parasites on the sweat and labors of others!"

"The inner wisdom, Vardek," said Kumara quietly, "is the truth. It is only a fantasy to those whose inner eyes are closed. It is the function of the priesthood to enlighten men's minds, not dominate them—to open their inner eyes."

"Inner eyes—rubbish! I have one pair of eyes only, and one pair is enough to see the temple for what it is, a leftover from an age when men were silly enough and primitive enough to believe your fantasies. The days of the priesthood are over, Kumara—we are no longer prepared to tolerate the existence of a temple that sucks a soft living from the people and gives nothing in return. Everyone on this island, whether he be Toltec, Akkadian, or Rmoahal, renders a service to the community—everyone, that is, except you priests! What does the temple give to Ruta—nothing! You take a tithing from every man's labors and give nothing in return—nothing save prophecies of doom, nothing save a long list of petty restrictions that forbids even the most simple pleasures of the flesh, nothing save the annual sacrifices of valuable animals, aye, and even men—you take with both hands and give nothing—nothing!"

There was dead silence in the hall after this tirade. The assembled officers were awed by the arrogance of their Lord Commander. No other man on Ruta would have dared speak so contemptuously to even a junior priest, let alone to Kumara of the Sea Temple.

"What you say is perfectly true for such as yourself, Vardek," said Kumara sadly, "for you have never wanted what we have to give. It is true that we of the priesthood do not contribute to the physical plane assets of Ruta, for that is not our function. It is our task to bring the Light of the Most High to the minds and hearts of men—to point the way of human evolution, to teach men how they may develop their innate spiritual qualities, to lead men to the truth. For such as you who reject the truth, Vardek, we must indeed seem as parasites."

"What truth?" sneered Vardek. "There is nothing to your so-called teaching save tales of fantasy. I do not care one jot for any priest who ever lived, or for any of your so-called truth!"

"What you choose to reject is your own affair, Vardek, but your continual opposition to the priesthood, backed by the power of your high position, is causing a rift between the temple and the people. Those who in their own small way are receptive to the truth are being dragged further and further into the darkness of your shadow. Choose the way of darkness for yourself if you must, Vardek, but you have no right to inflict darkness on others!"

Vardek leaned back on the cushions. "And if what you say is true," he said sneeringly, "if I am leading the people away from the temple, what do you think you can do about it?"

Kumara drew himself up and pointed an accusing finger at the Lord Commander of the Army. "You think you are all-powerful," he thundered. "But I tell you, Vardek, that you have not even begun to understand what real power is! This is your last warning—cease your war against the temple, or die! You shall not spread your darkness any further! Be warned now before it is too late!"

For a split-second, for one tiny unmeasurable moment of time, Vardek's mind was riven by an explosion of fear, but then suddenly he leaped to his feet and hurled his knife straight at Kumara's throat. Barely a dozen feet separated the two men—everyone in the room saw the blade leave Vardek's hand, and yet Kumara did not fall. Vardek had never been known to miss with a knife; his speed of reaction and deadly accuracy were almost a legend in the army; and yet, there the blade was, embedded in the solid wood of the great door, the hilt still quivering. It must have missed the old man completely by at least a foot.

Kumara shook his head. "You fool!" he said quietly, and turned and strode for the door. The two Rmoahal houseboys leaped to open the way, their eyes white with fear. When the great doors had thundered shut behind him, Kumara paused and sighed. He had hoped so much to have given Vardek pause for thought, but it seemed that any opposition whatsoever levied against the Lord Commander, this so-called marshal of Ruta, merely added fuel to the man's arrogance and indeed to his ambition. It seemed that there was no way of averting the doom that threatened.

The curtain to an alcove stirred, and a tall, flaxen-haired man stepped into the antechamber and came to kneel at the old man's feet. At first Kumara could not place him, and then suddenly he remembered.

"Ah, yes, you are Herakos, are you not, chief of the Akkadians."

"Yes, Kumara, and one who is loyal to the temple and to yourself."

"I am pleased to hear it. There are some who appear to be dedicated to other principles."

Herakos rose to his feet. He really was a giant of a man, towering a good foot above the High Priest. "If you mean that dog Vardek," he growled, "I will be more than pleased to dispose of him."

"You overheard?"

"I was on the rear balcony. Vardek's gatherings are not to my taste, and I always escape as soon as I can."

"Then why go to them at all?"

"Because it would be dangerous not to. Those who offend Vardek do so at the risk of their lives."

"So it would seem," said Kumara dryly.

"And some have been known to die."

"Such as?"

"Demian, for one, chief of the Toltec warrior wing and second-in-command to Vardek. Vardek's own servant, for another, for knowing too much. And a priest of the Sun Temple—all on that last campaign to Amaria."

"To say nothing of ten thousand Amarians themselves put to the sword," mused Kumara.

"And no doubt many others. Some say that King Baralda and Khamadek are numbered among his victims."

"And Baldek?"

Herakos shook his head. "No, he died because of his own arrogance rather than that of his father."

"And who next, I wonder."

"Perhaps yourself?"

Kumara smiled. "Vardek cannot kill me, but there is one who is in danger who must not die if we are to salvage anything of value from these dark times. Do you know Helios?"

"The new High Priest of the Sun Temple? I know of him, but I have not met him. Those who speak of him speak nothing but good."

"And they speak truly. He must not die, Herakos. I cannot go into all the reasons now, but believe me when

I say that more than you can know or imagine depends on his survival. He will need a personal guard, one of more than ordinary courage. Would an Akkadian chief stand guard over a Toltec priest?"

"If it is your command, Kumara."

"Even against high-ranking Toltecs?"

"Against anyone who threatens him."

The older man looked at him keenly. "Herakos, my own life and your life are of little value compared to his survival. This may mean your death."

Herakos smiled. "You are speaking to a warrior of Ruta," he said proudly.

"Then so be it. Guard him well, my friend."

The Akkadian drew himself up and saluted the great High Priest of the Sea Temple, and Kumara made the sign of benediction. "There is a blessing on all who serve, Herakos," he said quietly, "but for you and me that blessing may not come in this life, but come it surely will." He turned and crossed the foyer, passed the fountain, and glided between the great pillars and out into the night.

Herakos stood gazing after him until the figure faded in the darkness, and then he, too, left the house and crossed the plateau to the Sun Temple to find Helios.

In the great hall the assembled officers spoke in whispers, not daring to disturb Vardek, who sat silently brooding at the head of the table. Vardek had not uttered a word since Kumara had left. His face was dark with supressed fury, and then into his brain there crept a thought so foul that even he resisted it—at first.

At length he looked up and growled. "Banda, dismiss the men—the party is over. Pick six men whom you can trust and have them remain. I have work for you."

It was in the small hours of the morning when Kumara arrived back at the Sea Temple, for mountain paths are not sympathetic to old men's bones. He slept for three hours, and just before dawn he awoke and summoned Marah and Melchadek. "You watched in the mirror?" he said.

"We did," said Melchadek, "and the situation is even worse than we feared."

"Vardek's greed for power seems to be accelerating," said Marah thoughtfully, "and there is a note of desperation in his actions which seems quite out of keeping with his character."

Kumara nodded grimly. "You are quite right, completely out of character. I doubt that Vardek has any control left over his own thoughts and actions. The Dark Lords are driving him faster and faster along the path to destruction, and I believe that his very soul is beginning to crack under the strain. The last act in such a tale is always a desperate plunge into chaos and insanity, bringing not only death and destruction to themselves but to all around them. We can delay no longer."

"What would you have us do?" said Melchadek.

Kumara rose and went to the eastern embrasure. The sky was beginning to lighten. "Set the emigration in motion. Send your runners to the north. Have the ships brought around to the mouth of the Naradek. Warn those selected to stand by to embark during the hours of darkness tomorrow night. It is essential that every one is in the small boats and heading upriver to meet the long ships by midnight. Once the small boats are under way, Vardek's fleet in the harbor can then be scuttled. Secrecy is obviously essential. It is imperative that no word reaches Vardek's ear until it is too late, until his own ships are sunk. If he is able to launch even a half-dozen ships, then the enterprise is lost, for you will not be able to fight off trained warriors."

"It will be done."

Kumara turned to the High Priestess. "I am concerned, Marah, for the welfare of those under our care. Please make immediate arrangements to withdraw every priestess and seeress from the Sun Temple and bring them back here to the Sea Temple—everyone, that is, except Zesta. She has chosen to live by a code other than ours, so let her die by it also. I suggest that you delay the exodus until after midnight. Let them slip away one by one secretly, so as not to alert the guard."

She nodded. "It will be as you say."

"And the priesthood?" said Melchadek.

"They must remain and take their chances. Collectively they are responsible for the corruption of the Sun Temple, and therefore collectively they must bear the consequences." He turned to the embrasure again. "There is one sign still missing, and when that appears, the end is only a matter of a day or two, perhaps even hours. We have not yet heard the rising of the elemental forces which always precedes a disaster of this magnitude."

"But we have!" said Marah quickly. "At last night's evening ritual the Earth and Fire elementals were unusually active, and indeed unusually intrusive."

Kumara spun around. "Last night? But I felt nothing! I would have picked up vibrations even though I was away in the city."

"The signs were faint, Kumara," said Melchadek. "They could only be detected under ritual conditions, but they have been growing stronger ever since, and I detect a note of power and anger. Haven't you noticed how still the air and sea is, how oppressive? Fire and Earth are rising, and Air and Water are giving way to them."

"Yes, but I thought it merely my own gloom. How stupid of me! How burns the Eternal Light?"

Melchadek hesitated. "The one in the Sun Temple stands higher hour by hour, but that is usual at this time of year."

"How high?"

"I do not know—I will check."

"And the one in the Sea Temple?"

"It too is higher than I have ever seen it," said Marah.

Kumara drummed his fingers on the stone wall. "The physical flame which we use as a symbol of the inner light is actually burning gas that has risen to the surface from deep underground. The height and fierceness of the flame is an infallible guide as to what pressures exist in the very bowels of these mountains. Go, both of you, quickly. Observe the flames, work the elemental ritual, and report to me here as soon as you can. Meanwhile, I must confer with Narada. Go now, quickly!"

Marah and Melchadek withdrew swiftly, and once more Kumara turned to the eastern embrasure. The light was now strong; already the sun was exploring the mountaintops, and soon the morning mists would be driven from the land. Now that Melchadek had pointed it out, the oppressive atmosphere was indeed obvious. The air was still; not even the morning breeze was moving, and that was unusual. The sea, too, was quiet; hardly a wave could be seen. But this stillness was not that of peace and gentleness; it was a dark, heavy stillness, ominous, foreboding, and the more Kumara gazed upon it, the less he liked it.

He moved to his meditation couch, set the seals, and within seconds he was in the presence of Narada, the Elder Master, the supreme guiding intelligence of earthly humanity. They did not communicate in words but in shared created mood, shared states of consciousness. For two hours the High Priest remained supine, and then with a sigh he sat up, removed the seals, and summoned Marah and Melchadek again.

"It is as I feared," he said. "There is no way to avert the disaster. The forces invoked by Vardek and Zesta and all those at the Sun Temple must take their course. All we can do is salvage a few of value, as we have planned. Have you sent your runners to the north, Melchadek?"

"Yes, they left shortly after dawn. There is something . . ."

"And what of the Eternal Lights?"

"They are standing too high, far too high, both here and in the Sun Temple. And the Earth elementals are moving also. Even a layman could probably detect them now simply by putting his ear to the ground. There are faint rumblings deep within the earth, and they grow louder with each passing hour. But there is something . . ."

"Rumblings? It has gone that far, then!"

"Kumara!" said the High Priestess sharply. "You must listen to our other tidings—it is important."

"Tidings? What tidings?"

She took him gently by the arm. "Come with us—we have something you must see."

"Though we would give a great deal for you to be shielded from the sight," put in Melchadek.

"What is it?"

"Come," said Marah. "We can talk as we go." They led the old man from his chamber and down the great stone stairway to the central hall. "Barely an hour ago a party of warriors left three large bundles at our gates and then departed hastily."

"As well they might," said Melchadek.

"Bundles? What bundles?"

"You spoke earlier, Kumara, of Vardek plunging into chaos and insanity," said Melchadek. "I am afraid that it has already happened."

They crossed the great central hall toward a group of priests and priestesses. As they drew near, Kumara was alarmed to see the priestesses openly weeping, and then to his dismay he saw on the faces of the priests the expressions of revulsion and fierce anger amounting almost to hatred, expressions that he never thought to see within the precincts of the sacred Temple of the Sea.

He was bewildered. "What is this, Marah?" he whispered.

Marah drew him gently forward. "Here before you is the evidence of Vardek's insanity and of the chaos into which his soul has already plunged. Look!"

The priests and priestesses moved to one side, and there on the roughhewn flagstones lay the naked bodies of the three most junior seeresses who had been working in the Sun Temple. Not only were they dead, but their bodies had been mutilated to an incredible extent. Their hair had obviously been torn bodily from their scalps, their heads were covered in congealed blood and torn skin. Their eyes had been gouged out, and their faces were savagely burned almost beyond recognition. The skin over their entire bodies was lacerated from a thousand whiplashes. It was also obvious that all had been brutally raped. One had been practically disemboweled, another had had her fingernails and toenails wrenched away, and the third had no feet and her shins had been smashed into a mass of splintered bone and torn flesh.

On one of the bodies was a note which read: TO KUMARA, HIGH PRIEST OF THE SEA TEMPLE—BEHOLD THESE THY SERVANTS!

For a long time Kumara stood and stared in horror at the bodies. He had known them all. Many a time he had seen them at the dawn rituals going about their duties, and he had personally conducted the rituals of their initiations as they had risen grade by grade, and he had interviewed each one personally with Marah when they had been assigned to duty in the Sun Temple, and he could remember personally giving them the ritual blessing as they had set forth. And now this!

"By Narada!" he whispered. "To what further depths than this can any human being sink! It is indeed the time for this age of man to die!"

10

High in the Rutian mountains in a comparatively sheltered pass between twin peaks, three youths in the traveling robes of first-stage initiates lay panting for breath after a cruel climb from the foothills below. Presently one of them sat up and gazed eastward toward the Sacred Mountain and beyond it to the coast. Even at this distance the white dome of the Sun Temple stood out clearly in the afternoon sun.

"Do you know we are higher than the Sacred Mountain itself?" he said. There was a note of wonderment in his voice. "We are actually looking down on the topmost plateau. I have never been this high."

The other two scrambled to their feet to join him. "How far do you think it is?" said one of them.

"The Sacred Mountain? About ten miles, I suppose. It's quite remarkable how small it really is compared to these peaks. I wonder why it stands on its own, quite separate from the rest."

"Some upheaval in ancient times, I was told," said the third." Can you see the Sea Temple?"

The first one pointed. "Yes, there to the right of the Sacred Mountain, farther to the south."

For some minutes they gazed thoughtfully at their own temple, made diminutive by distance. "It seems so huge when you are in it," said the second, "but it really is quite small."

They were silent for a little while more, and then the first one said, "Melchadek once told me that the best way to judge anything is to stand back and look at it from a distance."

"You think the Withdrawn Temple is a small thing, then?" said the second. "You think it is trivial?"

The boy shrugged his shoulders. "If Melchadek were here, he would probably say that from this distance it is easier to realize that the temple is not the whole world but only a part of it. I think he would also say that the importance of anything is not relative to its size. The Temple of the Sea is small, but it is by no means trivial."

They digested this for a while, and then the third youth said, "Why wouldn't he let us take the coastal route?" He pointed to the east. "Melchadek, I mean. That way would have been much quicker."

The first youth was a year older than the other two, and although they were all in the first degree, he was held to be the senior because of his longer period of training. Because of this he was sometimes inclined to lord it over the others. He pointed to the south. "Isn't it obvious?" he said. "We would have had to circle the southern side of the Sacred Mountain before striking north, and that means we would have had to cross the harbor area before coming on to the coast path through the marshes."

"So what?"

"So that means that there would have been the risk of us being stopped by Vardek's men and questioned."

The second youth snorted defiantly. "I wouldn't have told him anything!"

"Nor I!" said the third.

The first youth plucked a blade of mountain grass and drew it through his teeth. "Did you see the three seeresses this morning? We would have been the next three bundles to be delivered. Are you sure you would not have talked?"

They remembered the three crushed and horribly mutilated corpses of their erstwhile sisters, and their eyes grew cloudy and their stomachs sickened at the memory of it.

"Too much is at stake for Melchadek to have taken even that small risk," said the first one, "and so we have come by this longer route. We have plenty of time. As long as we reach the secret fleet in time, all will be well."

"And if we don't?"

The first youth stood up abruptly. "If we don't, then the fleet will not sail, and thus there will be no emigration—and thus the teaching that has been given to man through the temple will perish along with Ruta itself. If we fail, then for century upon century man will live in darkness and corruption until he comes to understand enough to build a new temple and train himself to receive the inner wisdom again. That's what Melchadek told me before we set out."

The second youth scrambled to his feet, but the third remained seated. There was a strange expression on his face. "I have never felt important before," he said slowly. "The whole future—right here in our own hands!"

"As we said earlier," said the first one, "the importance of anything is not relative to its size, or even its position. Come!" he said sharply. "Let's not keep the future waiting!"

The three climbed their way out of the valley and up into the high mountain passes. For hour after hour they sped northward to where the secret fleet lay hidden in a tiny bay—and the responsibility of their task lay heavily upon them.

The sun withdrew behind the mountains, and the long shadows reached out to engulf the Sun Temple and the whole of the Sacred Mountain. They spread their fingers over Vardek's fleet drawn up in the harbor and then crept out to sea until all was blackness save the topmost peaks of the mountain chain, which remained a fiery orange for a time, until they too were overcome by darkness.

Helios stood in the shadows near the northern portal. "It is time," he said shortly.

The figure behind him nodded and slipped through the side door into the storehouse. The great room was stacked from floor to ceiling with huge hods of grain, hundreds upon hundreds of casks of wine, bolts of cloth, barrels of sweet-scented oils, great jars of honey, and a thousand crates and boxes and sacks stuffed with goods of every conceivable nature, the spoils of a year's tithing accepted as tribute from the peoples of Ruta. At the back of the storehouse, in a relatively clear area, were the hooded and cloaked figures of two dozen priestesses and seeresses, the entire Sun Temple complement, saving only Zesta herself.

Netziachos stepped out from the group and came to meet the figure. "Herakos?"

The huge Akkadian came up to her and took her arm. "Helios says it is time. Let them come one at a time, as arranged."

She nodded and beckoned Melandros. "Go with Herakos. Are you sure you remember everything?"

"Of course," the woman said calmly.

Though not the most senior priestess present, she had been chosen to go first because of her practical common sense, her calmness in an emergency, but above all because she had eyes as sharp as a cat's. Because of the need for secrecy it was impossible for them to go eastward by the main flagstoned road through the great Golden Gates and down to the lower levels the normal way. Instead they would have to go to the precipitous western edge of the plateau and down the plunging rocky path to the boulder-strewn Naradek far below. And because of the need for secrecy, they could carry no lights until they were below the shoulder of the mountain. Even in daylight it was a risky path to take; at night it was perilous. Earlier in the day Helios and Herakos had taken a great bundle of wax torches and had hidden them beside the path a hundred feet below the cliff edge. Melandros would have to make that journey in pitch darkness to find the torches and light one to act as a guide to those who followed.

There had been a fierce argument that afternoon when Helios had announced that he would go first to find the torches in the darkness. Finally Melandros had said, "It is not male strength that is needed, Helios, but a sure foot and a sharp eye, and mine are surer and sharper than yours! And besides, we have only two men to bear arms, should the guards arise. You and Herakos must remain." In the end Helios had to agree, though he liked it little.

Herakos took her hand to guide her, but she shook it off. "Let go, you great ox—it is I who should be guiding you!" And she swept past him and stepped outside to join Helios.

"Are you all right?" he whispered.

"Of course—why shouldn't I be?"

"It's not too late to change your mind and let me go first."

"Rubbish—it's not the first time I have gone walking in the dark. What of the guards?"

"One of them patrolled this area twenty minutes ago, but nothing since. The trouble is that they do not stick to a set routine. He could be back in five minutes or five hours—there is no way of telling."

"Then I had better go now."

"All right, then—good luck, Melandros. Take care."

The priestess smiled briefly, slipped through the portal, and disappeared into the darkness.

Toward the west the moon had begun to rise, a nearly full moon, and still waxing. Already the parapets of the outer wall were beginning to stand out in silvery contrast to the deep shadows in which Helios and Herakos were hidden.

Herakos touched the sword that Helios had buckled at his waist. "Can you use that?" he whispered.

"I've been through the training—everyone in the temple has to."

The Akkadian grunted disdainfully. His opinion of temple arms training was not high. "Have you ever killed a man in combat?"

"I have never killed a man at all, in combat or in any other way."

"Have you ever used it in a real fight?"

"Of course not—I'm a priest, not a warrior."

"Hmmmmm! In that case, if we have trouble with the guards, you had better leave things to me."

"My courage is not lacking, Akkadian—I will fight if I have to."

"I don't doubt it, but frankly I think you might get in my way. If trouble starts, you had better stand back."

Helios smiled in the darkness. "We will see," he murmured. "I think it is time to call the next one."

Herakos nodded and slipped through the doorway again, and a few seconds later another hooded and cloaked priestess emerged into the courtyard.

"You understand what you have to do?" Helios whispered.

The arrangement was that the second girl would go only as far as the cliff edge and report back if she could see a light below. "Yes, perfectly," the girl said.

"All right, off you go, then."

The girl slipped away in the darkness, and the two men waited with growing impatience for her return. "By Narada, she is taking her time!" said Herakos sharply, but at that precise moment the girl appeared.

"All is well," she said breathlessly. "I can see the light perfectly."

"Good—then off you go again. We will send one every two minutes, as arranged."

Over the next half-hour another dozen or so hooded figures slipped through the western portal. "It's almost too easy," whispered Helios. "So much for our so-called guard. Half of Vardek's army could slip into this temple without our precious guard knowing a thing about it!"

There were only six more to go when it happened. Suddenly a shout rang out, and a guard came up at a run. The girl froze by the portal.

"Who is that?" the guard shouted. "Identify yourself!"

The guard was coming from Helios' right to where the girl was to his left. He would have to pass them, but not close enough to seize him quickly. "Only one," whispered Herakos. "No problem."

"But silently, Herakos, silently, or we will have the whole Temple Guard upon us. He is not close enough— one clash of swords will wake everyone for a hundred yards or more!"

"Who is there, I said?" shouted the guard. He had slowed to a cautious walk.

The girl kept her head. She moved out of the doorway and came toward the guard and stopped immediately opposite where Herakos and Helios stood hidden. "Who dares challenge a priestess of the Sun!" she called out.

The guard came up to her. "What are you doing out here, priestess?" he growled.

"Going about my duties—what else!"

"At this time of night?"

"And who are you to question at what times we of the priesthood perform our duties! It is your duty to keep out marauders—do I look like a marauder?"

Cleverly the girl moved around a little as though to stand more clearly in the moonlight, but it had the desired effect of turning the guard so that his back was toward the storehouse.

"Don't bandy words with me, girl!" the guard growled. "You had better come with me and explain yourself to the captain." And he reached forward and grabbed her arm.

He was perhaps ten yards or so from Herakos, but the huge Akkadian reached him in five silent strides and slipped his forearm around the man's throat and snapped his neck as easily as breaking a twig. He picked up the body, grabbed the girl, and rushed back to the shadows.

Another voice called out from the night. "What's all the shouting about! Danek, are you all right?"

Helios stepped forward. "Yes, yes, I'm all right," he shouted. "I tripped and fell!"

"Clumsy oaf!" said the voice. "Keep it quiet or you'll wake the whole temple!" And they could hear him clump away back toward the guardhouse.

"Close!" whispered Helios feelingly. "Too close for comfort! Are you all right?" he said to the girl.

She was still looking up at Herakos in frightened astonishment. She had never seen a man killed before, and she could hardly believe that it had been done so quickly and so easily. "Yes . . . yes, I'm all right."

"You did well—that could have been nasty but for you. All right, if you are feeling recovered, you had better be off."

The girl nodded and slipped away again. There was no further trouble, and ten minutes later there was only Netziachos left.

"There is so much I want to say, Helios," she whispered, "but there is no time."

"We will have time enough later," he said gently. "Go now—you must not delay. The others are waiting for you, and you must all be at the Sea Temple by dawn, and you have a long way to go."

She flung her arms around him and kissed him and then turned on Herakos. "Guard him well, Akkadian," she hissed, "or I will have your life for it!" And she spun around, slipped through the portal, and vanished into the darkness.

Herakos chuckled. "And she would, too!" he said admiringly. "I like a woman with courage—you have chosen well, Helios!"

"Enough of that!" snapped Helios. "What are we going to do with him?" And he prodded the body with his foot.

"Leave him to me." The Akkadian picked up the corpse as easily as lifting a sword, swung him onto his shoulder, and followed the girl. Five minutes later he returned. "Since he was so anxious to interview the priestess, I have sent him after her," he said calmly, "but I fear that in my enthusiasm I sent him the quick way, straight over the edge!"

Helios smiled. "Good. Come, you had better sleep in my chamber for the rest of the night. There will be pandemonium at dawn when they discover their loss. Zesta herself is now the only woman in the whole temple!"

The sky was already beginning to lighten when Banda hurried into Vardek's house. "Is he awake?" he said to the guard.

"Been pacing his room all night," the man replied.

Banda grunted. "Conferences at midnight, conferences at dawn—when is a man supposed to sleep?"

When he was shown into Vardek's inner chamber it was obvious that the Lord Commander was in an angry mood. "Sit down, sit down!" he barked. "Any news from the Sea Temple?"

"None at all."

Vardek banged his fist on the table. "Incredible! We dispose of three of their seeresses, and they do nothing! Don't they care?"

Banda shrugged. "Probably, but what could they do anyway?"

"Something, surely! Even these scrawny priests must at least try some sort of retaliation! Are they just going to sit there idly while we dispose of them one by one?"

"So it would appear."

"I don't believe it! I don't trust these priests—they are brewing something, be sure of that. They must be! But we will not wait any longer, Banda. Get your commanders together, send the Rmoahals and the Akkadians back to their own people by noon—the work we have to do is best done by Toltecs. Have the Toltec wing ready by tonight; we take the temple by storm tomorrow at dawn. You have twenty-four hours to prepare."

Banda frowned. "Why reduce our ranks? Why send the Rmoahals and Akkadians away?"

Vardek stopped pacing and glared down at his second-in-command. "Are you questioning my orders?" he blared.

"Not at all," said Banda hurriedly. "I was merely asking your reasons."

"They should be obvious even to one of your limited understanding! Even priests are Toltecs, and I will not encourage Rmoahals and Akkadians to raise arms against Toltecs. We have over five thousand Toltecs under arms, more than enough to deal with one ridiculous Temple and its puny Temple Guard."

"I was not thinking of the attack," said Banda, "but of swelling the ranks of the Rmoahals and Akkadians below. If they were to unite they could raise five thousand to storm the plateau, and our five thousand would then be fighting on two fronts; and it was you, Vardek, who taught me never to fight on two fronts if it could be avoided."

"The Rmoahals and the Akkadians will never unite, they hate each other too much for that—and even if they proposed such a thing, it would take months of negotiations, wrangling, and arguments in their so-called councils before they could even appoint an overall commander-in-chief. The Rmoahals would never accept an Akkadian as chief, and the Akkadians would never fight under a Rmoahal."

"You are probably right," said Banda. "But I still feel uneasy at the thought of five thousand trained warriors at my rear."

"Oh, very well, if it will ease your mind, put one thousand to guard the Golden Gates. That will still leave four thousand to take the temple, more than enough."

"One thousand against five?" said Banda dubiously.

Vardek's temper suddenly flared again. "I did not bring you here to argue my orders but to obey them!" he roared. "And if you were anything of a commander at all, you would have realized that if they do unite and attack, which is only a remote possibility, then they will have to attack along the road in columns and so will not be able to bring more than a fraction of their number to the front of the fight at any one time, not nearly enough to trouble our rear!"

"Of course, of course!" said Banda hastily. "I was merely thinking aloud."

"Then don't think—just obey!"

Melchadek was ushered into the inner private chamber of Malekh, High Master of all the Akkadian craft lodges. "Greetings, Malekh," he said courteously.

"Greetings," said the old man. "Please be seated." He eyed the younger man shrewdly, but he was difficult to assess. Young certainly, but no youth—his face induced thoughts not of time but of timelessness. "Forgive me," the High Master said quietly, "but until yesterday I had not even heard your name. For one who stands so high in the priestly hierarchy, you are little known. I am told you stand at Kumara's right hand."

"That is one way of putting it," said Melchadek.

"And that you are to lead the emigration."

"No—Helios and Netziachos will lead as High Priest and High Priestess. I will go with them and serve in the same function for them as I have for Kumara."

Malekh was a little subdued by the aura of extreme authority—the younger man's voice seemed to emanate from some incredibly remote point in time. "I see; then you will be interested to know that the Rmoahal fighting wing passed through here an hour ago on their way to their homes below, and I understand that the Akkadian wing is on its way home also." He stared hard at the young priest. "What does this mean, Melchadek—what new foul thing is Vardek contemplating?"

"We believe he intends to attack the Sun Temple, probably at dawn tomorrow, and we believe he prefers to use only Toltec warriors to slaughter Toltec priests."

The High Master's eyes widened in horror. "Slaughter the priesthood—he must be insane!"

"Undoubtedly."

"But is there nothing that can stop it?"

Melchadek shook his head gravely. "Priests are no

match for trained warriors. Also there are only some
two hundred in the temple, including the guards,
against a five-thousand-strong warrior wing. There are
a few hundred civilians on the plateau outside the temple, but there is nothing they can do either. Only one
thing could stop Vardek, and that is if the Rmoahals and
Akkadians were to unite against him. Between them
they could put up nearly five thousand trained warriors of their own against Vardek's five thousand—an
even match."

The old man's eyes gleamed. "It is an attractive
thought. It is perhaps not the most diplomatic thing for
an Akkadian to say to a Toltec, but the dream closest
to every Akkadian heart is to see the overthrow of
Toltec domination on Ruta. Forgive me, but it is true."

"I am a priest first and a Toltec second, Malekh.
I know of this dream and share it. It is not in accordance with the principles I serve for one race to dominate another. At certain times in human evolution it is
necessary that one race take the lead, but never to
dominate."

The old man sighed. "An attractive dream, but one
that must remain a dream for the time being. I am the
leader of my people, Melchadek, but the Akkadians
would not follow me if I tried to lead them against
Vardek. Akkadian warriors would not turn against their
Toltec brothers-in-arms. When men fight together as
these have done, when they have risked death together, it forges a bond which is not easily broken. And
what incentive could I give them—to save the lives of a
relatively few Toltec priests whom even the Toltecs are
willing to slaughter? Forgive me, but they would not
do it. And the same goes for the Rmoahals. Dracombi
would not shed a tear if every Toltec and every Akkadian were to die tonight—indeed, that is the Rmoahal
dream, that they will inherit all Ruta. No, Melchadek, if
the survival of the Sun Temple depends on an alliance
between Rmoahal and Akkadian against Toltec, then
they are indeed doomed."

Melchadek nodded gravely. "That is our assessment
also."

"And forgive me again, but from what I hear they will be small loss to Ruta—the Sun Temple is not what it used to be. There was a time when it commanded the respect of Rmoahal, Akkadian, and Toltec alike, but not anymore."

"That is true. Because of their corruption they have brought this doom upon their own heads, but when they die, all Ruta dies with them, hence the need of this the third emigration, to save those of value. You in particular will be an invaluable asset in the new life."

"But I am not going."

The younger man frowned a little. "But why is that? You will be badly needed, if only to coordinate the efforts of your various craft masters."

Malekh shrugged. "As for that, there are several among them who could take over as high master. My place is here with those of my people who must die. Kumara would not choose otherwise," he said shrewdly. "I'll wager he is not going, nor Marah."

Melchadek smiled. "You are right; they both choose to remain."

"And so do I."

"So be it, but in that case you can render a very valuable service. Although your warriors will not attack Vardek, would they defend themselves if Vardek attacked them?"

"Of course, particularly if Herakos were here to lead them."

"That cannot be. His task is even more important. Helios is the one man who *must* survive. Didn't Kumara explain this to you?"

"Yes, but I was not happy about it. Times must indeed be bad when the only man you can trust to defend the life of a Toltec priest is an Akkadian warrior—and it is a sad blow to us to deprive us of our warrior chief —but we must make do as best we can. I will lead the Akkadian warrior wing myself if indeed we are attacked, though why Vardek would bother to attack the Akkadians is beyond me."

Melchadek rose. "The embarkation begins tonight, but it will take many hours to complete. Word is bound to reach Vardek's ear, and he will undoubtedly send a company of warriors to stop it. To do so, they must come down from the Golden Gates and pass through the Akkadian sector here—if you let them. If you, Malekh, refuse them permission to pass, they will attack you, and if your warriors resist, you may have the whole Toltec warrior wing about your ears. But whatever happens, they must not pass."

Malekh also rose. "No Toltec will pass through here, not if every Akkadian has to die to stop them. You may count on that!"

The news of the withdrawal of every priestess and seeress was quietly received. It had not been entirely unexpected. The story of the deaths and mutilation of the three junior seeresses had already crept from mouth to ear, and everyone had expected at least some reaction from the Sea Temple. The shame lay like a living cloud over the entire group of initiates. Such a withdrawal was a terrible stigma, an incredible indictment against the Temple of the Sun, and every priest of every grade felt the burden of that accusation as though it had been leveled against him personally.

At noon the Council of Priests met in the inner sanctum of the Hall of Learning to discuss the matter, though indeed there was little to discuss. What was written was written, and no amount of talk could erase a single line of it. After a subdued statement of facts the Council voted a decision and Zesta was summoned to appear before them. When she did so it was with an air of half-defiance, half-fear, with an admixture of guilt and insecurity.

"And what does the Council want with the High Priestess?" she said boldly. "Are you seeking a scapegoat for all this—am I to bear the burden alone?"

"Not alone, Zesta," said Helios quietly. "There is not a priest in the Sun Temple who does not share the responsibility of what has happened. We have all known and abhorred what was going on and yet each of us left it to someone else to deal with. Each of us could have done something within the limits of his grade, but we each failed to do so. The result of our negligence has been the murder of ten thousand Amarians; the murder of a priest, supposedly washed overboard; the murder of Demian, Vardek's erstwhile second-in-command; the murder of King Baralda; the murder of the captain of the King's Guard; the murder of the Lady Pirani; the murder of Khamadek, High Priest of the Sun Temple; the death of Baldek; the torture and murder of three seeresses who were under our care and protection—to say nothing of the foul and obscene rites practiced by Baldek and his followers within these very walls—and all because not once in fifty years has anyone had the courage to put a curb on Vardek's ambition! A terrible list of crimes, Zesta, and the responsibility of having failed to prevent any one of them is quite clearly ours, the Sun Temple priesthood."

"I am glad to hear you say so," she said calmly. For a moment a wild hope flared in her heart that she was not going to be called to account, but that hope soon died.

"However, your own position," Helios went on, "is quite different. While we are responsible for not having prevented the crimes, you, Zesta, encouraged, plotted, and even participated in many of them. Therefore it is the decision of this council that you be hereby removed from the office of High Priestess and banished from the temple for the rest of your life. A decree to that effect will be circulated within the hour. My own recommendation is that you go to Kumara and beg forgiveness."

"Never!" she said viciously. "I would sooner die!"

Helios shrugged. "It is either the mercy of Kumara or the mercy of Vardek. The choice is yours."

"Then I choose Vardek," she said haughtily. "He is a better man than all you priests put together!"

"Then so be it!" Helios summoned the captain of the Guard. "The Lady Zesta is no longer the High Priestess and is banished from the temple itself. Conduct her to her private chamber. You may allow her fifteen minutes to collect her personal belongings, and then you are to escort her off the premises. Please see to it that she is never allowed to set foot within these walls ever again!"

The captain made as if to take her arm but she shook herself free. "I will be back, Helios!" she snapped. "Be assured of that! And when I return, I will have Vardek and the whole army with me—and on that day I will personally see to it that you die a death so foul that men will speak of it with horror for centuries to come!" And she turned and strode for the door.

When the door had closed behind her, Deledian sighed and said, "Even now I find it difficult to believe that a high priestess of the Sun Temple could have fallen so low, and I fear that she meant every word regarding your own immediate future, Helios."

"No doubt she did, but I have a feeling that Zesta will return more quickly than even she supposes, and not quite in the manner that she has threatened. However, we will see."

Helios dispatched a guard to summon Herakos to the Council meeting. The elders raised their eyebrows at the sight of an Akkadian warrior chief in the temple, but they kept silent. A few minutes later the captain of the Guard returned to report that Zesta had gone.

"Good!" said Helios. "Now perhaps we can prepare ourselves. Firstly, I must advise the Council, and you, Captain, that Kumara has appointed Herakos, chief of the Akkadians, to be my personal bodyguard. Kumara seems to feel," he added dryly, "that I am in some danger."

"And he is right," said Deledian quickly, and the other members of the Council nodded in agreement. "And Kumara seems to have chosen well," he added, eyeing the stature of the giant Akkadian.

"He has indeed, and Herakos has already proved his value," said Helios. "Which brings me to you, Captain. I am afraid that Herakos and I owe you an explanation."

"Indeed, my lord?"

"You must be aware by now that one of your men is missing. I'm afraid that he stumbled upon one of the escaping seeresses and would have sounded the alarm if Herakos had not disposed of him."

"There was no other choice, Captain," Herakos put in. "If he had allowed the girl to continue on her way, he would be alive today. But he insisted on taking her to see you, and I understand that the normal procedure in such cases is for him to sound the nearest alarm."

"Which would have alerted Vardek's men and so would have jeopardized the entire exodus."

"But it was not my intention to kill him," said Herakos, "only to stun him, but his neck broke so easily in my hands."

The captain eyed the Akkadian, and in spite of himself he shivered a little—few necks would be safe in such giant hands. "Where is the body, my lord?"

"Over the cliff—we did not dare risk it being discovered by Vardek's patrols." The man was silent, and after a few moments Helios said, "Well, Captain, what say you to this?"

The captain smiled. "You need feel no worry on that score, my lord. I have long suspected him of being one of Vardek's men, but I could never prove it. It could even be possible that he was intending to take the girl to Vardek instead of to me."

Helios frowned. "Could he have been involved in the abduction of the three junior seeresses yesterday?"

The man shrugged. "We will never know, but he was certainly the most likely suspect."

"If you are right, Captain, then I shall feel no more remorse at his death. However, as you say, we shall never know. Anyway, here is Herakos, my bodyguard —not a man to trifle with. He has complete freedom of the temple—to go wherever he chooses, whether by day or by night. See to it that your men are advised."

"At once, my lord. Perhaps he would like to accompany me on my rounds. No doubt he will want details of our strengths and weaknesses."

"Thank you, Captain," the Akkadian said. "The sooner the better."

"You are expecting a fight?" said Helios.

The man nodded. "Yes, my lord, and so are you."

"You are right—which brings me to my next point. It is our opinion," he said, indicating the rest of the Council, "and the opinion of the Sea Temple, that Vardek will attempt to storm the Sun Temple, probably tomorrow—or if not tomorrow, then certainly very soon."

"It is tomorrow at dawn," the man said. "Banda has already let slip the word."

"Very well, then, here are your instructions. Get all the scribes and administrators, and their families, inside the Temple by midafternoon." He turned to Deledian. "Have the stores checked, give instructions particularly to fill every water cask in the temple. When that has been done, then close the great doors. Secure all embrasures, Captain, even those on the northern side, and deploy your men in siege positions. Report to me when all that has been done."

During the next two hours the temple buzzed with activity, and during it all Helios stood on the eastern ramparts gazing toward the warrior arena. One by one the scribes and administrators scurried toward the temple for refuge, and not once did any of Vardek's men interfere, even though word must surely have reached Vardek's ear by now. At last Herakos climbed the stone stairway to join him. "Is everyone in—is all secure?"

The Akkadian nodded. "Yes, it only remains to close and bar the great doors. Deledian waits your command."

Helios turned to the east. "Vardek's arrogance knows no bounds. I am perfectly sure he knows of our preparations and could have stopped them at any time these past two hours. He is playing with us—he wants us to tremble behind our barred doors, to spend the night in fear of his coming at dawn. Even now he still underestimates the priesthood. Very well, let us play out the game, Herakos. Come."

The Akkadian shaded his eyes. "Wait—what is that?" And he pointed to where a lone Toltec warrior came striding toward the temple with a bundle over his shoulder. The man stopped at the bottom of the great stairs, threw the bundle on the ground, raised his hand in a mocking salute, and strode away.

Helios turned to the stairway, and Herakos followed. They reached the courtyard just as two of the junior priests were carrying the bundle in. They laid it on the stone-flagged ground and stepped back. Deledian turned to them. "A message from Vardek," he said simply.

On the floor was the body of Zesta. A knife had been driven to the hilt between her breasts.

"That is Vardek's own knife," said Herakos calmly. "I recognize it."

Helios sighed. "I rather feared that Vardek would have no further use for her."

Deledian wrung his hands. "Another death! Every day the temple reeks of death!" He turned to Helios. "If you knew this would happen, then you have deliberately driven her to her death!"

"Peace, Deledian, peace! Her death is not on our heads. She had a choice—Kumara or Vardek. She chose, even as we have chosen. She has reaped the result of her choice, as we will reap the result of ours. But treat her body gently, let it be consumed by fire— there was a time when she was a worthy priestess."

He turned to the towering portal that bestrode the head of the giant stairs. "And then, Deledian, close the great doors. Our karma is soon upon us, I fear."

The sun had long set when Melchadek made his way down the lower slopes of the Sacred Mountain, heading for the Rmoahal sector at its foot. All about him was the brooding stillness of the darkness and the freshness of the Rutian air by night. Above him was the vast indigo canopy of the sky and the glittering brilliancy of the stars. As he drew near the Rmoahal compound the freshness of the night air began to be poisoned by the dank swamp mists that wreathed about the lower slopes.

The guard at the compound gates was alert and highly suspicious. There was an atmosphere in the air that had been making him increasingly nervous ever since he had come on duty. The impulse to plant his spear in the visitors's belly and ask questions afterward was very strong indeed. It was only the sight of the strange robes that made him hesitate. He had seen the white robes of the Sun Temple priesthood before, but this all-black robe and black hood was strange to him. It was as well he did hesitate, for when the stranger spoke it was in the Rmoahal's own guttural tongue, yet clearly he was a Toltec.

A few minutes later Melchadek was escorted under heavy guard to the shaman's hut. As he entered he heard a quick, smothered gasp from the far corner, and Melchadek smiled to himself. "Greetings, Dracombi," he said gravely. "A troublesome cough, I hear. You must let me send a potion to you."

"It is nothing," said the thick voice in the darkness. "A touch of swamp mist in my lungs, no more. Be seated."

Melchadek squatted on the dirt floor. "Do you know who I am?"

Dracombi chuckled. "No one moves in the night anywhere on Ruta without Dracombi knowing who moves and why. The dead keep watch for me. They told me a full hour ago of your coming. It is not often that a priest of the Sea Temple visits the Rmoahals."

The young priest smiled again. It had not been hard for the old rogue to guess that he had come from the Sea Temple. There were only two temples on Ruta, and the robes alone had told him that he was not from the Temple of the Sun. Dracombi was probably trembling right now lest he be asked to state his visitor's name and business. But he had not come to prick the old man's pride. Let him keep his mysteries; it did little harm. "You are well informed, Dracombi," he said quietly. "You are truly a great shaman. As you obviously know, my name is Melchadek and I come at Kumara's request to discuss grave business with you."

"And what can the Rmoahals do to aid the great Kumara?" The old man's voice was suddenly warmer, more friendly.

Melchadek shifted his position slightly. "Vardek has

sent the Rmoahal warriors back to their people, and the Akkadian warriors back to theirs. As you know, this is not because of any generosity on the Lord Commander's part."

"Vardek does nothing without payment," the old man agreed. "This we all know. Go on."

"The reason, as you also probably know, is that Vardek intends to storm the Temple of the Sun at the dawn and put the priesthood to the sword." There was silence for some time, and Melchadek waited patiently.

"This I also know," the old man lied, "but what has this to do with the Rmoahals? We are not of the Sun. You have your gods and we have ours. It has always been so."

"I, too, am a shaman of my people," said Melchadek. "I know that it has been a dream of the Rmoahal people since time began that they will one day throw off the bond of slavery, to free themselves from Toltec domination. I have come to ask whether Dracombi of the Rmoahals thinks that day has come."

Again there was a silence. The thought was a startling one to the old man. True, it was an old dream of the Rmoahals, but only a dream. "It is possible," he said cautiously, "but Vardek has many more warriors than the Rmoahals, and he controls the plateau. We would have to attack upward, and between us lie the Akkadians."

"Who are no friend to the Toltecs."

"And no friend to the Rmoahals either."

"Both Akkadian and Rmoahal dream the same dream, Dracombi."

"They are not slaves."

"But they groan under Toltec domination nonetheless, and they do dream the same dream as you. Tell me, Dracombi, is it not written that when two men dream the same dream they are as brother to each other?"

"And where is this thing written, Melchadek of the Sea Temple?"

"In the stars, Dracombi—it is written in the stars."

"And who can read the stars?" he said scornfully.

"I can," said Melchadek softly. "And I tell you of my own knowledge that it is so written."

Such was the authority in the young man's voice that Dracombi's heart leaped within his breast. "It is hard to believe," he said slowly.

"Perhaps so, but it is so written. Rmoahal is brother to Akkadian because they dream the same dream, but whether brother fights against brother or alongside him is up to Dracombi of the Rmoahals. Choose well, then, Dracombi, for these opportunities do not come too often, as you well know." He rose to his feet. "And now I must go." He walked to the door and paused. "As well as attacking the Sun Temple, Vardek may also lead his forces down to the lower slopes. If he does so, I have the word of Malekh, High Master of the Akkadian craft lodges, that the Akkadians will oppose him and refuse him permission to pass through their sector. Vardek will not tolerate such opposition. The Akkadians will fight bravely, Dracombi, but they cannot successfully oppose Vardek alone. But if the Akkadians and Rmoahals fought side-by-side, then who knows what great things you would achieve together. Choose well, Dracombi." And he stepped through the doorway and strode across the compound toward the great gates, and not a guard moved to stop him.

When darkness hid him from sight, Dracombi summoned the chief of the Rmoahal fighting wing. "Bulambi," he said slowly, "let the warriors eat their fill before dawn. There may be work for them to do before the sun is high."

Bulambi grinned in the darkness. He had been listening to the discussion in the shaman's hut and he knew Dracombi's cunning old mind very well—there would indeed be work to do.

Outside the Rmoahal compound, Melchadek picked his way across the lower slopes until he came to the flagstoned pathway that led down to the harbor area. He did not expect for one moment that the Rmoahals would join the Akkadians against Vardek, but all avenues to safeguard the emigration had to be explored.

At worst Dracombi might merely stay put and leave the Akkadians and Toltecs to fight it out. There was, however, just a chance that they would take at least some part in the day's events, and anything that would delay or hinder Vardek if only for a few minutes would be more than welcome. Nothing, absolutely nothing, must prevent the safe launching of the emigration. The death of ten thousand men would not be too high a price to pay.

The harbor was silent and dark. Melchadek frowned. Where were the guardlights? He could see the shadowy outlines of the long ships of Vardek's fleet drawn up alongside the harbor wall. There should have been at least three of Vardek's guards patrolling the area, each one with a flaxen torch, but there were no guards and no lights. He picked his way carefully to the pre-arranged spot and called a name softly through the darkness. Almost immediately a figure loomed up beside him. "You are late, priest," a voice whispered.

"A few minutes only; the night is dark. What is wrong—where are the guards?"

The Akkadian warrior captain chuckled. "We could not wait for you, priest, so we began without you. Do not look so alarmed. They are dead, all of them."

"And no noise?"

"Not a murmur."

Melchadek nodded approvingly. "You have done well—Malekh chose wisely." He looked up at the dark sky. "Even without the moon I judge it to be close to midnight now. Are the small boats drawn up?"

"Yes, all of them, but from the number of people who are going, it will take several trips to ferry them all to the mouth of the Naradek. It will be well after dawn before all are away. I hope your fleet is out there."

"So do we all, Captain," said Melchadek feelingly. "Give the signal to your men to begin scuttling Vardek's long ships, and send a runner to both Malekh and Kumara to tell them to start moving their people down. It will take about two hours to get them all safely down and into the harbor area."

"And half the Akkadian fighting force, twelve hundred warriors in all, will throw a ring of defense around the whole harbor area," said the captain, "to stop Vardek from interfering. This we have discussed a dozen times, priest, and still I say it is too small a force."

"Twelve hundred on the shoulder of the mountain, and twelve hundred here. Not enough, we know, but it is all we have. You will have to hold out for at least eight hours if Vardek forces his way down the mountain now. So pray you, Captain, that he sleeps at least a little longer before descending upon you!"

"That I will, Priest—and with feeling!"

Melchadek smiled. "Very well then, Captain, give your orders now. Let us not delay any further by even a minute."

Kumara stood with Marah in the center chapel of the Sea Temple that contained the Eternal Light. Normally the flame stood a mere two or three feet high, but now it towered above them to something like ten or twelve feet, and every so often a gush of extra flame would erupt from the well and spurt to twenty feet or more. The heat was intense and Kumara shook his head. "This stonework has withstood the rush of fire for untold centuries, but it will not last much longer at this rate."

"How long do you think, Kumara?"

"I do not know—a matter of hours, certainly. The whole heart of the mountain is being torn out by giant hands and squeezed upward toward us."

"In the bowels of the earth is the Living Fire," she said, quoting from an elemental ritual.

"Indeed, but the trouble is that it is not remaining in the bowels. It is rising toward us, and when it reaches the surface it will split the whole island into a million fragments!"

11

The Akkadian captain loomed up out of the darkness. "So far, all goes as planned, priest. The runners have been dispatched to Malekh and to Kumara —the first to go should be arriving within the hour."

Melchadek nodded. "There will be six hundred and forty souls altogether, Captain—twenty already on board the fleet, one hundred and twenty priests and priestesses, two hundred Akkadian civilians, and three hundred Toltec civilians—quite a few to handle."

"Which brings us," said the captain thoughtfully, "to the biggest problem of all—how to move three hundred Toltec civilians off the topmost plateau of the mountain right from under the noses of Vardek's guards!"

"We've been over the plan a dozen times and more."

"Oh, yes, we've been over it, but that of itself does not guarantee success."

Melchadek eyed the captain sharply. "You sound overly doubtful. Do you think we will fail?"

"We have succeeded a dozen times in our discussions, as you have said," the captain retorted, "but you will find it very different up there when we have to do it in reality. The slightest error in timing, the smallest cry, the faintest glimmer of light, a more than usually alert guard—any of these things could alert the whole army, and if that happens, not one of us will leave the plateau alive!"

"You are afraid?"

"Yes, of course—I always am before a fight. Any warrior worth the name knows the feeling of fear. The trick is not to let it influence your actions."

They were silent for a moment, and then Melchadek said quietly, "Tell me, Captain—you were one of the few Akkadian warriors, along with Herakos, who were invited to come with us on our journey to the new lands. Why did you refuse?"

The man shrugged. "Oh, many reasons, I suppose. Basically it is probably because I cannot accept that this whole island will be destroyed. I, too, can hear the rumblings beneath my feet—you don't have to be a priest to know that something is going to erupt at any moment. But I cannot believe that the whole island will go. There will be enough left to start again. Another reason is up there on the plateau—this might just be his day of reckoning, and if so, then I want to be among those who make it so."

"Vardek?"

The man nodded. "For too long he has strutted about this island like a god. His day has to come sometime, and maybe this is it. There will be a pitched battle before all this is over, and I might even be privileged to see him die; indeed, I have prayed to every god I know to let it be my hand that ends his life!"

"And for this you risk your own life?"

"Oh yes, priest, willingly—and there are many who think as I do."

Marah and Kumara left the Chapel of the Eternal Light and climbed the stone stairway to the western ramparts. "One of the things that I find incredible," said Marah, "is that three hundred Toltecs and two hundred Akkadian civilians have known of our plans for weeks, and yet not a single word has been leaked. It is proof of the wisdom of your selections."

"They were not all mine, Marah. Malekh chose most of the Akkadians and Helios most of the Toltecs."

"They were good selections."

"They were indeed, particularly those of Helios. If even one of his selections had been unwise, we would not have survived the first danger period." He pointed to the Sacred Mountain three miles away. "When Helios drew the Toltec scribes and administrators into the Sun Temple this afternoon, Vardek should have asked himself why three hundred apparently refused to accept the refuge offered. A careless word or even a gesture at that point would have roused his suspicions."

"Vanity?"

"Probably. It must have seemed to him that the

civilians were confronted with the choice of whether to show their allegiance to Helios and the Sun Temple, or to Vardek and the army. He must be feeling quite flattered that three hundred have seemed to choose him."

"Whereas in fact," she said thoughtfully, "outside the army itself only one chose to offer allegiance to Vardek."

"And was rewarded by a knife in her heart! Poor Zesta—was ever a priestess so misled! You saw it in the mirror?"

She nodded. "He did not even bother to listen to her explanation. He had already heard of her expulsion from the Sun Temple and she was therefore already of no further use to him. The moment she was ushered into his house—into the very room and to the very spot where you once stood, Kumara—he just simply drew his knife and threw it before she even had time to greet him, even as he threw a knife once at you."

"And this time he was not made to miss," he said heavily. "Poor Zesta—ambition makes a poor counselor indeed!"

One by one the Akkadian families were assembled on the road in the pitch darkness until all two hundred souls had been accounted for. No torches were allowed, lest they be seen from the plateau above, and in the darkness the children wailed in fear and could not be comforted. Malekh, the High Master, moved among his people with quiet words of hope and encouragement. "Take heart there, Danios—and you, Persepios. This night will not last forever. Tomorrow when the sun is high you will all be free men and sailing to a better life than you have had here. Take heart, my friends."

"If all goes well," one of them muttered.

Malekh frowned. "It will go well, Danios," he rebuked, "if all concerned make it so—including you. You are a fine craftsman, though a surly one. Think of the new temples you will build in the new lands, the new roads, the new craft lodges, and the new city. All will be new and fresh. Think of your new life, Danios, and take comfort."

"Tomorrow I may smile," the man grunted, "but today is not yet over. I could more easily smile today if I could be certain that there would indeed be a tomorrow for me or for any of us!"

One of the others laughed. "It's no good, High Master; every lodge has its man of gloom, and Danios is ours! All Akkadia has wondered how it is that such a surly man can carve a living joy into the stone he touches, but it is so. Perhaps he pours so much joy and beauty into his work that he keeps none for himself or for others!"

"And I have always wondered," Danios retorted, "how one who spends his life in senseless laughter, as you do, Persepios, can produce any worthwhile work at all!"

Malekh smiled. Danios and Persepios were the two finest craftsmen of stone in all Ruta and in due course would certainly rise to be craft masters of their art. Together they had grown up from childhood, together they had taken their apprenticeships, and together they had worked on the many projects entrusted to them. When the great carved stone portal of the Golden Gates was damaged by lightning, it was Danios and Persepios who together had repaired the damage so that no eye could tell the new carvings from the old.

"Peace, my friends!" Malekh laughed. "If this is indeed your last day, Danios, then all gloom is futile, and if it is not then any gloom at all is unworthy of the future that lies before you."

"I live today for today, High Master, and regardless of what the future may hold, it is today's events that affect me today. How can any Akkadian laugh at a time when our people are split in two, half to leave Ruta forever and half to remain, and with not one of us really knowing which half will live! Either you or I will die today, High Master, and neither prospect can raise a single smile in me."

Malekh took his hand. "You are a good man, Danios —and you too, Persepios. I spoke sharply just now.

Please forgive me. Will you perform one last task for me as your High Master?"

"Of course," said Danios gruffly. "What is it?"

"Lead my people down the mountain to safety. Danios shall represent the sadness of our parting, and Persepios shall represent the joy of your new life tomorrow. Will you do this for me, craftsmen?"

Danios grasped the old man's hand, made as if to say something, then turned and strode for the head of the column.

Persepios stepped forward and embraced the High Master. "He is full of love for you, Malekh, but cannot speak of it, even at your parting. You will remain in his heart all the days of his life."

"I know, I know," he said gently.

"And in mine, also, High Master."

"That I know too—and you and he in mine. Tell him, Persepios—tell him tomorrow, when you are at sea. He will want to know. And now, go you and lead my people to safety together."

Malekh gave the signal, the ranks of warriors presented the salute of honor, and the column moved off through the darkness down the mountain to the long ships and to the future that waited for them.

Dracombi stood at the door of his hut and sniffed the night air. There was more in the air tonight than merely the exodus of a pack of priests fleeing from an overdominant Toltec warrior chief—the very air and ground spoke of more portentous things. For the tenth time that night he knelt and put his ear to the ground and listened to the faint rumblings far beneath his feet. He rose and sniffed the air again. Was the mist more pungent than he remembered from yesterday? Was it hotter than he remembered? And the sea, too—why did the water move in that strange and restless way like a pot on a fire? And where was the moon, which should have been sailing full and clear across a starlit sky? Why had she hidden her face, and from whence had come those gray and swirling clouds? Too many questions, too many strange signs to decipher, but of one thing he was sure, one thing that every instinct in his being confirmed, that this dark night was the herald of a day in which great things would happen, and if so, then why should it not be a day in which the Rmoahal people would indeed rise up from slavery and overthrow the mighty Toltecs? Why shouldn't the Rmoahal dream come true, and why shouldn't he, Dracombi, be the one to make it so?

Bulambi came up out of the darkness and towered above him. "All is ready, Dracombi," he growled. "The warriors will rest now and rise a full hour before the dawn, as you commanded."

"Good, and then I, Dracombi, will lead them to greatness."

"Or to death!"

At first the old man could hardly believe that he had heard correctly. "What was that you said?" Never in all his time as shaman of the Rmoahals, a time that spanned the life of an ordinary man, had anyone ever uttered even a hint of criticism against him. "Take care, Bulambi," he added dangerously, "and remember that the dead have your soul in their care and that it is I who command them to keep it safe. One word from me and you die, Bulambi, and your spirit will be a plaything for the dead for all time! Take care, Bulambi!"

The huge chief of the Rmoahals trembled. The shaman's threats were no idle ones. He, Bulambi, had seen men die under the shaman's spells, die deaths so foul that even he, the greatest warrior of them all, trembled at the memory of them. "I do not oppose the shaman," he muttered, "but I do know that many a warrior will die in search of this greatness of yours."

Dracombi was not used to even implied criticism, but this was no time to quarrel with his warrior chief, the eve of the greatest battle that the Rmoahals would ever fight. "Have you then become afraid of death, Bulambi?" he jeered. "Do you now tremble at the thought of clashing spears?"

"Bulambi does not fear the battlefield, as you well

know, Dracombi," he growled, "but many of our finest warriors will die—perhaps too many."

"Too many? How can you speak of 'too many' when our freedom is at stake? It does not matter how many die if it secures our release from slavery!"

"It will be too many," growled Bulambi, "if there are none left to taste the freedom of which you speak!"

Dracombi struggled to keep his temper. Bulambi was the finest warrior chief that the Rmoahals had ever known. Under him every man fought like ten, and without him they would feel lost. "Tell me, great one," he said mockingly, "why you think that none would survive? What great spirit has come to you and whispered words of defeat? Tell me his name so that I may summon him from the dead to speak these dreadful words again! Speak, Bulambi, tell me what has caused you to tremble!"

"I do not tremble, Dracombi, and well you know it!" he growled angrily. "And it is to you that a great one has come and whispered false words!"

"The priest? The black-robed one from the Sea Temple?"

"I heard his every word, and he speaks lies! It is true that Rmoahal and Akkadian together might overthrow the Toltec, but what then? With our warrior force reduced, could we then stand against the remaining Akkadians? Remember, Dracombi, that a full twelve hundred Akkadian warriors will not be in the battle against Vardek on the shoulder of the mountain, but will remain in the harbor area, a short distance from this very spot on which we stand. What is to prevent them from storming this very compound? Who then could prevent them from slaughtering our women and driving off our cattle—and with our women gone, how could we then breed more warrior sons to continue the fight? He would lead us into death, this priest, and none would survive to taste this precious freedom!"

"He said that the Akkadian is our brother," said Dracombi softly, "because we dream the same dream of freedom. Would a brother creep behind our backs to take our cattle and kill our women?"

"Never in our history have the yellow-hairs ever called us 'brother' or even 'friend'!" Bulambi retorted. "Why now do they seek our friendship except to overthrow the red ones. When Vardek and the Toltecs lay dying, then the Akkadians will have no further need of their 'brother,' and then, Dracombi, they will turn on us while we are still weary from battle and far from our homes. I do not trust an ancient enemy who is too suddenly a friend!"

Dracombi smiled. "Your wisdom grows to match your strength, Bulambi," he said softly. "All this has come to my mind also. I said that tomorrow the Rmoahals will give battle, but I did not say against whom."

Bulambi frowned. "Your words have no meaning for me."

"Then let me explain. The Rmoahals will *not* join the Akkadians."

"Then to whom do we give battle?"

The old man bared his teeth in a hideous grin and whispered in his ear.

There was silence for some time and then Bulambi grinned hugely in the darkness and chuckled deep in his throat.

In deference to secrecy the bells of the Withdrawn Temple remained silent. The full company of priests and priestess was assembled in the great courtyard. Those who were due to leave, five score and four, were drawn up in ranks by the great gates. Those who were to remain, a mere two score and ten of the more aged and feeble, were seated in a half-circle behind a rostrum which had been placed in the very center. The two sections faced each other silently and sadly and waited for Kumara. At last he came, slowly and heavily, down the stone stairway and across the courtyard to the rostrum. The tall and regally beautiful Marah, High Priestess of the Sea Temple, came with him to guide his steps. Kumara, who had never hitherto worn his great age for other eyes to see, now wore it openly as a burden that had grown too heavy for his strength to bear. He who had always stood before them erect, strong, and full of vigor now seemed crushed with years. Marah helped him climb the steps of the rostrum and then stood back. Her eyes were dim with tears, and love, and pride, and unfathomable compassion for this great one who had borne the burden for so very, very long.

For some time he was silent, grasping the rail with trembling hands, his own eyes as moist as hers. At last he straightened up, and as he did so new vigor flowed into him. When he raised his arm it was a salute full of energy, a commanding salute of extreme authority. His voice rang through the temple as a clarion call that lifted every heart there assembled. "From those of us who will this day see the light face-to-face, I bring you greetings!"

"Greetings!" came the instinctive response from every throat.

"We who remain," he said more quietly, "have been granted the privilege of being allowed to lay down our burdens for a little while to rest—to die, even as our beloved temple itself will die with us. We have sailed the seas of this life for many a year engaged on the tasks entrusted to us, and now we are being allowed to return home to rest and gather fresh strength for the voyages to come." He looked around at the young faces before him and saw their tears. "Do not grieve for us, my friends," he said softly, "for we are going home, and we go with joy. It is we who have compassion for you, for it is you who must continue to live, it is you who must continue to bear the burden, it is you who are entrusted with the task of establishing a new temple in the strange lands to the east, it is you who must see to it that the light is not withdrawn totally from this world during the dark centuries to come, it is you who must be as a lamp set in the darkness for all men to see, and it is *we* who have compassion for *you!*"

He paused for a moment and then went on. "We know of the pain and hardship that you will suffer, we know of the long and seemingly unrewarding labor that you will have to undergo, and we know of the doubts and the weakening of faith that will often cloud your hearts and your minds. But we also know this, brethren of the Order of Narada, we *know* that despite the many mistakes that you will make you will, nevertheless, succeed in the phase of the great work that has now been entrusted to you. The light is being given into your care. You will be mocked and jeered at by those who think that they are a law unto themselves, and there will be many who will seek to destroy the light and yourselves, even as Vardek has tried to do here on Ruta. Also, from time to time, there will rise from your own ranks traitors who will seek to destroy you from within, even as Zesta and Baldek rose in the ranks of the Sun Temple. But despite all this, we know that the light has been placed in safe hands, we know that due to your care it will shine more abundantly among the nations of man, and we know that you will pass the teaching safely on to those who will come after you.

"Remember that religion is not the light itself. Religion is merely the outer form that contains the light, even as a lamp contains the flame. You will come into contact with other religions, each of which will profess to be the only true religion for mankind. You must remember that neither theirs nor yours has a monopoly on truth. *Any* religion that shows forth the light is a true religion, even if its ritual forms are different to all others.

"And remember, too, that as your knowledge and wisdom grow, the forms of your own religion must change to give a better expression of your new understanding. You must be constantly destroying the old forms and building new ones to contain your new ideas. Remember that any religion that does not change is one that is dying. Never be afraid to destroy the forms of your own religion, for if you do not, then the light will be withdrawn to seek a more adequate expression elsewhere, leaving your own religion as an empty shell with rituals that are but a mockery. The light is ever seeking greater and greater expression. See to it that you and your religion are adequate for its purpose.

"And never forget what has happened here on Ruta, and do not let the children forget it either. See to it that the record is available for all men to see for thousands of years, a record of what happens when priests and priestesses pay homage to the darkness that lurks in all of us, even the highest. Do not ever forget that Ruta's doom did not spring from the people or from the army, not did it spring from such as Vardek; the corruption sprang from within the temple, from the hearts and minds and attitudes of the priesthood itself!

"My brethren, the path that you tread is as straight as the blade of a sword and as narrow as its edge. Follow it steadfastly, looking neither to the right nor to the left, for on either side of the path are the lands of darkness from whence it is difficult to return if once you stray. Follow the path steadfastly and with honor even unto the perfect day which will surely come for each one of you. There is a blessing on all who serve!"

The venerable High Priest fell silent, and the robed priests and priestesses waited for him to continue. At last he looked up and said, "Go with the blessing of all of us who remain. Go with the blessing of the great inner plane beings who watch over us. Go with faith and go with hope!" He turned and stepped down from the rostrum unaided, and as he did so the great temple gates swung open. Kumara and Marah crossed the courtyard to the head of the stone outer stairway so that they could say their farewells to each and every one as the company of priests and priestesses moved out of the temple in single file into the darkness beyond. Netziachos was the last to leave, and she flung herself into Kumara's arms so fiercely that he staggered and almost fell. The tears were streaming down her face and she could not utter a single word.

"Peace, Netziachos, peace!" he said gently. "It is you and Helios who must now look after our people. My heart goes with you, child—farewell."

"And I will be in your dreams, Netziachos," said Marah softly. "If you need me, you have only to visualize my image and there I will be. My heart, too, goes with you and with all who set forth—farewell."

Netziachos turned and ran blindly after the others, and as the column moved through the darkness they heard from the temple behind them the strange and beautiful chant from the ritual of the fourth degree sung hauntingly and sadly by those whom they were leaving behind. The last two lines seemed to hang in the air all about them until long after they had left the Temple far behind.

Waft thou their souls down the River of Naradek.
Bring them to Light, and to Life, and to Love.

The first of the Akkadian refugees were already arriving in the harbor area, and without mishap. Those families with children were the first to embark in the fleet of small boats drawn up on the beach at the northern end of the harbor. The moon was still hidden behind swirling clouds, and the embarkation was carried out in pitch darkness.

"How goes it, Captain?" said Melchadek as a dark figure, cursing heavily, came stumbling through the darkness.

"The gods know I like children well enough, priest," he said wearily, "but these are fractious little animals!"

"It is strange for them, and frightening. They cannot understand."

"True enough. Anyway, they are all on board and ready to go. One hundred and twenty souls all told, in twenty boats. Six to a boat is enough when children are involved. The remaining eighty are all adults."

"Eighty Akkadians," mused Melchadek, "one hundred and twenty from the Sea Temple, and three hundred Toltecs. Five hundred in all remaining. We can risk only two more trips. From now on you will have to put fifteen to a boat."

"A tight squeeze."

"It will have to be. It will take two hours for the boats to paddle out and back again. Even three trips will take us until well after dawn. We cannot risk a fourth by cutting the numbers down—Vardek will be upon us even before the dawn. Give your orders, Captain—get this first wave away."

A few minutes later, amidst a bedlam of muffled shouts and curses, the squeals of women who had never in their lives set foot on a boat, and the cries and wails of bewildered children, the twenty small boats were thrust out into midstream to begin the long haul through the darkness downriver to the open sea. Among their number were six craftsmen of ships whose task it would be to bring the empty boats back upriver lashed together in single file ready for the second wave.

"So far, all goes well, priest," said the captain, coming up through the darkness. He was wet to the waist. "But if those screaming and helpless women don't cause a disaster, then it will be a miracle!"

"You have a poor opinion of women, Captain?" said Melchadek.

"They are all right in bed," he grunted, "or for cooking and rearing children, but they are fit for nothing else!"

Melchadek thought of Marah and smiled. Before he could say anything, however, a runner came through the harbor area. "A message for Melchadek!" he was calling softly. "A message for Melchadek!"

"Here! Over here!"

The man came up to them, still breathing heavily. "From Kumara to Melchadek, greetings!" he quoted. "Those chosen are now on their way to you." He hesitated for a moment, trying to remember the exact words. "From we who are already of the past, to you who are already of the future, greetings." He stumbled a little over his words. "Oh, yes, and then he said to tell you that there is a blessing on all who serve."

The captain shook his head. "Riddles! You priests do love your riddles! Why you cannot speak as other men do is beyond me!"

Melchadek ignored him. "When did they leave?" he said to the messenger.

"Scarcely an hour ago."

"So they will be with us within another hour. Good —the timing goes well. Come, Captain, let us to our next task."

The great Golden Gates towered above them so high that the topmost transverse beams were lost in the darkness of the night. The stone-flagged road rounded the shoulder of the mountain and ran the last hundred yards at a very steep angle up to the great gates. Over that last hundred yards the road climbed a hundred feet, a gradient that taxed even the strongest muscles. On one side of the road was a sheer drop two thousand feet to the boulder-strewn Naradek far below. The other side of the road hugged a smooth rock face that rose to the summit, to the plateau itself, as a vertical wall with not a crevice or a ridge to give foot- or handhold. That rock face had been kept deliberately smooth for centuries. Any invading army would not only have to attack up a very narrow and steep road, but would also have to batter down the gates themselves, for there was no other way of reaching the plateau—no other way that would be known to a mainlander.

The major portion of the Akkadian fighting force remained below the shoulder of the mountain. They would allow the three hundred refugees to pass through and then would close their ranks against any of Vardek's men who would seek to follow. Melchadek and twenty specially chosen warriors rounded the shoulder and climbed the last hundred yards to the great gates. The warriors hid themselves on either side of the gates, pressing themselves against the rock face so that they could not be seen from the watchtower above. Six of Vardek's men would be guarding the gates, only one of whom should be on the watchtower, alert. But even so, the task of breaching the gates was not an easy one, for they could not be opened from the outside. Massive though they were, the gates were beautifully balanced and could, by a system of chains and pulleys, be opened by one man alone, but that man had to be on the inside.

When the warriors were hidden, Melchadek and the Akkadian captain approached the towering gates. The priest stood boldly in the center of the road and held his black cloak slightly away from his body, and the captain hid behind him. From the spear slits in the gates themselves only one figure could be seen, that of a harmless unarmed priest.

"Guardian of the Gate!" shouted Melchadek. "Guardian of the Gate! Open up! I have urgent business with my Lord Vardek!" At first nothing happened, and then Melchadek could see a face at one of the slits. "Open up, I said! This matter is urgent!"

"Who comes at this time of night?" a surly voice answered. "Go away lest I put a spear in you!"

"I am Melchadek of the Sea Temple. I have an urgent message from Kumara, the High Priest, to Vardek, marshal of Ruta. Open up immediately— every second lost is vital!"

"All right, all right!" the voice grumbled. "Don't get yourself in a sweat! Wait a moment while I summon the guard."

"You dolt!" thundered the priest. "Do you think we have time to waste while you wake your drunken companions! Open up, I say!"

"I must summon the guard," the voice said stubbornly.

"If you waste one more second of my time, you oaf, I will have pleasure in informing Lord Vardek that when I arrived the guard was asleep and no one in the watchtower!" And he pointed upward. "Now, open the gates this instant!"

For a moment it seemed as though the man would still refuse, and the hidden warriors grimaced in the darkness. The Akkadian captain hidden behind Melchadek's cloak swore silently and fluently. But the threat had been an effective one. "All right, all right!" the voice muttered. "Calm down, priest—no need to go making threats!" And the face moved away from the spear slit. A few seconds later came the clanking sound of the gate chains, and as the great gates began to move ponderously open, Melchadek stepped forward through the gap, with the Akkadian captain creeping behind him. As they came through the gates, the captain leaped on ahead and rammed his short sword into the guard's back, and the man dropped without a sound. The twenty Akkadian warriors slipped in through the gates to join them.

The massive gates were open only a few inches. "Leave them like that," Melchadek whispered. "The fact that they are open may not be noticed from a distance. Get the other guards—quietly!"

The warriors slipped silently into the guard chamber, and before a single eye could open, began the slaughter. Most died without waking. Only one man burst from the chamber, his mouth gushing blood, but he too died before he had taken a single stride beyond the door.

"Good—well done, Captain," the priest said. "Now, remain here. If any of Vardek's men approach, they must die quickly, and above all, silently. I will summon the refugees."

He slipped away through the darkness and began to cross the plateau toward the houses and offices of the Toltec civilian administrators. At one point he paused and gazed ahead to where the Sun Temple stood barred and locked waiting for its fate. It gleamed white in the darkness, with a porticoed front and a domed roof. Great steps sunk into the sand led up to its entrance, where rose five pillars bearing its pediment. Melchadek sighed softly and then moved on.

The great house of the senior civilian administrator loomed out of the darkness, and Melchadek gave the prearranged signal and waited. The door opened a fraction and a voice said, "Who comes?"

"Melchadek of the Sea Temple. Are your people ready?"

"Yes, though few of us really believed that you would come."

"Then you will have learned a lesson in faith," he said simply. "Are all three hundred in there?"

"Yes."

"Good. Send them out one by one—quickly and

silently. The Akkadians hold the gates and wait your coming. Be quick!"

The door opened a fraction more, and a figure slipped out into the darkness, then another, and another. "Straight along the road," the priest whispered. "Hurry! The gates stand open, but not forever!"

For thirty minutes he stood silently by as the Toltec refugees hurried away one by one, and then, when only a few dozen were still to go, he approached the senior administrator and said, "Those who left first will be safely through the gates by now. I am leaving to join those who stand guard. Will you be the last to leave?"

"I will."

"Good, then I will look for you. When we see you approach, we will know that all are safe." He turned and joined the line of refugees. When he arrived at the great Golden Gates he saw a great many more Akkadians than the twenty he had brought with him.

"I brought up some reinforcements," the captain said. "We may have need of them. I have one hundred warriors here now."

"Very well, it is probably a wise move. How many refugees have gone through?"

"About two hundred. No trouble, none whatsoever."

"Good. One hundred to go. Another fifteen minutes, and we will have brought out all three hundred, without the loss of a single life!"

"None of ours, at any rate." The captain grinned.

At that precise moment the whole plateau, the great gates, the Sun Temple, the Toltec administration buildings, and the very road itself became bathed in a soft white light. The captain cursed and looked up to see the moon riding full and clear through a break in the clouds. "Look there!" he said, and pointed to where a long line of refugees could be clearly seen moving along the white ribbon of the road.

For a whole two minutes nothing happened, and then from the left came a shouted question. The Akkadian warriors moved forward toward the sound. Then came the clash of swords, shouts, and curses, and while one hundred refugees were still spread out along the road clearly visible for hundreds of yards, lights began to spring up in the Toltec warrior camp a half-mile away.

Another fifteen minutes would have seen them safe —a mere fifteen minutes—but already the harsh-sounding alarm was being sounded, and on the western rim of the plateau, near the Sun Temple, lights began to blaze in Vardek's house itself.

12

Vardek came bursting from his house, buckling on his sword as he ran. "Banda!" he roared. "Banda! By all the demons, where is that commander of mine! Banda!" It took him no more than ten minutes or so at a dead run to reach the warriors' quarters in the southeast segment of the plateau, by which time the entire camp was in an uproar, with men running in every direction, shouting and cursing, and above it all the alarm gong continued to pound harshly and deafeningly. Vardek grabbed the nearest warrior. "Where is Banda?"

The man shook his head stupidly. "I don't know, my lord," he stammered. "He went straight to the gates— that's where the trouble is!"

"Trouble? What trouble? Talk sense, man!"

"I don't know, but there is fighting!"

Vardek flung the man away. "You there, Captain. Pick fifty men and follow me! You there, throw a guard around this entire camp, and tell that fool to stop pounding that damn gong, the whole of Ruta must be awake by now! Stop these men scurrying about like frightened children! Get them to their positions! Move!"

The officers ran, shouting orders. Men responded, the gong ceased suddenly, men ran. "Captain!" barked Vardek. "Bring your men—follow me!" And he left the camp at a dead run with fifty battle-trained warriors at his heels. As he approached the great gates, he saw a desperate hand-to-hand fight going on between a few dozen Toltecs and what looked like at least a hundred Akkadians.

"Deploy your men, Captain," Vardek snapped. "I want those gates secure in ten minutes. You there— get back to the camp—my orders. Bring one hundred more men. All others to remain in camp. Alert! Move! Banda!" he roared, and a figure burst out of the melee and came hurrying up to him. "What is going on?"

The second-in-command was panting heavily. A great gash across his shoulder was flowing blood. Seven or eight Toltecs and as many Akkadians were already lying dead. "I still don't know!" he said breathlessly. "As far as I can make out, a detachment of Akkadians took the gates—probably by trickery—and slaughtered the guard company."

"Why?"

"I have no idea as yet, but we are trying to take one of the Akkadians alive, but they fight like demons. We trained them too well!" he added bitterly.

"When you get one, bring him to me! Who are those?" he said, pointing to the line of refugees.

"Toltec civilians—that's all I know. The Akkadians are trying to hold the gates until they all get out!"

"Has this whole world gone raving mad?" Vardek thundered. "Why should Akkadian warriors protect Toltec civilians? And why are Toltec civilians leaving the plateau anyway? What insanity is all this?"

Banda shrugged. "I've been a little too busy to ask polite questions," he said irritably.

"Get me at least one live one and kill the rest!"

"And the civilians?"

"Of course!" snapped Vardek. "But I want at least one of them alive as well. Get moving! Here come your reinforcements. Perhaps now you can drive these vermin out! Move!"

A hundred more of Vardek's men came swooping to the fray, and the Akkadians began to fall back toward the gates. As they did so, the last of the line of refugees, a dozen or so who were within a hundred yards of safety, hesitated as they saw the mass of struggling warriors edging toward the road in front of them. Some of them stopped, some turned back to flee, and some, a very few, made straight for the gates at a panic-stricken run. The Akkadian captain standing atop the gate-chain housing was shouting for the others to come on—there was still time—but they paid him no heed. He leaped to the ground with every intention of rushing out to rally the stragglers, but Melchadek grabbed him and pointed. "Look!"

Banda, too, had noticed the tail end of the refugee line scattering in all directions and had sent a dozen men to cut them down. "But they are defenseless!" protested the captain. "They'll be butchered!"

"It cannot be prevented," said Melchadek calmly. "We have done all we can. Recall your men, Captain. Get as many out as you can. We must close the gates in Vardek's face!"

The captain hesitated. He knew full well that some might not make it in time and would be trapped inside to be slaughtered. "Very well, priest—so be it!" And he leaped away, shouting orders as he ran.

A dozen warriors had remained by the gates, hurrying the refugees through as they came panting and staggering those last few yards to safety. Melchadek remained by the gate, motionless, arms folded, the one calm area in that sea of turmoil. One young woman carrying a child, breathless, frightened, clutched his arm. "My husband!" she screamed, and pointed back to where Vardek's men were already in among the panic-stricken remnants. He shook his head, gently prised loose her hand, and urged her through the gates. She clung on, but a warrior took her roughly and pushed her through. A middle-aged man, the senior administrator, his face red, gasping, came staggering up and almost collapsed. "Most!" he gasped. "Most of them! More than we expected!" Melchadek helped him to his feet and motioned him through, the very last of the civilians to reach the gates and safety.

"And now you," he said calmly to the dozen warriors. "Outside—stand ready to close the gates. As each of your companions comes through, he must join you. It will take fifty at least to heave it shut. Once the gate is closed, the spare swords are to be hammered into the ground up to their hilts, up tight against the gate itself, so that not even a hundred Toltecs could heave it open again. Go! You can tell the tale later of how a hundred Akkadian swords held at bay the entire Toltec fighting force!"

The men grinned and obeyed him, and Melchadek turned back calmly to watch the scene. Already a dozen civilians lay slaughtered, and as he watched he saw a woman, more fleet than the rest, finally be run down by a racing warrior. The man slashed his sword across her back. She stumbled, fell—the warrior grabbed her hair and hacked at her throat. Even at that distance Melchadek could see the blood spurt high as she sank down and sprawled lifeless in the sand. But he also saw two civilians, a man and a woman, together, perhaps man and wife, be taken, helpless, struggling but unhurt, back to the Toltec line.

The remaining Akkadian warriors, some eighty of them in line abreast, shields up in front of them as a solid unbroken metal wall, were falling back fast toward the gates. As another one fell, hacked to the ground, the line closed up, still moving backward. The advancing Toltec line, stabbing, cutting, thrusting, had perforce to advance stumbling over the dead, both Toltec and Akkadian. The captain was in the very middle of the line, shield up, sword thrusting outward, hacking, stabbing, his face and head covered in blood from a spear that had all but taken his life. Suddenly he barked an order, and the entire Akkadian line turned and raced for the gates, taking the Toltecs completely by surprise. At the gates a dozen turned at bay, shields up, swords out, while the rest slipped through the gates to safety. The Toltecs howled their rage and fell on the dozen furiously, but in that enclosed space they could put no more than a dozen or so of their own up front. An Akkadian fell, transfixed by a spear—a Toltec fell, his mouth gushing blood—another Akkadian staggered,

blinded by a sword slash across his eyes, his shield arm
fell, a spear thrust into his stomach—he charged blindly forward, momentarily scattering the Toltec line, dying
as he charged, falling, his arms flailing.

The captain seized this opportunity, barked another
order, and the remaining Akkadians turned and raced
the last few yards to the gates. Melchadek turned and
slipped through before them. "Close the gate!" he commanded. "Now!" And fifty or more Akkadians threw
themselves against the massive timbers and heaved it
inch by inch just as the last of their companions came
racing through. Three Toltecs also made it through before the gap became too narrow, but these died in
seconds, hacked to the ground by a dozen men. The
captain leaped to add his own weight to the heaving
line, and slowly, fraction by fraction, the great gates
closed in the faces of the howling Toltecs—and a dozen
Akkadian swords rammed home to keep it so.

The silence was eerie, almost unnatural. The wind
had dropped an hour ago, and the water was so
smooth and the night so dark that it was difficult to
tell how far they had come. In the prow of the leading
boat, Danios, the craftsman, was beginning to get a little
worried. They should have reached the sea by now,
but if this was the sea, then it was remarkably still
—and if so, then where was the fleet?

There was a muffled hail from the boat astern, and
an exchange of voices. One of his men came forward
and knelt beside him. "Persepios wants to know where
we are."

"Tell him we are at sea. Where else!"

"He has probably already worked that out for himself!"

"Then tell him to ask a more specific question."

"He already has. He wanted to know how long a small
boat loaded with women and children would continue
to stay afloat in the open sea if the wind suddenly
rises again?"

Danios smiled grimly. "Tell him that it is a good
question."

The man waited. "He wants an answer, Danios."

"So do I!"

"But what do I tell him?"

Danios turned and thrust his face close. "Tell him," he said irritably, "to keep paddling and to stop wasting my time with questions that he knows perfectly well cannot be answered! Just tell him to keep paddling!"

The flotilla slid on through the darkness with still no sign of the waiting fleet. One of the risks that Melchadek had taken was to give orders to the secret fleet that they must show no lights lest they betray their position to Vardek's lookouts on the plateau of the mountain. The risk that the small boats might not find the fleet at all had seemed small, but no one had bargained for so dark a night.

Danios counted one hundred more paddle strokes and then gave the order to give way. The twenty small boats came together, pitching and rolling slightly under the swell. Persepios' boat came alongside, and his friend leaped aboard. "Well, what now, Danios? Do we return, or what?"

"Return to what?"

Persepios ran his hands through his long hair. "I know, I know, but we can't just sit here and wait for the sea to finish us. If we return, then at least those on shore will know that all is lost and we can take part in the fight."

Danios pointed to the women and children. "Do they take part in the fight?" he said softly.

"No, but they may survive. Vardek is not stupid. Where is the future if it is not in the women and children! A great many warriors will die tonight. How will Vardek replace them without women and children?"

"If they were Toltecs, I would agree with you, but they are Akkadians, and I don't think Vardek cares one jot for the future of Akkadians."

"Then we die here at sea or die on shore—it doesn't seem much of a choice."

At that precise moment the darkness gave way to a soft silvery light. Persepios gave an oath and sprang to his feet, pointing to where the moon was riding clear and full in a break in the clouds. "The moon! By Narada, the moon!"

For a wild moment their hopes sprang high, but as they gazed seaward their hearts sank, for still there was no sign of the fleet from horizon to horizon—and then suddenly a shout, a chorus of shouts, fingers pointing, and there, close inshore, riding at anchor, were the long dark shapes of the seven ships of the secret fleet.

Vardek and Banda strode out onto the lookout point, a huge flat-topped boulder that jutted out from the very edge of the topmost plateau of the Sacred Mountain. From that vantage point could be seen the whole harbor area two thousand feet below, the long silvery ribbon of the Naradek as it made its way to the sea, and the sea itself for many a mile up the coast. "What is it?" growled Vardek. "This had better be important!"

The lookout guard swallowed nervously. "There, my lord!" And he pointed down to the harbor area, where even in soft moonlight it could be seen as a hive of buzzing activity. "I have counted nearly twelve hundred Akkadian warriors drawn up in a circle around the whole area, and there are civilians there too who seem to be waiting for something." He pointed out to sea. "And there, my lord—seven ships close inshore, and those tiny black shapes around them are small boats, I'll swear to it, a dozen or more!"

Vardek frowned. "What do you make of it? You've been watching!"

The man shrugged helplessly. "I don't know, my lord. At first I thought it was an invasion from the mainland, with the small boats bringing the warriors ashore, but that doesn't make sense. There are priests and priestesses from the Sea Temple down there in the harbor, to judge from their robes, as well as civilians. I think they are using the boats to get out to the fleet there, and the Akkadians are protecting them from interference. I think it is an escape, my lord, not an invasion."

"Escape from what?" said Vardek irritably.

"From you, Vardek," said Banda suddenly, "from

the army, and an escape from this so-called doom that is supposed to be hovering over Ruta."

"Rubbish! If that were the case, then why have they not used our own fleet?"

Banda rubbed his chin thoughtfully. "Because our own ships would need at least two days to prepare for sea, and we would hardly have granted them two days without interference. Indeed, two days would barely be enough. All the oars and the sails themselves are all in the storehouses, and there is no water or food on board any of them. They must have spent months building their own ships—probably up the coast somewhere; it would be easy enough."

"Bring the prisoners here!" barked Vardek suddenly. "We'll soon get to the bottom of this!"

The two Toltec civilians, brother and sister, and an Akkadian warrior were hauled roughly onto the lookout point. The warrior had a great gash running from his right shoulder down across his chest and stomach to his left hip. He was weak from loss of blood but still defiant. "The great Vardek is beginning to wake up at last!" he sneered.

Vardek pointed below. "Explain!" he said curtly.

The man shrugged. "What is there to explain? It should be obvious now even to you. The Sea Temple priesthood, with the help of Akkadian craft masters, built those ships there. They will carry the entire Sea Temple priesthood, plus two hundred Akkadian and three hundred Toltec civilians, to the strange lands to the east."

"Why?"

"Because the priesthood say that by tomorrow Ruta will no longer exist."

"And you believe them?"

The man hesitated. "Frankly, no, but many do."

"Fools!" He stamped his foot on the ground. "Isn't that solid enough for them! Do they think that this is all going to melt away by priestly magic—an entire island? Fools!"

"Maybe, maybe not," said the warrior sullenly. "But

I do know that all this"—and he waved his arm to the scene below—"has finally brought the Akkadian fighting wing to its senses. For too many centuries we have done your fighting for you, built your ships, built your roads and your fine houses, forged even the very weapons with which you fight, and as reward we have received nothing save your insults and your contempt, Vardek, but not anymore. There are two and a half thousand Akkadian warriors on Ruta, each of whom now wants only one thing from life, and that is to see you dead, Vardek!"

"Me?" he roared. "Do you think that a rabble of long-haired yapping dogs are any match for us Toltecs! By Narada, it seems that everyone on this damned island needs a lesson, and before this day is out, they will get it!" He turned to his second-in-command. "Banda, I will keep five hundred men only to take the Sun Temple, and by noon there will not be a priest alive here on the plateau. You take the rest of the army and teach those Akkadian dogs a lesson! Then get the fleet to sea. Never mind the sails, or the food and water. Break out the oars only. I want to see that fleet heading downriver by dawn. Catch those renegades. Kill every priest and priestess on board, and bring the civilians back. By Narada, I'll teach those fools to defy me! Do you understand?"

"Yes, Vardek. It will be done."

The Akkadian warrior smiled to himself—Banda might find it difficult to carry out his orders. He was going to meet one or two surprises on the way down the mountain, and even if he did win through, he might find it very difficult indeed to take a scuttled fleet to sea. But let him find that out for himself. The Akkadian glanced at the two Toltec prisoners. The girl was terrified, and so too was the boy. They knew that they were going to die—the knowledge was in their faces. It was different for him; he had spent all his life knowing that he was going to die. A warrior was trained from childhood to die with honor, with courage, and without fear.

"What shall I do with these?" said Banda.

The Lord Commander hardly glanced at them. "Kill them," he said, "and throw their bodies over the edge —they are of no use to us."

They died even before the import of his words could sink in. Banda signaled the guards, and they just simply thrust their swords into their backs, dragged the bodies to the edge, and tossed them over—a matter of a few seconds only.

The Akkadian sighed. His only regret was that he would not live to see Vardek die. But at least he could choose the moment of his own death and not wait tamely for a sword in his back. In a sudden swift movement he was free of the guards and ran the few strides to the edge of the precipice. "You too will die today, Vardek—be assured of that!" he said, and stepped calmly over the edge.

A dozen men clambered down the smooth rock face and yanked out the Akkadian swords that were holding the gates. The massive timbers creaked as the great gates swung open. The long columns of over five thousand battle-trained Toltec warriors began to move down the road with Banda at their head. A scouting party was sent on ahead but soon returned. "The road is barricaded with boulders," the senior among them said. "It will not be easy."

"How many Akkadians?" said Banda.

"Difficult to say—about twelve or fifteen hundred."

The Akkadians had just over two and a half thousand men under arms, as Banda knew. If there were twelve hundred in the harbor, then there must be twelve hundred here on the shoulder of the mountain. Twelve hundred against five thousand, but the road was narrow and he could not bring more than a tenth of his force into action at any one time—and the barricade made things even more awkward.

Banda gave his orders. The column halted, and Banda himself and his group of captains moved on down the road. As they rounded the shoulder, Banda's heart sank. The barricade was enormous, standing over twelve feet and comprising great boulders that had obviously been pulled and rolled down the mountain face. The Akkadians must have been working frantically to have achieved so much since dusk.

"Herakos!" he roared. "Herakos, show yourself! I would speak with you before it is too late! Herakos!" A figure rose on top of the barricade, and even at that distance and in that pale moonlight it was obvious that the figure was not the warrior chief of the Akkadians.

"I would speak with Herakos, old man—go and fetch him!"

"Herakos is not here!" the figure called. "You will have to speak with me!"

"And who are you?"

"I am Malekh, High Master of the Akkadian craft lodges. In Herakos' absence I command the Akkadian warrior wing!"

"Malekh!" one of the captains muttered. "What is that old fool doing leading warriors—he doesn't know one end of a sword from the other!"

"Maybe not," said Banda, "but he has twelve hundred warriors who do." Aloud he called out, "Where is Herakos?"

"In the Sun Temple," came the surprising reply.

Banda shook his head. He did not understand any of this, but if Herakos was absent, then so much the better. The Akkadians without their warrior chief would be the poorer force. "Tell your men to lay down their arms, Malekh, and dismantle this barricade. If you do, then I promise you that no harm will come to you or any of your men!"

"Toltec promises are worth nothing!" came the retort. "The barricade remains. Take it if you can!"

"I have five thousand warriors, Malekh. You cannot withstand us for long. All your men will die!"

"And many of yours too, Toltec!"

Banda was suddenly exasperated by the whole thing. "So be it then, you old fool!" he shouted. "By dawn there will not be a single Akkadian warrior left alive!"

A few minutes later the column rounded the shoulder and charged the barricade. Shields out, swords up, yelling ferociously, the Toltecs poured onto the barricade, climbing up, hacking and thrusting at the densely packed line of defenders. But the Toltecs were at a disadvantage. They had to climb upward, slowly, over piles of loose boulders, thrusting upward against figures that were only half-revealed behind the topmost line of rocks, climbing up against a forest of long spears that thrust downward against them.

And soon men began to die—a trickle of death at first as the fiercest and bravest reached the top, to be hurled back lifeless on top of those who followed; a trickle that became a river, and then a torrent of death. Soon the barricade was littered with Toltec dead, and so far not an Akkadian had died. But then one giant of a warrior picked up the corpse of his dead companion and with a mighty heave he threw the body up and over the top, scattering the line of defenders at that point, and the giant sprang into the gap, to be joined in seconds by a dozen more. And soon Akkadians began to die also, and the barricade began to run with blood.

The captain came up to Melchadek. "The fighting has begun! Five thousand Toltecs, the runner says. The barricades will not hold for long!"

"Long enough," said Melchadek. "Look there, Captain!" Rounding the bend in the river came the twenty small boats.

"By Narada—they're empty!" breathed the captain excitedly. "Your fleet is there!"

"I never doubted it. Get the next batch down to the beach—the eighty remaining Akkadians and two hundred and twenty Toltec civilians, three hundred in all —no more. That will leave fifty Toltecs to go with the priesthood on the last trip."

The captain leaped away, shouting orders. Melchadek nodded quietly to himself. The captain was a good man; it was a pity that he was remaining to die. He waited until the boats had grounded and until the next batch were all assembled and being helped aboard, and then he turned and crossed the harbor to where the Sea Temple priesthood were assembled, quietly waiting. "Greetings!" he said softly. "As you can see, all goes well. But we do not have much spare time. Those boats will not return until well after dawn. We have to hold off Vardek's army until then. Even now five thousand Toltec warriors are trying to break through the Akkadian line."

"Will they succeed?" said one of them quietly.

"Yes, eventually, but whether they break through in time is a question that none of us can answer. The Akkadians are brave warriors, but they are heavily outnumbered."

Netziachos stepped forward. "And what of Helios?" she said.

"He is still in the Sun Temple, as you know. At dawn he in the Sun Temple and Kumara three miles away in the Sea Temple will perform a joint ritual of invocation of the Elementals. Once that has been done, he will be free to make his escape as best he can—and don't forget that he has Herakos to protect him."

"One man against an army!"

"But the best there is. No one on Ruta is more fitted to the task than Herakos."

Netziachos looked grim. "Vardek intends to attack the Sun Temple at dawn. Helios and Herakos have not only to escape from a temple which is under attack, but also to make their way down the road through five thousand of Vardek's men, through a full-scale raging battle, and reach the harbor here before the boats return! It is asking too much!"

"Whether it is too much, only Narada knows. We can only wait and pray." Melchadek could see that the girl was near to tears. He took her hands and drew her away from the others. "Netziachos, I cannot believe that Helios is fated to die here on Ruta, and you must not believe it either."

"But he—"

"And furthermore," he went on firmly, "you are the new High Priestess. It is up to you to set an example of courage and indeed of faith!"

"It is not easy. . . ."

"No one said it was going to be easy! Kumara and Marah had sufficient faith to choose you as High Priestess, and I believe they could have made no wiser choice. Don't let us down. Believe in the ultimate success, believe in it firmly and unwaveringly, and it will surely come to pass."

She blinked back her tears. "I'm sorry—it's just that I have never been through anything like this!"

"Nor have any of us. Some of the junior seeresses must be feeling very frightened. A word from you would give them courage."

"Yes . . . I'm sorry . . . I'll do what I can." She took his hand. "Thank you, Melchadek—I'm all right now," and she turned and rejoined the others.

Melchadek stood watching her moving among the junior seeresses, her head high, a smile on her lips, speaking calmly now to one, now to another. He nodded to himself, satisfied. Her moment of near crisis had come and gone.

The captain came up to him. "Right, that's the second lot away."

Melchadek turned and saw the flotilla of small boats once more set off downriver. He looked at the sky. The moon was low and already the eastern sky was pale. "It will be first light soon, Captain. See to it that your men are fed."

"Yes, now would be a good time, though most of them will not feel like eating while their companions are fighting. They feel that we should go to their aid."

Melchadek shook his head. "The harbor area must be defended, and no more than a few hundred can be in the fight at any one time. Our plan is still the best."

"It doesn't feel like it, just sitting here," and he strode irritably away to supervise the ration issue.

Thirty minutes later came a shout from the guard, running figures, more shouts, and the captain ran to investigate. Melchadek followed him more slowly. At the outer perimeter of the harbor area a man was gesticulating excitedly. "What is it, Captain?"

The Akkadian turned, his eyes gleaming. "The Rmoahals are coming!"

Even as he spoke, the first of the long column of giant black Rmoahals rounded the base of the mountain. At their head was a litter bearing the wizened form of Dracombi, and beside the litter strode Bulambi, the most terrifying warrior in all Ruta. Six abreast the warriors strode, their plumed headdresses tossing, their skins glistening with animal fat. As they drew level with the Akkadian outpost, Dracombi signaled the column to halt. "Ho, priest!" he called. "As you see, the Rmoahals listened to your words and found them good."

"What's all this?" the Akkadian captain whispered.

"Reinforcements, Captain," the priest said calmly. "I did not want to raise your hopes by mentioning it earlier, but the Rmoahals are marching to join the Akkadians against the Toltecs." He stepped forward onto the road. "Greetings, Dracombi," he said gravely. "Your warriors are a welcome sight."

"There are some who will not welcome us!" the old man chuckled. "How goes the day?"

Melchadek pointed upward. "On the shoulder of the mountain, five thousand Toltecs attacking down against twelve hundred Akkadians. Make haste, Dracombi!"

"The Rmoahals are not slow to battle!" he retorted. "Send one of the yellow-hairs ahead with the news lest those above think we come as enemies not as friends."

The captain grinned and barked an order to a near-by warrior, and the man set off at a run. He turned to the shaman. "Malekh, the High Master, commands our forces above. He will welcome your help."

"We dream the same dream, yellow-hair. Ask the priest there." And he waved the column forward.

Over two thousand Rmoahal warriors the captain counted as the long column moved on up the road. "More than enough!" he said gleefully. "The Toltecs' reign on Ruta is surely ended now!"

Melchadek looked up at the sky. "It is dawn, Captain," he said quietly. "The dawn of the last day."

But the captain did not hear him.

13

Marah and Kumara stood on the rostrum in the Hall of Learning in the great Sea Temple and faced the assembly of priests and priestesses who had elected to remain. A shaft of early sunlight crept in through the eastern embrasure, highlighting the dancing motes of dust. The faces of the assembly were grave.

"It is dawn," said Kumara simply. "The dawn of the last day. All that needs to be said has already been spoken. Marah and I have one last task to perform, but you are all free to spend these last moments as you wish. We have achieved a great deal, and I thank you for your help, your loyalty, and your trust. There is also a great deal that has not yet been achieved, but this must be left for those who come after us."

He paused for a moment and then said quietly, "The seedbearers have set forth, and we who nurtured that seed can now rest from our task knowing that we have not failed."

He and Marah stepped down from the rostrum and passed among them saying their farewells. When they had gone, those who remained split up quietly. Some retired to their private chambers to meet their end in meditation; some gathered quietly together in group prayer; and some went out from the temple to walk among the mountain flowers in the sunlight on this the very last morning of their world.

Helios and Herakos stood on the eastern ramparts of the Sun Temple. The early sunlight was strong in their eyes. Below them, outside the temple, Vardek's men waited for the command. "How many do you make it?" said Helios.

The Akkadian shaded his eyes. "Just over five hundred, which means that over five thousand have been sent to take the harbor."

"Will the Akkadians hold out?"

"Long enough."

Helios smiled. "At least we are sure of one thing—everything must be going as planned, otherwise Vardek would not have detached almost his entire army. Come, it is time to go."

He and Herakos made their way down the stone stairway to the great courtyard below. There the frightened priests were milling about, not knowing what to do or where to go. The Temple Guard were waiting quietly at their posts, a strong detachment by the great doors themselves. "The guards bear themselves with more dignity than these so-called priests!" said Helios disgustedly.

"There are some without fear," said Herakos, pointing to where the Council members had gathered quietly to one side.

Deledian broke away from the group and came over to them. "Greetings, Helios—and you too, Herakos."

"Greetings, Deledian. You and your council seem to be the only priestly men in this entire temple!"

Deledian glanced at the milling horde. "Try not to judge them too harshly, Helios. They are young and afraid of death."

Helios snorted. "A man who is afraid of death does not make a good priest! Is everything ready here?"

"As ready as we will ever be. The Temple Guard are all in position, and some of the younger priests will bear arms alongside them. Will you call them together and tell them of the emigration and that they were considered unworthy to be included?"

"No. It will be no comfort to them to know that others will survive while they die, nor would it serve any purpose that I know. They have lived in ignorance, let them die in that same state!"

Deledian hesitated. He had a reverence for the truth, and it seemed to him a grave injustice to keep the truth from those about to die—but then he sighed and nodded. As Helios said, such a truth would bring no comfort. "In that case there is nothing more we can do save wait. You are still going to perform the special ritual?"

"Yes, in my private chamber, and I must away to it

now. Farewell, Deledian. You are one of the few here in the Sun Temple who is worthy of the name of priest. As to the rest, give them what comfort you can when the time comes. They will die hard, I fear, and there is nothing you and I can do to stop it!"

"Farewell, Helios," the old priest said quietly, "and you too, Herakos. We will keep Vardek at bay as long as we can. My thoughts go with you!"

The dead littered the barricade on both sides, and Malekh watched men die by the score. Never in his long life had he ever seen a battle, nor even seen a single man die violently. Like others, he had listened to the warriors' tales of battles fought on the mainland to the west, tales of courage and of death, and he had seen the half-healed wounds of those who had lived to tell of it. But the tales were told by those who had exultingly survived, and as such they spoke of courage and of honor and of the glory of battle—but there were no tales from the dead, no stories from those whose entrails were ripped from their bodies to spill bloodily to the ground to trip their owner as he tried to fight on, no tales from those who knew the staggering and blinding pain of a spear thrust that smashed the ribs and drove on inward to split the heart asunder, and no stories of honor from those whose limbs had been hacked from their bodies and who had been left to die the slow foul-smelling death of rotting flesh as they lay amidst the carnage and corpses of a morning's glory. Malekh had listened to the tales of those who had survived, and in his secret heart he had often envied the warrior life, and now at long last he had tasted the experience for himself, and it had left him gasping and shaken, filled with a horror that he could not have begun to describe.

During those first few seconds of carnage on top of the barricade he had been sprayed with blood from the torn throat of a Toltec warrior who had died at his feet, and he had been violently and retchingly ill, vomiting again and again until there was nothing left to bring up, and still men continued to die all around him, hacked to the ground, their chests torn open, their throats gaping, tongues protruding hideously in death, blind eyes glazed and open, hands tearing at the jagged rocks in their death throes. He had cried out agonizingly, gasping for air that did not reek of blood, and they had borne him gently away down off the barricade to a safe spot at the rear. A young, warrior, barely seventeen, had gazed down at him pityingly. "He should not be here, poor old man! Why don't they take him below!" And they propped him up against a rock and left him to watch the horror.

The Toltecs had gained a footing on the very top of the barricade. A giant warrior, his sword flailing, had already hacked the life from three defenders, and more Toltecs were scrambling to join him. The young Akkadian, who only a few seconds ago had been helping to carry Malekh away, was now back on the barricade, scrambling upward toward the giant. He poised for a moment and then sprang the last few feet up and under the giant's guard, desperately thrusting his sword into the Toltec's stomach. The giant roared in agony, plucked the youth from below him, swung him up bodily over his head, and hurled him to the ground below. Malekh saw the boy's head smash against a rock, saw the brains spill out of the cracked skull, saw the white splinters of bone thrust out through the cheeks as the jawbone was crushed, saw the eyes wild with desperate pain at that moment of death, and Malekh rolled over and was sick yet again.

But the giant, too, paid for his bravery. In order to pick up the boy, he had dropped his own sword, and now a trio of more battle-hardened warriors were upon him. He plucked the boy's sword from his side, but before he could use it, an Akkadian knocked it from his hand. A spear thrust into his throat. A sword slashed across his chest, and he grabbed at it blindly, tugging it from the defender's grasp, slashing his own fingers on the blade as he wrenched it free. Another sword slashed at his knees, a spear buried itself deep in his chest, and with a wild bellow he came lunging down the barricade, Akkadians cutting and stabbing at him as he fell—and with blood pouring from a dozen mortal wounds he crashed to the ground and died on top of the body of the boy he had slain but a few seconds earlier.

A shout from the rear, a runner came panting through the ranks. "The Rmoahals are coming!" he cried out. "Hold on a little longer! The Rmoahals are coming to join us!"

The Akkadians took fresh heart. A captain barked an order, and a few minutes later, when the column of black Rmoahals arrived, the Akkadian ranks opened to let them through. Dracombi's litter was set down in the very middle of the Akkadian force. "Greetings, Malekh!" the shaman cackled. "The Rmoahals are come to release you from your dream!" And before anyone could stop him, the giant Bulambi strode over to the Akkadian High Master, lifted his head, and slashed his throat from ear to ear. Malekh, High Master of the Akkadian craft lodges, felt the agonizing pain of death, a pain that burned like sharp ice. His eyes turned to the boy, and in that moment of time he experienced the truth that had lain behind all the warriors' tales that he had heard, the pain, the blood, the agony, the sweat, and the filth of battle; and then came the roaring in his ears, the blackness that welled up inside him, the terrifying gulf of nothingness into which he fell shrieking and gasping, the scene vanishing as he slid into a warrior's death.

Even as Bulambi had strode toward the High Master, the Rmoahals had turned and sprung upon the Akkadian ranks. Too quick, too suddenly treacherous for instant reaction; in those first few seconds, a hundred Akkadians died, battered to death by the giant Rmoahals; then a hundred more, and yet another hundred, and still the Rmoahal column was arriving. With the Toltecs above them, and the Rmoahals among them and below them, the Akkadians had nowhere to retreat. Butchered, slaughtered, hacked to pieces, the remnants of them were split into separate groups, each group desperately fending off the shrieking battle-crazed Rmoahals.

On top of the barricade, Banda signaled for the Toltecs to stand firm—let the Rmoahals finish them off. He stood and watched the last few minutes of the utter carnage below. He saw group after group be swamped and overrun by the raging Rmoahals. He saw individual Akkadians try to run, only to be pulled down and slaughtered. Death after death he watched, until the roadway for a hundred yards and more was piled high with bodies; and he saw rivulets of Akkadian blood cascading down the rocks, to pour over the edge of the precipice and redden the mountainside for yards below.

And when it was finally over, all twelve hundred Akkadians had died. Not one remained alive on the mountain.

And the dawn of the last day had barely begun.

Kumara lit the four candles and placed them with considerable care at the four Cardinal Points, placing them in the *exact* positions required. Marah lit the Eternal Light and placed it reverently on the altar that stood in the exact center of the room. Kumara took his position in front of the eastern portal, and Marah sat herself in the chair in the south. From the thurible on the altar rose the smoke of sweet-smelling incense.

The ritual was about to begin.

In the Sun Temple, three miles away, Helios motioned Herakos to remain on guard outside in the corridor and then entered his private chamber and closed the door behind him. He slipped off his ordinary robe and put on the special ritual cloak. He lit the incense first and placed it on the altar, then the Eternal Light, and then the four candles. He, too, then took his position by the eastern portal.

Kumara, High Priest of the Sea Temple, stood silently in front of the eastern portal deep in meditation, visualizing every detail of Helios' private chamber, three miles away, and visualizing Helios himself.

Helios, High Priest of the Sun Temple, similarly stood silently in front of his eastern portal and visualized Kumara and Marah.

Both priests remained silent for many minutes, building the inner state necessary for their work. The forces began to gather, swirling and intermingling between the two lodges.

Helios was aware of his own lodge, and superimposed on it was his visualization of Kumara and Marah. Similarly, Kumara and Marah were aware both of their own lodge and their visualization of Helios. Gradually, as their visualizations increased in clarity and intensity, the outer plane reality of each became fused with their inner visions such that the two became indistinguishable. For all practical ritual purposes Kumara, Marah, and Helios were in the same room together, performing the same ritual. Such was the degree of reality that Helios found that he had to step back from the east because Kumara was already there. He turned and sat himself in the chair in the west.

They paused for a few moments, cementing this fusion more firmly, and then Kumara turned and faced the east. He raised his arm and described the opening pentagram seal. His voice rang with power and authority, and on the inner Helios and Marah were aware that the massive eastern gate had swung ponderously open, allowing a flood of force to pour through.

The lodge was vibrating intensely, the atmosphere almost crackling with the forces invoked. Helios could feel it physically in the tips of his fingers and at the back of his neck, and his whole being was vibrating with the power of it. He shifted his position slightly and flexed his hands to get rid of the tension that had crept into them. It was vitally important for him to be poised, alert, but relaxed. He had taken part in some powerful rituals in his time, but never anything like this.

Kumara turned to face the altar. He raised his arms high, and then in an incredibly powerful and vibrant voice he began to intone the ancient ritual invocation of the great kings of the Elementals, and as each one answered, the very elements themselves surged up under the impact of the forces unleashed. The very earth beneath their feet rumbled ominously—the sea itself and the waters of the Naradek began to convulse and seethe restlessly; the fire and molten rocks below the surface oozed up more hideously under the suddenly

increasing pressure—and the very air itself quivered
and shimmered with the portent of things to come.

The Elementals had answered.

Vardek stood on a mound and directed the attack.
Half-an-hour earlier twelve men had raced up the giant
stairs to the great doors. Kneeling, their shields held
above them to fend off the hurtling spears from the
Temple Guard on the ramparts above, they had lit an
enormous fire of brush and logs against the timbered
Sun Temple doors; and now they waited for the flames
to eat their way through.

Frantically the defenders poured caldron after caldron of their precious water down from the ramparts,
but such was the angle of the wall that very little found
the fire itself, nowhere near sufficient to quench the
flames. The captain was standing grim-faced at a narrow
enbrasure to the left of the doors surveying the scene
outside. Deledian came up to him. "Will the doors
hold, Captain?"

The man grunted. "They would, if left alone—the
timbers are too thick to go on burning after the fire outside has died down—but they are weakened, and Vardek has a battering ram."

Outside, fifty men were manhandling an enormous
contraption up the great stairway. It consisted of a massive tree trunk slung from a vast wooden cradle, sus-
pended from the center pole itself.

A few minutes later a great booming crash reverberated throughout the temple. The milling horde of
priests froze, terrified, and then scattered in all directions, frantically searching for a place to hide. Deledian
and the other Council members remained in the courtyard, standing with arms folded, calmly waiting for the
inevitable. Again the battering ram thundered against
the doors—and again, and again—and at each blow the
great doors shuddered and buckled inward a little
farther.

Suddenly, from behind them, from within the temple
itself, came a crashing roar and the sound of falling
masonry. A young priest dashed into the courtyard.

"Come quickly—the Eternal Light has burst its well! Come, come quickly!"

Deledian turned and hurried after the youth. They ran as fast as they could down corridor after corridor, deep into the temple, until they came to the central chamber that housed the Chapel of the Eternal Light, a stone chapel some ten yards in diameter that contained the well that was fed from underground springs of oil. Deledian stopped, aghast. The entire chapel had been torn apart, and blocks of masonry lay scattered everywhere. The well housing itself had collapsed completely, and in its place was a gaping hole in the floor through which there rose not the normal gentle flame but a raging, blazing giant that rose up in a deafening roar twenty feet to the ceiling itself. Deledian gazed upward, horrified, to where the great gout of flame had already blackened the roof of the chamber for yards around. He knew instantly that no masonry could withstand that heat for long and that soon the roof itself would collapse. The youth beside him tugged him away. "We must get out! There's nothing we can do here!" The heat was intense, and already it was difficult to breathe. "We must get out!" the youth shouted again, and tugged him back into the corridor and away.

Another priest raced up. "The lake!" he shouted. "The lake is boiling! What is it, Deledian—what is it?"

Deledian pulled himself together and hurried through the temple and up the stone stairway to the ramparts above, and there his eyes could hardly believe the staggering sight of great spumes of steam that rose from the lake half a mile away on the other side of the plateau. Through the steam he thought he could see great clouds of smoke and ash that were not coming from the lake itself but from farther on, probably from the very edge of the plateau, perhaps from below the edge, from a vent in the side of the mountain. Steam and smoke were writhing together and rising in great clouds that were rolling across the plateau. Already the plateau in that direction was dark, as the clouds hid the sun. Deledian leaned over the ramparts. Below him, some of Vardek's men were pointing, shouting, and he could see Vardek himself racing up the great steps, sword in hand.

"Get that ram going again!" Vardek bellowed.

"But the clouds!" one of the captains protested.

"I said, get that ram going again! Never mind the damn clouds—it's just a priestly trick to frighten you!" Vardek was beside himself with rage. All his life he had dreamed of destroying the temple, and nothing was going to rob him of this final triumph. "Get back to your posts! I will kill any man who disobeys. Move!"

The warriors reluctantly turned to the task again, and the ram crashed against the great doors—and again, and again. The warriors were sweating, frightened, glancing back over their shoulders to where the great clouds were rolling inexorably toward them. Suddenly the great transverse main beam of the massive doors splintered, snapped, and the ram drove home through the smoke and flames and tore a great hole. Frantically the warriors heaved back the ram for another blow. They were now suddenly desperate to get inside, frantic, terrified. Again the ram crashed home, and the jagged hole grew larger.

Inside, in the courtyard, the captain of the Temple Guard steadied his men. He had thirty guards only to fend off the main frontal attack. Not enough, he knew. He had another twenty men stationed around the perimeter of the temple keeping watch at the embrasures. He was sorely tempted to withdraw them to help fight off the frontal attack, but he did not dare. Vardek had thrown a ring of warriors around the entire temple, maybe a hundred men, no more. Not enough to launch a secondary attack, but enough to ensure that the Temple Guard would have to split its force, and secondly and more importantly, enough to ensure that no one could escape—Vardek did not want any of these so-called priests to slip away through any of the rear embrasures.

The captain of the Guard grunted to himself; Vardek knew his business, all right. "Steady!" he warned. "They will be through at any moment."

"Five hundred of them!" said one of the men. "It will be quite a party!"

"They can't all come through at once. We'll be all right!"

"But if they—"

"Hold your tongue! Here they come!"

The ram jerked free. The gaping hole was now blazing, and great clouds of smoke were pouring into the courtyard. Oblivious of the fire, a figure came leaping through the gap, to be cut down instantly, then another, and another. "Pile those bodies up!" the captain roared. "Block the gap with their own dead!" His men leaped to obey. Again the ram came crashing through, slightly to the left of where it had been before, and the hole gaped wider. A guard screamed and went down as the ram smashed his skull to splinters of white bone. The ram withdrew and crashed through again, and the planking split still further. Two warriors came leaping through the gap, and then two more. The captain raced forward, sword up, and there began a desperate hand-to-hand struggle. He felled one attacker with a slashing downward stroke that all but severed the head, but two more leaped through to take his place. One of his own men went down, his throat spurting blood. "Forward!" he roared. "Block the gap!" The guard pressed forward, pinning the attackers against the doors. Four of Vardek's men died under a hail of spears and swords. The bodies began to pile up. Attackers came leaping through, to stumble awkwardly on their own dead. Another guard went down. A shouted order from outside, and the attackers withdrew, those that were still alive. Momentarily the gap was free. The captain frowned, and then suddenly he understood. "Back!" he roared. "Get clear of the gap!" But even as he spoke, it was too late. A dozen spears, thrown together, came whistling through the gap, and six guards went down in a struggling, screaming heap. Another dozen spears, and while the guard were still disorganized, two of Vardek's warriors came leaping through again, then another two, and then two more, until a dozen raging warriors were inside. The guard recovered and charged forward, but it was too late. Another six came clambering through, but these did not join the fight. While the first twelve were fending off the guard, these six turned their attention to the doors themselves. They hacked at the splintered planking with their swords, ripping away the half-burned wood, and when all was clear, they threw themselves on the massive inner locking beam and heaved it out of its retaining stanchions. The guard fought desperately, but they could make no headway against the twelve specially chosen giant Toltecs who barred their way. Six more guards were already down, and the captain knew that the end had come. The attackers flung the locking beam to one side and then heaved against the huge timbers of the doors themselves. At first they would not budge, but then slowly, fraction by fraction, they creaked open, and there on the atrium outside, feet apart, a great sword in his hand, stood Vardek, with nearly four hundred men at his back.

The temple was wide open.

Banda signaled to one of his captains. "Get this barricade cleared away. Send a runner to Vardek to tell him what has happened." The captain hurried away, shouting orders, and the Toltec warriors began to toss the boulders over the precipice. Banda clambered down the barricade, flanked by two captains, and approached the shaman's litter. "Greetings, Dracombi," he said carefully. "The Toltecs give thanks to the Rmoahals for their aid."

The roadway for a hundred yards was piled high with Akkadian dead. The old shaman shrugged. "We took ten minutes to do what would have taken you all morning, Toltec!" he retorted.

Banda nodded. "The Rmoahals are great warriors, truly."

"The best on Ruta."

Banda frowned and felt suddenly exposed. He fingered his sword and glanced behind him at the barricade. It would be several minutes yet before it was cleared. He could not afford to antagonize the Rmoahals. "Great warriors, truly," he repeated.

"The best!" the old man insisted.

Bulambi, the giant warrior chief of the Rmoahals, came up to join them. "And we still thirst for battle, Toltec. Look there!"

The battle-crazed Rmoahals, their eyes still on fire, were dancing crazily among the Akkadian dead, still hacking at the bodies with their spears. Instead of their battle lust dying down, it seemed to be increasing. Banda was suddenly nervous. "There are twelve hundred Akkadian warriors in the harbor area, Bulambi. We go to destroy them. Will the Rmoahals march by our side?"

"The Akkadians are soft and die too easily," Bulambi growled. "We need something stronger to test our warriors."

"And we have marched by your side too often, Toltec!" snapped Dracombi.

Banda tried to put a brave front on it. "You would be foolish to march against the Toltecs," he warned. "Many of your warriors will die!"

"And many of yours too, Toltec!" The old shaman grinned evilly. "It is not important how many die, but how many survive. Perhaps there will be enough Rmoahals left to be masters of all Ruta!"

Banda glared at Bulambi. "Enough of this nonsense!" he snapped. "We march on the Akkadians whether you are with us or not!" And he turned and strode for the barricade, his two captains on either side.

Dracombi muttered an order, and two spears flashed out and the two captains fell, transfixed. Banda turned. Bulambi grinned, raised his spear, and hurled it through the Toltec's chest. Banda fell to his knees, the great spear rammed right through his body, its point sticking out of his back. He tried to say something, but the blood gushed into his mouth. A great howl of triumph rose up from the Rmoahals, and they came charging forward.

The senior captain on top of the barricade barked an order, and the Toltecs hastily regrouped to meet the attack. The howling, raging Rmoahals swarmed up the barricade, to be met by a forest of Toltec spears. Such was the impetus of the attack that the first wave of Rmoahals cleared the top of the barricade in seconds, but not without paying a heavy price. Two dozen of their number lay dead and dying among the boulders, though twice that number of Toltecs lay with them.

The senior Toltec captain, now suddenly finding himself in sole command of almost the entire Toltec fighting wing of nearly five thousand warriors, barked another order, and a wave of Toltecs poured up the barricade and regained their position at the top. The Rmoahals howled their rage, and a second wave came leaping to the attack, with Bulambi at their head.

Suddenly the very ground beneath their feet began to shake, and loose boulders came crashing down the mountainside, to smash in among the struggling warriors. The battle paused as men clung to the rocks to keep their balance. More and more violently the earth shook, until it was no longer possible for a man to stand upright. The warriors, both Toltec and Rmoahal, clung to the ground, suddenly terrified. Boulders continued to crash down among them, and men screamed in agony as their legs or arms were crushed by the hurtling rocks.

Then, as suddenly as it had begun, the tremor ceased. The warriors dazedly picked themselves up, all thoughts of battle gone. Someone shouted, men were pointing upward, and there, high above them, rose great clouds of steam and smoke and ash. The Rmoahals began backing away down the barricade, and as another tremor briefly shook the earth, they howled their fear, hurled away their weapons, and began to stream back down the roadway.

A runner came racing into the harbor area and came up to where Melchadek and the Akkadian captain were standing. "Treachery!" he blurted out. "The Rmoahals attacked us from behind!"

The captain grabbed the man. "What's this you say? Make sense, man!"

"The Rmoahals attacked the Akkadians, I tell you!" he gasped. "I saw it with my own eyes! There is not a single Akkadian left alive on the mountain!"

The captain's face went ashen white. "All of them?" he whispered. "All twelve hundred?"

The man nodded. "I saw it all. They didn't stand a chance. They thought the Rmoahals were coming as friends, so they let them through. Once inside our ranks, the Rmoahals just turned and fell on our people. They were taken completely by surprise. They didn't stand a chance! The Toltecs just stood and watched! I did not stay to see whether Rmoahal would fight Toltec or whether they would march together!"

The captain spun around to Melchadek. "So this is the result of your diplomacy, priest—twelve hundred dead! Why couldn't you have left well alone!"

"Because we knew," he said quietly, "that the Rmoahals would never stand idly by while a battle was being fought. We knew they would march, but we did not know against whom. I tried to influence them in favor of joining the Akkadians, but obviously they chose otherwise."

"And now Malekh and twelve hundred Akkadians are dead, and you stand as calm as if we were discussing the weather. Doesn't anything stir your damn blood, priest?"

"I am calm because it would serve no purpose to be otherwise."

"You would be more stirred up if it were your damn priests who had been slaughtered!"

"I might remind you, Captain, that at this very moment Toltec warriors are slaughtering the Sun Temple priesthood, and few will be left alive from that either!"

"All right, all right! Just let's hope the Toltecs and the Rmoahals fight it out. If they join forces, they'll run through us in a matter of minutes. Twelve hundred against five thousand was bad enough, but twelve hundred against more than seven thousand will be impossible!"

A young priest came hurrying over. "The boats are coming!" he said softly.

Melchadek turned, and there, rounding the bend in the river, came the flotilla of small boats. "Good. Tell Netziachos to get our people down to the beach. Tell her we must not waste even a single minute. I will meet her there." He turned to the Akkadian. "About thirty minutes, Captain, and then we will be away."

At that precise moment voices shouted, men stood up, pointing. High above their heads from a vent in the side of the mountain great billows of black smoke were belching out into the morning air; and beyond it, from the topmost plateau, there rose great clouds of steam. The earth suddenly trembled, and men were flung to the ground. Melchadek and the Akkadian captain clung to a rock as the whole island shook violently and roared as if in pain. The noise was deafening, appalling, and the hideously unnatural shaking of the ground robbed a man of any chance to think clearly. They could only cling on, terrified, shaken and pounded as loose boulders came crashing down the mountainside and into the harbor area among them. But as swiftly as the tremor had struck, as suddenly it was still again. The men picked themselves up dazedly. The smoke and steam were still billowing above them, but at least the ground was still.

Melchadek's one thought was for the boats, but to his relief, they were still afloat. The waters of the Naradek were now churned and violent, but at least the river was still there and not sucked dry through a sudden underground rift. The boats were slewed sideways against the far bank, but he could see Danios and Persepios getting them around and under way again. They would need another thirty minutes to arrive, embark the priesthood, and shove off again for the last trip, but there was no way of telling whether they would be granted that time.

The Akkadian captain climbed to his feet. "I can't say that I enjoyed that at all," he said feelingly, "but if that is the extent of the disaster you predicted, then I think that a great many men have died for nothing!"

"That was only a herald, Captain," said Melchadek shortly. "The main tremor is still to come."

Since the Akkadian warriors were stationed around the perimeter of the harbor area and thus closer to the mountain, it was they who had taken the brunt of the avalanche of loose boulders that had come crashing down. Three men were dead, and a dozen lay badly injured. The priesthood, as far as Melchadek could tell, had escaped unscathed—they were all moving down to the beach, and none of them seemed to be needing any assistance.

"All our men dead, Captain?" one of the men shouted, pointing up the mountain.

"Yes," he said shortly. "You will be able to take revenge very soon now."

"What about our women and children?" another shouted.

"We will know soon enough," he said. "And if they have killed our women, then all the more reason for revenge! Stay at your posts—you'll get action soon enough!"

The boats grounded on the sandy beach, and Danios and Persepios leaped ashore and came splashing through the shallows. "I thought that was going to be the end!" said Danios sourly.

"So did many others," said Melchadek. "Are all on board the fleet?"

"Yes, no problem. Having done it once before, the second trip was much quicker."

"Good. We need every minute we can gain. The Rmoahals marched up the mountain road, slaughtered all twelve hundred Akkadians, and may have joined the Toltecs. We could have over seven thousand warriors on top of us at any moment!"

"All twelve hundred!" Persepios said, aghast. "And Malekh!"

They were silent for a few seconds, and then Danios shrugged and said, "Ruta itself will take care of Rmoahal and Toltec alike. Let's get moving before we too are numbered among the victims."

A bedlam of shouts rose up from behind them. They spun around, to see the staggering sight of the entire Rmoahal fighting wing, the finest warriors that Ruta had ever known, in full flight down the mountain road, their eyes glazed with terror. Melchadek saw the Akkadians brace themselves for the attack, but the Rmoahals swept on past the harbor and raced on around the mountain and down to their own village in the swamplands. At the rear of the column was the giant, Bulambi, no less terrified than his warriors. He and a dozen men were hurrying down as fast as they could with Dracombi's litter. It was a tribute to the old shaman's power over his people that they were even more terrified of him than they were of a mountain that shook; otherwise they would have abandoned him long ago.

The Akkadian captain seized his opportunity, barked an order, and as the rear of the Rmoahal column drew level with the harbor, a hundred Akkadians leaped over the barricades and fell on the Rmoahals.

Netziachos came hurrying over. "Where is Helios?"

"I don't know, and I am afraid that we cannot wait for him. Get our people into the boats—yourself as well."

"But we can't just leave him here!"

"We cannot wait, I tell you! Would you risk the lives of the entire priesthood because of one man! Get to the boats—we have no time to lose! Quickly now!" Malchadek turned to Danios. "Get ready to shove off, but wait for me!" And he turned and hurried across the harbor. By the time he reached the barricades, it was all over. Fifty or more Rmoahals lay dead or dying on the roadway. Among them was Bulambi, his giant body hacked almost to pieces. Dracombi's litter lay sprawled at the side of the road, and the shaman's body, its head severed, lay among the carnage.

"A small revenge at last!" said the Akkadian captain grimly. "Without Dracombi and Bulambi, the Rmoahals will be easily dealt with tomorrow."

Melchadek looked down at the tiny, insignificant corpse of Dracombi. For seventy years and more he had been the power behind the Rmoahals—Dracombi, the Eyes Through Which the Dead Look Out; tiny in stature by any standards, he had held the Rmoahal people in his grasp since his youth, and even the Toltecs had feared him.

"Saluting a fellow priest?" said the captain.

"He was the shaman of the Rmoahals," said Melchadek. "In his own way he was a great though misguided man. If only men like him and Vardek would lead their people on the true course of their evolution instead of following their own personal ambitions, what strides humanity would make! He could have been greater than he was, Captain, but Dracombi of the Rmoahals was nevertheless a great man."

At that moment more shouts came, men pointing, and around the bend in the road came the Toltecs. Unlike the Rmoahals, they were not fleeing in terror but came in steady, organized columns, their captains at their head. The Akkadian captain shouted an order, and once more his men streamed back into the harbor to take up their positions behind their barricade.

The Toltec columns halted. The senior captain, now a commander, stepped forward. "Who commands the Akkadians?" he said in a strong voice.

The Akkadian captain stood up. "I do, Toltec."

The Toltec commander glanced around at the Rmoahal dead, the barricades, and the ranks of Akkadian warriors. There was no sign of weakness or fear that he could detect. Beyond the Akkadians he could see the masts of Vardek's fleet at anchor, and to the left on the beach he could see the group of priests and priestesses climbing into a flotilla of small boats. "Tell your men to surrender."

The Akkadian laughed. "Akkadians do not yield to Toltecs, commander, and twelve hundred of our dead companions cry out for revenge!"

The commander turned and growled an order. The Toltec ranks opened up, and three women were thrown forward to the ground. They were completely naked, their hands tied behind them, their long fair hair spilling in the dust. "Your women and children are safe, but they will die if you do not surrender—and where is the future of your race without your women!"

There was an angry muttering in the Akkadian ranks.

"And what are your terms if we surrender?" the captain shouted.

"I am sure our Lord Vardek will be merciful and will spare all your lives. Only a very few Toltecs have died—few enough for us still to be merciful."

"We do not trust the word of a Toltec commander, nor the mercy of Vardek!"

The commander shrugged. "I will give you five minutes to consider your position—five minutes, no more."

The Akkadian captain stepped down from the barricade. "At least it gives you time to get away, priest."

Melchadek frowned thoughtfully. "It is we priests whom Vardek wants dead. Surely the commander must know that. Why is he giving us time to get away?"

The Akkadian smiled. "He thinks to pursue you in one of Vardek's ships."

"But they are scuttled!"

"Yes, but he doesn't know that."

They both instinctively turned to where Vardek's long ships lay against the harbor wall. To an experienced seagoing eye they were obviously a lot lower in the water than they should be, but to a landsman's eye they must look perfectly normal.

Melchadek smiled. "What will you do, Captain?"

"You'll see." He turned and sprang onto the barricade. "Toltec!" he shouted. "The word of an Akkadian means a great deal to us. We have given our word that we will hold the harbor until the priests have left in their boats. Once they are in midstream we will surrender, provided you allow us to keep our weapons and let us join our women on the shoulder of the mountain. Do you agree?"

The Toltec commander smiled sardonically. "We agree," he shouted. "But they have five minutes—no more!"

The Akkadian captain leaped down from the barricade grinning broadly. "The man is a fool! You will get clear and we will be allowed up the mountain— and on the plateau is Vardek, with no more than four or five hundred men. I may even realize my ambition to see Vardek dead!"

"So you will not change your mind and join us?"

"Not now, priest, not now! Come, the sooner we can get you away, the sooner we can get after Vardek."

The two of them hurried down to the beach, where the last of the priests were being helped into the boats. Only Netziachos remained on the beach. They quickly explained the terms of the so-called surrender. ". . . and so you see, Netziachos," said Melchadek gently, "if Helios is still alive, then there will be twelve hundred Akkadians on their way to rescue him."

"I would go with the Akkadians, then," she said.

He shook his head. "You know that's impossible."

She sighed heavily. "I suppose so, but it goes against my every instinct to leave without him." She looked up at the Akkadian. "Do all you can, Captain—you don't know how important he is to me personally and to this entire emigration."

"I will do what I can. Farewell, priestess."

Malchedek helped her into one of the boats and then turned back to the Akkadian. "Farewell, Captain. We could have done with men such as you with us."

"And if things had been different, I might have come. Farewell."

The two grasped hands briefly, and Melchadek stepped into the leading boat. Danios shoved off, and the lead boat swung out away from the shore, the others following. Soon the entire flotilla was in midstream and heading downriver. Once clear of any possible pursuit, the flotilla paused to watch the scene back in the harbor area. They saw the Akkadian captain giving orders to his men and saw the barricades come down. The Akkadians formed into two ranks and marched out of the harbor area and through the Toltec ranks.

Suddenly Melchadek leaped to his feet. The Toltecs had learned their lesson well from the Rmoahals. As the Akkadians passed through the Toltec ranks, Melchadek saw the commander turn to his captains and growl an order, and the entire Toltec force of five thousand fell on the Akkadians. Netziachos cried out in horror as she saw the Akkadian captain be the first to fall. Even from that distance they could hear the shrieks of dying men and the clash of swords.

The Akkadians were split into separate groups, as they had been on the mountain, and each group dwindled rapidly as man after man was cut down by the raging Toltecs. The horrified priests and priestesses could do nothing as men died by the scores less than a hundred yards away. Melchadek saw the Toltec commander leave the melee with fifty men and come racing through the harbor to Vardek's fleet of ships, and he clearly heard their howl of rage as they discovered that each and every ship had been scuttled.

Netziachos was too full of horror to scream. "But what will happen to Helios now?"

Melchadek took her hand gently. His eyes were full of sorrow. "There is nothing we can do now. You must accept the fact that there is little hope of his escape." And he turned and quietly gave the order for the flotilla to give way and head out to the fleet that waited for them.

14

Vardek the Butcher and four hundred of his men went rampaging through the Temple of the Sun, and the priesthood began to die. They died as they had lived, some quietly, calmly, some babbling for a mercy that they knew they would not get, some dragged shrieking from their hiding places, some recanting desperately but futilely; and some died bravely with swords of their own in their hands.

Deledian was the first of the priesthood to die. He did not run, but waited in the courtyard, arms folded, calmly watching the Temple Guard be butchered before his eyes, and calmly he waited as Vardek himself came bursting through the melee and hacked him down almost without pausing.

"Get me Helios!" Vardek roared. "Alive!"

His men poured through the temple, but although priest after priest was slaughtered, no Helios could be found. And then, seeking life, a babbling, terrified priest told of Helios' private chamber, and died with his betrayal scarcely past his lips.

In his private chamber, in the closing stages of the joint ritual, Helios, High Priest of the Sun Temple, faced Kumara, High Priest of the Sea Temple, three miles away, for the very last time. They did not speak, but simply nodded gravely to each other. They had done all that they could do. Nothing now remained to be done save to seal the two lodges, make the reverse circumnambulations, and each to retire quietly to his destiny, Kumara and Marah to the release of death, and Helios to join the exodus if he could. With Kumara's vibrant voice intoning the closing seals, Helios allowed his inner vision to fade, and he returned to full consciousness in his own private chamber.

During the later half of the ritual he had been aware as if from a great distance, of the booming sounds of the battering ram as it had pounded against the temple doors. That sound was now gone, and Helios knew that Vardek and his men were inside the temple. He would have to be quick if he and Herakos were to escape the holocaust that was to follow.

He opened the door and beckoned to Herakos. "Come quickly. We have no time to lose!"

At that moment two of Vardek's men came raging around the corner and stopped dead on seeing the huge Akkadian warrior chief. Instead of retreating as expected, Herakos leaped upon them and cut them down before they could even lift a sword in defense, but as he did so, six more warriors burst into the corridor through the far door. "Back into your chamber!" Herakos growled. "Get ready to close and bar the door!"

The six warriors were advancing cautiously. The corridor was narrow, and they could advance only two abreast, and the leading pair were reluctant to come to grips with the giant Akkadian. Their two dead companions were sufficient evidence that odds of two to one were no guarantee against such as Herakos. But as the Akkadian was backing warily away, Vardek himself burst into the corridor and came storming through his own warriors, throwing them aside in his raging eagerness to get at Herakos and Helios. Vardek was insane with rage. His face was red with apoplectic fury, the veins standing out clearly beneath his skin. His one and only all-enveloping, consuming desire was to get at Helios and tear him apart with his own hands.

The moment Vardek came raging into the corridor, Herakos instantly turned and leaped into Helios' private chamber and slammed the door behind him. Before Vardek was even halfway along the corridor, Helios had quickly slipped the bar into place, and the enraged Lord Commander flung himself against the door uselessly. They could hear his bellowing rage and the thunder of his fists on the thick paneling, and could also hear him roaring orders to his men.

"He appears to be somewhat anxious to meet me," said Helios dryly.

"And he will if we do not hurry," the Akkadian growled. "That door will not delay them for long. Get the rope."

Earlier that day they had secretly brought up a coil of rope from the storehouse and had secured one end to the inside buttress near the embrasure. They looked out through the slit to the ground thirty feet below. There should have been at least four of Vardek's guards in sight, but only two could be seen. The other two must have fled at the sight of the great clouds of steam and smoke.

The embrasure was set in the western outer wall of the temple, a hundred yards from the edge of the plateau. The semisecret trail that the priestess had used when they had escaped secretly from the Sun Temple plunged down the western face of the mountain. Helios pointed to a spot a few hundred yards farther to the right. "The trail starts there where that large boulder rests. But what about the guards?"

"Leave them to me. I will go first." And the Akkadian picked up the coil and fed it through the embrasure until it hung to the ground. A shout came from the two guards below, but no others responded to their call—there were still only the two. Herakos grunted in satisfaction. He hoisted his bulk through the embrasure and began to lower himself down the outer wall hand-over-hand. The guards saw him coming and drew their swords. To them it seemed an easy task to kill the Akkadian when he had descended to within range—the fool's sword was still in its scabbard—but they were only guards, not too intelligent, and with little imagination. When Herakos was within twelve feet of the ground, he simply grasped the hilt of his sword, let go the rope, and plummeted down, wrenching his sword free as he fell, and crashed squarely on top of the two men. In a matter of seconds they were both dead. Herakos wiped his sword and beckoned for Helios to follow.

As Helios reached the ground, there was a thundering, splintering crash from the room above—and then another, and another—and then the raging figure of Vardek appeared in the embrasure, sword in hand. "We'll have to leave the rope. Come on!" And they raced for the plateau's edge. Helios was not used to this physical exertion. By the time they reached the giant boulder that marked the beginning of the trail, he was already gasping painfully for every breath he took. Behind them, Vardek too had reached the ground and was charging after them. "Come on, come on!" Herakos growled. "This is no time to rest!"

The mountain trail plunged precipitously down, zigzagging from left to right. At times the path came to an abrupt halt, and they had to lower themselves down over a mass of tumbled boulders or negotiate a seemingly impassable ledge before picking up the trail again. They were moving as fast as they could, but the sounds of Vardek's crashing pursuit were growing louder with every moment. "He must be mad!" Helios gasped.

"Perhaps mad enough to kill himself," grunted Herakos.

By the time they were halfway down the mountain, Vardek was only a few yards behind them. Helios' breathing was now a rasping wheeze, and there was a stabbing pain in his side. "It's no good, Herakos—I must stop soon!"

"A few more seconds!" the Akkadian urged. "You must!"

They dropped down yet another steep slope and staggered onto a ledge some twenty yards long and a dozen feet wide. "This will do," the Akkadian said. "I will fight here." Helios staggered to the far end of the ledge and collapsed. Herakos drew his sword and turned to face the way they had come.

Vardek's fury was still on him. He came slipping and sliding down the last slope, crashed onto the ledge, and without any hesitation whatsoever he flung himself straight at Herakos. The warrior chief of the Toltecs versus the warrior chief of the Akkadians—this was the fight that every man on Ruta would have given a great deal to see. Vardek was a small man, barely five and a half feet, a good foot shorter than the Akkadian. But though short in height, his girth was immense. His skin was dark and gnarled with muscles, and his entire body was matted with thick coarse hair. He was without doubt the strongest man on Ruta, but he was not so quick on his feet as others, and his lack of reach was a serious disadvantage. Normally such a slow man would be easily dealt with, regardless of his strength, but Vardek had an utterly fearless animal ferocity that few men could withstand. His method of attack was simple and direct. He always charged straight at his man at full speed, relying on his strength and ferocity to carry him through any defense to get to close grips. The whole front of his body was a mass of scars that had been inflicted over the years by a hundred adversaries as they had slashed at him to halt his charge, but no man had ever lived to boast that he had wounded Vardek, for once Vardek was in close, no man had ever held out for more than a few seconds against his incredible strength and the utter barbarity of his animal ferocity.

Herakos, fair-haired and clean-skinned, adorned with the purple shoulder sash of his rank, stood over six and a half feet. He was as light as a jungle cat on his feet, and equally dangerous. So fast was he for so big a man that there was not even a single scar on the whole of his body. He was not as strong as Vardek, but certainly twice as fast. He was a cool, thinking warrior. What he lacked in ferocity he more than made up for in speed and cunning.

Vardek charged straight at him, and Herakos only just managed to wheel aside in time and slash at the Toltec as he passed. A great gash opened suddenly across Vardek's shoulder and upper arm, but he scarcely noticed it. He spun around and charged again. Herakos' sword leaped out and under the Toltec's shield and bit deep into his side. But Herakos had committed himself with that lunge, and Vardek was now close in. The Toltec dropped his sword, wrenched the Akkadian's shield away, snatched out his dagger, and drove for the throat. Herakos desperately wheeled aside, slashing at Vardek's face and head, but although the dagger did not find his throat, it did drive sickeningly into his shoulder. Vardek clung on with one hand to stop the Akkadian from leaping free, and with his right hand he stabbed again and again at the Akkadian's chest. Such was their position that Vardek could not get the dagger lower to go for the heart, nor high enough for the throat, but four times the blade bit into Herakos' upper chest and shoulder. Vardek was in so close that Herakos' right arm and sword was behind Vardek's back, and try as he might, he could not free his arm to use it. In desperation he dropped his sword, grabbed at Vardek's hair, and dragged him backward, tripping him so that Vardek staggered and fell. Herakos leaped away, snatched for his shield, and whirled about just in time to meet Vardek's second attack. Swordless, with only a small shield against a dagger, he tried to leap aside as Vardek came plunging in. He could not get completely clear, but he did manage to take the dagger's point in the middle of his shield. The dagger spun off the metal shield out of Vardek's hand and fell to the ground. Herakos took the opportunity to snatch up his sword and leap back to compose himself. Vardek would have charged again instantly, as was his custom, but now he was without his shield, his sword, and indeed his dagger. Even Vardek would not charge unarmed. Instead, it was Herakos himself who now charged forward. Vardek snatched up his dagger and shield and whirled to meet the attack. Herakos did not charge to close grips, but slashed at the Toltec as he passed, but Vardek took the stroke safely on his shield. Both men paused now and began to circle each other warily. It was unusual for Vardek to pause at all during a fight. His method was a whirlwind to the finish, but he had not come up against a warrior such as Herakos before.

The fight had lasted barely twenty seconds, and the unarmed Helios was staggered, dazed, and utterly appalled at the ferocity of the clash. Like Malekh, his knowledge of fighting and battles was secondhand. This was the first time that he had ever personally seen a real fight to the death, and the animal ferocity of it appalled and sickened him. Both men were streaming blood from wounds any one of which would have put Helios or any other priest on his back for days. The sword thrust in Vardek's side would have killed any lesser man outright, and so too would the four dagger wounds in Herakos' upper chest. It was unbelievable that so many deadly wounds could have been struck in so short a time, and unbelievable that both men were still on their feet.

At that precise moment the very ground beneath their feet began to tremble. Helios looked up, startled. The great clouds of steam and smoke were still billowing from the plateau above. The trembling increased rapidly to a shaking, and loose stones began to trickle down the slopes. Vardek and Herakos stopped circling. The shaking grew until it was difficult to keep upright. Herakos staggered and fell to his knees. Vardek saw his chance and started toward the Akkadian, but he too staggered and fell. Helios clung to the ground. The roaring sound of the tremor filled their ears until they could no longer even think clearly. The shaking grew more and more violent, until it seemed as if the entire mountain must collapse in rubble. Larger and larger boulders were beginning to crash down the mountainside. One huge juggernaut smashed onto the ledge, tearing away a great slice of ground before plunging over the edge and down to the Naradek, still a thousand feet below. The tremor lasted for a few minutes only, but during that time the three men knew a terror that they had not experienced before. At last the shaking ceased, but still the boulders were raging down the mountainside. Vardek ignored them. He picked himself up and charged forward at Herakos again, but it was a foolhardy move. A small boulder struck him in the back and sent him sprawling. Before he could rise, another and larger runaway came thundering down the slope, smashed squarely on his pelvis and upper thighs, and then rolled on over the edge down to the lower slopes. Vardek screamed hideously as the boulder struck him, and then was silent. Helios was nearly sick. He could see that Vardek's pelvis and thighs were smashed so severely that splinters of bone were sticking through the flesh in several places. Not only that, but the boulder must have struck over a wider and higher area for the Toltec's side and abdomen had split open like an overripe fruit.

Herakos picked himself up and staggered toward Helios. The blood from his chest wounds was pouring down his body as though it would never stop. Suddenly Helios cried out and pointed. Herakos turned, and there, unbelievably, Vardek had begun to crawl toward them. He was dragging himself forward inch by inch by his hands. His eyes were glaring with an unquenchable hatred. It was incredible that the man was still alive. His broken legs were trailing behind him, and the entrails were being squeezed from his body as Vardek pulled himself over the rocks. The two horrified men stood paralyzed, unable to take their eyes off the crawling figure whose hatred for them was keeping him unbelievably alive. Vardek had crawled several yards before Herakos pulled himself together. The Akkadian ran over to him and plunged his sword into Vardek's back to finish him off, but still Vardek would not die. If anything, his hate-crazed eyes were brighter than before. Again Herakos drove his sword in, and again, and again—and at last the light began to fade from Vardek's eyes. His squat and ugly body convulsed in one last sickening heave, and then his arms collapsed, his head fell forward, and his eyes finally glazed over with death.

Vardek was dead! Even seeing his body lying there, it was still difficult to believe. Helios still half-expected him to rise up even now and pursue him. Vardek was dead! The source of all Ruta's troubles was gone, finished. Mass murder, priest-killer, king-poisoner, temple-destroyer, torturer—dead, gone, finished! It was unbelievable!

Herakos took him by the arm and drew him away. The Akkadian then bent over the body and ripped away the tunic. "Help me bind these wounds," he growled, "or I'll soon be joining him."

Helios shook his head to clear his fuddled thoughts. "I'm sorry. I've never seen a man die violently before. Here, let me do that."

"And you won't see one die again quite like that!" the Akkadian said feelingly. "I have never known a man to have so strong a hold on life. The boulder took his life and saved mine. I would never have beaten him."

Helios tore the tunic into strips and made a rough bandage for the Akkadian's chest and shoulder. "How do you know? You might have won."

Herakos shook his head. "No. There is no man alive who could have beaten Vardek. I know that now. I am a warrior—believe me, I know!"

The bandaging finished, they made their way on down the mountain. Now that they were no longer pursued, they could take it at a slower pace, but even so the trail was no easy one to follow. Helios marveled that the priestesses had come this way, and at night too. By the time they reached the base of the mountain, Helios' breathing was again a painful, rasping wheeze. But the Akkadian was in even worse shape. His face was ashen gray, and every few minutes he coughed violently and spat blood. One of the dagger thrusts must have pierced the windpipe, and if blood was seeping into the windpipe and down to the lungs, then Herakos was in very real danger of drowning in his own blood. The exterior bleeding had not eased either. The blood was still oozing through the bandages and running down his body.

"I will never make it on foot around the mountain," he said. "You had better leave me here."

"We don't have to go on foot. Rest yourself here." The young priest propped the Akkadian against a rock at the edge of the river. "I will be back in a little while."

A few minutes later Helios returned, walking along the edge of the river, pulling a small boat. "I hid this some weeks ago—for emergencies. I didn't even tell Kumara or Melchadek about it. Come on, let me help you in."

Around the other side of the mountain where the harbor lay, the River Naradek was broad and deep and slow, but here close to where it came tumbling down in waterfalls from the inland mountain range, it was much narrower, faster, and more shallow, with jagged rocks sticking up above the surface. Helios tied the boat to a rock and helped the Akkadian into the stern. "You take it easy." He untied the boat, but before he cast off he stood for a few moments staring across the river and up into the low hills where the Sea Temple lay. "The finest man I ever knew," he said softly, "and for that matter, the finest woman, are up there with others waiting to die." He stared hard at the hills, and for a moment he could almost see Kumara and Marah sitting calmly and patiently waiting for the end.

The Akkadian grunted. "It is easier to die than it is to live."

Helios looked at him. "That's what Kumara always said. A fool can die but cannot live—a wise man can live but never die. I never really understood it until now."

"Had we not better get going?" the Akkadian said.

Helios smiled. "Yes, you're right. It will take us fifteen or twenty minutes to paddle around to the harbor. If the priesthood has already left, then we can paddle on downriver and out to the fleet. Once there, the healers will soon have you well again."

Herakos shook his head. "You cannot fool a warrior about death, Helios. I do not think I will live through this day."

"Nonsense!"

The Akkadian smiled but did not answer. Helios cast off, and soon the tiny boat was hurtling down the Naradek around the mountain to calmer waters. Helios was worried about Herakos. The Akkadian was right —he was close to death, and they both knew it.

Fifteen minutes later they rounded the bend and came in sight of the harbor, and as they did so Helios stopped paddling. "We're too late. Look!"

Ahead of them they could see that the beach was clear of boats and that no priests or priestesses were on the harbor wall. The emigration must have gone as planned. But it did not look as though Helios and Herakos would be allowed to join them. The angry Toltec warriors had built themselves a crude raft, presumably with the ripped-up deck planking of one of Vardek's scuttled ships. They had even stepped a small mast and had jury-rigged a small mainsail. They were just in the process of launching it as Helios and Herakos had come around the bend. They were obviously intending to give chase to the priests, and with a sail and twelve men paddling they could certainly travel faster than a flotilla of small boats. Obviously the priests had escaped only a short time before; otherwise the Toltecs would not have thought they had a chance to catch them.

One of the warriors shouted and pointed straight at them. The Toltec commander looked up and then came racing down to the beach. Helios bent to the paddle again, but it was obvious that the raft would reach midstream before Helios' boat could pass that point.

"Stop!" said Herakos. "You don't have a chance. Listen to me!"

He spoke rapidly and earnestly, and Helios kept shaking his head. "No, no—I won't let you!"

"What other alternative is there! Your way we both die. My way, at least one of us will get through. Don't give me any arguments, Helios. Kumara charged me with your life. I am not going to fail in my promise to him just because you cannot accept the reality of the situation! You may be the High Priest, but this time you are going to take orders from me! Now, paddle— and don't let me have any more arguments!"

They were rapidly drifting down to the raft. Helios hesitated but then smiled softly. "Kumara could have chosen no finer and no braver man than you, Herakos. I consider it a deep honor to have known you."

"And I you, priest. Now, paddle or it will all have been a waste of time!"

Helios snatched up the paddle, and the boat picked up speed and raced toward the raft. Herakos stood up in the stern. He settled his shield more firmly in his left hand and drew his sword. As the boat came up to the raft, Helios dug his paddle hard on the port side. The boat slewed sideways, and as it did so, Herakos roared the Akkadian war cry and leaped the gap and landed on the raft in the midst of twelve surprised and suddenly terrified Toltec warriors. As planned, Helios bent to the paddle again and the small boat shot past the raft and on downriver. Helios back-paddled immediately and turned to watch the scene behind him.

Herakos had taken the Toltecs completely by surprise. Five men were already in the water, and three of them were sinking, obviously either dead or badly wounded. Even as Helios turned his head to watch, he saw the Akkadian's sword slash down the Toltec commander's guard and then run him through the chest. The commander dropped his shield and his sword and toppled overboard. The remaining six Toltecs were obviously terrified. They did not want to face the raging Akkadian, but they had little choice. Herakos had already suffered a half-dozen more wounds, and by this time the blood was gushing quite freely from his mouth. He uttered his bellowing cry again and charged down upon the remaining Toltecs. Two went down before his sword, two turned to jump overboard rather than face him, but the remaining two stayed to fight. One of them dropped to his knees and slashed at the Akkadian's legs. Herakos came crashing down, but as he fell, he dropped his sword and snatched his knife, and the man died before he could even feel triumphant at having brought the warrior chief down. The remaining man stood paralyzed, and that moment of indecision cost him his life. Herakos lunged upward with his knife, and the man slipped to his knees clutching his stomach and rolled slowly over the side into the river.

The raft was cleared save for Herakos and two dead Toltecs, but already more warriors were swimming out from the beach to take him. The raft was listing badly. It had been hastily jury-rigged in the first place and could not take the treatment that it had received in the last few minutes. Already one corner of it was awash, but it was nevertheless still serviceable. If the Toltecs could regain possession, they could still take up the chase. Herakos knew it, and he had begun to hack at the thongs that held the planking together, and as each thong parted, the raft sank a little lower in the water. Herakos continued to hack at the thongs until it was obvious that the raft was beyond salvage, and then he paused. He lay near the mast, his head down, the water already washing over his body. The water around the raft was red with blood, his own and the Toltecs'. His chest heaved, and he retched violently, and the bright blood gushed from his mouth. He raised himself up on one elbow and raised his right arm aloft, the fist clenched, the Akkadian sign of victory. Helios stood up in his own boat and raised his own arm aloft in reply.

The raft sank lower and lower, until finally Herakos of the Akkadians sank beneath the waters of the Naradek. His promise to Kumara had been fulfilled.

Ten million years had passed since the old volcano had spouted fire, but now it stirred again and trembled with inner passion come suddenly to life. Great clouds of smoke and steam billowed from its topmost mouth, but the main force of its passion was still oozing hideously upward from within.

The flotilla of small boats ran down to the fleet, and the priesthood embarked on to the ships that were to be their floating homes for many a month to come. Melchadek himself was the last to board. He hurried aft to where the old Akkadian craft master of ships stood at his post. This was the man who had built the fleet and who had brought it down the coast to lie in wait for the refugees. Melchadek smiled as he grasped the old man's hand. "The plan has succeeded because of you, old man. We owe you much."

"There were others," the old man said laconically.

"True, but their efforts would have been in vain but for the part that you have played."

The Akkadian shrugged. "I have built some ships— so what? I have been building ships all my life."

Melchadek smiled. "My thanks anyway, old man," he said softly. "But now we must make haste. Get the fleet under way. The sooner we are farther out to sea, the better."

At that moment a voice shouted, then others, and Melchadek spun around to see the staggering sight of a great gout of flame and ash burst through the topmost plateau of the Sacred Mountain. Even from that distance they could see the great white dome of the Sun Temple flung into the air as though it were a toy. The whole plateau became a raging sea of fire, and then they could see the first sluggish, ponderous waves of molten lava spill up and over the precipice and down the sides of the old mountain. Another voice shouted, men pointed, and there to the right, farther inland, they could see other gouts of flame rush into the morning air. The Sacred Mountain was not the only peak to feel the rush of elemental passion. Quickly, very quickly indeed, the whole scene changed before their eyes. From a green and luxuriant island the ancient kingdom of Ruta became a raging mass of flame and fire. Molten lava was pouring down toward the sea at a dozen different points, and already the day had darkened from the clouds of ash that hid the sun.

As the lava hit the sea, great clouds of swirling steam hid the coastline. Only at one point was the coastline clear, at the mouth of the Naradek itself, and they knew that soon great waves of near-boiling water would be rushing downriver to the cooling sea. All eyes, however, were riveted on the topmost plateau of the Sacred Mountain. The temple had gone, and the whole plateau was a lake of seething lava, but the great Golden Gates still stood, and as if by a quirk of godly humor, the sun was lancing through the clouds of ash and lighting up the great gates so that they shone most gloriously in that dreadful holocaust. For thousands of years the gates had stood as a mighty symbol of the Toltec empire, but now they too began to be swallowed by the flame and fire. Slowly, ponderously, almost with a glorious dignity of their own, the great gates began to lean over, slide, and fall majestically over the plateau's edge, to vanish forever in the sea of flame below.

Netziachos stood on the poop deck high over the stern of the ship. The tears were streaming down her face as though they would never stop. Melchadek went over to her and gently took her arm. Although crying bitterly, she was, however, calm and controlled. She turned to him. "I have been watching Helios die," she said simply.

At that moment another voice shouted, and again the crowd that lined the ship's rail was pointing excitedly—and there, at the mouth of the Naradek, was a small boat. "By Narada!" breathed Melchadek. "It's Helios! It must be!" He turned to the ship master. "Give way, helmsman—run down to that boat!"

The old craft master demurred. "It is dangerous. The water there will be boiling soon."

Melchadek hesitated. The man was right. The certain loss of one life against the possible loss of hundreds. Netziachos clutched his arm. "You can't, Melchadek—not again!"

"You're right. This time the risk is worth it." He turned to the ship master again. "Tell the other ships to head out to sea, but take this ship down to that boat!"

Orders were shouted, and the lead ship turned ponderously about and headed back to land. Even as they began to move toward the mouth of the river, they saw the great waves come sweeping down the Naradek, the steam swirling from their near-boiling crests. The boat was right at the mouth of the river, and the waves were sweeping down toward it. But as the mouth widened, the waves lessened in height until by the time they reached the boat they were a mere two or three feet high, but even so they picked up the boat and spun it crazily about, and they could see the man clinging desperately to the thwarts. If he should fall overboard into that raging, near-boiling water, he would die instantly. The great ship swung down nearer and nearer until they could see that it was indeed Helios, their High Priest.

The waves had raced on past the small boat and had now reached the ship itself, and the stream writhed against her sides. The old craft master calmly spun the wheel and brought the ship around to within a few yards of the boat, and within seconds it was alongside and Helios was being hauled on board.

"Give way!" shouted Melchadek. The great sails cracked, and the ship turned ponderously to port and headed for the open sea.

Netziachos flung herself into Helios' arms, too full of emotion for words. "Steady," he said gently. "It's all over now."

"I thought you were dead!" she cried.

"Dead? Didn't I promise that I would see you again?" He smiled and kissed her gently.

Melchadek came up and took his hand. "Greetings," he said gravely.

"Greetings," said Helios.

The fleet stood out to sea. Behind them the great clouds rose higher and blacker and hid the raging island from their sight. All day the fleet stayed hove-to, and all the following night, and when the dawn came, they looked out over an empty sea. The twin islands of Ruta and Daiteya, the home of the ancient and mighty Toltec empire, had vanished from the face of the earth, and there was not even an atoll left to prove that they had ever existed.

Helios stood on the poop deck and searched the empty sea. "Will men ever believe that it ever existed?" he said softly.

"It does not matter whether they do or not," said Melchadek gently. "The important thing about Ruta is what we carry in our own hearts. If men can believe in the teaching that we can pass on to them, what does it matter if they think of Ruta as a legend to amuse the children?"

"But will they believe the teaching? We are going to strange lands to live among strange and alien people. Will they believe us?"

"Let us go and find out," said Melchadek softly, and the fleet turned ponderously into the morning wind and headed toward the sun.

And behind them the sea rolled emptily.

ABOUT THE AUTHOR

PETER VALENTINE TIMLETT was born in London in 1933. A former jazz musician, Mr. Timlett has traveled widely, living for several years in Australia. *The Seedbearers,* his first novel, was prompted by his interest in the occult. At present he works for a large British publishing house and lives in Bedfordshire, England.